The New Start

Boz Bostrom

Best Wishes!

Boz

Praise for *The New Start*

Often, authors will seek quotes from "famous people" to help pro-mote their book. I was blessed in that many people took the time to read and provide input on early drafts of the manuscript. They are my "famous people."

"Quite possibly the most interesting book about auditing ever written."

– Chris Condon, auditor

"Only Boz Bostrom can take something as seemingly benign as accounting and turn it into international-thriller material. Murder, suspense, intrigue, cooking the books . . . all written to grab you from the first sentence in Grisham-esque fashion."

– Mike Enke, executive manager

"First book that made becoming a CPA seem cool. Stayed up half the night to see what Johnny and Katie would do. Couldn't put it down."

– Jake Kirsch, software engineer

"If you love Vince Flynn and John Grisham, add Boz Bostrom to your list of favorite authors! You won't want to put this book down—and will be rooting for these auditors right down to the last brawl."

– Katie Doerer, campus recruiter

"The first accounting book I was actually excited to read."

– Maria Van Hove, auditor

"You need a top-notch auditor to account for all the twists and turns in this gripping portrayal of green meets greed."

– Derek Debe, scientist

"Plenty of action and romance, unlikely heroes and villains, plus national and international intrigue."

– Elena Sánchez Mora, Hispanic Studies professor

"A book that combines my love for accounting and my love for reading? This is every nerd's dream."

– Hailey Sabin, auditor

"Totally engaging and entertaining."

– Heidi Gandsey, sales

"When auditors go bad. An enjoyable, behind-the-scenes suspense tale."

– John Holland, attorney

"This was a true page-turner. Boz sprinkles in just the right amount of character development, accounting, and suspense to make this one hell of a story. I look forward to reading about Johnny Fitch's next adventure and following along as Boz builds this accounting adventure series as only he can."

– Will Gillach, lifelong learner

"To those who think accounting is boring, you need to read this book!"

– Grant Fuchs, auditor

"Find a comfy chair and prepare to shift to the edge as Boz's accounting drama roils the pages."

– Doug Wolff, dentist

"A gripping portrayal of the unexpected darker side in the seemingly mundane world of accounting."

– Mark Burns, attorney

"A Boz Bostrom accounting book > any other book about accounting."

– Jake Thorsten, tax associate

"I couldn't put this book down and finished in less than 48 hours. While you may think action-packed and accounting seem oxymoronic, Bostrom marries the two seamlessly. After reading this book, you'll associate accountants with James Bond more than pocket protectors."

– Daniel Tripicchio, international tax manager
and co-founder of "hangtime"

"I do not normally read novels, but before long I was hooked and read straight through to the finish."
– Tania Gómez, Hispanic Studies professor

"I've cried staring at accounting books before but never because I was sad I reached the end. *The New Start* is a top 10 must read!"
– Kristin Rezac, auditor

"An exhilarating international page-turner that seamlessly blends auditing, martial arts, and romance—what more could anyone possibly want (outside of a second novel)?"
– Ben Trnka, accounting and finance professor

"A must-read book outlining what happens when greed and opportunity intertwine in the financial world. Johnny is demeaned and betrayed but is relentless in his pursuit of truth in spite of obstacles he confronts."
– Mort Bostrom, retired financial fraud investigator

"As a strictly artistically minded individual (and the author's daughter), I wasn't anticipating how wrapped up in this book I would become. It's engaging from cover to cover, even with all the numbers. Take a chance on this tale of justice and love!"
– Sofia Regina, musician and writer

"He was deemed a good international tax man, a gifted professor and advisor, but I will add that he is a great storyteller. Who knew my 'boring accountant' would be such a Renaissance man?!"
– Kacey Bostrom, student affairs professional

"I felt like I was reading an actual book. After 20 percent, I stopped thinking about the Boz connection and got lost in it. If I wrote a book, that would be my aim."
– Craig Parsons, retired CFO

This book is dedicated to Jake, Hailey, Maria, Chris, Kristin, Grant, and all other New Starts.

May your first years be somewhat less adventurous than Johnny's.

PROLOGUE

Ciudad Juárez, Mexico
September 1, 2018

Jorge González pressed the red end-call button at the bottom of his iPhone and stared at the blank screen. He stood up in his office on the second floor of the manufacturing plant and stared out the large window that overlooked the operations below.

He had watched this facility being built from the ground up. In the beginning, it had been 10,000 square feet and had employed 20 people. Now, nearly 1,000 people worked in the 300,000-square-foot plant. Out his window, Jorge saw efficiency and positivity. Production hummed along at the highest rate ever. They were at a record 188 days without an injury on the job, a number that grew by the day. His employees—many of whom were his friends, his cousins, and children of his friends and cousins—were making a good and honorable living. The facility had pulled many people out of poverty, and it made substantial contributions to the community; a local park displayed the company's name. Jorge was known as one of the finest general managers in all of Juárez.

They had a sister facility in Reynosa that was about half the size and had about a third of the people. Jorge remembered being insulted when it had been suggested that the Reynosa facility be constructed as a complement to the plant in Juárez because a single facility "bore too much risk to the supply chain." People in suits over 1,000 miles away who had never been to Juárez had asked, "What if there's a fire or a natural disaster?"

"Nonsense," Jorge had replied. "The facility is completely

secure, and disasters are rare in Juárez. Do you think we'd be hit by a hurricane? We're fifteen hours from the coast. You're crazy!"

"We will make you general manager of that plant as well," they had responded. "We will increase your pay by thirty percent."

With that, Jorge had relented. His pay had been increased to nearly 1.6 million Mexican pesos, or about $80,000 USD. That was a lot of money in Juárez, and all of it was necessary for Jorge. A recent divorce had cleaned him out, and his daughter was battling leukemia. Health care wasn't covering the services she really needed.

Jorge set his phone down on his desk and considered the new offer he had just received. This wasn't a matter of another moderate raise; it involved a much higher sum with incredible stakes. The offer on the table was $5 million plus expenses. His task was as simple as it was complex.

Spend the next 16 months making the Juárez facility as profitable as possible. Then, blow it up.

CHAPTER 1

Cleveland, Ohio
September 30, 2018

She had asked him to sit on the steps and stay still, so he did. He found it hard, nearly impossible, to say no to her. He had adored her for the 14 years he had known her, despite how different she was from him. His hair was short. Hers was long. His body was tight and firm. Hers was soft and gentle. He loved math, numbers, and sports. She loved words, music, and art.

He sat with his feet a bit more than shoulder-width apart and was leaning slightly forward, his forearms resting across the inside of his thighs and his hands clasped. He was looking off in the distance, a bit to his right, not really at anything in particular.

"I'm about done," she said without prompting. She was sitting at a table about 10 feet in front of where he sat. She looked up at him and then back down as she made some quick but calculated motions with her left hand. She was a lefty, like many great artists.

"No worries," he replied. "Take your time." For her, he always had all the time in the world.

A couple of minutes later, she set her pencil down, looked up at him, and smiled. "All done," she said proudly.

"Do I get to see it?" he asked.

"Not yet." She gently rolled the picture up and secured it with a piece of twine and a simple knot. She walked over to the steps and handed it to him. "You can look at it after I'm gone."

"I'm going to miss you, Dani," he said softly, rising to his feet. She turned away, and he noticed her head drop a bit. He put the drawing in his left hand and put his right arm around her shoulder. She leaned into him, her head pressing into his side.

"Let's walk a bit," she said. And so, they strolled around the square, listening to musicians and watching children play in the splash pad.

They had arrived in the city the morning before to move his belongings into his apartment—his new home. Their parents had bought a house in a small town 22 years earlier, shortly before he had been born. It was the only home he had ever known.

He was the oldest, which meant he had always been the most intriguing to his sister, the youngest in the family. Because of the age difference, they'd only recently felt like they were getting to know each other. And now he was leaving.

They stopped and listened to a musician. When the song finished, Dani's brother approached and tossed a ten-dollar bill into the guitar case while asking, "Know any Van Morrison?"

The musician smiled and said, "Sure do."

When the chorus began, Dani's brother softly took her by the hands. He gently swung her back and forth, giving her a spin here and there. When the song ended, he gracefully dipped her, and a few onlookers politely applauded.

Dani pulled herself toward him, buried her head in his chest, and squeezed tightly. He squeezed her back and then picked her up and twirled her around once. She laughed in delight like she always did when he picked her up. He set her down, picked up the drawing, and walked her toward the curb, where a car pulled up. Dani had insisted on some final time alone with him, so the rest of their family had gone for a drive.

Their parents and brother got out, and the family had one final group hug of sorts. He shook his head no when his dad asked if he wanted a ride home, and then he held the door for Dani. She got in and gave him a smile as she wiped a tear from her eyes.

"You be careful," she said.

He nodded and grinned. "I'll see you in a few weeks."

He had plenty of time to kill, so he walked the four miles back to his apartment, taking in the sights along the way. He had lived in Cleveland for two months the previous summer during his internship, but this time the move was permanent. When he entered his apartment, he suddenly felt very alone. He carefully took the twine off Dani's drawing and opened it up. There he was, Johnny Fitch, sitting by himself in front of one of Cleveland's tall buildings. It was beautiful.

CHAPTER 2

Cleveland, Ohio
October 1–2, 2018

The next morning, Johnny walked across Cleveland's Public Square. The splash pads were turned off, the musicians were still sleeping, and his sister was back in their hometown, likely getting ready for school. He entered the Stone Tower and got off the elevator on the 17th floor. He saw the familiar desk with its handsome wood finish, marble countertops, and the initials *JPG* in large silver letters. Behind the desk, where she had been sitting last summer and for the past 23 years, was Val, the spirited receptionist.

Val was on the phone when she saw him, and she wrapped up the call with her customary "Thank you for calling JPG." He loved listening to her voice; it was friendly and warm.

"As I live and breathe. Johnny Fitch!" Val exclaimed as she leaped to her feet. "Welcome back!"

Val circled to the front of her desk and stretched out her arms. Johnny embraced her and gave her a good hard squeeze. Although he had only been in the office about once per week last summer, they had connected. Perhaps it was because he would go out of his way to greet her on the days when he had come in. His dad had always told him to be kind to others regardless of their social status: "Do it because it is the right thing to do, but then watch how people treat you in return."

"There's a fresh batch of Sumatra," Val said. He and Val were coffee buddies. He had been a Folger's guy during most of college, but when he'd stopped into a coffee shop in the North

Beach district of San Francisco on a work trip during his internship, he'd become addicted to the full-bodied Sumatra roast. He'd brought some back to Cleveland for Val, and she'd also become a fan. Since ordering coffee was one of her many duties, Val had added Sumatra to the supply list, but she only made it on days that Johnny came into the office.

Johnny filled a cup and, as always, left no room for the pollutant that others referred to as "cream." He headed to the training room 15 minutes early. He was always early. Running late made him anxious. He remembered how nervous he'd been when he'd started his internship, but the experience had given him confidence. If he put in the work, he knew he could hang with the best, so he strolled with the confidence of someone who had "been there, done that."

When he arrived in the training room, he saw only one other person. He went over to introduce himself.

The other guy said, "I'm Nicholas Montgomery, from *the* Ohio State University." He looked Johnny up and down. "Did you intern here last summer?"

"Yeah, luckily they decided to take me back," Johnny said, using self-deprecation to break the ice.

Nicholas didn't laugh. "I was part of the global internship program and spent the summer in Barcelona," he said importantly.

"That sounds like a party." Johnny smiled.

"I was there to work," Nicholas replied, staring too long.

Johnny was desperately trying to think of how to end the conversation when he felt a tap on his elbow. He turned and was thrilled to see that it was Katie Doyle. Katie and he had worked on the same account for a week last summer, and Johnny had felt instantly attracted to her. She was smart, beautiful, and kind—the full package.

They hugged in the way that friends do, and behind Johnny, Nicholas said, "The firm frowns on office romances."

Johnny pulled away from Katie and gestured toward Nicholas. "Katie, this is Nick."

"My name is Nicholas," he corrected in a nasally voice as he extended a hand to Katie and then walked away without looking back at Johnny.

They chose seats far from Nicholas's, and soon others began to wander in. There were 33 of them in all. They would be called the "New Starts" until another batch of New Starts arrived next fall.

Johnny made his way to the food table and grabbed a banana nut muffin, figuring that it contained at least 700 calories. On his way back to his seat, his gaze lingered on Katie, who was chatting with another New Start. His attraction to her last summer had been stunted by the inconvenience of her boyfriend. Shortly before her postgraduation rock-climbing trip to Spain, however, Johnny had noticed that she had changed her Facebook relationship status to "Single." Pictures of her summer escapades had been free of any male companions.

As he sat down, Katie turned to him. "You nervous?" she asked.

Johnny shrugged. "I was nervous last year before my internship, but now that I've seen what the work is like, I'm feeling confident. How about you?"

"About the same. You passed the CPA Exam with flying colors, I assume?"

"I still have to take Reg," Johnny replied, referring to one of the four sections on the CPA Exam. "It's definitely the toughest for me. I always thought tax sucked, but studying for law is worse."

Katie smiled and said, "Yeah, maybe you'll only get a 90 on that one."

Johnny brushed off the compliment. His friends all thought he was a brainiac, but the truth was his intelligence was merely somewhat above average. His scores for the other three parts of the exam had been in the mid-80s, sure, but he had studied nearly double the recommended time. "You wrap it up yet?" he asked Katie instead.

"One left for me, too," she replied. "I tried to take Audit right after graduation, but I didn't study much and barely missed it with a 74." Johnny winced in sympathy. "But I've gotten the other three out of the way and am retaking Audit on Saturday."

"I'm taking Reg on Saturday as well, at the Middleburg Heights location. How about you?"

"Same place!"

"Maybe I'll see you there." He smiled.

"It's a date!"

Johnny blushed. Luckily, the training began, and the awkward moment passed.

Bob Grayson, the office managing partner, was at the podium, and any New Starts still standing quickly took their seats. They all quieted down in a hurry, partly out of respect and partly out of eagerness to hear what he had to say. Bob commanded any room he entered. Rumor had it that he was on the very short list of potential candidates for CEO of the entire firm.

"Welcome to JPG," Bob said. "On behalf of the rest of the partners, we are excited to have you join us. JPG stands for Johnson, Preston, and Graham. Herman Johnson founded the firm back in 1938 and over the next five years recruited Lawrence Preston and Oliver Graham to join him. Early on, the three men understood that accounting is enormously complex and that growth means access to a diverse group of minds. Contrary to many firms, they focused on organic growth because acquisitions can be very tough on culture. JPG has made a few small acquisitions but is the only top ten firm which has not gone through a significant merger. The result is a culture and pride that is unmatched at any other major accounting firm. As you know, we are currently the fifth largest firm in the world, and we are growing much faster than the four larger than us."

The New Starts remained transfixed as Bob continued. His voice was rich, and he spoke with a passion that made Johnny ready to dig in immediately. Johnny felt proud when Bob said JPG was attracting the best clients in the country and was hiring the best talent to support them. Johnny found himself nodding as Bob wrapped up: "We hope you found some time to enjoy yourselves this summer in between taking sections of the CPA Exam. The economy is strong, and business is booming. JPG generated record profits last year, and morale is high. You are starting your careers at the perfect time."

After Bob, another partner walked to the podium. Maureen Davis was the head of the Cleveland audit practice. At 36, she was the youngest partner, and she was also the first female partner in the Cleveland office regardless of service line. Her meteoric rise had resulted in her admittance to the partnership after only 13 years. She had a reputation as an ass kicker and a brilliant leader, someone who completed audits under budget without skipping any steps. She had an uncanny ability to motivate her team with her intelligence and enthusiasm, and Johnny wanted to work on her accounts.

"I remember when someone asked me why I stayed in a boring profession like accounting," she said to the New Starts. "I told them that without reliable information, investment and lending would stop and the financial markets would collapse, taking the economy down with it. Nothing boring about that."

The New Starts applauded.

Training continued until 5:00 p.m., at which time the New Starts strolled across Public Square to Merton's, a warm pub specializing in premium craft beers on tap and large food portions. The entire back room at Merton's had been reserved for JPG, and that was where the New Starts met their "buddies." Johnny's buddy was Will Stevens, a handsome and chiseled senior associate from a small town two hours south of Cleveland. Johnny had seen Will at a couple of events the previous summer but didn't know him too well yet.

"What are we drinking?" asked the server.

"Bud Light," Johnny replied.

Will cut in. "You're not in college anymore, and the firm is buying tonight. You don't have to drink that crap." Will said to the server, "He will have a local IPA."

Johnny chuckled. This was something he had learned last summer: at JPG, they worked very hard and got treated well in exchange.

Johnny looked around the room. They were an impressive group. JPG had developed a reputation as the up-and-coming firm, the place where you wanted to work if you had a growth and leadership mindset. Many of the very best students selected JPG over the historically more prestigious Big Four firms because JPG selected only fast-growing clients with complex issues. In fact, if a client stopped growing, JPG would often resign as their auditor. "Annuities seem nice," he remembered hearing Maureen say, "but if we hire strong people and they become bored, they will leave."

In the college recruiting process, New Starts had to demonstrate that they could perform at a high level academically while maintaining a busy schedule. A 4.0 student who wasn't involved beyond the classroom wasn't likely to get a job at JPG. Hard work was expected, so the firm wanted to hire people who were used to being busy and didn't need a lot of downtime to be happy. There was personal time to be had, but it was your responsibility to find it, not the firm's.

This happy hour reflected that culture. It was loud, really loud. The JPG group didn't often rest at five, so when they did, they made it count. But they also wouldn't be a group that would stay until Merton's closed at two in the morning. They would hit it hard for a few hours and then get to bed so they could be up by 5:30 a.m. for their morning workouts.

Nicholas Montgomery went home before eight after consuming four glasses of water and a plain chicken sandwich. He made a point of letting the partners know that he wanted to get rested up and be alert for training in the morning. Katie left around nine. By ten o'clock, the back room at Merton's was empty except for Will and Johnny.

Will seemed to need very little sleep. On a night like tonight, he would catch a Lyft home after midnight and be on a run or lifting weights less than six hours later. Everyone at JPG operated at a high level, but Will perhaps functioned at the highest level of them all. "God blessed me with a pretty big battery," Will liked to say.

Will and Johnny stayed late. *Monday Night Football* was on in the background, and second-year quarterback Patrick Mahomes led the Chiefs to a furious fourth-quarter comeback over the Broncos. But Johnny wasn't watching the game. He was asking Will question after question about what life would be like at the firm and how he could live up to JPG's high expectations. Will poured knowledge into Johnny, and Johnny soaked it up.

The next morning, Johnny stepped out the front door of the Hampton House Apartments in Cleveland's Edgewater neighborhood and broke into a light jog. The first few steps were torturous, and he thought he might vomit. But as the fresh air raced into his lungs and the Tylenol circulated through his veins, he slowly began to feel better, and the damage done by the night before began to heal. He had chosen an apartment near Lake Erie, or "the Lake," as the locals called it, and an out-and-back run through Edgewater Park was almost exactly three miles. A handful of other early risers were out for jogs and powerwalks, and he did his best to smile and wave at any others whose paths he crossed. At the end of his run, he found a quiet patch of grass and practiced kata, a pattern of martial arts movements.

By the time he arrived at the office at 7:50 a.m., he had already consumed two cups of coffee and emptied what seemed like half a container of Visine into his eyes. When Val handed him a cup of Sumatra, he breathed a sigh of relief.

Johnny ran into Will in the restroom. "How ya feeling, Fitch?" Will asked.

"Never better," Johnny lied.

Will's responding roar of laughter hurt Johnny's head. The truth was that Johnny still felt waves of nausea, but he didn't want to let Will down. He felt an inexplicable need to prove himself.

"Got in three miles this morning. How about you?" Johnny asked.

"Attaboy, Fitch. I hit the weights but kept the volume down on the earbuds!"

Johnny laughed, but not too loudly. He'd had two pints of IPA for every one of Will's, and he felt silly for having gotten plowed in front of his "buddy" on his first day of work.

He walked into the training room, where Nicholas

Montgomery was already sitting front and center. While the other New Starts were in the allowed training attire of jeans and collared shirts, Nicholas wore dress pants and a jacket. "Dress not for the position you are in but for the position you want," Johnny overheard him say.

The day's training was a crash course on audit processes at JPG. These were things most of the New Starts had been taught in college and had learned in their internships the previous summer, but the firm liked to start everyone at the same level, which meant making sure they mastered the fundamentals. Johnny sat at a table with Ben, a friend from college. Ben was sharp but kind of squirrely—Johnny was sure he had undiagnosed ADHD.

Will led the morning session. "You need to get documentation for everything," he explained, "and you set the tone from the start. I once had a client ask me to 'trust him,' that what he was telling me was accurate. I said, 'Mr. Jones, with all due respect, the only person I trust completely is my grandmother, and I still ask her for documentation. She once told me that she won a chocolate chip cookie bakeoff when she was in high school. I told her I needed proof. The next time I was over, she gave me her certificate and a whole ice cream bucket full of homemade cookies.'"

The New Starts laughed, and Johnny marveled at how Will owned the room. People looked at him in some form of awe. It was as if everyone in the room wanted to either date him or be his friend. Will was brilliant and carried himself with a great deal of confidence. Someone who didn't know him might have thought it was arrogance except that he was simply too likeable. "He's got real swagger," Ben said softly. Johnny took mental notes on the way that Will spoke in hopes that he could emulate him.

That night, Johnny went home and spent five hours alone in his apartment studying for the CPA Exam. Dani had left him an empty picture frame, and he put her drawing into it and set it on his kitchen table—the first piece of art displayed in his new home. He looked at it often, not to see the sketch of himself but to feel less alone. When he looked at the picture, he felt his sister was there with him, watching over him and keeping him safe.

CHAPTER 3

Cleveland, Ohio
October 6, 2018

On Saturday, Johnny showed up at the Middleburg Heights CPA Exam testing center a half hour before noon, and Katie arrived a few minutes later. She had her long brown hair pulled back in a ponytail and wore black yoga pants and a sweatshirt that had the logo of her college on the front. She normally wore contacts, but for the exam she had on a pair of dark brown glasses, which Johnny found attractive.

"How ya feeling?" he asked her.

"With the amount I studied, I better pass," she replied. "I've heard it's awful to try to take a CPA Exam once we get busy. How do you think you'll do?"

"I'm feeling good," he said with forced confidence. The truth was that he never felt confident before a performance of any sort. He got anxious before exams, he dreaded giving speeches, and he'd often felt sick before his high school wrestling matches.

As they were making idle chitchat and waiting for the exam to begin, Nicholas walked out of the testing center. He was dressed in a full suit and tie. "Dress well, test well," Johnny had heard him say multiple times the day before. The popular expression, of course, was "Dress good, test good," but Nicholas had pointed out to anyone who would listen that it wasn't grammatically correct.

"How did you do?" Johnny asked politely and instantly regretted it.

"I expect I did well enough," Nicholas said smugly.

"Well enough for what?" Katie asked, and the drop in her

face indicated that she likewise instantly regretted it.

"The Selles Award," Nicholas said. "I got 98s on Audit, Reg, and FAR. I only need an 89 on the BEC. So yeah, I'm pretty confident I've got the firm's $25,000 bonus for Selles Award winners locked down."

When Nicholas was out of earshot, Johnny said, "What a nerd."

"We're all nerds," Katie replied.

Johnny laughed softly and rubbed the back of his neck.

Johnny took all four hours allotted to him; he was a slow test taker. He saw Katie walk out with about 15 minutes to spare. He was delighted when he got to his car and found a text from her: "Drinks to celebrate (hopefully) being done?"

He clicked on a thumbs-up emoji but then changed it to a beer-mug emoji. He then did a search for GIFs with the word "Cheers" and clicked on one of Leonardo DiCaprio toasting with what looked like a big wine glass. He looked at it and shook his head, deleted the GIF, and typed, "Love to." He didn't want to come across desperate or cliché or dorky. He then deleted the text and replaced it with "Sounds fun. Where at?"

An hour later, after stopping home to change into fresh clothes, he walked into Masthead Brewing Company. Katie was already there and waved to get his attention. Her yoga pants had been replaced with dark blue jeans, and she seemed to have put on a touch of makeup and lipstick. Her studious eyeglasses were nowhere to be seen. Her T-shirt was a solid burnt orange.

"Great color on you," Johnny said as he gestured toward her shirt.

"It's my favorite," she replied.

"I can see why," he replied with a grin.

Johnny and Katie walked to the bar to place their order.

Katie went with the Endless Bummer, a "sessionable saison," the beer menu said. Johnny was also about to order the Endless Bummer, like he normally would, when he remembered Will telling him he had to step up his beer game. He ordered the Jalapeño IPA, and he liked to think that Katie's nod meant she was impressed by his choice.

"Any food?" the bartender asked.

Katie looked at Johnny. "You have time? I don't have any other plans tonight."

Johnny had been planning to meet a few college buddies later to watch the Ohio State Buckeyes football game but figured they'd probably forgive him if he skipped just this once. Actually, he didn't care if they forgave him or not. If Katie wanted dinner, they were going to eat dinner.

They decided to split an Everything Pretzel and a Jerk Chicken Pizza, which was prepared Neapolitan style. Over dinner, Johnny asked, "How was mountain climbing this summer?"

"Rock climbing," she corrected.

"Aren't they pretty much the same thing?"

"You do taekwondo, right?"

"Karate," Johnny replied. Katie simply smiled at him, and he said, "Touché. So, how was rock climbing this summer?"

"I loved it," Katie replied. "I went to Siurana, Spain, in the Tarragona mountains. The rock is limestone, and there are many steep climbs and overhangs."

"I'm getting nauseous thinking about it." Johnny squirmed.

"But you're okay with other people trying to kick and punch your face in?"

"Yes, but that all happens on solid ground. If I get hit, I don't have far to fall."

Katie laughed.

"How did you get into rock climbing anyway?" he asked.

"Growing up, I was hard core into gymnastics. I lived in the gym, and I loved it. But when I was fourteen, I grew five inches in a single year, and I could no longer do the things I was used to. I got so frustrated that I gave up gymnastics altogether and started playing volleyball. I went to a volleyball camp at a college one summer, and they had a rock-climbing wall. It was intense, and I guess you could say I was a natural. I still had good body control and hand strength from my gymnastics days." She smiled briefly, perhaps wrapped up in nostalgia, and then asked, "How did you get into karate?"

"When I was eleven, the school bully was picking on my best friend, Pete, who has asthma. I stepped in, and the bully challenged me to a fight. I accepted, partly because I wanted to defend Pete but also because I was a pretty good wrestler, so I figured I could get him on the ground and make him give up. Well, we squared off and he popped me right in the nose. Blood splattered all over, and a teacher came in to break us up. I realized then that I could defend myself on the ground but not on my feet. Boxing really wasn't an option at that age, so I picked up karate."

"Are you still close with Pete?"

"He went to college at Stanford and now works in private equity in San Francisco. Even though we don't talk as much, I still consider him my best friend."

"Do you miss not having him around?" Katie asked.

Johnny swallowed and said, "Yeah, I do."

"What belt are you?"

Johnny looked down at his waist and said, "I'm pretty sure this is a Kenneth Cole."

Katie laughed, leaned in, and said, "C'mon. Really."

"I got my black belt when I was fourteen, and next year I'll get promoted to something called fourth-degree black belt."

"You still train?"

"There aren't a lot of adults who stick with it, so I mainly instruct the younger kids. If I'm in town, I teach maybe twice per week, although that could be tough now with the long hours at JPG. I enjoy sparring. Every Tuesday night a group of more seasoned instructors from the area get together after school closes, and we mix it up a bit."

"Like a modern-day Fight Club?" She grinned.

Johnny laughed. "I suppose a little bit, but it rarely gets out of hand. There are a couple women who join us. I tried to go easy on one once. She clobbered me and told me if I ever did that again she would break my nose."

"I love it!"

"Yeah, it is a fun release. I try to spar in a few tournaments per year."

Katie cocked her head, and Johnny admired her long brown hair as it brushed against her orange shirt. "So you're kind of a badass?" she said.

Johnny laughed, pleased but embarrassed, and quickly changed the subject. "I know we've only been on the job a week, but any thoughts on how long you'll stick around JPG?"

By this time, Katie was on her second beer, an Imperial Winter Stout, which boasted a staggering alcohol content of 11.6 percent, nearly three times that of macro brews such as Coors Light and Bud Light. She took a sip and replied, "I'm hoping I can make it five years, and then I'll move into something else."

"Why's that?" Johnny asked before taking another bite of the pizza. "The hours?"

"Not really. I've always felt like I can separate myself by simply outworking everyone else." Johnny nodded, as he had often felt the same way. "I look at the partners, though, and don't think I could ever get to their level—they are brilliant. I would hate to bust my butt for fifteen years and then be told I wasn't going to make partner. I'll make manager, and then, with the JPG name on my resume, I should have a lot of options."

"What do you mean you don't think you could get to *their* level?" Johnny reached out and grabbed her hand for a moment before realizing what he was doing and slowly pulling away. "You are the smartest one in our class!"

"Not smarter than you or Nicholas Montgomery," she replied.

"First," he said, "you are a hell of a lot smarter than me. And Nicholas may be smart, but he will rub people the wrong way; I can't tell if he is a jerk or a dork or maybe both. But people are drawn to you. You win them over. You are serious when needed but also know how to relax. And you have the best smile." He instantly felt awkward. Katie's smile was something he found irresistible, but it had nothing to do with her ability to become a partner. He felt he'd made an ass out of himself and grinned sheepishly.

"That means a lot. Thank you." She reached out and took his hand, but this time neither of them pulled away for a good long while.

A bit after nine o'clock, they left the bar and were walking down the sidewalk, a couple of feet between them. They both moved slowly as to seemingly extend their time together.

"This is me," Katie finally said, gesturing to an apartment building on the right side of the road, the Lumen at Playhouse Square.

When she looked back, Johnny had taken a step closer to her and taken her hand in his. She looked at him for a long moment and then leaned in and pressed her lips to his for a second, maybe two. She released his hand, turned, and walked toward the building.

Johnny was staring, transfixed, his mouth half open, as she opened the building's door and turned to look at him. She saw the look on his face and grinned before walking inside. "Thanks for a great evening."

CHAPTER 4

Las Vegas, Nevada
October 7, 2018

Bob Grayson, leader of JPG's Cleveland office, walked out of McCarran International Airport and into the short line for taxis. He had mainly switched to Uber or Lyft like seemingly the rest of the tech-savvy population, but he still found it easier to take a taxi when leaving an airport.

The Las Vegas skyline quickly came into sight. It was much less impressive during the day, which was why he usually preferred to arrive in the evening, but this time the choice had not been his.

Within 15 minutes, he was dropped off in front of the Mirage. It was one of the oldest hotels on the strip, and it was his favorite. He remembered staying there right after it was built in the fall of 1989. At that time, it was the largest hotel in the world, boasting over 3,000 rooms. In its early years, the Mirage had featured the Siegfried & Roy Show, filled with magic and wild animals. It had hosted boxing matches involving superstars such as Sugar Ray Leonard and Evander Holyfield. Its grand architecture had landed it roles in many films, including *Ocean's Eleven, The Wolf of Wall Street,* and George Strait's *Pure Country*.

Bob checked into his room, tossed his suitcase onto the bed, and made his way down to the sportsbook. He paid $50 for VIP seating, which included all the Jack and Cokes he could drink. He had missed the earlier-starting football games but arrived in time for the second slate. He wagered $500 on the Brady-and-Belichick-led Patriots to cover the 10-point spread at home over

Andrew Luck and the Colts.

Bob's love of football season had nothing to do with the sport itself and everything to do with the gambling opportunities it provided.

When the Patriots went up by three touchdowns with seven minutes to go, he felt confident and decided to bet on the Rams to win the Super Bowl. Their two-point win earlier in the afternoon had moved them to 5–0. The Rams hadn't scored fewer than 33 points in a game all season and looked unstoppable. Bob had told himself to only bet what he won, to cap it at the $500 he would win on the Patriots game. Perhaps it was the six Jack and Cokes, or perhaps it was just Vegas, but he instead put $5,000 on the Rams at 3-to-1 odds, a bet he would lose a few months later.

When Bob arrived back at his seat after placing his bet, the spot next to him was taken, as he'd expected it would be.

"Winning tonight?"

"So far, so good, Sage," Bob replied as a deep pass put the Colts at the one-yard line. He doubted that Sage was the man's real name, but it didn't matter. He knew to give Sage what he wanted, and things would be fine.

"Do you have it?" Sage asked.

"Of course," Bob replied as Andrew Luck hit Eric Ebron on a short touchdown pass to pull the Colts within 14 points. If the Colts were to recover the onside kick and score, they would cover the spread, and Bob would be $500 poorer. He wasn't anxious; $500 was a small bet for him. Bob pulled an envelope out of his pocket and slipped it to Sage.

"Is it all here? All fifty grand?" Sage asked. When Bob nodded, Sage asked, "You have a plan to pay it off?"

"What do you care?" Bob replied. "You can't beat five percent interest per month."

The balance was indeed $1 million. Sage's boss had finally capped him off even though he had never missed a single interest payment before hitting the $1 million mark.

"True," said Sage, "but the boss would still like to see you start to make some progress."

Patriots safety Nate Ebner fell on the ensuing onside kick. When Brady took a knee for the second time and the clock ticked toward zero, Bob stood up. He handed Sage his ticket, saying, "Apply five hundred to the balance."

As he walked away, he heard Sage call out in a cold voice, "See you next month."

CHAPTER 5

Atlanta, Georgia
October 7–19, 2018

The morning after the CPA Exam and Johnny's date with Katie, the Cleveland New Starts flew out to Atlanta. There, they went through two more weeks of training with other New Starts from across the nation and from select cities around the world. Johnny and Katie were in separate training groups and thus saw very little of each other during their first week in the Atlanta suburb of Stone Mountain. Training lasted from eight to five every day, and many of the New Starts got in a workout or caught up on social media for a couple of hours before meeting at the conference center's dinner facilities at seven. Drinks were free, and there was a different theme every night in the bar: karaoke, one-hit wonders, classic rock, international, country, and '80s music. Part of the reason for sending the New Starts to training was for them to bond and get to know each other and to meet other New Starts from JPG's offices around the country and world. A tight-knit group would be more collaborative and welcoming of working long hours together.

The firm brought in an outside speaker on Friday afternoon to talk about ethics and professional conduct. Johnny and the other New Starts had seen this topic on the schedule and assumed the worst—that it would be a boring session flipping through laws, rules, and regulations. While there was a bit of that, the speaker also mixed in several real-life cases of CPAs who had gotten caught up in ethical scandals. One module that particularly captured Johnny's interest was on insider trading.

"When you work with publicly traded companies, which most of you will do at least some of the time, you will be exposed to confidential information a minimum of four times per year, when the company releases earnings," the speaker explained. "It is critical that you do not share this information with anyone except those on your immediate engagement team. Let's go through an example.

"When medical giant Johnson & Johnson released earnings for the first quarter of 2018, they indicated they expected annual sales of about \$81.5 billion and adjusted earnings of about \$8.10 per share. In July, Johnson & Johnson released its second-quarter earnings and again provided guidance on full-year expectations, with sales decreasing to the \$81 billion range and adjusted earnings increasing to about \$8.12 per share. How do you think the markets reacted?"

"Not much movement," Nicholas, always eager to please, called out.

"That's right," said the speaker. Nicholas smiled smugly, and a couple New Starts rolled their eyes. "The share price initially bumped up by three percent, but within three days it was almost back to where it was previously. On the day of the release, share volumes were up maybe fifty percent over normal, which may sound big but actually is much smaller than expected at the time of an earnings release.

"Now the thing is, about a week or so before earnings were released, J&J management as well as their auditors knew this information. Management prepared the press release and provided it to the auditors for review. This press release is an example of 'inside information,' and trading on this information is illegal. In this example, the risk of insider trading was likely lower, as those who saw the earnings release in advance would have expected very little stock price movement and thus little opportunity to profit.

"Now, let's look at an example from Grubhub. On July 24, Grubhub's stock closed at just over $109 per share. The next day, they closed at nearly $135 per share, a one-day increase of 24 percent. Why did you think that was?"

"Strong earnings release!" blurted Nicholas.

"You all have your laptops and smart phones. Check it out," the speaker replied.

Within a couple of minutes, the noise level in the room grew loud as the New Starts searched for Grubhub's most recent earnings releases and began comparing the expected revenue and adjusted EBITDA to the actual reported revenue and adjusted EBITDA. Looking at the first-quarter earnings release on his laptop, Ben said to Johnny, "For the second quarter, they expected revenues of about $232 million and adjusted EBITDA of $62 million."

Johnny replied, "In their second quarter, they reported actual revenues of nearly $240 million and adjusted EBITDA of over $67 million."

"They kicked some ass." Ben smiled.

"How about full-year guidance?"

"In their first-quarter release, they expected annual revenues of about $947 million and adjusted EBITDA of about $252 million. I imagine they increased it in the second quarter?"

Johnny nodded. "In their second-quarter release, they said they expected annual revenues to be about $975 million and adjusted EBITDA to be about $263 million."

"They kicked some *serious* ass."

"So now do you understand why their share price skyrocketed overnight?" the speaker asked, regaining control of the room. "It obviously was going to increase; it was a question of how much. Someone could have profited on this by purchasing shares or call options in Grubhub and would have had very low risk with a lot of upside." The speaker paused and then asked, "Who was aware of this information before it was announced?"

"Certain members of management and the auditors," replied Nicholas Montgomery.

"That's right," said the speaker. "And if they had acted on that information, they would have been guilty of insider trading." The speaker then showed several slides of individuals who had been convicted of insider trading and the punishment they faced: prison, restitution, fines, and loss of professional licenses.

The speaker looked out into the crowd of New Starts. Johnny felt like the speaker was looking right at him as he concluded, "Most of you are going to be reviewing confidential information on a regular basis. What should you do?"

Nicholas Montgomery started to say something when Ben looked his way and said, "Shut the hell up."

A hush fell over the room, and Nicholas glared at Ben. Ben glared back.

"That's right," the speaker said finally. "When you receive inside information, instead of talking about it, you should shut the hell up, and do not discuss earnings with anyone not directly on the engagement team."

The tension in the room was released and some laughter ensued, laughter from everyone except Nicholas.

The firm had six hours of training scheduled on Saturday, including a working lunch, which was JPG's subtle way of setting high expectations. By the time two o'clock rolled around, the New Starts were ready to escape the Stone Mountain Marriott and get into the big city.

Johnny's training group had grown somewhat close, and the 16 of them had lined up an overnight trip into downtown Atlanta. Their plan was to party it up and stay near downtown on Saturday night and then attend the Falcons game against the Tampa Bay Buccaneers on Sunday before heading back to the facility for another week of training. Johnny had invited Katie and one of her friends to join in the fun.

The firm provided limo transportation, and they all cracked their first beer on the ride into the city. When they arrived in Atlanta an hour later, the limo's cooler was empty.

Katie was the first to check in at the downtown Hilton. Johnny was still in the lobby when she texted and asked if he wanted to meet in the café. Johnny gave her the simple thumbs-up emoji just as Ben walked up.

"Let's grab a beer at the bar," Ben said.

"I was going to meet Katie."

Ben shook his head and said, "Bro, plenty of time for that later. I'm buying the first round."

Johnny was conflicted but then texted Katie back. "Told the guys I'd meet them at the bar. Come join us!"

When Johnny got to the bar, two JPG members from Switzerland were holding court. Pierre and Cedric were their names, although they referred to themselves as the "Swiss Frères," or Swiss Brothers. Johnny didn't care for the way they tried to capture all the attention and how they swore like sailors, so he did his best to ignore them. Once the full group had assembled, including Katie and her friend, the Swiss Frères led the charge out of the hotel bar and over to Max Lager's, a restaurant and brewery located in the heart of downtown Atlanta. Johnny tried the Hop-splosion!!! IPA, which had an alcohol content so high that they would only serve it to him in a 10-ounce glass, and he had to order refills more frequently.

A while later, the Swiss Frères led them to a Spanish tapas bar for dinner. The host reorganized several tables for them in the main dining room. Two servers stopped by to take their drink orders, and the Swiss Frères quickly decided that they would be shifting to red wine—just house red wine, though, since they had not yet received their first paychecks.

The group was growing louder by the minute, and the Swiss Frères began yelling at the servers to hurry up. When the manager came over to ask them to quiet down, Cedric replied, "They always tell me that America is the land of customer service. I say that is bullshit. Show me some damn service."

Cedric thought he was being funny; the manager did not. The 18 of them were soon back out on the street, half-drunk and hungry.

"Stupid Americans," muttered Cedric under his breath.

"Knock it off," Johnny said.

"Or what?" Pierre, Cedric's much larger partner in crime, stepped close to Johnny.

"Or you'll be picking your sorry ass up off the pavement," Ben chimed in.

"That's enough," yelled Katie as she stepped in between them. Pierre shoved Katie aside and stepped closer to Johnny, fists raised.

Johnny watched Katie go flying and felt his blood boil. "Stop." He raised his hands, palms facing Pierre. He had rehearsed this drill thousands of times in karate class, though he'd only had to use it on the streets on a couple prior occasions. His left hand went in front of his face, his right hand a bit lower, as he stepped his right foot back and somewhat behind his left, narrowing the target he presented.

"Stop *this*," snarled Pierre as he pulled his right hand back slightly and then began to hurl it forward. Even with a few beers under his belt, Johnny saw it all happen in slow motion. Pierre was big, slow, and sloppy. Johnny stepped toward Pierre while clenching his left fist and sharply swinging his left forearm outward. In one motion, he smashed his left forearm into Pierre's right forearm, stopping his punch, and then slid his left arm around Pierre's throat while stepping behind him. He used his left hand to grab his right bicep and then pushed Pierre's head forward with his right hand. Johnny pulled his shoulders back, effectively cutting off circulation to Pierre's arteries.

Cedric stepped in front of Katie, toward Johnny, as he balled his right hand into a fist. Katie grabbed his hand and pulled back hard before he had a chance to sucker punch Johnny. Within five seconds, Pierre slumped in Johnny's arms. Johnny released the pressure and quickly, but gently, set Pierre on the ground.

"You killed him!" yelled Cedric as he leaned over his friend's body. But as quickly as he'd lost consciousness, Pierre regained it, and his eyes fluttered open. Johnny stood back as Cedric helped Pierre to his feet, and then the two of them walked the other way, with Cedric talking in French and gesturing wildly.

"I told ya!" Ben yelled after them.

Katie's friend whispered in her ear, and Katie said, "I think we are going to go back to the hotel now."

"Can I walk you back?" asked Johnny.

"Sure," Katie said, just as her friend coldly said, "No thanks."

"Okay, we'll see you tomorrow," Johnny said in his best effort to hide his disappointment. Katie gave him an apologetic shrug.

The rest of the evening was a blur to Johnny. After dinner

the group hit a nightclub, and by one in the morning, the only ones left standing other than Johnny and Ben were Emily and Kim from JPG's Austin, Texas, office. Johnny was dead on his feet and ready to call it a night when Emily and Kim asked to go to one more bar. They ordered a round of beers, and Emily grabbed Ben's hand and led him onto the dance floor.

When they were alone, Kim said to Johnny, "What you did to Pierre—that was incredible."

Johnny simply shrugged.

"Could you have killed him?"

"I suppose," replied Johnny, "but that's not the point. That move abruptly ends a fight without doing any real damage. When the person quickly regains consciousness, they realize they better just leave."

"It was so hot," Kim said, putting her hand on his arm. Johnny blushed. "Do you and Katie have a thing going?"

Johnny hesitated for a second and then said, "Not really. We're just good friends."

As soon as the words left his lips, he questioned his response. Did kissing Katie count as a thing? It had been a week since that night, and they hadn't really had a chance to talk about it. Would Katie have responded differently?

"Good," Kim replied, and the word hung in the air.

An hour later, they took a Lyft back to the Hilton. Emily and Ben were making out in the back seat, oblivious to how uncomfortable they were making the driver. Johnny was in the front seat, and Kim had reached forward to wrap her hands around his chest. He had mixed feelings about it. Random hookups weren't his style—and thoughts about Katie still swirled in his head—but the alcohol had largely numbed him.

When they got back to the hotel, Emily and Ben walked

hand in hand toward the elevators, Johnny and Kim following closely behind. In the elevator, Emily pressed button 15 and Ben pressed 22. When the elevator dinged at 15 and the door opened, Johnny expected the ladies to step out. However, Ben stepped out with Emily, leaving Johnny in the elevator with Kim.

"Have a good night, buddy," Ben said with a wink.

"What?"

As the door closed, Kim slipped a hand under Johnny's shirt and said, "Looks like you are stuck with me."

Johnny exhaled softly, closed his eyes, and tried to think. He and Katie had had a single date. Kim was drop-dead gorgeous, almost modelesque. Plus, she was from another office, and he would not likely see her again.

They strolled back to his room, and he slid the key into the door. She walked into the room first and within seconds had let her dress fall to the floor, exposing her toned and tanned body. Her skin color blended nicely with her long, straight brown hair. She turned and walked back toward him. Slowly, even reluctantly at first, Johnny began to kiss her. Eventually, the warmth of her skin and the scent of her body won him over.

A few minutes later, he received a series of texts: "Can't sleep. Hope you guys made it back okay. Breakfast at nine? P.S. You are a true badass."

Johnny didn't see the texts until he awoke the next morning at nine thirty, by which time Katie had texted him two more times and tried calling once. Johnny grimaced but didn't reply to her. He wasn't sure what to say. He was pretty sure he was still half-drunk and needed Gatorade and Tylenol.

He'd also received a text from Ben a bit after nine that said, "Let me know when you guys are decent. Need a clean set of clothes for the day." Johnny figured he should walk Kim back to her room and retrieve Ben in person. The elevator was empty when they got in on the 22nd floor. Kim pressed button 15, and the elevator began to descend as she nestled into Johnny. He put his arm around her. Her hair smelled good, like the rest of her. The elevator stopped on the 17th floor, and when it opened, Johnny saw Katie's face and sobered up in a hurry.

Katie got on the elevator and smiled brightly. "I've been trying to get a hold of you." But then, she noticed that Johnny and Kim were together and that they were disheveled. Katie's expression turned into a mix of disbelief, sadness, and anger. She stood to the side and stared straight ahead at the door. Silence hung in the air.

When the elevator opened on the 15th floor, Kim awkwardly said, "Um, I think I'll go myself. I'll tell Ben to come back to your room, Johnny."

Katie had tears in her eyes by the time the elevator door closed.

"Look, Katie—" Johnny began.

"I don't want to hear it. It's fine. It's not like I'm your girlfriend."

"But Katie—" Johnny cut off as the elevator stopped on the fourth floor and a couple of Falcons fans, fully clad in black and red, got on. When the elevator reached the ground floor, Katie bolted and was out the front door in a flash. Johnny called after her and tried to follow, but she was long gone.

Later that day, four seats were empty at the Falcons game. The Swiss Frères were nowhere to be found, and Katie and her friend had returned early to the training facility. Kim sat on Johnny's left, and a woman with a Falcons cap and too much eye makeup sat on Johnny's right. Try as he might, he couldn't focus on the game and couldn't make much substantial conversation with Kim. It was a miserable three-and-a-half hours. At one point, the woman to Johnny's right leaned in to ask him about something that had happened in the game. As Johnny was explaining, Kim pulled him back, looked at the woman in the Falcons hat, and said intensely, "He's with me."

Emily watched it happen and later mentioned to Johnny, "Kim can get very intense when she wants something . . . or someone."

The Falcons had been up by five when Jameis Winston led the Bucs 68 yards in 70 seconds to set up one final and crazy play—a quarterback draw—from the 21-yard line. Winston lateraled the ball to Mike Evans. Evans then lateraled to Desean Jackson, who seemed to have a clear path to the end zone. Jackson dropped the ball, however, and it fell out of bounds, ending the game.

When Johnny got in the limo later that afternoon to ride back to the training facility, the driver asked, "Some finish to the game, huh, bud?"

Johnny numbly realized he had no idea who'd won.

Katie completely ignored Johnny the entire final week in Atlanta. After a couple of unsuccessful attempts to talk with her, Johnny gave up. Kim, sensing that Johnny had feelings for Katie, eventually ignored him as well, and in what seemed like the time it took a hungry dog to devour a piece of meat, Johnny went from having two women interested in him to none.

Ben spent every free moment with Emily, so Johnny ended up spending evenings with new friends from across the country and even, one evening, with Nicholas Montgomery—partly out of a desire for companionship and partly because Ben and Emily were using the hotel room after dinner. Although Nicholas didn't drink, that didn't stop Johnny from throwing down several pints of beer. Nicholas was direct and at one point said, "You realize you are basically drinking alone, right?" Johnny ignored him and asked the bartender for another.

The only good news was that the reason the Swiss Frères were missing from the football game was that they had apparently been arrested after a brief scuffle with nightclub security. A partner at JPG later bailed them out of jail and then promptly fired them. *Good riddance*, thought Johnny when he heard the outcome.

At three on Friday afternoon, the week mercifully came to an end, and Johnny and the other New Starts returned to their respective cities. They were quickly staffed on clients, many of whom were going through third-quarter earnings releases. Evenings of debauchery were replaced with nights of eating takeout and working late. The honeymoon period was officially over.

When CPA Exam results were released some time later, Johnny (who passed Reg with an 85) heard through the grapevine that Katie passed Audit with an 88. He texted her a quick "Congrats," but she didn't reply.

The next day, an officewide memorandum was circulated with the title "New Start Wins Selles Award." Of the 75,000 people who took the CPA Exam in 2018, fewer than 150 averaged higher than 95.5. Nicholas got a 99 on his final section of the exam and was instantly $25,000 richer. Johnny asked Nicholas if he wanted to get the New Starts together to celebrate.

"No thanks," Nicholas replied. "Very busy with work and a couple important clients right now."

Johnny shook his head and told himself to watch his back

around Nicholas; he seemed to stop at nothing to be the best.

CHAPTER 6

Ciudad Juárez, Mexico
October 25, 2018

Jorge thought of the first time he had met Bruno, although he now wondered if that was the man's real name. Six months earlier, Jorge had been going for a midday walk to grab some lunch from a local restaurant when a car screeched to a halt next to him. Two men jumped out and, recognizing him as the general manager of the plant, said they needed $5,000 to provide him with protection. Jorge tried to ignore the men and continue his walk, but they grabbed him. They punched him a couple of times and promised that worse things would happen to his workers if he did not pay the protection money. Jorge didn't know what to do, but luckily, he didn't have to decide, because right at that moment Bruno showed up. Bruno quietly pulled a gun on the men and told them that if they ever bothered Jorge again, he would end them. The men scurried away, and Jorge did not expect to hear from them again.

Over the past six months, Jorge and Bruno had developed a friendship of sorts. They'd shared meals and attended some fútbol matches together. Bruno said that he was from Mexico City and that his company had business in Juárez, although he was always very vague and spoke with more of an American dialect than one from Mexico City. Jorge was nonetheless quite grateful for the way Bruno had handled the situation with the two men and helped prevent corruption at Jorge's plant, and he genuinely enjoyed Bruno's company. As a result, he had been shocked when

Bruno called him at the beginning of the month with the offer to blow up the facility.

Bruno had given Jorge until the end of October to consider the offer. Jorge went into the factory every day and watched his team work. They were being paid a solid wage, working conditions were good, and they were quite happy. They did good work for the factory, in part because they were treated well but also because they were grateful to have the work. Unemployment in Juárez, while low, was creeping up in the manufacturing sector. Violence had increased in Mexico's drug cartels, and US companies were increasingly outsourcing manufacturing to China and other low-cost countries. There had also been a major shift in the US tax system, including a staggering drop in the corporate tax rate from 35 percent to 21 percent, causing some US companies to keep manufacturing at home.

On the last Friday in October, Jorge spent a long time staring out his office window at the production floor. Even though he knew what the result would be, he picked up his phone and checked his bank balance, which was less than the $9,000 his daughter needed for the second of her eight chemotherapy treatments. Jorge needed money, and he needed it now. Bruno knew this and had promised that, of the $5 million payout, Jorge would receive $100,000 when he agreed and the remainder when the task was complete.

"Family over all else," he remembered hearing his grandfather say on many occasions.

"Always do the right thing." That was one of his father's sayings.

Normally, the two mantras were aligned and led Jorge to a clear solution when making tough decisions. But this time, he felt they were pulling him in opposite directions. Both men had passed away, and Jorge wished he could talk with them now.

If he did not accept the offer, Ana's next round of chemo would be delayed until Jorge could save up enough money. His credit cards were maxed out. There was a reasonable chance that he would not be able to afford the treatments and Ana would die.

If he accepted the offer, Ana would get the care she needed, but those on the factory floor in front of him would be out of work for at least several months. He tried to rationalize it, saying that another company may pick them up or that the government may step in to help them out, but he knew that was highly uncertain. He closed his eyes, thought about it one final time, and picked up his phone.

"Hello," Bruno answered, and Jorge could feel him smiling through the phone. "I hope you have made a wise decision."

"I have," replied Jorge.

He hoped his grandfather could forgive him for siding with his father just this once.

Jorge could feel Bruno's smile disappear when he said, "I can't help you. It's not right." He would sell his house, save every penny he earned, and find odd jobs to do on Sundays, his only day off. Hopefully one eight-treatment round of chemo would be enough, because Jorge had no idea how he would pay for a second round.

"I was afraid you would say that," said Bruno, "but I understand."

Jorge exhaled, feeling instantly better about his decision. "Thank you."

"But there is something *you* must understand before I let you go."

"Yes, Bruno. What is it?"

"You are no longer under my protection."

The line went dead, and a few moments later, Jorge felt a presence in the doorway. He turned to find the two men who had approached him on the street six months earlier. He had no idea how they had gotten into the facility, but one thing was clear: that night six months ago had all been a setup to get Bruno close to Jorge.

One of the men put his index finger to his lips and handed Jorge a picture of one of Jorge's cousins who worked at the plant. "You will leave now and never come back. If you return, your cousin's legs will be broken. We will start with him and work our way to those closest to you." With that, they walked out the door.

Jorge sat in his office, completely stunned. He was in a no-win situation and couldn't think straight. If he quit, he would have no money, and Ana would die. If he tried to return, Bruno's men would rain chaos.

Jorge left and wandered around the city aimlessly. He didn't want to go home right away. Ana would ask him what was wrong. Even as she battled her cancer, Ana spent more time worrying about her father than her own health. When he eventually arrived home at seven in the evening, he found Ana had dinner waiting for him, as she often did. She told him that having a purpose took her mind off of her disease and off of her pain.

When they bowed their heads to pray over the meal of pan-fried arrachera with chorizo and queso blanco, Jorge felt tears rush to his eyes, and he told himself to get it together.

"Is everything okay, Papá?" Ana asked him with concern.

"Yes." He gave her a strained smiled. "Everything is going to be fine. I'm so happy to have you with me."

The next morning, Jorge dropped Ana at her mother's home and went straight to Tito's, a bar he used to frequent. The owner, Miguel, was working, as he always was.

"Jorge, my friend, I thought I would never see you again. How long has it been?"

Jorge looked at Miguel. "Last week, I celebrated three years of sobriety. I am cured and am ready to enjoy alcohol again."

Miguel's face dropped. "My friend, I can't serve you. I watched the alcohol destroy you. It cost you your marriage, your money, and almost your child. Don't do this, amigo."

Jorge replied angrily, "Either you serve me, or I will find some place that will."

"Stay here, and I will serve you. I will serve you coffee, and you can tell me what is happening," Miguel pleaded, hands folded in a prayerful pose.

"I need tequila," replied Jorge through clenched teeth.

"You won't get it here," Miguel replied, dropping his hands to his sides.

Jorge turned from the bar and angrily kicked a table, sending chairs flying, as he walked out.

Twelve hours later, Jorge staggered toward the front door of his home. He had found a place that would serve him. The owner of that bar also knew of Jorge's alcoholism but cared more about his pocketbook than helping Jorge preserve his sobriety. Jorge had once heard that if he started drinking again, it would be as if he had never stopped. He had heard correctly. He threw down cheap shots of tequila at a rate even he had never done before.

As he neared his front door, he saw two men walking down the sidewalk, coming his away. One of them stepped to the side to make room for Jorge, who simply made himself larger and threw his shoulder into the man. The two men turned and stared at him as he slurred, "What are you looking at?"

"Just take it easy, güey," the larger one replied.

"Take this easy, güey," Jorge slurred again, louder this time, as he drew his right hand into a fist and flung his arm wildly toward the larger man's face. The man easily stepped aside, and Jorge's momentum caused him to fall awkwardly forward. The men looked down at him and shook their heads before simply walking away.

Jorge made his way into his house and fell onto his couch.

The next evening, Jorge was showered and sober. He would be leaving soon to pick up Ana, but first he dialed a number on his phone.

"I knew you'd call back," Bruno said. "You will do it, won't you, Jorge?"

"Yes," said Jorge as he exhaled softly. "Yes, I will."

"Good. Very good. I will send you the hundred grand within a day, and Ana can receive the care she needs." Bruno paused and continued, "But you must know one thing. If after you spend the money on her treatment you change your mind about blowing up the facility, it won't be the cancer that kills her."

"Hijo de su puta madre," snarled Jorge, but the line had already gone dead.

CHAPTER 7

Cleveland, Ohio
November 2018–March 2019

Will Stevens had started his career at JPG four years ago. He came from a small town, had gone to a small college, and had somehow ended up in a big city. He was used to knowing everyone in tight-knit communities, and he'd gotten to know about everyone at JPG as well. He was heavily involved in recruiting, was a formal assigned mentor to five associates, and acted as an informal mentor to many more.

Will was well liked by just about everyone in the firm because he was genuinely kind and treated others well regardless of their position. He came from a farming background and thus was no stranger to hard work. He arrived every morning by seven o'clock, regardless of how late he had been working or socializing the previous night. He often worked through lunch, raiding the vending machine or scrounging for leftovers from a meeting. Despite this, he rarely missed a happy hour and started many, where he always had a drink in hand but was rarely intoxicated. With the exception of upgrading his beer selection from Bud Lights to IPAs, he had maintained his small-town roots.

Many new associates looked up to Will. Johnny perhaps even idolized him and Will thought very highly of Johnny in turn. Johnny always volunteered to take on the ugly projects—the stuff that no one else wanted to do. Will likened it to cleaning up cow manure and felt that anyone who was willing to wade through shit was worthy of serious investment.

Because of that, when the firm won a new client of some

prestige and Will was staffed as the lead senior associate and acting manager, he asked Johnny to be on the account. PurePower manufactured batteries primarily for smart phones. Its top-end batteries sold for double that of its competitors but lasted for more than twice as long. Consumers seemed happy to pay for this premium, and the company's sales had increased over 60 percent in the past two years. Apple and Samsung were PurePower's two biggest customers, and whenever they placed an order, it was larger than the one they had placed just before.

PurePower had outgrown its previous auditors, so the company put its audit up for bid with the big firms. JPG won, which wasn't a surprise based on the reputation the firm was developing, and was set to guide PurePower through its initial public offering. The hours were crazy. Each Monday, the firm would send an automated email to the New Starts that listed who had the most charge hours from the previous week. Initially, Nicholas Montgomery's name was listed every week, but once PurePower got rolling, Johnny found himself "winning" some of these weekly battles.

Will pushed Johnny very hard and always demanded more of him. Many times, Johnny felt like he couldn't find an answer, but Will refused to let him off the hook. On one occasion, Johnny complained that a client wouldn't return his calls, emails, or texts. Will asked if he had considered visiting the client.

"You want me to stalk him?" Johnny asked.

"I want you to get the information," Will replied.

And so, Johnny found himself in the client's conference room at six in the morning, waiting until his client finally arrived three hours later. Johnny intercepted the client at the coffee station and got the information he needed. Will was proud of him and took him out on the town that evening.

Despite the long hours, Johnny was having a blast. He felt like he was really making a difference in the world. His work would help PurePower attract investors, raise more capital, and improve the function of personal technology. More importantly, he got to work side by side with Will and learn from him—learn about the way Will's mind operated when information was murky, about how Will wrote emails, about how Will treated the rest of the team, about how Will researched issues, about how Will talked to the client.

Every Friday, the PurePower audit team knocked off at five o'clock sharp and hoisted a pint or three at Sonrisa, a quaint Mexican joint that introduced a new margarita at least once per month. On the February day that PurePower completed its initial public offering and started trading at a price of $45 per share, the company's executives, referred to as the "C-suite," were at the New York Stock Exchange to ring the opening bell. The audit team watched the festivities and took great pride in the $800 million raised that day. PurePower provided guidance that it expected earnings of $0.27 per share for the first quarter of 2019 and $1.25 per share for the year.

At the end of Johnny's first busy season of work, his charge hours second only to Nicholas Montgomery, Will called him in for an annual review. The review was glowing, and Will's final comments were "I am giving Johnny the highest rating possible because he does not accept defeat and always finds creative solutions. He will get the job done every time. He delivers what he says he will do. I would like to have Johnny staffed on all of my jobs."

Will saw a smile creep onto Johnny's face as he read those words.

"Any questions or concerns?" Will asked.

"It's flattering," Johnny replied, "but honestly, it almost seems too nice. I make too many mistakes."

Will looked intently at Johnny. "You make mistakes because I give you the most challenging work. If I gave you the same type of work I give to other associates, you wouldn't make any mistakes. But you also wouldn't learn nearly as much."

"Why are you investing so much in me?" Johnny asked, a bit embarrassed.

"You are the best associate that has ever worked for me. I plan to be at this firm a long time, and I want you right there with me." Maureen had said similar things to Will when he was a New Start. Will had found it empowering, and it had pushed him to another level. He hoped it would do the same for Johnny.

"Okay," said Johnny. "I won't let you down. But you always have to be there to mentor me."

Will nodded. "Deal."

Another one of the New Starts, Josh, was also staffed on the PurePower account. Josh had attended the University of Cincinnati, where he'd been a poor fit. Josh wasn't confident enough to introduce himself to many new people and had gotten lost at such a large school. His high school girlfriend had also attended the university, which was probably the reason he had enrolled, and they'd lasted until the start of the spring semester. She'd decided that she wanted to experience college independently and had slowly begun spending less time with him. Josh had felt her slipping away and gone all out on Christmas gifts, charging way too much on his credit cards. She'd dragged him along until mid-January and then broken up with him via text on a Tuesday evening.

Josh had never fully recovered from the breakup. He'd felt

rejected, and not for the first time. When he'd been eight years old, his parents had gotten a divorce, and his dad had stopped showing interest in him. To his dad, Josh and his younger sister were simply child support payments. His dad had missed most of his ball games and piano recitals and didn't celebrate Josh's birthday and other special days with much excitement.

After the breakup, Josh had gone to class and pulled good grades but spent a lot of his free time in his single dorm room playing video games against his online friends. It was somewhat of a mystery how he'd gotten hired at JPG without the typical stacked resume. In truth, an uncle who was a chief financial officer at a prospective client had called in a favor.

Josh was second-guessing his decision to join the firm a few months into his time at JPG. It appeared that the audit rooms were popularity contests at times, with a person's charm and communication skills being valued as much as their technical skills and ability to get work done. Josh still enjoyed accounting but envied those individuals who worked at his corporate clients, those who worked the eight-to-five job alone in their cubes and then got to go home. He figured he would last a year at most at JPG, and possibly only through busy season, before making the switch out of public accounting.

So when Bob Grayson began showing a real interest in him, Josh lapped it up. PurePower was the biggest new client the firm had won in a while, and Bob was involved in staffing it. Maureen Davis was the signing partner. Will was about six months away from making manager and was the lead senior and acting manager, and Johnny, Josh, and Angela, a highly regarded experienced associate, were the three associates on the account.

Bob personally stopped by Josh's desk in early December to let him know he would be added to the PurePower account. Bob told him that he had been making a great impression on others and that he was needed on this very important client.

When Bob suggested putting Josh on the account, Maureen balked. PurePower's management team was outgoing and engaging, and Maureen wanted a team that would be similar. Josh was kind of a wallflower. Bob insisted, saying that Josh would bring balance to the team and was a good associate to simply put his head down and get work done. He was a "yes" man, Bob said, and every team needed one of those.

Maureen balked again, saying that she hadn't risen quickly to the partner level by surrounding herself with "yes" men. She wanted more people like Will and Johnny who would challenge the status quo when needed. She suggested adding Katie Doyle, another rising star, to the account instead of Josh, but Bob said, "No, it's already been decided. It's done."

Maureen thought more about it and decided to confront Bob directly. "This doesn't make any sense at all. It isn't like you to override my decision. Is something wrong?"

"Not at all," Bob said. "I had a discussion with Josh's uncle, and he indicated that Josh was only having a so-so experience with JPG. Giving Josh an experience like this will make his uncle happier and give us a better shot at winning business from his company. Everybody wins."

Maureen nodded. "That makes sense. When did you turn into such a schemer?"

Bob smiled. "I've still got a few tricks up my sleeve."

CHAPTER 8

Las Vegas, Nevada
April 8, 2019

Bob Grayson settled in at the Mirage and within five minutes had received, and drained, his first cocktail. His nerves had never been higher, and it was going to take all the Jack Daniels in Clark County to settle him down. At the beginning of March Madness, he'd bet $25,000 on Texas Tech, a No. 3 seed, to win it all. It wasn't so much that he liked Texas Tech. He had never been to the school's campus in Lubbock and had only started following their basketball team this year. Rather, he felt that, at 40-to-1 odds, they gave him the best chance to erase his million-dollar debt in one fell swoop.

Bob had taken notice when the Red Raiders had smashed the Kansas Jayhawks by 29 points in late February during an impressive nine-game winning streak to end the regular season. He'd liked that they had Jarrett Culver, one of the top players in the country. When they'd lost their opening game in the Big 12 Tournament against a lowly West Virginia team, Bob had liked that as well. It had made their March Madness odds much more attractive from a gambling perspective, and he'd guessed that it would make the team hungry. He'd been right. Texas Tech had won their first five games of the tournament by an average of 14 points. Now, Virginia was all that stood in the way of Bob and the $1 million that he would use to fully erase his debt, a burden that weighed on him heavier with every passing day.

Bob thought about what erasing the debt would do to his life. He had once been an attractive man in every sense of the word. He had been sharp and fit and had treated others well. When he looked at a young professional like Will Stevens, he felt as though he were looking at a younger version of himself. But with the mounting debt had come irritation, distraction, and several added inches on his waistline.

He'd always enjoyed casual sports betting, but it had been nothing serious. In 1991, as a New Start at JPG, he'd been asked to join a fantasy football league. He'd enjoyed the challenge of trying to outsmart the other owners in his league. It was the first time he remembered doing any sort of gambling.

In the year 2001, on the 10th anniversary of their league, Bob's start class had held their fantasy football draft in Las Vegas. It had been the first time Bob had ever been to Sin City. Holding the fantasy football draft in Vegas had been such a hit that the tradition continued to this day.

From the first trip, Bob had loved Vegas, with its the lights and the energy. At first, he'd kept his betting relatively under control. He'd brought $1,000, and when it was gone, it was gone. Sometimes he'd left ahead, whereas other times he'd lost it all within 24 hours. In those cases, he'd spent his time hanging by the pool, walking the strip, and catching some of the incredible shows.

It was 2010 when he'd first started to turn. He'd lost the $1,000 fairly quickly, so he'd headed to the cash machine and pulled out $1,000 more. When that $1,000 had been gone, he'd pulled out another grand, which he'd also lost. A couple days later, when she'd been balancing their family checkbook, Bob's wife had asked him about the withdrawals. Bob had lied and told her that they were for friends who would quickly pay him back.

"Which friends?" she'd asked, and Bob had become cryptic. She'd known all his friends. She had been in their start class at

JPG and had left the firm after eight years, when they had gotten married and decided to begin a family.

In 2011, Bob had declared that he wanted to bring $5,000 to Vegas. He was pulling in excellent money as a partner at JPG, and their family could afford it, he'd argued. His wife had balked, not because of the amount but because of the trend she'd been noticing. Bob had brought the $5,000 anyway, and they'd had a big fight when he'd returned.

On the 2012 trip to Vegas, Bob had met a bookie. For the first time, Bob had been able to place sports bets from the comfort of his own home. He wasn't necessarily a poor bettor, but if one stays with it long enough, the bookie's cut—the "juice"— eventually catches up. He also tended to make larger bets when he was drunk, bets based on emotion instead of logic. His losses had started to mount, although they'd hurt his pride more than his pocketbook.

In 2014, he'd returned from Vegas, and his wife had given him an ultimatum: stop gambling or she would leave and take their three teenage daughters with her. Bob had stopped for a few months, and their family had enjoyed many great times together, but when March Madness had come around, he'd broken down and bet on a dozen of the games, losing $10,000. His wife had held true to her word and called a lawyer, and Bob had been served with papers a few months later. He'd kept their home and JPG capital account, while she had taken everything else. After she'd left, he'd had no reason to stay in check, and his addictions to both alcohol and gambling had exploded. He'd begun running a balance with his bookie. He could have been able to pay it off, but it would have meant spending less on gambling and booze. On a typical NFL weekend, it'd been common for him to wager $100,000.

He had begun to attend AA and Gambler's Anonymous meetings after March Madness in 2017, when his gambling debt had risen to $400,000. For a few months, he'd again stayed clean of both addictions. Maureen had set him up with her older cousin, and Bob had been in love for the second time in his life. He'd aggressively paid down his gambling debt and had been looking forward to a new life. Against his better judgment, and against his new girlfriend's wishes, he'd joined his JPG start group on their annual pilgrimage to Vegas for their fantasy football draft. He'd vowed to stay sober and stay out of the casinos. But he hadn't been open with his buddies about the extent of his struggles, and they'd pressured and poked at him until he'd broken. Things had quickly spiraled out of control, his new girlfriend had left him, and things had spiraled even more. When he'd lost $200,000 on the Patriots in Super Bowl LII, his gambling debt had reached $1 million, and his bookie had cut him off. Bob had missed his next interest payment and been visited at home by Sage, one of his bookie's goons. Two cracked ribs later, Bob had decided to not miss any further interest payments.

Midway through the first half, Virginia was up by 10 points over Texas Tech, and Bob's anxiety was through the roof. He was going through a double Jack and Coke every 20 minutes. Texas Tech battled back to take a slim lead late in the first half, but when Virginia hit a three-pointer to reclaim the lead at just before half-time, Bob cursed loudly and slammed his glass down on his table. Ice went flying.

"Ahhh, you bet on the Red Raiders tonight," a familiar steely voice said.

Bob looked left and nodded at Sage, who sat down and ordered a club soda. Sage was dressed smartly, as he always was, but Bob could sense the muscles rippling underneath the sports-coat.

The second half was agonizing. Virginia built a lead of 8 or 10 points and then Texas Tech whittled it down, but then Virginia built the lead back up. With just over 5 minutes to go, Texas Tech started to battle back. Jarret Culver's teammates chipped in, and then Culver himself gave the Red Raiders the lead with 35 seconds to go on a beautiful spinning layup. Bob leaped to his feet and yelled, "Yes! Yes! Yes!" as spit flew from his mouth. He felt physically lighter, as if the million-dollar debt were an anchor tied to him that was now being cut away. He told himself that this would be it—if he won, he would be completely done with gambling.

"Virginia is one-and-a-half-point favorites," Sage said. "How much do you stand to win if Texas Tech holds on?"

Bob ignored Sage and continued to focus on the game. When Virginia missed a jumper, Bob, already on his feet, leaped a few inches off the ground with his arms in the air, as far as his belly would allow. Sage grinned in amusement at the spectacle. Bob seemed to have almost no remaining athletic ability at this point in his sad life.

"I didn't bet just this game," Bob replied in a rabid voice.

Sage asked, "You picked Texas Tech at the start?" When Bob nodded, Sage probed, "How much?"

"Twenty-five," said Bob.

Sage checked the odds, and his quick computations showed that Bob stood to win $1,000. Sage found it odd that Bob would be so excited at that amount. When Bob looked at him with wild excitement in his eyes, Sage realized that "twenty-five" meant "twenty-five thousand" and that Bob's million-dollar debt was 22 basketball seconds away from being paid off.

When Virginia hit a game-tying three-pointer with 12 seconds to play, Bob screamed a vulgarity. Jarrett Culver had two chances to win it in the final 5 seconds but came up empty both times. As they waited for the teams to begin overtime, Bob handed Sage an envelope with $50,000 in cash.

"This month's interest," Bob said, foaming at the mouth and almost panting like a dog.

"Tell you what," said Sage, putting the envelope in his jacket pocket. "If Texas Tech wins and you hand me the million-dollar ticket, your debt will be paid off, *and* I'll even give you this fifty thousand back."

Bob grinned at the thought of leaving Vegas $50,000 ahead instead of $1 million behind, although he imagined he would spend at least $5,000 of that at a strip club and on a prostitute.

The first few minutes of overtime were a back-and-forth affair, but when the Red Raiders' efforts to close the gap to one point with 30 seconds to go was unsuccessful, Bob slumped in his chair. When the Cavaliers hammered home a dunk to extend their lead to eight points with under 15 seconds to go, Bob knew it was over. The clock hit zero, and Virginia celebrated its first-ever national title while Bob stared at the large TV screen in disbelief.

Sage gave him all of 30 seconds to sulk and then said, "We need some progress. Major progress."

"I make good money," Bob said, "but it all goes to taxes and interest."

Sage folded his arms and replied, "Then you need to make more money. Find a new way—and your debt is proof that gambling is not your strong suit."

"What do you want from me?" Bob asked, nearly in tears. "I give you almost my whole salary. My home is mortgaged to the max."

"You may need to retire and cash in your capital account."

"I'm too young. I have ten years left before I should retire. I'd be giving up more than ten million dollars in wages."

"Your problem, not ours," replied Sage. Bob stayed silent, and Sage said what he had been planning to say all along: "You do have one more asset."

Bob looked at him, confused.

"You have access to information. Information you could use to make a lot of money in a very short period. Starting this month."

Bob looked out through his drunken gaze, mouth hanging open as if he were not smart enough to close it, and realized what he was being asked to do. "I can't do that," he whispered.

"Actually, you *can* do it," said Sage coldly. "And you *will* do it. When I see you next month, you will bring an extra fifty thousand. If you don't want to do that, you can retire and pay us out of your capital account. If you don't want to do either, I will hurt you"—Sage paused—"worse than before." He stood, patted Bob on the shoulder, and walked out of the Mirage.

CHAPTER 9

Cleveland, Ohio
April 18, 2019

In mid-April, PurePower management had finalized the draft of the company's first-ever earnings release. At the time of its IPO, PurePower had provided guidance of $0.27 per share for the first quarter, and soon they would be releasing information that easily surpassed that estimate.

Bob Grayson had always made a point of visiting the office's most important clients, so he ventured out to PurePower on a Thursday afternoon. He spent a few minutes talking with PurePower's CFO and controller and then spent a couple of hours in the audit room, not doing anything important but simply making his presence felt. He looked around the room and was amused at what he saw. He wondered if he was in an audit room or a Costco. One whole shelving unit was full of drinks and snacks, almost all of which bore the popular Kirkland brand. He also noticed an abundance of whiteboards filled with undecipherable writing. There was a big round table in the middle that seated about six auditors comfortably but, in the midst of the busy quarter-end, was seated for eight.

Bob settled into an open chair next to Angela. He had trouble connecting to PurePower's Wi-Fi. "Damn internet," he muttered.

"This is usual," Will said in an IM to Johnny, suppressing a grin.

At about three o'clock, all team members except the associates went into a meeting with the controller, which left Bob alone in the audit room with Angela, Johnny, and Josh.

Bob looked at Josh and felt guilty. He had put Josh on the account in order to impress Josh's uncle, and now he was considering how to use Josh for different reasons. But, he told himself, he had no other choice.

Bob pulled two twenty-dollar bills out of his wallet. "Johnny," he said, "I noticed a Dairy Queen down the road. Why don't you and Angela go grab some treats for the team?"

Angela was a bit surprised that Bob had asked her instead of Josh, given that she was more experienced, but she was feeling somewhat left out of the meeting with the controller, so she complied and joined Johnny in a quest for Dilly and Buster Bars.

When it was only Bob and Josh left in the audit room, Bob asked, "You holding up okay, Josh?"

"Yeah," Josh replied. "It has been pretty grueling. It seems like we went straight from the IPO to this first-quarter review, so there hasn't been much of a break. But I see the light at the end of the tunnel. It is only a couple weeks away."

"When earnings are released?"

"Yeah."

Trying not to sound overeager, Bob asked, "Have you received a draft of the earnings release yet?"

"Yeah, just this morning."

"Have you read it yet?"

"No, not yet. I've been trying to wrap up a couple things related to deferred taxes. I think Will is having Johnny tick and tie the release."

Bob sensed a hint of dismay in Josh's voice. In truth, Josh could tell that Johnny was Will's favorite, and that often made Josh feel like an outsider. Bob considered how he could use Josh's insecurities to his advantage.

"Have you ever read one of those reports before?" Bob asked.

"In training, yes."

"I mean in real life, in real time, when it matters. Aren't you curious to see how the company is doing?"

Curiosity wasn't Josh's strong suit, so he simply said, "I guess."

"Pull up the report, and I can show you what to focus on."

Josh suddenly felt uneasy. The voice of the ethics trainer rang in his memory: "Do not discuss earnings with anyone not directly on the engagement team." Bob wasn't really on the team. But Bob, the office managing partner whose interest in Josh was pretty much the only thing Josh enjoyed about his job, was sitting five feet from him. Josh wasn't about to say no. He pulled up a private network that only the PurePower auditors had access to and opened the earnings release.

Bob scooted his chair over and pointed at the screen, saying, "Here. Here is where you focus. The release says that earnings are thirty cents per share in the first quarter and are expected to rise to thirty-two cents in the second quarter. Full-year earnings are expected to be a dollar thirty-eight per share. All of those figures are higher than guidance provided at the time of the IPO, so they are doing great. So great, in fact, that I expect the underlying numbers to be clean. I get most nervous when a company meets earnings exactly—it makes me wonder if they had to play accounting games to get there. But companies don't usually play accounting games to blow earnings out of the water like PurePower is doing." Bob paused and then said, "Well, go ahead and close that down now. We wouldn't want the wrong people to see it."

Josh nodded and thanked Bob for the impromptu training.

Will had been too busy talking with Johnny to explain this, so it was nice to learn, and Josh felt a stronger connection between his work and the real world.

When Johnny and Angela returned with an assortment of DQ treats, Bob grabbed a butterscotch Dilly Bar and bid the team farewell. A few minutes later, Maureen and Will got back from their meeting with the controller.

"Where did the DQ come from?" Maureen asked.

"Bob Grayson's treat," Johnny said.

"He didn't stick around for it?" Johnny shrugged and Maureen said, "Josh, grab the door please. Okay, we had a meeting with the controller and went through the earnings release." She gestured to the three associates. "I will now take you through it, but I must be crystal clear on one item: you may not show this to anyone, obviously no one outside of JPG, but also no one else at PurePower and not even anyone else at JPG. It is highly confidential, and the stock price will move because of this release. Heck, if Bob Grayson was still here, I'd have to ask him to leave before showing you. Got it?"

Josh froze. Certainly Bob knew the policy, so why had he asked to see the release? It was because he was educating Josh, right?

Johnny and Angela said, "Got it." Josh stared off in deep thought.

"Got it, Josh?" Maureen repeated a bit sternly.

"Oh, yes, of course," Josh said.

"Great. Now, the most critical item to focus in on is earnings per share," Maureen began, and Josh did not hear another word she said.

About a week later, PurePower released its earnings, and its share price shot up from \$46 to \$55 per share, an increase of about 20 percent in one day. The atmosphere at PurePower was electric, and everybody, including the auditors, was on cloud nine. As was Bob Grayson.

CHAPTER 10

Cleveland, Ohio
May 14, 2019

Although JPG expected hard work, they nonetheless took the time to celebrate it. Many people throw around the phrase "Work hard, play hard," but those at JPG truly lived it out. Every year on the second Tuesday of May, the firm had a party to celebrate the end of busy season—they called it the Spring Bash. Most firms had parties on April 15 to celebrate the end of tax season, but many CPAs were too burned out at that point to properly enjoy them, and the auditors were knee deep in first-quarter earnings. By mid-May, the tax team had recovered, and the auditors were finally finished with their big push from year-end through quarter one. Kids were still in school, so summer vacations had not yet begun. It was the perfect time to gather the group together. If things were going well, as they usually were, mid-year bonuses were often paid out at the party.

What actually happened at these parties was unknown to the New Starts. It was an unwritten rule that the party not be talked about in front of them: "What happens at the Spring Bash stays at the Spring Bash."

The firm chose a Tuesday night so that they could hold the party at the Rock & Roll Hall of Fame on the shores of Lake Erie. Tuesday was the only night when they could find both space at the Hall of Fame and a big-name band at a reasonable price. The stature of the band was often dictated by the financial performance of the firm. Everyone knew the year had been good, so people were excited to see which band would be featured. Rumor had it that the party cost $500,000, which seemed like a crazy price for 300 professionals, but administrative staff were also invited, and after the awards ceremony, spouses and partners were welcome to attend, so over 500 people would enjoy the event. Someone once pointed out that the price tag was about $1,000 per person, to which Bob Grayson replied, "That's about two billable hours apiece. I think we can handle it."

Most of JPG's employees worked in the office that day, and at a quarter to five, a large contingent made the 15-minute walk to the Rock Hall, strolling down Saint Emily Avenue and hanging a left on East Ninth Street. The Rock Hall opened for JPG at exactly 5:00 p.m., and the partygoers kept the bartenders hopping and tipped them well. At seven, dinner was served with a choice of filet mignon, lobster, or both, if preferred. Johnny was seated with a group of New Starts, including Katie, although she was on the other side of the table, stuck next to Nicholas Montgomery. Nicholas was babbling about something, likely something unimportant, and Johnny felt bad for Katie.

At eight, Bob Grayson walked to the podium and the room fell quiet. The New Starts were not sure what to expect—this was the portion of the party that was not talked about.

"On behalf of the rest of the partners at JPG, welcome to the Spring Bash. This has been a banner year for the firm, both nationally and in our local office. No other firm is doing the caliber of work we are doing or having as much fun in the process. We have the best people and are delivering the best results. I am pleased to report that our net fees this busy season were up over twenty percent compared to last year, and our client satisfaction ratings have never been higher. Thank you all for your outstanding efforts.

"I know you all want to get to the party, but first we have some business to take care of. Tomorrow is May 15, which is payday. You will all notice an extra five thousand dollars in your paychecks as a bonus for outstanding performance over these past few months."

Cheers, hoots, hollers, and thunderous applause ensued.

"And now," Bob continued, "the awards."

Bob handed out the Outstanding Senior Manager and Outstanding Manager awards. Both went to professionals on the tax side that Johnny had never met. Will won the Outstanding Senior Associate award, which came as no surprise to anyone, and while on stage, Bob also handed him the Most Charge Hours award. Outstanding Experienced Associate came next, and Angela was announced as the winner.

"The final award is for Outstanding New Start," Bob said.

Johnny perked up when he heard the name of the award even though he didn't fully realize how coveted the award was. It labeled the winner a golden child of sorts, and the winner often got the early bead on the best jobs and quicker promotions. Johnny didn't have any illusions that he would win. Though he felt Katie was deserving of the award given the way she energized any team she was on, he was sure that the award would go to Nicholas Montgomery, who was second only to Will in terms of charge hours and was still fairly fresh off winning the Selles Award.

"This year's winner has been a workhorse." Johnny watched as Nicholas sat up in his chair. "This person went above and beyond with everything we asked them to do." Nicholas buttoned his coat. "And they did outstanding work on one of our office's most important clients." Nicholas, who had been working on the American Bank account, casually ran his fingers through his hair.

"The 2019 Outstanding New Start is"—Johnny watched as Nicholas took a short breath—"Johnny Fitch."

Johnny's eyes widened. He felt as if he had been awakened

from a trance. He looked across the table. Katie looked impressed, and Nicholas Montgomery looked as if he had been punched in the gut.

"Get up there, man," Ben laughed as he gave Johnny a firm elbow to the arm. Johnny awkwardly rose and walked to the stage as loud applause filled the room. Bob presented him with a plaque and handed him an envelope. As they were shaking hands, a photographer snapped a couple of pictures, to be posted within the hour on the firm's internal home page.

Johnny heard some rustling on the stage behind the curtain, and Bob said, "Now, Johnny, would you please introduce tonight's entertainment?" Bob handed Johnny a half sheet of paper and whispered, "Read this with some good enthusiasm."

Bob walked off the stage, and as Johnny looked at the sheet of paper, his eyes widened. He mustered as much energy as he could in saying, "Ladies and gentlemen of JPG, please welcome to the stage, all the way from San Francisco . . . Train!"

The curtain opened, everyone leaped to their feet, and Train started in with their recent hit "Play That Song." Johnny quickly hopped off the stage and walked back to his table, enjoying slaps on the back and excited handshakes from his older colleagues. When he got to his table, Ben asked him what was in the envelope. Johnny shrugged and opened it up to find a certificate that stunned him. It was for an all-inclusive vacation package to Dubai: two business-class tickets on Emirates Airlines; seven nights in the Burj Al Arab, one of the most expensive hotels in the world; and a $1,000-per-day allowance for meals and excursions. All in, the vacation had a value of $25,000, and JPG would cover all income taxes due on the award.

Ben pursed his lips together, and his eyes got wide. "I don't suppose you're taking me?"

Johnny laughed but was embarrassed and quickly slipped the envelope into his jacket pocket. He looked across the table, saw Katie, and wished he hadn't messed things up with her so that maybe she would have joined him. She looked radiant as she chatted with another New Start.

Then Johnny's gaze drifted to Katie's right. Nicholas's chair was empty.

The rest of the evening was outstanding. The guests of JPG employees arrived. Train played straight for 90 minutes, and other than Nicholas, not a single person left before their set was done. There was dancing and drinking and laughter. A night like this would keep people at JPG despite the high stress and heavy workload. They worked hard, but they got rewarded.

At one point, Johnny exited the men's room as Katie was exiting the ladies' room, and they nearly bumped into each other.

"It's the big star!" Katie said.

Johnny blushed and smiled. "Thanks."

"What was in the envelope?"

"A vacation package for two," he said, wanting to downplay it a bit. "Honestly, Katie, I thought you should have won. You are already taking on the role of acting senior, and everyone loves working with you."

Up until that point, she had still seemed a bit guarded with him, but she noticeably softened when he said that. "Well, maybe you'll have to take me with on the vacation then. As long as there is some rock climbing involved." She laughed.

Johnny's mouth dropped open. Spending a week in Dubai with Katie was about the best thing he could imagine.

Katie noticed his expression and pulled back a bit. "I was just teasing you," she said softly.

"Were you?" Johnny asked softly as he took a step closer.

Katie stood still. She didn't step toward him, but she didn't step back either.

Just then, they heard heels clicking on the floor. They both pulled away, and Maureen turned the corner.

"Hey, you two," Maureen said. "Congrats, Johnny."

"Thanks, Maureen," he replied.

"Did you win this award in your first year?" Katie asked.

Maureen shook her head and said, "They first threw this party and created these awards the year after I was a New Start. Bob Grayson told me I was the inspiration for it, as they wished they'd had something in place to recognize me. I don't know if that's true or if he was just being nice. I guess I like to think it's true. But what is absolutely true is that I wish we had two of these awards to give out because, Katie, you were also very deserving."

"Told ya," said Johnny.

Train started in on their first number-one hit, "Drops of Jupiter," and the three of them dashed back to the dance floor. When the song ended and Train feigned that their show was over, the JPG crew called for "One more song! One more song!" During the encore performance, Will was called upon to join lead singer Pat Monahan in singing "Hey, Soul Sister." Johnny enjoyed seeing Will, the office superstar, become a rock and roll superstar on stage.

When Johnny caught a Lyft home that evening, he felt so content with where he was at. He worked for a great firm and was making a difference. He had the vacation of a lifetime coming up. He was being mentored by the coolest cat around. Things even seemed to be smoothing out with Katie. Life was very good.

CHAPTER 11

Ciudad Juárez, Mexico
June 4–6, 2019

Juan Carlos was abnormal for an IT guy. He liked to look beyond computers, the cloud, and networks and learn about business operations and processes. While he had majored in computer science at the University of Texas at Austin, he'd also enjoyed elective courses in operations management, supply chain, forecasting, and cost accounting. He listened to corporate earnings calls to learn how the company was faring and was probably one of a handful of people who would read the company's annual report and proxy in their entirety every year. Given his broad knowledge, he often identified systems improvements that made business sense. For this, Jorge had always highly valued Juan Carlos. He spent more time mentoring Juan Carlos than perhaps any other employee at the plant.

It was perhaps because of this business acumen that Juan Carlos noticed strange things happening at the Juárez plant in 2019. Decisions that seemed financially savvy on the surface lacked a long-term focus, which was very different from how Jorge had historically operated. In years past, Jorge had bought the nice equipment, even if it cost more, because it lasted longer. He'd spent more on repairs and maintenance, even when they seemed unnecessary, in order to prevent equipment breakdowns. He'd borrowed for the long term, even when interest rates were higher, to aid in financial security. He'd compensated employees wisely, even above market levels, to receive more effort and loyalty. He'd chosen more expensive insurance policies to protect the business he had built up. He'd been conservative in accounting. Finally, he'd supported the local community through charitable efforts, if not because it was the right thing to do then because it would mean the community would stand by the company.

Jorge had a great deal of autonomy because he had delivered such stellar performance over the years. "The Untouchable," some liked to call him. Because he had always been about the long term and focused on his employees, everyone loved him. But over the course of six months, nearly every decision Juan Carlos saw Jorge make was focused on the short term, which made no sense.

The change in focus had started when Jorge purchased equipment that was selling for 20 percent less than a competitor's product, even though its expected life was only half as long. Then, a five-year bank loan at an interest rate of 6 percent had been restructured as a one-year loan at a rate of 4 percent even though interest rates were rumored to be on the rise. Maintenance expenditures had started to decrease, offsetting, for now, an upward tick in failure rates. Jorge had even switched the accounting firm that handled the statutory audit, choosing the lowest bidder even though they seemed to lack the required experience. Jorge had promised staggering raises of up to 30 percent if 2019 performance exceeded that of expectations. Oddly enough, he'd eliminated the 10 percent holiday bonuses people had become accustomed to, promising that the company would more than make up for it early in 2020.

Jorge provided monthly financial updates to all his employees and showed how they were continuing to exceed targets. Morale had never been higher. Despite this, Juan Carlos felt Jorge was building what was referred to as "a house of cards."

Early one evening, Jorge saw that Juan Carlos was one of the last ones working in the administrative offices. As was not uncommon, Jorge stopped by to greet him. "Hey, Juan Carlos," he said. "Going to be an all-nighter for you?"

Juan Carlos laughed, but not because the question was absurd. He worked all-nighters a couple of times per year. At 28 years old, he was still fairly early on in his career and sacrificed much of his free time to continue learning about the company and work on special projects. "Not all night," he said. "Maybe another hour or two."

"I appreciate your efforts very much, and I will see to it that you are extremely well compensated in 2020."

Juan Carlos smiled and then said, "Jorge, may I ask you something?" He detected a hint of stiffness in Jorge's posture, but Jorge nodded, so Juan Carlos said what was on his mind. "Sometimes it seems like we are going all in on 2019." Jorge looked at him without replying, so Juan Carlos continued, "Some of our investments and decisions seem to be designed to maximize profits and cash flow in 2019, and I always thought of us as a company with a long-term focus. I was wondering if we have shifted our strategy."

Jorge smiled and stepped back. He grabbed a chair from a neighboring cube and sat down. "You have always been a great thinker, Juan Carlos, and that is why I like you very much. We've made some subtle changes that are indeed more short-term focused. Our people are vastly underpaid, and I'm going to change that. Our laborers work so hard for about three US dollars per hour, whereas in the US they would make four to five times that. I told headquarters that I wanted to give my team large raises. At first, they laughed at me and said that our pay is above average for Juárez, but then we started negotiating. Please keep this confidential, but if we hit certain metrics this year, next year raises will be fifty percent."

"Haven't you been telling people thirty percent?" asked Juan Carlos.

"Yes, because I want some wiggle room, both if we come in a little short and if headquarters decides to screw us over. But we are indeed on pace to meet our goals and grant fifty percent raises next year. I will also have some slush money for outstanding performers, and I sincerely expect your raise to be at least sixty percent. You are one of our very best employees."

Juan Carlos grinned in embarrassment and then quickly started doing the math in his head to calculate how much extra cash that would be each week. Truthfully, he didn't have any needs that were going unmet, and most of his raise would probably be invested in the stock market. But perhaps he would take a long vacation next summer. He had one cousin in New York City and another in Los Angeles, and the thought of a cross-country road trip thrilled him.

"What will happen to our 2020 results?" Juan Carlos asked. "Will they fall off and our raises be cut?"

"Not at all," said Jorge. "Morale will be outstanding, and productivity will reach an all-time high. I firmly believe that with our high productivity, we will more than offset additional spending we will need to do in 2020 to account for some adjustments we have made in 2019."

"That's wonderful," said Juan Carlos. "I can't wait."

Jorge smiled. "Speaking of productivity, I was wondering about something. It is easy for me to monitor the people on the floor, but I've always been curious about those in offices, how efficient we are there. How much productivity do you suppose we lose to web surfing?"

"Without naming names, probably anywhere from five to thirty percent."

"Would it be easy for you to give me a weekly report of where we seem to be losing the most productivity?"

"It would be an estimate, but yes, I think I could. We can identify which employees are most often browsing sites that are clearly not work related."

"Thank you," said Jorge. "Would some argue they are working from home?"

"We actually monitor home internet use as well if they are using company-provided laptops, so if they are doing a lot of company-related work at home, we could tell that, to some extent. They are told this when they start, but occasionally we get someone surfing porn at home from a company machine, and we send them a message."

"So if I'm checking the fútbol scores at home, you would know that if I am using a company laptop?"

"In theory, yes." Juan Carlos laughed. "But we run a different report for off-site internet use. It is mainly to detect very malicious sites, like pornography, as well as keywords such as 'bribe,' 'kill,' 'blackmail,' and so forth."

Later that evening, Jorge sat in his easy chair and opened his personal laptop. He looked at his internet history, with the repeated searches involving the word "bomb," and was relieved no one else could see it.

Two days later, Jorge sat in the oncologist's office with Ana and his ex-wife. While he often hated the woman and knew that she often felt the same way about him, they'd agreed to always be kind to each other in front of Ana. They chatted about Ana's summer schedule and firmed up dates for their respective summer vacations with her. The oncologist entered the room and shook hands, first with Ana and then with her parents. He sat down, and they all looked at him earnestly. The doctor had a file open in his hands. He shut the file and laid it on the table next to him. Jorge gripped Ana's right hand, and Ana's mother gripped her left.

"Ana, I have the results of your three-month bloodwork." Jorge held his breath as the doctor continued, "I am so pleased to say that the chemotherapy treatment worked. Your cancer is completely gone. We will need to continue to monitor to you through monthly testing, but I am very optimistic that you have beaten this."

With those words, Jorge and his ex-wife leaned into Ana in a group hug of sorts. When they pulled apart a bit later, Ana leaped from her chair and into the arms of her doctor. As they stood to leave, Jorge also embraced the doctor and said, "Thank you for saving my daughter."

The doctor smiled and said, "She is a tough and courageous girl."

Ana walked out of the doctor's office holding the hands of both of her parents. To an outsider, they looked like a typical, happy family. Jorge walked them to his ex-wife's car and held the door for Ana as she climbed inside. He shut the door and walked around to the back of the car where his ex-wife was standing.

She spoke gently to him, "Jorge, I never thanked you for paying for Ana's medical care. I know how expensive it was. How did you ever manage it?"

Jorge had been expecting this question at some point and had rehearsed his answer. He didn't want to lie, but he certainly couldn't tell the whole truth either.

"I had to borrow some, and I also picked up a special project."

Ana's mother moved close to him, took his hand in hers, and then pulled him in, hugging him as tightly as possible. It was the first time she had hugged him since before he had been served with the divorce papers.

"Thank you," she whispered. "Thank you so much."

Jorge hugged her back, gently at first, and then more firmly.

They released their embrace a few seconds later, and Jorge noticed that Ana was watching through the back window of the car, smiling in delight. He waved as their car pulled away, and Ana waved back. Jorge went for a long walk through Ciudad Juárez's Parque Central and did his best to keep his mind off his "special project," if only for a few hours.

CHAPTER 12

Las Vegas, Nevada
June 12–13, 2019

Bob Grayson was 35,000 feet in the air, somewhere above Western Colorado, when slight turbulence woke him from his long nap. He was on a United airplane headed to Vegas. He tried to fly United whenever possible because he was a Premier 1K member, the highest possible status on the airline. With that distinction, he often got free upgrades to first class, as was the case on this trip.

He fondly remembered the days of flying with his friends to Vegas. They would book their flights very early and take over most of the first-class section. The trip out was always the best, full of anticipation and excitement. They would plan those trips for months and count down the days. Now, Bob dreaded the trips to Vegas. To avoid a paper trail, Sage's boss demanded the interest payments in cash and had selected Vegas as the handoff spot.

Bob became lost in thought, as he often did, wondering how this would all end. After paying taxes and the interest payments to Sage, he had surprisingly little to live on for a man whose gross pay was slightly north of $1 million per year. He was due to take over leadership of the entire central region in September, and with that would come a 20 percent pay raise, but even then it would take him several years to pay off his debt. At Sage's request, or more like his demand, he had used his access to information to earn an additional $50,000 in late April, and he'd brought it with him when he'd visited Sage in May.

It was so wrong, something Bob couldn't believe he had

done. Yes, he'd broken a federal law, but more than that, he'd broken trust. His clients trusted him, the members of the firm trusted him, and anyone who relied on the integrity of the accounting system trusted him. He had violated that trust. He shook his head and held on to the only thought that would ease the guilt: he wasn't directly stealing from anyone. It was stealing, yes, but it was from a faceless stock market. No one was really getting hurt, right? Not like he would if he didn't comply with Sage's demands.

The plane touched down, and within 40 minutes, Bob was checked into his room at the Mirage. He wouldn't be meeting Sage until tomorrow, so he had an evening to enjoy himself. He dined at the hotel's Cravings Buffet and noted how his stress was destroying his health. He had gained 30 pounds in the past 12 months, and his doctor was warning him to watch his cholesterol levels. If only he could rid himself of the debt! He would then have the mental energy to exercise and eat right.

He had made a moderate wager on tomorrow's game, and the anticipation was making him uneasy. He stayed out of the sportsbook altogether and found a $25 blackjack table, which was the minimum bet needed to get a decent game. There, he found a group of four young men in their early 20s who were in town for a small bachelor party. They reminded him of himself in his younger years. They hadn't played much blackjack and asked Bob a few questions about strategy. He taught them and felt like a father figure of sorts. The five of them sat at the table for nearly three hours. Bob broke even, and the four young men each left over $300 ahead. They high-fived Bob when they got a blackjack and hugged him when they left. They exchanged phone numbers and promised to stay in touch, though Bob doubted he would ever see them again. He slowly sipped two Jack and Cokes during the time and called it a night shortly before midnight. He couldn't remember the last time he'd had that much fun.

The next evening, Bob found his way to the VIP section of the Mirage's sportsbook and began sipping Jack and Cokes. It was game six of the NBA finals, and he was feeling optimistic. At the start of the playoffs, Bob had placed a large wager on the heavily favored Golden State Warriors. They'd made it to the finals but then had been down three games to one in the best-of-seven series. When Kevin Durant had gone down with a ruptured Achilles in game five, Bob had shuddered but then watched in amazement as Stephen Curry and Klay Thompson, the "Splash Brothers," carried the Warriors to a one-point victory. Games six and seven were at home, and with the nucleus having won three titles in the past four years, odds were on the Warriors' side. They were favored in game six by three and a half points and would again be favored in game seven once that time came.

Midway through the third quarter, the familiar figure sat down next to him.

"Good evening, Sage," Bob said pleasantly even though he hated the man.

Sage nodded and replied, "Good evening." Bob noticed that Sage never used his name. He supposed that was because Sage wanted to depersonalize the bloodshed if it came to that.

The waitress stopped by and asked Sage if he would like something to drink. Sage simply shook his head from side to side, an indication to Bob that Sage wouldn't be staying long.

"Do you have it?" asked Sage.

Bob reached into his coat, pulled out an envelope, and handed it to Sage.

"Any extra in here?"

"Not this time," said Bob.

"Not this time, not any time," Sage said with a piercing stare, seemingly forgetting the extra $50,000 that Bob had paid him last month. "The next time we meet, there better be extra."

"I tell you what," said Bob. "When the Warriors win this series, you can have my ticket. It will be worth thirty grand."

Sage cocked his head a bit and snarled. "Thirty grand! The Warriors were two-to-one favorites. You bet twenty thousand with the hopes of winning ten? You idiot! You could have paid us the twenty grand and been on your way to satisfying your debt."

"It was a good bet," said Bob as he gestured at the massive, 85-foot projection screen in front of them. "I didn't count on the Durant injury last night, but look, the Warriors are ahead."

"By a point," snarled Sage. Just then, Steph Curry drove the lane, and six trademark, lightning-fast Warriors passes later, Klay Thompson nailed the open three-pointer, giving him a game-high 28 points with 15 minutes still to play.

"By four points." Bob smiled smugly. A minute later, Bob smiled again as the Warriors stole the ball and flew up the floor. When Curry dished the ball to Thompson, all of Oracle Arena was on their feet, as was a buzzed and overweight man at the Mirage.

What happened next left Bob collapsed in his chair. As Klay Thompson rose to throw down a monstrous dunk, he was bumped at his apex by a Raptors player. Landing awkwardly on his left leg, Klay crumpled to the ground, clutched his left knee, and began rolling around in agony. Bob's horror grew as a run by the Raptors lost the Warriors their lead. He held his breath as, with under 10 seconds to go, Steph Curry rose for a go-ahead three-pointer, Bob's last chance for redemption. But Steph missed the shot, and Bob's $30,000 ticket became worthless in an instant.

Sage simply shook his head. "Next month you have another opportunity. The boss wants a hundred grand extra."

Bob had known this was coming. He'd planned to protest, but now that Sage was looming over him, he simply nodded glumly. "I can do that."

"A hundred grand extra," Sage continued, "and a phone call."

Bob cocked a quizzical eyebrow in Sage's direction.

"A phone call with the information you are acting on so we can get in on the action ourselves."

Bob rose, took a deep breath, and exhaled. "I can't do that. It will increase the risk too much." He turned and walked into the restroom. He splashed water on his face and stared in disbelief into the mirror. The nightmare kept getting worse.

He dipped his head toward the sink to splash more water onto his face and didn't see or hear Sage enter the restroom. Sage quickly checked to make sure Bob was alone and, when satisfied that he was, stepped silently toward the sink and grabbed the hair on the back of Bob's head with one hand.

In a previous life, Sage had been a marine. Now, he worked for one of New York's five mafia families. He was six foot four with 230 pounds of solid muscle. He moved with the grace of a tiger and had ferocity to match. Sage raised Bob's head and then slammed it into the faucet one time and then another as bloody water filled the sink. Sage whispered, "You can do it, and you will," before slipping out of the bathroom and the Mirage.

When Bob flew home the following afternoon—with two large bandages on his face—he decided it was time to up the stakes. "Go big or go home," the saying went. That evening, he called one of his friends who worked in private equity and asked if he had any foreign connections. An hour later, Bob was on the phone with a man in Switzerland, hammering out the details.

CHAPTER 13

Cleveland, Ohio
July 16–18, 2019

It was mid-July and the PurePower team was knee deep in the second-quarter review when Josh asked if he could take off a bit early for the auditors' softball game. He had gotten almost all his work done for the day and promised to work for another hour or so after the game, so Will gladly obliged. Will had high expectations, but he knew that everyone needed an outlet and made accommodations whenever possible.

Bob Grayson had encouraged Josh to join the softball team, to get out of his comfort zone and meet some of his coworkers. Josh hated it, but he did it to please Bob. He played right field and batted last. This was the final softball game of the year, meaning it was likely the final softball game he would ever play. He was still waiting for a good opportunity to come along so he could leave the firm.

Josh arrived nearly an hour early for the nine o'clock game, and to his surprise, Bob Grayson was already there. Bob had shown up near the end of a few of the previous games with a cooler full of beer—"trunk treats," Bob called them—for the team to enjoy afterward, but he'd never come this early.

Bob was sipping on a gas station fountain soda pop. The scent of whiskey wafted toward Josh's nose.

"Hey, Josh. Last game of the year. Did you enjoy the season?" Bob asked.

"Yeah, it was pretty good," Josh lied.

"Did Will Stevens give you any grief about leaving early?"

"No, I told him I'd have everything done for him."

"That's good. I'm very proud of you, Josh. You are doing a great job at the firm and really stretched yourself by joining this team."

Josh simply nodded, not sure how to respond.

"I bet you even read the second-quarter earnings release as soon as the draft came out!"

It wasn't really a question, but then, it wasn't *not* a question either. Josh didn't know how to reply, but he had read the release, so he simply said, "Yeah, I did."

Bob got really friendly and, lowering his voice, said, "Well, let me hear your analysis. Let's see if you remember anything I taught you."

Josh had been planning for this moment for quite some time. If he didn't follow the script in his head, he'd probably mess it up, so he started talking. "Bob, Maureen told us that we can't talk about earnings to anyone, not even you."

"Excuse me?" Bob asked, his voice rising.

"Yeah, we can't show the release to anyone or talk to anyone about it." Josh hesitated, not sure he should say the next part, but he'd rehearsed it, so he continued, "I assume you know this, so I'm confused why you asked to see the earnings release last quarter."

Bob got right in Josh's face. "What exactly are you accusing me of?"

That part wasn't in the script, and Josh froze. He felt like he was about to vomit. "Nothing. I'm sorry."

Bob hesitated and then said softly, "I was trying to teach you something. I have been investing time in you, trying to help you learn and get out of your shell. I am insulted that you would question me."

Josh gulped. That was also not in the script. Bob walked away and pulled out his phone. Josh feigned stretching as he watched Bob out of the corner of his eye. After a few minutes, Bob returned.

"Josh, two things: First, I know you've been thinking of leaving public accounting. Well, you're in luck. There is a company in town called Chalton Enterprises. Ever heard of them?"

Josh had no idea how Bob knew he was looking for other jobs, but he had heard of Chalton, so he just answered the question. "Yes."

Bob continued, "They have an opening for a staff accountant. One of my friends is the controller there, and I told him he couldn't find a better person for the job than you. Ten percent raise, minimal overtime, your own cubicle, and so forth."

Josh was a bit taken aback, but after this exchange, he now loved the idea of getting away from Bob Grayson almost as much as he loved the idea of getting away from JPG. "I'll definitely look into it," he said.

Bob took a step toward Josh and said, in a low voice, "You don't understand, Josh. You don't insult me like that without facing consequences. You are done at JPG, effective immediately. Don't go to PurePower tomorrow. Drop off your laptop at our downtown offices and email your resignation to HR. Take the job at Chalton if you like, or look for something on your own, but you're done here."

Josh bit his lower lip and nodded.

Bob stepped to Josh's side, put his arm around him, and pulled him in close. "Oh, and the second thing: if any, and I mean *any*, of our conversations ever get repeated, I will make sure you never again work as an accountant in the state of Ohio. Am I clear?"

Josh, panicked, simply said, "Yes, sir."

"And if your uncle asks why you left JPG, you say you weren't cut out for the intense environment of public accounting."

Josh was confused why his uncle was being brought into this, but he wasn't about to ask Bob any questions, so he simply nodded.

"Good."

Bob began walking away. After a few steps, he turned on a dime and came close to Josh again. Gone was the affable man who used to check in on Josh and coach him. The man standing before Josh now, with his tensed demeanor and penetrating, glassy-eyed stare, was a monster Josh wanted to be as far from as possible.

Bob slowly shook his head from side to side and said, in a very low and guttural voice, "You messed with the wrong person."

Spit flew from his lips and into Josh's eye. The spit mixed with tears as Josh simply nodded again.

Shortly thereafter, some of Josh's teammates began to arrive. They were laughing and joking and, as usual, tried to engage him. Josh faked it the best he could, although he was still shaking inside from the encounter with Bob. Normally a poor softball player, Josh was even worse that night. He went into the seventh inning hitless in three at-bats and made a brutal error that led to three unearned runs in the fifth inning. JPG was down by one run in the bottom of the seventh inning, with two outs and runners on second and third base.

Josh swung at the first pitch, which was well out of the strike zone, and hit nothing but air. "A walk brings up the top of the order," a teammate called out. Josh heard that, froze, and simply stared as the opposing pitcher delivered a perfect strike right down the middle of the plate. Josh struck out looking, and JPG finished the season second in the league.

Josh dropped off his laptop at 8:01 the next morning, immediately after emailing his resignation to HR. He didn't pursue the offer with Chalton but did find a job as a staff accountant with a small company a month later. He had to take a 20 percent pay cut, but he never saw anyone from JPG again.

He did, however, make one final phone call to someone at JPG before he forgot about the firm forever.

The next day, Johnny was knee deep in the second-quarter review when Bob Grayson asked him if he could come into the office to meet with a potential new hire. "You're the best associate we have," Bob had said when he'd called Johnny to make the request, "and we really want this woman. Just be yourself."

Johnny had only met Bob Grayson a handful of times, so he felt honored to have received a personal call. Bob had previously had very little time for Johnny the couple of times they had crossed path during PurePower's IPO, when Bob had been called in because of his expertise with merger and acquisition issues. Then, during the firm's volunteer day last month, Bob had spent close to an hour talking to Johnny. Perhaps Bob was showing him more attention because of the success of the PurePower account, which had given the office a ton of credibility and cash flow. Or perhaps the newfound attention stemmed from Johnny's Outstanding New Start award.

When Johnny showed up at the office at seven thirty the following morning, Bob was there to greet him.

"Thanks for coming in during this hectic time, Johnny," Bob said as he shook Johnny's hand. "The candidate should be here shortly."

"No problem," said Johnny. "Happy to help."

"So, how is life at PurePower?" Bob asked.

"Great but busy. They've grown so fast that they are a bit understaffed. It's a messy review."

"I hear the company is doing well, though," Bob replied.

"I guess."

"What do you mean, you guess?" Bob asked with a slight edge in his voice. "You review their earnings release before it goes out, don't you?"

"Well, of course," said Johnny, a bit embarrassed.

"I hear they are raising guidance again," Bob said nonchalantly, in the same way he might say he was thinking about eating a ham sandwich.

Johnny hesitated. Maureen had been clear that earnings information couldn't be discussed outside the PurePower audit team. But Bob already seemed to have the information, so Johnny simply nodded and said, "Yeah."

"Good for them," said Bob. "And good for us; maybe we can raise our fees next year."

Just then, Val arrived. "Keep up the good work," Bob said to Johnny as he walked away.

While Val brewed the Sumatra and Johnny waited to meet with the recruit, he worried a bit that he shouldn't have given Bob that confirmation. Perhaps Bob was testing him and he'd failed. But nothing seemed to come of it. He met with the recruit, a high-performing and ambitious woman who was entering her junior year at Bowling Green (which boasted one of the top accounting programs in the state), and went on with his day.

A week later, PurePower reported earnings of $0.36 per share, beating the forecast of $0.32 per share. The company also raised its annual guidance, now expecting earnings of $1.50 per share. Its share price increased by 15 percent, closing the day at $65 per share, easily an all-time high.

A few days after the earnings announcement, Bob Grayson flew to Las Vegas and gave Sage an envelope containing $150,000 in cash, roughly $50,000 of interest and $100,000 toward debt repayment. His debt was down to less than $850,000. This time, Bob simply flew in and out of Vegas and didn't stay overnight. He didn't drink or gamble, and he never let his guard down.

96 — Boz Bostrom

CHAPTER 14

Ciudad Juárez, Mexico
August 1, 2019

Jorge dropped off Ana at her mother's home and was at the plant by ten. He got to the office and read reports from the previous day. Production was stellar, as it almost always was, and there had been no safety concerns to speak of. He had a standing all-employee meeting at 3:00 p.m., when the shift changed. He had thought long and hard about how to make his announcement without causing alarm. He was the sole communication between the Juárez plant and the parent company's headquarters in Ohio, and he wanted to keep it that way. The last thing he needed was one of his team members suspecting something unusual and placing a call or sending an email to the US.

He began with a general performance update, which was all good news, as usual. He then transitioned and said, "We have been performing at such a high level, and US management has such confidence in us, that we are going to scale back production of the X+ model for the next few months. Demand for the model has temporarily slowed, and they are currently sitting on a high level of inventory of X+ batteries in the US. Demand for X batteries has greatly increased, so we are going to shift more of our efforts there. Due to the bottleneck on the X production machines, that may require a third shift as well as work on Sundays, and those of you who volunteer to do that will be compensated for the less desirable shifts. We also have a lot of interest in our higher-margin contract manufacturing work for third parties, so some of you will be reallocated there. Once demand has stabilized for the

X+ model, we will go back to manufacturing those. US management asked if we could make this change, and I assured them we could. We have a nimble and superior workforce, and I am confident we will step up to the challenge. We are fully on pace to meet the goals we discussed, and I anticipate we will be able to provide the raises and benefits at the start of 2020 that I have previously communicated. Keep up the great work!"

The meeting ended, and the workers dispersed in a happy mood. The type of work they did didn't matter a whole lot as long as they got paid. Many of them didn't understand or fully appreciate the difference in the X and X+ battery models. The need to have some members work odd shifts was also met with positivity, as those who chose to do so would get paid more. There may even end up being competition for those spots. Life at PurePower Mexico was good.

After the meeting, Jorge called Enrique and Raul, the two who oversaw packaging of the X batteries, into his office and asked them to be seated. "Guys, as we expand our efforts into contract manufacturing, I really need some of my best people in that area. I would like to move you there and have you supervise overall production. This is a promotion, and you will receive an immediate ten percent raise. Same shifts, just a different part of the facility. Sound good?"

Both Enrique and Raul smiled hugely, and they gladly accepted. Ten percent went a long way in Mexico. Before long, Jorge dismissed them. Fifteen minutes later, Manuel, Roberto, and Tomás, the three García brothers, entered. They were not currently employees of PurePower.

"Here's the deal, guys," Jorge began. "You will oversee packaging for the new X batteries on the overnight shifts and on Sundays. Every battery that gets produced in those times will be packaged in X+ materials. Absolutely no one can find out that we are doing this. Your contract is for six months. At that time, you will be done with the company. You will be paid well, and if you complete your work properly, on February 15 you will each receive a thirty-thousand-dollar bonus. Got it?"

Manuel and Robert looked to Tomás, the eldest and leader of the three.

"This sounds risky, like fraud," Tomás said. "For that we need a larger bonus. Fifty thousand for each of us."

Jorge made a show of picking up his phone and asking the three brothers to leave his office for a couple of minutes. When he opened the door for them to return, he didn't invite them in. "It's a deal. But if you mess up, you get nothing."

The brothers nodded and left.

When Jorge shut his door, he exhaled. The increased bonus they'd negotiated didn't matter. Jorge hadn't even called anyone to ask if it was okay. By February 15, the facility would be gone, as would Jorge.

Bruno was the one who had told Jorge to make the shift in manufacturing, and it had two purposes. First, in the unlikely event that the explosion did not work, PurePower would run out of the necessary batteries, and the impact on their worldwide business would be devasting. Second, this change would keep manufacturing costs lower, temporarily increasing PurePower's profit. Jorge had no idea why a short-term increase in profits was important if the facility was going to be destroyed, but he didn't really care. He was simply following orders. In six months, he would receive $5 million. He was going to talk about imminent danger and convince his ex-wife to join him and Ana in beginning a new life together, far from Juárez.

CHAPTER 15

Cleveland, Ohio
August 30–31, 2019

It was noon on the Thursday before Labor Day when Johnny walked onto the elevator on the 17th floor of the Stone Tower. When the elevator stopped at the 16th floor, Johnny thought nothing of it; elevators tend to do things like that at lunchtime. But when the door opened, he saw Katie for the first time since the Spring Bash. His eyes lit up whenever he saw her, and this time was no exception.

She greeted him with a friendly "Hey, stranger."

"Yeah, it's been a while. Good to see you," he said.

"Meeting someone for lunch?"

"No, just grabbing a sandwich. Trying to get some work done so I can take tomorrow off."

"Me too," she replied. "Any plans for the weekend?"

"Ben rented a cabin and is having a few people up."

Katie paused, and he realized that the thought of Ben probably made Katie think of Emily, and the thought of Emily probably made her think of Kim.

"Just a boys' weekend," he added. When the elevator opened at the ground floor, he allowed Katie to walk out first in a gentlemanly mannerism he had learned from Will. "Want to grab something at Bonnie's?"

Katie paused, then said, "Sure."

Johnny ordered a club sandwich, she a turkey with swiss, and they walked out to Public Square, which was bustling on that gorgeous late summer day. For a while, they talked about work. Katie had been focusing on the health care industry and was making quite a name for herself. Many people found the industry's operations complex and difficult to understand because of its heavy usage of computer systems. Katie spent a lot of her free time studying and was quickly becoming versed in how companies generated profits in that industry. There was talk of asking her to join a select team in Pittsburgh, where JPG was planning to open a new office, its 43rd. Johnny felt torn about that. He wanted the best for her but didn't want her moving away. He still held out slim hope that someday he could make things up to her. Simply put, he still had a big-time crush.

"Any rock climbing this summer?" he eventually asked.

"Yeah, I went to Red River Gorge in Kentucky back in June. It was awesome."

As she raised her sandwich to her mouth, Johnny looked at her hands and realized he had never noticed them before. They were incredibly strong, though still soft in appearance.

"How about you?" she asked. "Has anyone punched you in the face recently?"

Johnny laughed and said, "There was a big tourney in Washington, DC, earlier this month that I participated in."

"You win?" she asked.

"No." Johnny shook his head. "It would be very unlikely I would ever win one of those things. Some of the guys have sponsors, fight year-round, and don't get distracted by earnings releases and internal control reviews. If I get a good draw, I can win a couple matches before getting smoked."

"Was it a good draw in DC?"

"Not at all. I got matched up against one of the best in the world. He eliminated me in less than a minute."

"You went all the way to DC for a minute of fighting? Was it a waste?" she asked.

He shook his head. "Nah, because when I sign up for a tourney, it forces me to train hard, which is good for me. Plus, it was a fun little road trip with my sister."

"I didn't know you had a sister."

"Yeah, Danielle. We call her Dani. My parents had my brother and me four years apart and thought they were done. Dani came another four years after that. We are eight years apart, and I didn't spend as much time with her as I could have growing up, so I try to take her on adventures when I can. We had a great time exploring DC. We are polar opposites, and she helps keep me grounded."

Katie smiled. "Maybe sometime you can teach me how to fight, and I'll teach you how to climb."

"I'd like that." Johnny saw this as in invitation to make amends, and he softly said, "I need to apologize for what happened in Atlanta."

Almost as if she had waited for this day, Katie replied, "No need. We only had one date, and it wasn't like we were exclusive or anything."

Johnny leaned toward her a bit and said, "Katie, what I did was wrong. I cared for you, and I got carried away."

"Carried away," she said dispassionately. "So that's what it's called these days." Johnny bit his lip. Her pain was palpable as she continued, "So when we kissed goodnight after we celebrated taking our final sections of the CPA Exam, was that also you getting carried away?"

Johnny flashed back to that night and could still taste Katie's lips on his. "No, not at all," he pleaded. "I had feelings for you. I *have* feelings for you."

Johnny watched as Katie stared off in the distance toward three children playing with a long jump rope, and he noticed how beautiful her brown eyes were. "What are you thinking right now?" Johnny asked tenderly. He reached his hand toward hers and stopped when they lightly touched.

"I'm thinking that I have to get going," Katie replied. She wrapped up what was left of her sandwich and stood up.

Johnny started to rise, and she quickly said, "No. Don't."

He ignored her plea and reached a hand toward her shoulder. She held out her palm toward him and said, "I can't do this. Maybe part of me wants to, but I can't." She turned 180 degrees and began to walk away. She tossed a couple bucks in a musician's guitar case, and he interrupted his song to give her a quick thanks.

Johnny watched her leave and realized that one night in Atlanta had likely permanently ruined his chances.

"I feel ya, bud. Love's tough," the musician said.

Johnny grimaced. "You can say that again."

Johnny rose early on Friday morning, went for a three-mile loop through Edgewater Park, and packed a bag for the boys' weekend. Shorts, T-shirts, sandals, a swimsuit, and a few toiletries were all he needed. He threw his bag and golf clubs in the trunk of his Toyota Corolla, stopped at the local gas station for a fill, a donut, and some coffee, and started the two-hour pilgrimage east.

He thought about calling Katie and twice even picked up his phone to do so, but both times he set his phone down again, unsure of what he would say. He finally did call. After four rings he got her voicemail, and he hung up. He cranked XM radio's Alt Nation station, new alternative rock, set the cruise at 79, and drove on.

When Johnny pulled into the cabin, he saw Ben's SUV

parked in the gravel driveway. He parked alongside it, grabbed his bag, and walked toward the front door. He opened the front door and was greeted with a resounding "Surprise!"

Surprise indeed, as standing with Ben were not two other guys from their start group but Emily and Kim from Austin. It had been about 10 months since that night in Atlanta, but Kim still looked fantastic. She had dated a bit but hadn't found anyone she liked better than Johnny. As for Johnny, it seemed that his chances with Katie were slim. So here they stood, together again.

Kim walked swiftly toward Johnny and threw her arms around his neck. He hugged her back but felt more uneasy than excited. Johnny looked toward Ben and caught his eye and shot him a quizzical look. Ben noticed the look and said, "Ladies, let me show Johnny the boat. Maybe go change and we'll take a ride in a few minutes."

As they walked through the backyard and down the hill to the boat, Ben said, "What's wrong, man?"

"Why the hell didn't you tell me about this?"

"Because you'd have gotten cold feet. You haven't dated anyone since Atlanta. You need to get back in the game."

"I'm actually feeling fine on the sidelines right now."

"Bullshit. You need to get some action. You're too pent up. Kim's hot, she's cool, and she's really into you. Just have fun this weekend and worry about the future later."

Johnny was silent for a few moments. "I had lunch with Katie yesterday," he said finally.

Ben sighed. "Oh man, I thought that ship had sailed."

"So did I, kind of. But when I saw her, I wanted to be with her."

"So what happened?"

"She's still pretty bitter about Atlanta."

Ben hesitated. "Well, no one is going to tell her about Kim being up here, so enjoy the weekend with Kim and worry about Katie later."

They heard some laughter in the distance and turned around to see the women walking down the hill. Emily had on a red bikini; Kim's was brown and made her body look even more tan and toned.

"Just enjoy it," Ben repeated, and he walked up the hill toward the women.

CHAPTER 16

Cleveland, Ohio
September 6–October 26, 2019

On the Friday after Labor Day, Johnny was back in the office. Fridays in the office were jeans approved, so Johnny donned a polo and a pair of Levi's. Around ten thirty in the morning, Johnny was intently focused on a complex XLOOKUP formula in Microsoft Excel and didn't hear Bob walk up to his cube.

"Johnny Fitch!"

Johnny startled to attention and smiled. "Hi, Bob."

"Everything going okay with PurePower?"

"Yeah, I'll be back out there in a couple weeks and will probably be there for about a month over quarter-end."

"Great. You a Browns fan?" Bob asked.

"Of course."

Bob tossed a pair of tickets on Johnny's desk and said, "Enjoy the game," as he walked away.

Johnny picked up the tickets: 40-yard line for Sunday's opener against Tennessee. He stood to thank Bob for the tickets and to ask why he was receiving them, but Bob was gone.

On the last Monday in September, 37 wide-eyed and eager roughly 22-year-olds were seated in the training room at JPG. Johnny and his friends were no longer the New Starts; a new batch of New Starts had arrived. They first listened to Bob Grayson, who gave an inspiring welcome about the firm's history, its successes, and its philosophy. They then listened to Maureen Davis, who talked about the audit practice and the importance of learning. Maureen then welcomed the next speaker, who she referred to as the Outstanding New Start from last year's class.

Johnny walked to the podium, looked out at the group, and smiled. He remembered sitting in their spot, eating a banana nut muffin and soaking up as much wisdom as he could. The last year had been intense, with many highs and only a few lows. He gestured to a woman in the second row and, with well-rehearsed words, began to speak. "One year ago, I was sitting in your chair. Sometimes it seems like it was yesterday, but then I reflect on how much I have learned and how much I have grown. The best thing I did was find a great mentor.

"Will is very sharp, but he separates himself in the way that he carries himself and cares about his work, his clients, and his team. When I am talking to Will, he makes me feel like the most important person in the world, and I know others feel the same way. He makes me want to be a better worker and a better person. He also makes me want to be a better leader, to have others look at me the way I look at him. While he is the hardest-working person in the office, he is never too busy to teach me or to grab lunch or a beer and counsel me. He is investing in me, and if I have done one thing well, it is that I have leaned into him as much as possible. I have let him teach me, let him guide me, and let him prepare me for a bright future with JPG. So find your mentor and lean into them." Johnny paused for effect. "But you can't pick Will. He's mine."

The New Starts laughed.

A few weeks later, in late October, Johnny was knee deep in the third-quarter review. The quarter-end was an unusually busy one for PurePower. They had completed an acquisition, and the target company was a family-owned business that did not maintain GAAP-based financials, the standard required of publicly traded companies like PurePower. Johnny spent the better part of two weeks reviewing the PurePower controller's best attempt at the target's opening balance sheet. Much of that work had happened during the due diligence phase of the acquisition, but there were still some loose ends to tie up. Will gave that task to Johnny, of course, because Will gave all the tough tasks to Johnny.

Will tolerated errors and gave Johnny a lot of freedom, but he told him, "Keep me in the loop with any problems. If you aren't getting the information you need from the client, I want to know about it." When Johnny had sent an email to the wrong person at the client, Will forgave him. When Johnny had asked the arrogant CEO who he was, rubbing him wrong, Will forgave him. But when Johnny had once sat on information, not bringing Will into the loop quickly enough, Will criticized him heavily. Johnny never made that mistake again.

The long hours meant that tension in the audit room got high at times, but Will did a great job of keeping everyone grounded. They had fitness challenges, weekly meditations, and even an essential oil diffuser in the audit room. Maureen had given Will a liberal expense budget for staff morale, so lunch and dinner were brought in every day. At three every afternoon, Will held a short trivia contest, and the winner received a bottle of craft beer (to be consumed off-hours).

On Fridays, work ended at five o'clock. Will would bring his team to Sonrisa and stuff everyone in cabs at the end of the night with instructions about what to wear on Saturday. Hawaiian day, athletic day, glory days: the theme was always something different.

Five days before the third-quarter earnings were to be announced, Will asked Johnny to review the press release.

PurePower was raising its earnings guidance yet again, this time by over 20 percent. Sales were increasing, but interestingly, "manufacturing efficiencies" were driving huge margin improvements. At the time of the IPO, PurePower was forecasting operating margins for the year of 28 percent, but the recent guidance expected margins to be a phenomenal 33 percent.

The company's IPO had not only raised capital, but it had also raised awareness of PurePower's batteries. Orders were through the roof, especially for the X+ batteries, and product could not be produced quickly enough. PurePower management was regularly checking in with the general manager at their Juárez facility to make sure production of X+ batteries stayed at a high level.

At one point, Will asked the client how often they visited Juárez.

"Just once or twice per year," they replied. "They keep delivering great results, so we basically try to stay out of their way."

Will saw risk in that approach and decided a visit to Juárez would be in JPG's best interest.

One evening, at about nine o'clock, Johnny was verifying the accuracy of the numbers in the press release (a process auditors called "tying out") while watching some Monday night football. His phone buzzed, and he did not recognize the number. He debated whether to answer it and ultimately pressed the green talk button.

"This is Fitch," he said, not taking his eyes off the television.

"Johnny, it's Bob Grayson."

Johnny sat up and hit the mute button on the television, shocked that the newly appointed managing partner for the central region was on the other end of the phone.

"Hi, Bob."

"Yes, I am sorry for contacting you this late, but I must make a staffing request of our national office in the morning. I'm wondering if you think we'll need more people on the PurePower account next year. I'll ask other team members as well, but I like to get thoughts from people at different levels."

Although it was a little odd, Johnny felt a sense of pride that Bob wanted his input. "We were stretched about as thin as possible this year, and everyone says they are going to start doing a bunch of bolt-on acquisitions. I assume we'll need to increase our budgeted hours next year by thirty percent or so."

"Okay, thanks. That is helpful information. Does the company seem to be doing all right?"

"I guess," said Johnny. "Everyone keeps raving about them."

"They going to increase guidance again, I suppose?"

"Yeah," said Johnny. As soon as the word left his lips, he questioned himself again.

"That's good," said Bob. "Very good. When our clients do well, we do well. Well, I think you answered my question. Thanks, as always, for your hard work. After earnings are released on Friday, make sure to catch your breath this weekend. Go grab a nice dinner and put it on your expense report. If anyone squawks, tell them I approved it."

After they hung up the phone, Johnny kept the game on mute while he thought. Bob had sounded different when he'd asked about PurePower's earnings guidance. It was as if he'd been nervous but trying to sound casual at the same time. Unsure what else to do, Johnny turned the volume of the TV back on and completed his tie-out of the press release.

The next day at work, Johnny thought occasionally about his conversation with Bob and tried to figure out what about it was unsettling him. His head was still a jumbled mess when he left the client site at eight at night, so he drove straight to the karate school in Parma. Eight instructors had shown up to spar: a perfect number. After a few minutes of warm-ups, they broke into groups of four.

The rules were that you sparred each person in your group, round-robin style, and then the winners of each group would meet in the nightly championship match. Two points were awarded for a kick and one point for a punch, with the fighters resetting after each point. The winner was the one who scored the most points in the three-minute round. In tournaments, rounds were only two minutes, but they pushed themselves harder in training. Johnny won his first three matches, although none of them were easy. In the championship match against Brent, he had a 9–6 lead with 30 seconds remaining. A hard right hand by Johnny had broken a strap on Brent's helmet, and Brent called a time-out to put on a spare.

Johnny had a couple of minutes to relax, and thoughts of Bob Grayson crept back into his mind. It finally dawned on him. After the markets had closed the day before, PurePower indicated it would release its earnings Friday morning instead of Thursday morning as originally planned. The company needed a bit more time to get the auditors comfortable with the accounting for its recent acquisition. This change in timing hadn't even been brought up in the audit room. Johnny only knew because he'd overheard it mentioned by the controller while waiting for the elevator that evening. But Bob had told Johnny to grab a nice dinner after the earnings release on Friday. How had he known that information?

Brent interrupted his thoughts. "I'm ready. Let's finish this."

Johnny nodded and the center referee started the match back up. Brent blitzed Johnny and punched him in the head four straight times, pulling out a 10–9 victory.

"What the hell, Fitch?" cackled another instructor. "You died out there."

"Too many big lunches, dinners, snacks, and not enough time on my feet." Johnny forced a laugh.

In truth, thinking about Bob had thrown him completely off his game.

On Friday, before the markets opened, PurePower released earnings and revised full-year guidance significantly upward. PurePower's stock price skyrocketed, and the company was the New York Stock Exchange's top stock gainer of the day.

When the PurePower audit team went out to celebrate the end of another quarter of earnings on Friday evening, Will noticed something off about Johnny. He was distant and drinking more than usual. It wasn't celebratory drinking; it was drinking to get drunk, to escape something. Johnny was also staring at the college football game on the television instead of chatting with his teammates like he normally did. So when Johnny went to use the restroom, Will decided to follow him in.

They stood side by side at the urinals, and Will asked, "Everything okay, man?"

Johnny wobbled a bit as he glanced over at Will. "Yeah, just tired. Rough quarter."

A short while later, Johnny excused himself from the party and caught a Lyft. Will followed him out, and as Johnny got into the car, Will said, "If you need to get something off your chest, let me know." Johnny drunkenly nodded back. The cab dropped him off at home at nine, and he was asleep five minutes later.

The next morning, Johnny woke a bit before seven. Despite some cobwebs, he felt pretty good after sleeping for nearly 10 hours—a side benefit of passing out early, he figured.

It was a perfect October morning, 60 degrees with the sun peeking over the horizon, and Johnny decided to go for a run to clear his head. As he set foot after foot on the running trails of Edgewater Park, he couldn't stop thinking about Bob Grayson. Was it possible that Bob was using Johnny for stock tips? How could Johnny find out? This was crazy. Bob was the central region managing partner and seemed to be an honest guy.

Johnny was on the second half of his first loop, a mile from home and near the park's large pavilion, when an idea hit him. He dropped the hammer and was pouring sweat by the time he entered his apartment complex. He sprinted up the stairs, taking the steps two at a time. He burst into his apartment and hustled over to his laptop. A minute later, his jaw dropped.

Will was still in bed when his phone buzzed.
"Can you talk?" It was Johnny, out of breath.
"Sure," Will replied. "What's up?"
"Let's meet at the Starbucks off Clifton," Johnny replied.
"What's going on?"
"I'll be there in twenty minutes" was all that Johnny said.

Johnny, still wearing his sweat-soaked running gear, was already in the back corner of the Starbucks and staring intently at his open laptop by the time Will walked in. Will stopped at the counter and ordered a large Sumatra (Johnny and Val had hooked him), then sat down across from Johnny.

"Well?" Will asked.

Johnny took a deep breath. "When is the last time you talked with Bob Grayson?"

"Probably a month ago."

"He didn't ask you earlier this week about staffing PurePower next year?"

"What? No. Johnny, what the hell is going on?" Johnny looked around nervously and Will repeated, a bit more slowly, "Johnny. What the hell is going on?"

Johnny told Will about the two unusual conversations he'd had with Bob Grayson. Will listened intently, never interrupting, and kept nodding. When Johnny finished, Will said, "Thanks for telling me that, man. Sounds weird, but I've always thought Bob was an odd guy. And nosy. Definitely nosy. I bet that's what it is, Bob being nosy. Probably nothing to worry about."

Johnny turned his computer around and simply said, "That last conversation was Monday evening, October 21."

Johnny had pulled up a history of the share price and trading volumes of PurePower over the last month. As expected, the stock price jumped on Friday, October 25, after earnings were released. But then Will realized what Johnny was getting at. PurePower traded somewhere in the vicinity of 500,000 shares per day, give or take 50,000 shares. But on Tuesday, October 22, share volume was 725,000 shares. It returned to normal on Wednesday and Thursday before spiking as expected on Friday. Tuesday had been a normal day in the markets in general. But something happened at PurePower. More specifically, someone was trading on PurePower.

Will glanced at Johnny, who said, "There were 225,000 extra shares, and the stock price went up 23 points on Friday. That's 225,000 times $23 per share—about $5.2 million."

Will glanced back at the laptop and sat back in his chair. He took a sip of piping hot Sumatra as Johnny continued, "I went back and looked at my previous conversation with Bob. On July 17, when I met Bob in the office before the markets opened, the share price was $56. Average share volume around that time had been about 500,000 shares per day. The next day, 700,000 shares were traded, and again, the markets were normal that day in terms of both pricing and volume. A week later, the stock price jumped 9 points when earnings were released. That's 200,000 extra shares times $9 per share—about $1.8 million."

Will, always quick-witted and known for saying the right thing at the right time, was silent. His mouth hung half open, and he only moved to take another sip of Sumatra.

"Say something, Will," Johnny pleaded.

"Holy shit" was all Will could muster.

"Say something else."

"Okay. It's possible that what you are saying is true. Let's go through it all again, more slowly this time, and think about any other possibilities."

For the next two hours, which included another tall cup of Sumatra, a blueberry muffin for Will, and a fried egg bagel for Johnny, they hashed through things: motives, misinterpretations, possibilities, consequences, and the like. In the end they concluded that one thing was quite feasible: Bob Grayson was involved in a multimillion-dollar insider trading scheme, and Johnny had helped him pull it off.

CHAPTER 17

Cleveland, Ohio
October 28, 2019

The following Monday afternoon, Will swung into JPG's main office in the Stone Tower. Although Bob now managed the entire central region, Bob still considered Cleveland his home base.

The light was indeed on in Bob's office as Will walked down the hall. Will felt his heartbeat accelerate and his breathing become shallower. "Get it together," he whispered to himself. He paused 10 feet from the door and closed his eyes, taking a deep breath.

"Everything okay, Will?"

Bob's booming voice startled Will out of his trance. While Will had been collecting himself, Bob had walked out of his office.

"Oh, sorry, Bob. I'm a little anxious. Can we talk for a minute?"

"Of course," Bob said and stepped aside to let Will in. Bob shut the door and plopped into his high-back mesh chair. After a minute of idle chatter, Bob asked, "What can I do for you?"

"Johnny Fitch talked to me," Will began, and he thought he saw Bob's eyes tighten, if only a bit. "He is somewhat uncomfortable that you've been asking him about PurePower, as he thinks that's confidential information."

Bob's eyes tightened for sure this time as he leaned back and folded his arms. "What's your point, Will?"

"I'd rather you direct any questions to me." Will exhaled,

relieved he had made his request.

"I see," said Bob. "You don't trust the central region managing partner."

"It's not that. It's that Johnny is still fairly new and, like many New Starts, wants to follow every rule to a T."

Bob slowly nodded affirmatively and replied, "This younger generation is too concerned about rules, processes, and bullshit like that. Back in my day, we worked hard, collaborated, and got the job done."

Will decided not to reply and inhaled as he brought his lips together.

"But that's fine," Bob continued. "I thought he was one of us and enjoyed the personal attention, but I will direct my questions to his big brother instead."

Will let the comment pass and simply stood up and said, "Thanks." He began to walk out of the office, and right about the time his hands touched the doorknob, Bob spoke again.

"Hey, Will." Will turned to look at Bob. "The next time Johnny has a problem with me, tell him to grow a pair and come talk to me himself."

Will nodded his head once and quickly exited Bob's office.

The next morning, Bob flew to Las Vegas and gave Sage an envelope with $250,000 in cash. Bob now had more than that. Much, much more. He'd considered paying off the entire debt, but he'd decided on a different use for the cash, one that would set him free forever. Once again, the trip to Vegas was an in-and-out day trip. Bob didn't have anything to drink, didn't place any bets, and didn't even use the restroom. He never took his eyes off Sage.

Sage said, "You did good work for us last week. The boss is very happy."

"Good enough for you to wipe off my remaining debt?" Bob asked.

Sage laughed coldly. "Not that good. Let's spread the balance over two more quarters. You will continue to call us with the information you are acting on. Then we will call it good."

Bob said, "I can do that. But we may have a problem. I need you to do something for me."

After Bob explained what he needed, Sage nodded. "Consider it done."

"Don't go overboard on this one," Bob said firmly.

Sage just stared at him.

That evening, Bob pulled off the interstate after a long day of travel and drove down Gates Mills Boulevard. He loved that road with its beautiful homes on either side. He turned off the boulevard into the city limits of Pepper Pike, one of Cleveland's most ritzy suburbs, and before long saw his house up ahead. It was a gorgeous house, boasting over 5,000 square feet and a very open floor plan. It had an obscene number of windows, something his ex-wife had insisted on when they'd built the home in the mid-1990s. Many times over the past few years, as his gambling debt had mounted, he'd considered selling it, but in the end he couldn't stand the thought of separating himself from the last remaining memory of his family, and he held out hope that the familiarity of the place would draw his daughters back one day.

As he went to turn left into his driveway, he noticed a car parked across the street, which was odd. He then saw a lone figure sitting on his front step. He stopped short of his garage and called out, "Who's there?"

"Bob, it's Maureen."

Bob put his car in park and exited as calmly as he could. He was feeling quite uneasy but knew he couldn't show it.

"Maureen, it's ten o'clock on a Tuesday night. Why are you sitting on my front steps?" he asked.

"Where were you today?" she asked.

"I had to fly to Chicago for a client proposal."

"Which client?"

"It's confidential."

"Cut the crap, Bob. How was Vegas?"

Bob stood silently for a few seconds. Softly, he asked, "How did you know I was in Vegas?"

"I know a lot more than that."

"I don't know what you're talking about." His pulse began to race, and his breath became short. He didn't even recognize his own voice.

Maureen ignored his deceit. She had been expecting it. "A couple months ago, a friend saw you on a flight home from Vegas and said it was clear you had been beaten up. I noticed you worked from home for the next week, citing a cold, unusual in the middle of a hot summer. And then, a week later, I got another call, from Josh, the former staff member on the PurePower account who mysteriously resigned without warning or explanation. I guess you've been snooping around."

"Josh," Bob muttered.

"I've also noticed that trading volumes have been way up on PurePower before earnings are released. At first, I thought it was just speculators, but the numbers seemed high even for them. I figured someone was getting in on the action, maybe the friend of someone in controlling or the distant relative of a board member. But then I put two and two and two together. I know what you're doing, and given your history with gambling, I can guess why you're doing it. How much do you owe?"

Bob's initial impulse was to lie, to deny it tooth and nail, but the truth was that Maureen was much smarter than he, and she would see right through his bullshit. He was exhausted and tired of running. Tired of looking over his shoulder. Tired of wondering when Sage was going to assault him next. Tired of wondering if every call that came in was the FBI, SEC, IRS, DOJ, FINRA, or any other governing body with an acronym. And so, he told the truth.

"Six hundred and forty thousand dollars."

Maureen nodded. "I was afraid it would be even larger." She looked off into the distance for a moment. "You recruited me. You groomed me. You made me who I am. You went to bat for me against the sexist bastards on the leadership team when I was up for partner. You are my role model and one of my best friends."

Bob remained quiet, tensed for the squad cars he was sure would come blazing up at any moment.

"When will the six forty be paid off?" she finally asked.

"Two more quarters," he replied.

"And then you'll stop?"

"Yes. I swear I will be done."

Maureen got up and walked past him into the driveway. Before disappearing into the night, she said, "Out of respect for all you have done for me, I'll give you two more quarters. If it continues past that, I will have no choice but to call the authorities." Bob nodded gratefully as she continued, "I was always concerned about your gambling. That must stop as well. If I ever hear of you purchasing another lottery ticket, playing in a fantasy football league, or even just playing pull tabs at the bar, I will make the call."

Bob got choked up. "Thank you, Maureen. I am so sorry to let you down."

She walked away without acknowledging his weak apology.

Bob went inside and, hands shaking, poured himself a strong Jack and Coke. He felt that he had narrowly dodged a bullet. He didn't know why Maureen was giving him a second chance, but it didn't matter. He was still safe. For now.

He collapsed onto the sofa and flipped on game six of the World Series. Earlier, he had put $100 on the Nationals to beat the Astros and keep the series alive. Sure enough, with the stakes so small, he won the bet.

CHAPTER 18

Westerville, Ohio
November 2, 2019

It was the first basketball game of the year in Columbus's north-ern Westerville suburb. The Westerville College Sand Gazelles were playing Saint Paul University, a team from Minnesota.

Sophomore accounting major Billy Fitch felt nervous as he went through warm-ups. He had played hundreds of basketball games in his life, thousands if he included pickup games, but this one felt different. He had been a highly touted recruit and gotten about a dozen minutes a game playing for Westerville the year before. As a freshman, he'd been asked to control his game: shoot the open three and play solid defense. This had been a bit limiting for a player who'd been used to being "the man" his whole life, but he'd gradually accepted the role. All had gone well until the final regular season game against top-ranked Loveland. Coming down on a rebound, Billy had landed on the foot of an opponent and suffered a high-ankle sprain. Westerville had lost that game, which had cost them a share of the conference title. Then they'd been upset in the first round of the conference tournament, a game that Billy had also missed, and it had ended their season.

Now in his second season, Billy was probably good enough to be in the starting lineup, but the coach was deferring to a senior who had put in his time. This disappointed Billy, but instead of grumbling, he'd simply increased his effort. He was the first one to arrive at every practice and the last one to leave. His already strong game had started to improve even more. The coach told him to be ready for heavy minutes, and Billy aimed to play so well that the coach would never take him out.

As Billy drained a long three to end warm-ups and headed to the bench, he looked into the stands and saw his parents, older brother, and younger sister. His parents and sister always attended his games, so he kind of took that for granted, but it meant a lot to see his brother. Johnny lived two hours away and put in long hours at the office, so Billy knew it wasn't easy for him to get away.

Four minutes into the game, Westerville was down by five points, struggling to put the ball in the net. The coach gestured toward Billy, who took off his warm-up shirt, checked in at the scorer's table, and entered the game at the next whistle. He was going to come out firing and make everyone in the arena notice that he was ready to play a leading role.

Initially, the game seemed faster than he remembered, and on his first possession playing defense, he was a step slow chasing his man through a series of picks and watched helplessly as his man knocked down a jumper from the elbow. Billy shook his head as he ran up the court. He threw a bad pass on the next possession. Saint Paul picked it off and flew up the other end of the court, ending the fast break with a thunderous dunk.

When Westerville brought up the ball again, Billy caught the pass coming off a screen, open from three, and eagerly rose to take the shot. He rushed it, without reason, and it missed, the ball barely hitting the back rim before clanging out of bounds. After Saint Paul scored again to increase their lead to 11, Westerville's coach called for a time-out. Billy walked back as a heckling fan from Saint Paul called out to him, "Nice shooting, Seventeen."

Billy's head was hanging low when his coach intercepted him and said, "Billy, listen to me. Settle down and play basketball.

I'm keeping you in the game, and you are going to make your next shot. I believe in you."

Billy nodded. As he left the bench area, he shot a glance up into the stands. His sister Dani was intently drawing in her sketchbook, as it seemed she always was. Johnny flashed him the thumbs-up sign and mouthed, "You got this." Billy nodded back and took his place on the floor. The coach called a play for Billy coming out of the time-out, a very high pick that would likely cause his man to slide under the screen instead of fighting over it or switching with his defender.

Billy took the ball and watched a teammate come out to set the screen to Billy's left. As expected, Billy's defender started to slide underneath. Billy took one dribble left to sell it and then dribbled once back to his right. He was four feet beyond the three-point line, but that didn't matter. He rose in the air and felt like he was floating. The moment the ball came out of his hand, he knew he didn't even have to watch it; it would be good. He watched it anyway, and it sailed through the hoop, touching nothing but net.

Billy hit four more three-pointers and threw down a monstrous windmill dunk after stealing a bad pass by Saint Paul's point guard, giving Westerville a one-point lead. After Westerville forced a bad shot by Saint Paul, Billy brought the ball up the court. Saint Paul immediately sent a double team at him. He dished out of the double team and then ran for the corner, his man staying with him the whole way. Westerville whipped the ball from man to man as Saint Paul desperately tried to rotate while not losing sight of Billy. Billy cut toward the basket as a teammate got the ball wide open at the free-throw line. But the teammate didn't shoot or drive to the basket. Instead, he let Billy pick up another screen and pop open by a hair from the opposite corner. Billy caught the ball and rose to shoot as the defender jumped in his face. He was falling away a bit, right into his team's bench. It would have been a horrible shot under any other circumstances, but when you were this hot, you kept shooting. When the shot went through, extending Westerville's lead to four, Saint Paul's coach called another time-out, and the arena erupted. Billy didn't need to walk back to the bench—he had landed there—and his teammates pounded on him in celebration.

Billy had scored 20 points in only five minutes, hitting seven straight shots, including six from three-point land. He eventually missed, but by then the momentum had changed. His teammates were playing with confidence and Saint Paul's spirit was broken. Westerville won by 18 points, and Billy finished with a game-high 27 points.

Westerville's coach gathered the team in the locker room after the game. "Great job tonight, guys. That's the kind of effort we need to bring all year. And Billy, feel free to get hot like that anytime." His teammates laughed and pounded on him again, and then they all went back into the arena to greet their families and friends.

Billy chatted briefly with a couple of friends and then walked over to where his family was standing. He shook hands with his dad, and his mom and sister Dani pulled him in for a hug. Then he turned toward his brother, who extended his hand and said, "Little brother, that was one of the coolest things I have ever seen. Well worth the two-hour drive."

Billy grabbed his brother's hand and pulled him in for a strong embrace. "Thanks, Johnny. It means so much that you came down here."

Johnny was leaving the arena when he heard a voice call out, welcoming him back to Westerville: "¡Bienvenido de nuevo!"

Johnny spun around and smiled when he saw Elena, his favorite professor from his college days. A couple of quick steps later, he was leaning down to give her a gentle hug.

"It's my first time back since graduation," Johnny said. He remembered seeing Elena on graduation day and how she'd teared up a bit when they'd said goodbye.

"Let's walk," Elena said, "and you can tell me what you've been up to."

For the next 30 minutes, they reminisced and strolled around the campus that Johnny had called home for four years— or more like three and a half years, as he'd spent one semester studying abroad in Chile. Elena, who taught Spanish, had been the study abroad program director that year. Johnny remembered how homesick he had felt while in Chile and how Elena had always been there to lift his spirits. Johnny had continued to go to her for guidance even after they were back in the US. The next year, when he'd ultimately had to choose between an offer from JPG and an offer from a Big Four CPA firm, it was Elena's advice he'd sought.

As they walked, Elena asked him how his new job was going. Did he feel like he had made the right decision going with JPG? Though part of Johnny wanted to tell her about his current struggles involving Bob Grayson, he told her about the positive things instead: he was doing interesting work and had found a wonderful mentor. She seemed glad to hear he was doing well.

When they arrived back at the arena, Elena said, "Make sure to let me know the next time you are on campus for a visit. While I don't know much about accounting, I've lived a lot of life. Any time you need someone to talk to, you know where to find me."

"Gracias," Johnny replied.

CHAPTER 19

Ciudad Juárez, Mexico
November 4, 2019

Jorge had once imagined that receiving the news of Ana's cure from cancer would be one of the best days of his life, and it truly had been, but every day thereafter had been worse because the deadline was drawing closer. In August, he'd called Bruno and asked to change the plan, promising to set a payment schedule to pay Bruno back for the $100,000 advance with a healthy rate of interest. Bruno had simply laughed at him, and later that evening, his two thugs had stopped Jorge on his way home from work and smacked him around a bit.

In September, Jorge had tried to make plans to escape Juárez with Ana. He'd found a small town in Belize where they could start a new life and had been in the midst of trying to figure out how to convince Ana's mother to join them when he'd received a call from Bruno. As if reading his mind, Bruno had warned him that if he ran with his family, Bruno would find them and kill them slowly.

Out of options, Jorge continued working on a plan to blow up the plant and coped the way he used to: with tequila. He raised his empty glass and the bartender brought over the bottle to fill it again. Jorge looked at the liquid. It was golden in color, meaning it was cheap. He didn't have money for better brands.

His ex-wife called, wanting to transfer Ana to private school and asking if Jorge could pay for it. Jorge asked her why she couldn't get a second job to help cover the cost. That led to yelling, a bit of swearing, and a hastily ended call. Jorge missed the old days of rotary phones, when you could make a point by slamming down the receiver when you were ticked off. Perhaps it was better this way, though. He would still need her cooperation if he wanted to leave Juárez with Ana after the project was complete.

Jorge continued to order tequila until nearly midnight, when the bartender came over and said he needed to close. Jorge found a late-night taco stand and ordered four tacos to carry home. He stuffed his face as he walked, portions of the tacos spilling down his shirt and onto the street. He staggered into his house, plopped down on his easy chair, and turned the TV to the rerun of a fútbol match played earlier that evening. He grabbed two beers from the fridge but was passed out in his recliner before even finishing half of the first one.

Sometime around two in the morning, an idea roused him from his sleep. He read up on the use of ammonium nitrate in the Oklahoma City bombing and, after scribbling some illegible notes in a special notebook, closed his internet browser and laptop. He shut off the TV and went to sleep in his bed. When he got up the next morning, he was hungover and disorganized. He staggered to the side table next to his easy chair, grabbed his work laptop—which was resting on top of his personal laptop—and went to the plant.

The next evening, Jorge looked on his personal laptop for the previous day's Google searches related to ammonium nitrate. None were to be found, and this confused him. He tried a few things to find his searches but didn't have any luck. Eventually, he shrugged and, assuming it had all been a drunken dream, found the information he wanted with fresh searches.

CHAPTER 20

Cleveland, Ohio
November 5–9, 2019

On a Tuesday evening, Johnny and Will were the last two working at PurePower's corporate offices in Parma. In five days, Will would be flying out to Ciudad Juárez, and Johnny was envious. Maureen had finally decided that JPG needed to investigate the production facility and warehouse in Mexico, since having only two production facilities posed a significant risk to PurePower and, in turn, to JPG.

"Any chance you need someone to go along and carry your suitcases?" Johnny remarked while packing up his things around seven o'clock.

Will laughed. "I didn't get my first international trip until last year. Your time will come. Plus, you have a free trip to Dubai anytime you want! When you going to take that one?"

Johnny shrugged. He really didn't have any plans and still wasn't sure who he would take with him. Possibly his brother or sister. He still dreamed of taking Katie, but after their last encounter, the chances of that seemed about as good as Nicholas Montgomery agreeing to accompany him. "You sure you don't want me to stick around tonight?" Johnny asked instead.

"Nah, go on and get out of here. Go get a workout in and do some bicep curls for me." Will grinned.

A half hour later, Johnny found himself at the gym working with free weights, the only real kind of weights, in his opinion. Ironically, it was during a set of hammer curls that he first saw Katie's familiar long brown hair. She was doing lunges with alternating legs. Her form was perfect, and he realized he had never seen her in workout attire before. He stared somewhat trans-fixed in her direction and quickly tightened up his own form and body in case she looked his way.

He went to the weight rack to set down his dumbbells just as she did the same.

"Hey, Johnny," she said, eyes lighting up in recognition.

"Hey, Katie," he replied. "It's been a while. Come here often?" He cringed, realizing he had used one of the oldest and cheesiest pickup lines in the book.

Katie cocked her eyebrow. "I joined at the first of the month. Wasn't digging the vibe at my other gym."

Johnny nodded, trying to appear casual instead of awkward. "What do you think of the vibe at this one?"

"So far so good."

Her smile was polite, but there was something more to it that made Johnny blush. He tried to quash his growing elation.

"How much you got left?" she asked.

"Just a couple more sets," he replied. "How about you?"

"Just a few sets of pull-ups. Good for the rock climbing, you know?"

"How many can you do?"

"Why do you ask? Think you can beat me?" Katie tilted her head playfully.

Johnny had picked up the dumbbells to do another set of hammer curls, but he set them down quickly. "Only one way to find out."

"Loser buys the protein shakes after?"

He usually sparred with his fellow karate instructors on Tuesday nights and hated to miss it, but he recognized Katie's invitation as the peace offering that it was. He thought for all of a millisecond before saying, "You're on."

They walked over to the pull-up bar, and he gestured toward it. "Ladies first."

She took off the somewhat looser shirt she was wearing and tossed it to him. "Hold this for me," she said.

As she ripped off pull-up after pull-up wearing only a black sports bra, Johnny marveled at her figure. Her back and shoulders were incredibly ripped, and her stomach was flat. She struggled with pull-up number 14 and got halfway up on number 15 before she gave up and lowered herself to the floor.

He handed her shirt back. As she pulled it back on, she asked, "Think you can beat that, or are you going to concede and buy me my shake?"

Truthfully, Johnny doubted he could match what she'd just done, but he'd never backed down from a challenge and wasn't about to start now. He took his own T-shirt off, tossed it to her, and winked. "Hold this for me."

"Smart ass," she replied, grinning.

Johnny hadn't done pull-ups in quite a while, but the required muscles were in pretty good shape due to a regular dose of weights, karate, and kata. The first 10 flew by. He felt himself start to struggle on number 11 and then struggle some more on number 12. He barely got his chin over the bar on number 13 and relaxed for a moment when he lowered his body.

"Give up?" Katie asked.

"Never." Johnny closed his eyes and exhaled deeply, focusing hard. He pulled himself up and cleared the bar for number 14 with a couple of inches to spare.

He lowered his body, and she tossed his shirt back to him. "A tie! I guess we go Dutch."

"I hate ties," he said. "You know how the saying goes: 'A tie is like kissing your sister.'"

"Good thing I'm not your sister."

Johnny felt his pulse begin to race. Was that flirtation in her voice? "Shower first, then protein shakes?" he managed to ask.

"Well, I'm not showering with you, but otherwise, yeah," she replied. "Give me fifteen minutes."

Johnny's heart about pounded out of his chest, and he stood there for a moment while she walked away.

After showering, Johnny stopped at his locker. He was still daydreaming about his upcoming minidate with Katie. Absent-mindedly, he glanced at his phone. He was surprised to see he had over 20 new messages. Perplexed, he scrolled backward through questions that wondered, "Is he going to be okay?" "Who did it?" "Which hospital is he at?" Finally, he made it to the original message, sent from Maureen, and discovered that all the commotion was about Will. He hurriedly texted Katie, put on his clothes, and, forgetting to put on deodorant, rushed to the hospital.

At eight o'clock, Will had been the last one to leave PurePower, as usual. He had been busy tying up documentation for the third quarter and planning his trip to Mexico.

He'd walked down the staircase and out the front door into the crisp November air. It was a clear night with a light breeze, and he'd taken a deep breath of fresh air after having been holed up inside for the past 13 hours. He'd walked to the outdoor surface parking lot, which had been empty except for three other cars scattered about the lot.

A black Chevy Silverado had been parked alongside Will's red Jeep Wrangler. Will had walked between the two vehicles toward his driver's side door and hit the unlock button on his key fob. He'd opened the back door and set his laptop bag down on the seat. He'd closed the door with his left hand and had looked up in time to see an orange club swinging at his face. He'd tried to move his head and raise his hand at the same time, but it had been too late. The club had struck him on the right temple, and he'd crumpled to the ground, immediately unconscious.

A PurePower security guard doing regular rounds had found Will's limp body at about nine o'clock. The guard had recognized Will and known his name because Will had always gone out of his way to greet the staff at PurePower. The ambulance had come within four minutes, and after determining that Will did not have a neck or back injury, the paramedics had rushed him to the hospital. After the ambulance had pulled away, the guard had called the human resources director at PurePower, who'd fortunately had her phone on her. The HR director had called PurePower's controller, and the controller had called Maureen.

By the time Johnny arrived at the hospital, Maureen and other members of the firm were already there. Instinctively, Johnny hugged Maureen and started to get choked up. "I'm sorry. I should have stayed with him."

"It's not your fault," Maureen said, obviously a bit shaken herself. "I was told to wait here and that a doctor would be along shortly."

Within a few minutes, a doctor came to give them an update. While it was still early, Will would likely make a full recovery. He had a fairly severe concussion and some swelling on the brain, but there were no indications of permanent damage. As there was nothing else they could do, it was decided that Will's coworkers would head home and that Will's younger brother Aaron, who had arrived shortly after Johnny, would text them as soon as anything changed.

It was 2:00 p.m. the following afternoon when Will finally woke up, gauze wrapped around his head and a tube sticking out of his arm. His head throbbed, and when he opened his eyes, his vision was blurry. Aaron was dozing in the seat next to him. Will tried to speak, but barely any sound came out of his mouth. He tried again and got a bit louder, and then on the third try he finally mustered up the energy to make a sound loud enough to wake Aaron.

"Hey, big brother!" Aaron exclaimed.

Will grimaced, and Aaron immediately felt bad. "So sorry," Aaron said in a much quieter voice. "I'm excited to see you."

Will nodded shallowly a couple times and then asked, "What happened?"

"Do you remember anything?"

Will shut his eyes for a second and shook his head slowly. "No, and don't make me think. It hurts too much."

Aaron smiled, pleased that his brother's wit was still intact. "You got mugged in the parking lot of PurePower last night. Looks like the thug hit you hard once in the head and that knocked you out cold."

Will nodded, having no recollection of the attack. "What did he take?"

"Not much, actually. Seems like only your cash. Your wallet was found at the exit to the parking lot with the credit cards still in it. Your phone was still in your pocket, and your laptop was still in your back seat. Pretty weird if you ask me. People don't carry around much cash these days. I'm not sure why the guy would go through the risk of whacking you for only a few bucks."

Will nodded, a bit more groggily this time, and closed his eyes again. Before drifting off, he said, "Aaron."

"Yes?"

"I'm supposed to go to Mexico next week. Tell Johnny to take my place." With that, Will fell back asleep.

A short while later, Johnny received a call from Maureen.

"Can you go to New York tomorrow?" she asked.

"What?"

"Will woke up and requested that you take his place on the Mexico trip. You need a Visa to do work in Mexico, and given the late notice, you'll have to visit the Mexican consulate in New York."

"I can't go anywhere with Will still in the hospital," Johnny stammered.

"I understand," Maureen said slowly, "but Will seems to be on the mend, and the work goes on. Let's book your trip to Mexico. If Will's condition starts to worsen again before you leave, we'll cancel the trip."

Johnny was silent for a few seconds, too many thoughts racing through his mind. Finally, he replied, "Okay."

Johnny went straight to the hospital after returning from New York. Will was sleeping, but Aaron was still at his side.

Will had had a good day. The swelling was going down, and so was the pain. His memory was coming back, although he still didn't remember much about the attack. He was convinced the weapon was orange, but he also remembered a flash of green. A police officer had stopped by for the second day in a row. Carl was his name, although he seemed less enthused about finding the attacker now that Will was on the mend. Too much crime, too little staffing. It was probably just a thug Carl had arrested before.

When Johnny stopped by the hospital again on Friday night, Aaron had barely left Will's side and was in dire need of a shower and a change of clothes. Aaron thanked Johnny for coming and promised to be back in time to hunker down for the night shift.

At about nine o'clock, Johnny was in deep focus reading Will's notes about shipping logistics in preparation for the Mexico trip when a soft whisper startled him.

"Hey, Johnny," Will said.

Aaron had warned Johnny to speak softly, so Johnny tempered his enthusiasm and gently replied, "Hey, Will."

"You look funny." Will smiled.

"Thanks." Johnny grinned back. "The doctors say that there's some swelling on your brain that's going to impact your vision for a few days. How's the head?"

Will squinted a bit. "I feel like shit."

"So, what do you remember?"

"I remember Aaron was here earlier. What day is it anyway, and where is he?"

"It's Friday evening, three days after the attack. Aaron went home to shower and change clothes. Believe me, he needed to."

Will smiled. "That's nice. Aaron told me I got mugged. I'm not sure if I remember it or if I only remember it because Aaron told me. Things are pretty fuzzy."

"Do you remember telling him I should go to Mexico?"

Will smiled. "Yeah, I think so. Say, this was all your doing, wasn't it? You were jealous of my trip, so you had me taken out?"

"You're on to me," Johnny said.

"This is going to reflect poorly on your next performance review," Will joked.

"You really don't remember anything about the attack?"

Will closed his eyes and thought for a moment. "About the only thing I remember is that he hit me with something orange. Orange and very hard."

"That's what Aaron said. But an orange club? That's not

very easy to conceal," Johnny said, thinking out loud.

At that moment, there was a knock at the door. Johnny turned to look, but Will couldn't muster the energy. "Who's there?" he asked Johnny.

Johnny swallowed. "It's Bob Grayson."

Will's eyes tightened. He couldn't remember the attack, but he did remember the recent conversation in Bob's office. He hadn't told Johnny about the conversation yet; he hadn't wanted to worry him.

"I'm not feeling so well," he told Johnny. "Can you call the nurse?"

When Johnny stepped out of the room to call for a nurse, Bob walked around to the other side of the bed so that he could see Will's face. "This is really unfortunate, Will."

"It sucks," replied Will.

"Yeah, it is really unfortunate. This didn't have to happen." Bob stared Will dead in the eyes. He took one step closer, and Will started to panic, unsure of what Bob meant.

They were interrupted as Johnny returned with a nurse. "Good to see you awake, Will. How are you feeling?"

"I'll be going now," interrupted Bob Grayson. "I only wanted to make sure you were okay." As he walked toward the door, he turned to Johnny. "Have a good trip to Mexico."

"Thanks" was all Johnny could think to say.

Johnny watched the nurse check Will's vitals and give him a couple of pills—"For the pain," she said. When she left, Will said to Johnny, "I don't want to alarm you, but something's not right with Bob. He might suspect we're on to him."

"Do you think he was behind this?" asked Johnny.

There was another knock at the door. "Mr. Stevens, may I come in?" It was Carl, the police officer.

Will nodded at Johnny, and Johnny nodded at the officer. "I want to ask you a few more questions to see if you remember anything more about the attack."

"Did you find the guy?" Will asked.

"Not yet, but we are still looking into it," the officer said without much conviction. "The security tapes aren't clear, but it looked like a clean-cut guy in his mid-30s. Olive skin and dark hair. Tall, muscular, and very fit, moved swiftly. Probably comes from an athletic or military background."

Aaron returned as Will told the officer as much as he could remember, which wasn't much. After they were done, Will looked at Aaron and Johnny and said, "I don't feel that well, guys. I need to close my eyes for a bit." Within 30 seconds he was asleep, and Johnny figured he should get going. He'd have to find out more about Will's observations of Bob Grayson later.

The next day, Johnny was working with Angela to prepare for his trip. Angela, who was more senior than Johnny, had helped Will with all of the original preparations (at one point, she had even been planning to go with, though a personal conflict had ultimately come up). She helped Johnny understand all the things he needed to accomplish while at PurePower Mexico.

Johnny tried to focus, but he kept thinking of Will. The way the police officer described the attacker, he almost sounded like a professional. Could this have been a targeted instead of a random attack?

That evening, Johnny went to the hospital determined to talk to Will about his suspicions and to finish their conversation about Bob Grayson, but to his dismay, Will's parents were there. They had just gotten back from a trip to India, and Will's mom wasn't leaving her son's side.

"You got hit by an orange club?" she asked Will. "I've never seen an orange club before. I usually think of those black billy clubs that cops carry around."

Will closed his eyes and thought for a moment. "It's coming back to me."

"What's coming back to you?" she asked.

"I think it was a baseball bat. An orange baseball bat with green lettering."

Will's mom said, almost at a whisper, "That could have killed you."

Johnny turned his head and looked out the window into the hospital parking lot. It was dark outside, and a black bat, though unusually large, would have been tough to see coming. But an orange bat? That would stick out. No thug in his right mind would use something that flashy and memorable. Johnny began to doubt even more that the attack was random.

Johnny stuck around for an hour hoping to get a chance to talk to Will alone, but eventually he announced that he needed to get going so he could rest up before his early flight in the morning. He looked at Will. "I haven't done one of these audits before in the United States, let alone Mexico. I sure wish you were going along to mentor me. Any advice?"

Finally, Will asked his parents for a couple of minutes alone with Johnny. "You'll do great," Will started out reassuringly. "Maureen knows how to sniff out big risks, so follow her lead.

"PurePower is totally reliant on these two manufacturing sites, so if they have any control weaknesses, it could come back to haunt them big time. You will want to focus on things that would inhibit the subsidiary from delivering quality product to PurePower.

"Also, some Mexican companies play by different rules

than we do in the United States. The crime rate is fairly high in Juárez, not only with theft and violence, but also with corruption and bribery. I want you to try to figure out if PurePower is making payments to get things done."

"Isn't that a violation of the FCPA?" Johnny asked. The Foreign Corrupt Practices Act of 1977, he recalled, had made it illegal to bribe government officials.

"Yep, and the companies that do it know it, but some feel they have to do it in developing markets like Mexico."

"Okay. Wait, if the crime rate is high in Juárez, why is JPG letting us go down there?"

"What, you don't want to go on the trip anymore? There's still time. I could try to convince Angela to skip her stuff and take your place," Will teased.

"No, it's not that. I'm really excited. I'm just a bit surprised that JPG is having us go down and not simply using our local team."

"We do use our local team a lot, and we had to ask for special approval to make this trip. That is part of the reason Maureen is going. She's really hands on for a partner. She told firm leadership that if we couldn't make at least one trip down there, we should perhaps drop PurePower as a client altogether. Too much risk. Leadership approved the project after she said that. Just stay off the streets at night, especially if you are alone."

"The other night, you were going to tell me more about Bob Grayson," Johnny prompted.

Will sighed. "That's going to be a longer conversation, and I don't think my mom will leave me alone that long, nor do I know if I can stay awake. They have me completely drugged up. Let's chat on that when you get back. You'll be two thousand miles from him for the next week, so things should be fine. When do you get back?"

"Friday around seven."

"Sounds good. I should be out of here by then, so let's plan to grab a late dinner at Merton's. You can tell me how the trip went, and I'll tell you more about Bob."

"Good plan," Johnny said as he extended his right hand.

Will grabbed his hand, started to pull, and said, "Bring it in." They hugged, or as much as they could hug while Will lay in a hospital bed.

Later that evening, Bob's phone rang. It was Maureen. Bob answered, but before he could say anything, Maureen said, "What did you do to Will?"

"*I* didn't do anything," Bob replied.

"Don't screw with me, Bob. What did you 'have done' to Will?"

"He was snooping around. I found a guy and told him to scare Will a bit and send a message. He said he panicked at the last minute and hit him too hard."

"You told a guy to hit Will with a club?"

"Well, I guess it was a baseball bat—"

"A baseball bat!" Maureen yelled. "Give me one reason why I shouldn't turn your ass in right now."

"I'm as upset about this as you are."

"I hardly believe that. No more violence, or I make the call."

The phone went dead. Bob breathed what felt like the millionth sigh of relief he'd given in the last year. He was surprised, again, that Maureen was giving him yet another chance. This time, though, he began to question why.

Recalling the days when he'd been fit and would go for jogs to process tough information, he put on a light coat and a pair of sneakers that he'd barely used and began to walk through his neighborhood. By the time he returned home, he had reached only one possible conclusion: Maureen had already made the call and was working with the authorities. They were going to take him down. He needed about six months to pull his plan off, but he wasn't sure if he had that much time.

CHAPTER 21

Ciudad Juárez, Mexico
November 10–14, 2019

Luckily for Johnny, when Maureen's assistant booked the flight for him, only seats in business class remained. It was a grueling trip—100 minutes from Cleveland to Atlanta, 4 hours to Mexico City, and then 3 hours more to Juárez—and though partners automatically flew business class, the seating arrangement was more controversial for staff members. Clients often balked at the thought of paying for a $2,000 flight for a 23-year-old "kid." With business class being the only option, there didn't have to be any debate about whether Johnny would be allowed to upgrade.

The flight from Cleveland to Atlanta was predictably uneventful, and after a short layover, Johnny was onboard a Boeing 757. He had heard great things about international flights, but this plane was more basic. It was nice in business class, but it still had the normal two-seats-by-two-seats configuration. Johnny had an aisle seat and was happy to have a slender woman next to him so he wouldn't be jockeying for elbow room.

Maureen was back one row and across the aisle. She also had an aisle seat, and a serious-looking businessman sat next to her. The flight attendant offered Johnny fresh-squeezed orange juice or champagne. Maureen had chosen the champagne, so Johnny decided to follow suit. A different flight attendant offered him a hot, damp towel, and he wasn't sure exactly what to do with it. The guy across the aisle noticed his apprehension and said, "It's for your face."

"Thanks," Johnny replied. "First time for me in business class."

The man smiled and replied, "You'll get used to it quickly."

Shortly after takeoff, the flight attendant took Johnny's dinner order, brought him a plate of warm, mixed nuts, and refilled his plate when he scarfed the first batch down in a couple of minutes. The in-flight entertainment system had about 100 movies to choose from. Johnny enjoyed movies related to martial arts, so *Fighting with My Family* caught his eye. He thoroughly enjoyed it. Dinner was a well-prepared salad, warm bread, and a shrimp pasta. The flight attendant recommended pairing it with a sauvignon blanc, and Johnny enjoyed two glasses. New York cheesecake was for dessert, and the flight attendant recommended pairing it with a small glass of port. Johnny was indeed getting used to business class quickly.

He had picked up a Vince Flynn novel at the airport, having read a couple and enjoyed them before. He wasn't sure where this one fell in the series but was sure Mitch Rapp would kill a lot of bad guys. He wasn't more than 15 pages into the book when he felt his eyes getting heavy.

He woke up after an hour both dehydrated and with a large urge to use the restroom. On his way back to his seat, he glanced in Maureen's direction and noticed that she was awake and using her laptop. She had a reputation as a partner who never stopped working, so it didn't surprise Johnny to see her pecking away. When she noticed him, she lightly jerked her neck in a way that beckoned him to stop over.

"Hey, Maureen," he said when he reached her seat.

"How's business class?" Maureen asked.

"I feel spoiled," Johnny replied sheepishly.

"I know what you mean," she said. "PurePower has to sell

a lot of batteries simply to cover our plane tickets. We better do good work for them."

Johnny nodded, and she asked, "When is the last time you saw Will?"

"I stopped by the hospital last night."

"His brother Aaron has been sending me updates. Sounds like he is getting better?"

"Yeah, fortunately. That was pretty scary for a while."

Maureen nodded. "Did he leave pretty good notes for this trip? I mean, do you feel prepared?"

Johnny smiled. "For sure. Will is big on documentation. He always says to document things assuming you will get hit by a beer truck and someone else will have to look at it next year."

Maureen chuckled. "He may have to change that to assuming you will get hit by a baseball bat."

Johnny smiled and then suddenly found himself choking up. "I'm sorry. It's all so new right now," he said.

"My fault. 'Too soon,' as they say. Well, thank goodness he's getting better," Maureen said. "I'll let you get back to whatever you were doing. I just wanted to say hi."

Johnny walked back to his seat and opened his own laptop, figuring it would look good to Maureen if he was working—maybe it would help justify his expensive business class seat. He was trying to understand an Excel model Will had started. The file had been saved at 7:55 p.m. on Tuesday, so Will had been working on it right before he'd left and was attacked. The model had something to do with the manufacturing capacity of the Mexico subsidiary and how that tied into potential profits of PurePower. Will hadn't gotten a chance to finish the model, and the purpose of a sensitivity analysis stumped Johnny. He was deep in thought when the flight attendant interrupted him. "Anything to drink, sir?

A glass of wine, or perhaps a Bloody Mary to help you wake up?"

Johnny smiled and said, "Just some sparkling water, please." When he looked back at his Excel spreadsheet, his focus narrowed. But he was no longer looking at anything on the spreadsheet. He was thinking hard about Maureen's comment about the baseball bat. Will hadn't recalled that the attacker had used a baseball bat until last night. Maureen hadn't been there. Had she talked to Will since then? It seemed doubtful given how early their flight from Ohio had left.

A few hours later, the plane touched down in Mexico City. As Johnny and Maureen were walking through the concourse toward their third and final flight of the long day, Johnny nonchalantly asked, "When was the last time you talked to Will?"

"Well, I actually haven't seen him since the day after the attack," Maureen replied. "Aaron has been keeping me up to speed."

"When is the last time you talked to Aaron?" Johnny asked.

"I think we exchanged texts around dinnertime a couple nights ago. Why do you ask?"

Johnny was stunned and didn't know what to say.

"Why do you ask?" Maureen repeated.

Johnny thought quickly. "Oh, he made a lot of progress on Friday, and his memory is getting much better. I wanted to make sure you knew."

Maureen knew about the baseball bat even though she clearly hadn't gotten that information from Will or Aaron. The information must have come directly from the attacker, or from someone connected with the attacker. Someone like Bob Grayson.

Johnny met Maureen in the lobby of Hotel Lucerna for dinner later that evening after they had checked in. Though he now suspected she was involved in Bob's illegal activities, he had decided to act normal around her. He had no other choice.

They met up with Juan Carlos, who worked in IT at PurePower Mexico and was going to serve as their escort of sorts for the week. Juan Carlos was young, single, very social, and enjoyed hosting the few guests who came to the facility. He took them to Dos Amigos, a restaurant that was popular with Americans. Their dishes had enough local flavor to make Americans feel like they were engaging in the culture but were served with much less heat than the locals preferred. It offered "a soft launch" into authentic Mexican cuisine, Juan Carlos told them.

They got back from dinner around nine, and Johnny had some time to kill.

He first emailed his former Spanish professor Elena. "I am in Mexico on business. What part are you from?"

He was surprised when she replied almost instantly. "Ciudad Juárez."

"I am in Ciudad Juárez right now!" he emailed back.

"Wow! So many memories. I haven't been there in more than ten years. I hope you enjoy your time. Be safe, and don't go out alone at night."

Johnny then popped open Facebook. He really wasn't active on social media but had an account so he could "stalk" some of his friends, as people liked to say.

"Hey, world traveler," came an IM. It was from Katie.

"Hey, there!" Johnny wrote back.

"Amazing that you are in Mexico. I get to spend a couple nights in Dayton this week."

"I bet the pollution won't be as bad in Dayton," he countered.

"Whatever. I can't believe what happened to Will. Is he

going to be okay?"

"Looks that way."

"Any muggers over there where you are in Juárez?"

"Ha, I imagine there are. But I don't think I will be walking around at night by myself much. They have booked our schedule pretty tight on this trip."

"When do you get back?"

"Dinnertime on Friday."

"Our start group was thinking of getting together for drinks Friday night."

"Count me in," he wrote and then quickly backtracked when he remembered his plans with Will.

"We can invite him if he's up for it," Katie suggested. "I'm sure everyone would like to see how he is doing."

Johnny thought for a moment. He wanted some time alone with Will to talk about Bob Grayson and his rising suspicions but didn't want to make it obvious, so he agreed.

Katie signed off with a simple "It will be good to see you . . ."

Johnny wanted to ask her what she meant by that but instead replied with a simple "You too."

The thought of seeing Katie perked him up. The next morning when the fitness center opened at 5:30 a.m., he was ready. He did a couple extra sets of bicep curls and a couple extra sets of ab crunches. He felt like a dork because they wouldn't make any noticeable difference in the next few days, but he did them anyway.

On Tuesday morning, Jorge, PurePower Mexico's general manager, brought Johnny on a tour of the Juárez manufacturing facility. The math was fairly simple. PurePower planned to sell about 20 million batteries in 2019. Assuming the facilities in Mexico operated all 365 days of the year, they would need to produce about 55,000 batteries per day to satisfy the inventory needs of the parent company. Johnny's task as an auditor was to find out if this was possible.

On the tour, Johnny learned that PurePower made two types of cell phone batteries: the X and the X+. The X model, the initial battery PurePower had produced, was made with lithium ion. It was a much lower-end battery but was still used when price was more important to a customer than performance. The X+ model relied on a copper foam substrate that came from copper antimonide, a compound that was generally mined and manufactured in Mexico. The X+ batteries were the best on the market and lasted two times as long as the lithium-ion batteries.

Jorge showed Johnny the supply of raw materials and explained how the materials were processed by highly specialized machines. The machines for the X and X+ batteries appeared similar but had some critically different components. There were two X-battery machines in Juárez and two in Reynosa. The four X-battery machines could process a battery every 10 seconds, so if needed they could produce 33,000 X batteries in a day (after accounting for about an hour of maintenance per day). That exceeded the parent company's demand of 22,000 X batteries per day, so the machines operated from about 6:00 a.m. to midnight Monday through Saturday. Jorge also increased or decreased production at times to manage the amount of extra inventory stored in Parma. The goal was to always have an additional two months of inventory in storage.

There were six machines that produced X+ batteries, and all were located in Juárez. Due to the increased risk this posed, six months of inventory was kept on hand in Parma. When new machines would need to be purchased down the road, they would likely be delivered to Reynosa to further manage the risk. The

X+ machines could also process one battery every 10 seconds, so daily production of nearly 50,000 was possible. Since demand was only about 33,000 per day, the X+ machines also ran from 6:00 a.m. to midnight Monday through Saturday.

"How much does one of the new X+ machines cost?" Johnny asked Jorge.

"About five million dollars," Jorge replied.

"And if the company wanted another one, how quickly could it have one made?"

"Our vendor says they can make one in six weeks, four weeks in an absolute emergency, but they ask us to allow three months because they have a pretty big backlog."

"What if there's a fire?" Johnny asked.

Jorge laughed at him like he was an idiot. "Small fires can happen in a Mexican manufacturing facility, but look up." Jorge pointed to the ceiling. "There are many sprinklers. The fire would not last long."

Another section of the plant was a mishmash of equipment, less organized and standardized than the main battery-producing area. Jorge explained that this area was used for contract manufacturing work for other companies when they got ahead of schedule for the parent company or when the workers really wanted overtime. This portion of the plant seemed cramped to Johnny. The machines were very close to one another, and workers were periodically bumping into each other. Johnny saw two workers, trying to get through the same tight aisle, bump into each other and drop a couple of boxes.

"The inspector is fine with these tight working conditions?" he asked.

"We assured him that we will start using more of the facility for PurePower and less for third-party contract manufacturing in the first quarter of 2020."

"And that was okay with him?"

Jorge looked at Johnny and smiled. "At first the inspector was not fine with that. But we persuaded him."

Johnny hesitated. "How did you persuade him?"

Jorge's smile stayed firm as he said, "Let's say we have a budget for times when we need to persuade the inspector."

Johnny was really taken aback, although he tried not to show it. Jorge had just confessed to bribing a government official.

Jorge saw Johnny's posture change and added, "We do that very, very rarely."

"About how much per year?"

Jorge thought for a moment, realizing he perhaps shouldn't have admitted to the bribery. "Less than five thousand dollars in total this year. Before I took over as general manager, it was more common. I have whittled it down to almost nothing and expect the amount to be zero by 2021."

At the end of the tour, Johnny was convinced that Juárez was more than able to satisfy the inventory needs of the parent company. The bribery, however, concerned him. He brought up his findings to Maureen and asked, "What do we do?"

"Right now, nothing," Maureen answered. "The bribes are immaterial. When business is conducted in developing markets, it is almost impossible to eliminate all bribes. I get most concerned if bribes are paid to win contracts, as the law prohibits 'obtaining or retaining business.' But paying a small bribe for a safety inspection is a different story. It's questionable whether that violates the Foreign Corrupt Practices Act. Thanks for catching that, though. I will have a conversation with Jorge later."

He was surprised about Maureen's nonchalant attitude toward the bribe. That Maureen didn't want to sound an alarm or do anything to harm PurePower further raised his suspicions that she was in on the insider trading with Bob. He made a mental note to talk with Will about it when he got home.

On Wednesday, Johnny and Maureen met at length with Juan Carlos and Felipe, who worked with Juan Carlos in IT for the facility. Felipe fit the stereotype of an IT professional—brilliant but with mixed social skills. They spent time talking about controls and processes, and Johnny came to the conclusion that Juan Carlos and Felipe were quite good at their jobs.

That evening, Juan Carlos invited them out to dinner at a place where there were only locals. A more senior member of the PurePower finance team also joined them. Maureen spent much of the time chatting with him, which left Johnny and Juan Carlos to enjoy warm conversation over cold Bohemia beer. Johnny had liked Juan Carlos a lot the first time they had gone out to dinner, so he was grateful to have the chance to get to know him better.

"How do you like working at PurePower?" Johnny asked.

Juan Carlos tipped his head back a bit. "I love it."

"Love," Johnny repeated, lingering on the word. "That's a strong emotion."

"The company saved me," Juan Carlos explained. When Johnny cocked his head, Juan Carlos said, "The cartels are pretty bad here in Juárez. I got pulled into a gang when I was fourteen years old. We fought other gangs all the time, and it wasn't pretty. One of my close friends died in my arms after a drive-by shooting. My mom was desperate to get me out of Juárez. She knew I'd get killed if I stayed here."

Johnny marveled at how nonchalantly Juan Carlos said that. He couldn't imagine such a life.

"PurePower had a partnership with the University of Texas in Austin," Juan Carlos continued, "and through a great scholarship, I went to school for only a thousand bucks a semester. They also promised me a job after college, assuming I did well enough. I did, and I've worked here ever since. Jorge really took me under his wing."

"That's so wonderful." Johnny smiled.

"Yeah. I owe so much to my mother. Every boy should have a mother like I have. But I also owe so much to the company. I will defend it at all costs."

Johnny noticed that Juan Carlos used the word "will" instead of "would," as if an attack was imminent, but he chalked it up to an English–Spanish translation issue of sorts.

They continued talking. Johnny described his family to Juan Carlos, who seemed intrigued that one of Johnny's siblings was a star athlete and the other an artist.

"Which one do you get along with better?" Juan Carlos asked.

"Growing up, it was Billy. We are closer in age and had much more in common. In recent years, he's been so busy with sports, girlfriends, and his buddies that I've probably spent more time with Dani. She sends me texts all the time—sketches she has done and songs she has written."

"I always wanted to have a sister," Juan Carlos replied.

"You mentioned your mom—do you have any other immediate family members?"

Juan Carlos shook his head and said, "My mom had me when she was eighteen. She and my dad tried to make it work, but eventually they drifted apart, and my dad left town. My mom never married or had any more kids. I see her at least a couple of times per week, including church every Sunday."

Within a few hours, Johnny and Juan Carlos had developed a unique bond based on their shared values of loyalty to and love of family. At the end of the night, they hugged in farewell, and Johnny felt like he was saying good night to a longtime friend.

On Thursday, Johnny and Maureen's final full day in Mexico, Juan Carlos popped into the audit room to ask if he could pick up lunch for them. "That would be wonderful," Maureen said. A half hour later, Juan Carlos came back in with three Styrofoam boxes and asked if he could join them. Near the end of lunch, Juan Carlos picked up his cell phone, said an audible "Hmm," and set it back down. "Our city fútbol team has a match tonight. A couple of friends and I are going, and I guess we have one extra ticket. I know you are busy, but the game doesn't start until eight, so would one of you like to go?"

Maureen saw Johnny perk up a bit. "You should go," she said.

"Are you sure?" Johnny asked. "We are busy, and I don't want to leave you alone."

"I'll be fine," she replied. "I have a lot of work from clients back home to catch up on anyway."

As excited as he was to spend time with Juan Carlos again, Johnny was even more thrilled at the idea of getting away from Maureen for an evening. As the days went by and his suspicions grew, it was becoming harder and harder to act natural around her.

Around seven o'clock in the evening, he took a taxi back to the hotel and quickly changed into more casual clothes before Juan Carlos arrived to pick him up. The game was a short drive away, and they were in their seats about 10 minutes before the match started. Juan Carlos's friends had picked up a couple extra street tacos and beers, which Johnny consumed quickly.

The stadium held nearly 20,000 fans and was at capacity on that gorgeous evening. The match was quite interesting, and the atmosphere was unlike anything Johnny had ever experienced at a professional sports game. The fans spent the entire match on their feet, chanting and singing in a beautiful spectacle.

Following Juan Carlos's lead, Johnny cheered for the Juárez team, more commonly referred to as a club. It had only been in existence for five years, after a previous team representing the city had disbanded. This was the first year the club was participating in the Liga MX, the top soccer league in Mexico, and they gave the Tigres from Nuevo León a run for their money. The Tigres led 2–0 until Juárez scored a goal on a penalty kick in the 90th minute. Juárez put up an intense fight during injury time but never put the equalizing goal in the back of the net. For Johnny, it was one of the most unique cultural experiences of his life. Juan Carlos seemed somewhat more distant and preoccupied, but Johnny figured that was because he had seen many matches like this before.

After the match, Juan Carlos asked Johnny if he wanted to get a quick beer. They went to Dos Amigos and each ordered three tacos al pastor and a cold Bohemia beer. As they entered the restaurant, Juan Carlos's preoccupied air turned into downright edginess that Johnny didn't know what to make of. To lighten the mood, he copied Juan Carlos in putting not one but two lime slices in his beer and said, "Tacos three times today. A good day."

Juan Carlos feigned a smile. Johnny watched as his eyes danced around the restaurant.

"Is everything okay?" Johnny asked finally.

Juan Carlos didn't reply immediately. His eyes dropped to the table, he took a sip of his beer, his eyes glanced to the street, he fiddled with his napkin, and then he took a larger gulp of beer.

Johnny watched him but didn't say anything.

Finally, Juan Carlos asked, "Can I confide in you?"

"I think so," Johnny replied. "I guess it depends on what it is. Is it related to PurePower?"

Juan Carlos hesitated and said, "It may be." He paused and continued, "As part of our role in IT, Felipe and I monitor websites our employees visit. I mean, we're not constantly watching them, but once per week we run a report. You'd be amazed how many people are looking at job posting websites. I think morale is good here, but I guess people are always curious what is out there."

"That's what you wanted to tell me?" Johnny asked, a bit perplexed.

"No," replied Juan Carlos. "I also get a listing of how much time our employees spend online. We had one guy who was probably spending half his day online, messing around on political and sporting news websites. We talked to him about it, and it scared him straight in a hurry. He never goes online for anything personal anymore."

The server brought the tacos al pastor, and Johnny asked for another round of Bohemia, which they both put two lime slices into. They ate and drank in near silence for the next 10 minutes, simply observing the tables around them.

"Juan Carlos, what is it that you want to tell me?" Johnny asked, pushing his empty plate to the side.

Juan Carlos fidgeted and looked out into the street. He brought the dark brown bottle of Bohemia to his lips and watched a boy run by dribbling a soccer ball. A younger boy ran helplessly after him, asking him to slow down. Juan Carlos then shifted his gaze across Johnny and to the other side of the restaurant, toward the kitchen. There was a post-match rush. Several employees were moving quickly, and the man at the grill moved adeptly from item to item, checking and flipping, checking and flipping. Juan Carlos then looked back at Johnny and took another long pull off his beer bottle. He set the beer bottle down and began to speak.

"I came in one day early last week and took a quick look at the web surfing log. I saw a series of Google searches related to ammonium nitrate, how to obtain it, how much is needed, and how much it costs."

He paused and Johnny took this as a cue to jump in. "What's ammonium nitrate?"

"Most people wouldn't know, and most people would have flown right past it, I suppose. But I always enjoyed the sciences. I thought of a career as a chemist before settling on computers." Juan Carlos cleared his throat nervously. "Ammonium nitrate is a chemical compound used in fertilizer. By itself, it is relatively harmless. However, it can also be used in explosive devices, including bombs. Our employee Googled the cost to purchase ten tons, or twenty thousand pounds, of ammonium nitrate. I did the Google search myself and saw that the cost is about six thousand dollars."

Johnny nodded but wasn't completely sure where this was going.

"So someone is curious about bombs," Juan Carlos continued. "Maybe it is simple curiosity, I don't know. But then I saw a Google search for the amount of ammonium nitrate to blow up a three-hundred-thousand-square-foot building. At first, I didn't understand the relevance, but then it dawned on me that our facility is three hundred thousand square feet."

Johnny pushed his chair back from his table a few inches and exhaled. He then scooted forward and leaned in close to Juan Carlos. "You think someone, an employee, wants to blow up your facility?" he whispered.

Juan Carlos nodded.

"But to get ten tons of anything into the facility would be

a major undertaking. There's no way that could happen without Jorge noticing."

Juan Carlos nodded glumly and then drained what was left of his beer. When he set the empty bottle down, he simply stared at Johnny. Johnny stared back and bit his lip as he thought hard about what this all meant. His eyes wandered aimlessly around the restaurant. He wasn't seeing anything; he was simply thinking. Suddenly, he blinked and focused his gaze on Juan Carlos. "It was Jorge who was doing the Google searches, wasn't it?"

Juan Carlos squeezed his mouth together, teeth touching and lips pursing ever so slightly. He stared back at Johnny for several seconds and then replied, "Yes. And it made sense. Jorge has changed over the past several months. His decisions have become so shortsighted. He used to be so positive—an inspirational leader—but he has gotten increasingly distracted and angry. That hadn't made sense to me before, because we are setting performance records, and though Jorge has a daughter with health issues, she has greatly improved."

Johnny wondered if he looked as bewildered as he felt. "What are you going to do? Do you confront Jorge? Do you go to the police? Do you call PurePower headquarters?"

"Felipe and I discussed this at length. The notion of Jorge blowing up the facility makes no sense to us. The plant is his life. He has watched it grow and takes immense pride in it. He is a man of the highest character and integrity. We figured he must have just been curious, maybe even thinking about how to defend his facility from an attack. We decided to give him the benefit of the doubt and simply ask him about it. Felipe said he'd have the conversation. He said he would leave my name completely out of it and say he found it himself."

Juan Carlos paused for too long, so Johnny was forced to

interject. "And what happened?"

"It was early yesterday evening when Felipe decided to talk to Jorge, after virtually everyone else had gone home. You, Maureen, and I had already left for dinner. Felipe said he would call me later to let me know how it went." Juan Carlos paused, and Johnny thought he saw a tear forming in his left eye. "He didn't call, and when I got home at ten, I texted him. He didn't reply, and this morning he never showed up. I texted him and called him a few times and didn't get a reply. The security tapes from after six last night are deleted, and the report showing Jorge's Google searches has vanished. I don't have a copy."

"You think Jorge did something to him?"

"I really don't think Jorge would hurt him, but I also didn't think Jorge would be planning to blow up the facility. I just can't believe this. Jorge is like a father to me." Juan Carlos paused and swallowed hard before continuing, "I think there is a real chance Felipe is gone, and I don't have any evidence to prove it or to prove that Jorge did the searches for ammonium nitrate."

"Will you go to the police?" Johnny asked.

Juan Carlos shook his head. "Mexico has many wonderful people and many honorable police officers, but not so much in Juárez. Many of the police here are crooked, accustomed to being paid off by the cartels. If Jorge is up to something, I'm sure he is paying off the police. If I go to the police, I will be dead before I leave the station."

"Does Mexico have an FBI of sorts, and could you go to them?"

"Kind of. We have the Policía Federal and the CNI, which is our equivalent of your CIA. However, with the logs now gone, I have zero proof. They are woefully understaffed and would probably just laugh at me."

"Do you want me to go to the authorities in the US?" asked Johnny.

"Maybe. That is why I told you. I can't think of anything else to do, and I'm afraid of talking to people down here."

"But what would I say to the FBI? 'I don't have any evidence, but the general manager of a manufacturing plant in Mexico is going to blow it up'? Yeah, I'm sure they'd jump all over that one and rush right in to help."

"I'm sorry. I should not have told you. I just don't know where else to turn."

"Can you just . . . walk away?"

"I couldn't bring myself to do that. I told you, PurePower saved my life. And I can't let Jorge go through with it. I need to save him."

"Save him?" Johnny asked in bewilderment. "He is the one who's behind this."

"No, there's someone behind him pulling the strings. There has to be."

"So what are you going to do?"

Fear filled Juan Carlos's eyes. "I have no idea."

Johnny wasn't sure what to say or do, so he simply said, "This is a lot." He got up, ready to walk out into the street. He needed to move so he could think.

"Let me give you a ride back to the hotel," Juan Carlos said as Johnny laid $12 on the table to cover the bill.

"It's okay," said Johnny. "I want to walk for a while."

"Juárez can be dangerous at night," Juan Carlos cautioned.

"So can I." Johnny smiled and distractedly raised his fist before heading out.

Johnny began a brisk walk back to his hotel. It was about 11:30 p.m., and the Hotel Lucerna was about a 20-minute walk away. It was a beautiful evening despite the chaos inside Johnny's head. He already had his own troubles with Bob keeping him awake at night. What was he supposed to do now that Juan Carlos had told him PurePower Mexico's beloved general manager was planning to blow the plant up?

Frustrated, he distracted himself by looking at the buildings he passed. He was staring at a sign that said "Lechería," pretty sure it was a dairy store, when two men stepped out of the shadows of an alley.

From the moment he saw them, Johnny knew something was off. He remembered Will's words: "Stay off the streets at night, especially if you are alone." Too late to change that now.

The men fell in behind him, and a third man stepped out of the shadows of the next store and stepped directly in front of him. Johnny waited.

"Your wallet and your phone," the man said.

Johnny looked at the man in front of him and quickly turned to look at the two behind him. They were probably about 20 years old, the type of people Juan Carlos would have become had he not gone to college. None of them had weapons out. They were likely banking on numbers to get him to quickly relinquish his possessions. Johnny thought for a moment. Could he take them? Maybe. Was it worth the risk? Absolutely not.

He reached with his right hand into his back pocket to hand over the items, but the men had been waiting for him to move one of his hands out of defensive position and behind his back. He heard a change in the breathing of the taller man behind him and instinctively stepped to the side. The man, who had been mid-lunge, brushed past.

In that moment, Johnny knew the decision of whether to fight or flee was no longer his. They had made it for him.

In a three-on-one fight, movement was key: moving to get all three attackers in front and then continuing to move until two were behind the other one. That would turn it into a one-on-one fight, if only for a moment. Johnny quickly shuffled about 10 feet backward, and predictably, all three men began to advance. When he got some distance, he took two hard steps to the right so that the shortest of the three men was now the only one in front of him.

In a three-on-one fight, it was also about keeping it a kicking game as long as possible. Punching would bring him too close to the attackers; the other two could grab him while he fought off the one. So Johnny waited as the shortest man advanced. Johnny had long been taught that martial arts was for defense only, and while that was true, sometimes the best defense was a good offense. Johnny stepped forward and launched a devastating side kick right into the man's nose. It was a move that would never have worked against an opponent in the ring. It was sloppy, and opponents in the ring tended to be more cautious. But this was on the street, and the shorter man wasn't expecting to get kicked in the nose. The kick made a sickening noise when it landed, and the man went down in a heap.

Johnny quickly retreated a couple of steps and watched as the two remaining men spread out, trying to get on either side of him. One was taller and one was thicker, and both looked mean and pissed off. Johnny darted back and forth a bit but couldn't change the angle.

Within seconds, both men would rush him, and he wouldn't be able to deliver a powerful blow to both at the same time, so he decided to bait them.

Johnny rushed the taller man, who backpedaled a bit, and threw a left hook, not really intending it to connect but hoping it would serve as a distraction, which it did. The taller man backpedaled a bit further and put his hands in front of his face. Without looking, Johnny turned and began a front snap kick, knowing the thicker man would be rushing him. How quickly the man rushed would dictate whether Johnny's kick connected with groin, ribs, or face. As it turned out, the thicker man was a bit slow, and the kick connected square with his jaw, sending him down 10 feet away from his smaller companion.

Johnny turned just in time to see a blade coming at his neck. He ducked under the blade and caught the taller man's forearm in his right hand. With his left hand, he delivered two quick strikes to the ribs, which weakened the man's entire body. Johnny then twisted the man's arm behind his back, and within seconds, the knife fell harmlessly to the ground. Maintaining the pressure, Johnny forced the man to the ground. Rage filled Johnny as he quickly debated what to do next: break the man's arm, repeatedly smash his head off the pavement, or walk away.

Johnny's decision was made easier when he heard the steel-on-steel cocking of a gun. "Let him go," a voice said. The thicker man was still out cold, but the shorter man, the one Johnny had sent down with a side kick to the face, was standing 10 feet away, blood pouring out his nose, down his chin, and over his clothes. He had a pistol in his hand.

Johnny released the pressure on the taller man and slowly backed away.

"Against the wall," said the shorter man, pointing to the side of a building.

Johnny slowly walked to the side of the building, terrified. "Please, sir. You started this. Take my wallet, take my phone, and leave me alone."

The two men whispered and then Johnny heard the taller one say, "Mátalo." Johnny remembered that "mata" meant kill.

He was out of options and about out of time when he saw flashing lights and heard the blaring of a car horn.

Juan Carlos had bid farewell to Johnny and watched him walk away. Although Johnny insisted on walking home alone, Juan Carlos was not at all comfortable with it. The gangs of Juárez would be out and about. Juan Carlos got in his car and began to drive home, tapping his steering wheel nervously. He had about reached home when he whipped a quick U-turn and pressed the accelerator. He was going to find Johnny and drive him home, whether his new friend liked it or not.

Juan Carlos was driving quickly and peering down the streets when he saw commotion in the dark. Instinctively, he turned toward it, his high beams on. When he got a block away, he recognized Johnny's shirt and saw him on top of another man. Two others lay on the ground, but then one of them rose and pulled something from his waistband and pointed it at Johnny. He saw Johnny stand up and move toward a building. The two men were talking, one of them with his arm extended toward Johnny. Juan Carlos didn't know what they were saying, but he hit the gas, laid on his horn, and began flashing his lights.

Johnny watched as the car steered onto the sidewalk and the two men fled down an alleyway. They left their thicker friend still lying unconscious on the pavement. The car narrowly missed the man and came to a screeching halt right next to Johnny. Johnny had been half blinded by the car's flashing lights and was unsure what was happening until he heard Juan Carlos yell, "Get in!" He flung open the car door and jumped in. Juan Carlos hit the gas and Johnny struggled to shut the door.

It took Johnny several seconds to catch his breath. When he

finally spoke, he said, "You saved me."

Juan Carlos simply nodded

"Do we go to the police?"

Juan Carlos shook his head. "They would do nothing. They are afraid of the gangs."

"Am I safe at the hotel?" asked Johnny, feeling emotional.

"Yes, they wanted some quick cash. They will move on to their next victim."

Johnny took a deep breath and exhaled loudly. "Earlier, you told me you had no idea what to do about Jorge and the bomb. I want to help you."

Juan Carlos replied, "This could get very dangerous. Maybe think about it."

Johnny looked out the window and saw Hotel Lucerna in the distance. He stayed silent for a minute and then said, "I've thought about it. I'm going to help you. Just say the word."

CHAPTER 22

Cleveland, Ohio
November 15–16, 2019

The travel back to Ohio the next day was long but uneventful. When Johnny and Maureen got to baggage claim, Maureen's bag was the third one off. She said goodbye to Johnny, thanking him for pitching in at the last moment and for working hard on the trip. Johnny hadn't told her what he had learned from Juan Carlos the night before. He still didn't trust her and wanted to talk to Will first.

A half hour later, Johnny was the only one waiting when the baggage carousel stopped. His bags had never been lost before, and he felt violated even though he subconsciously knew that was silly. He filled out a missing baggage report with the unenthusiastic worker in the lost baggage department, and it was close to eight thirty in the evening when his Lyft finally pulled into Merton's for his outing with his start group.

His start group was in a side room, and the volume of the conversation told Johnny that they had been there awhile. When Johnny walked in, they all started yelling in Spanish to him: "¡Bienvenido! ¿Cómo estás? ¿Quieres cerveza? ¿Cuántos tequilas?" Ben and Nicholas Montgomery were on the end of the table closest to him. Katie was at the far end, and Will was in the middle along with a few others.

Johnny reached across the table and shook Will's hand. "Great to see you out of the hospital."

Will smiled and replied, "How were the tacos al pastor at Dos Amigos?"

Johnny hesitated and wondered how Will knew he had eaten at Dos Amigos and what he had ordered. Will noticed his hesitation and explained, "I texted Maureen and asked her how the trip was going. She told me you were headed to a place called Dos Amigos for dinner."

Johnny exhaled, smiled, and nodded. When had he gotten so paranoid?

When the server stopped by, Johnny realized he was famished. He ordered the fish tacos and Bohemia beer and was a bit underwhelmed with both. Will could see him eating without much joy and said, "Not quite as good as Dos Amigos?" When Johnny shook his head side to side and asked why not, Will, sipping ice water due to his recent brain trauma, replied, "Same actors, different stage."

Ben raised his glass in the air and said, "Everyone, I have an announcement to make. This is our first time together not being the New Starts. We survived our first year."

"Hey, I wasn't a New Start," Will said.

"Okay, we're kind of like a band, then. Will and the New Starts. Sounds catchy."

"Cheers," they said in unison as they clanked mugs and took a strong pull out of whatever they were drinking.

At one point, Katie got up to use the restroom, and she gently touched Johnny's shoulder on her way by. He gave it a minute and then quietly slipped out of his chair and waited outside the restrooms, which were out of the view of the others. She emerged shortly and smiled at him, "Waiting to use the ladies' room?"

Johnny grinned. "Nah, just waiting to chat with the lady."

"Well, what should we chat about?"

"You still owe me a protein shake," Johnny said.

"We tied! Don't you remember?"

"Remind me." He leaned casually back against the wall and crossed his arms.

"You said a tie was like kissing your sister," she said playfully as she stepped forward.

Johnny pushed off the wall and stood straight up, inches from her. "And you said it was a good thing you aren't my sister."

He stared into her familiar brown eyes, and she didn't look away.

"Excuse me," said a nasally voice. Nicholas was walking past to use the restroom. Before entering, he turned and said, "This really isn't the place for those kinds of shenanigans."

Katie blushed under Nicholas's stare. "Meet you back at the table," she said to Johnny and walked away.

Johnny followed Nicholas into the restroom, and they stood side by side at the urinals. "Can't you mind your own business?" Johnny asked.

"Can't you keep your private life out of the public?" Nicholas replied.

"Sure thing, Nick."

"My name is Nicholas."

"I know," Johnny replied sarcastically as he washed his hands and walked out the door.

Johnny returned to the table, hoping to catch up with Will or perhaps flirt more with Katie. Instead, the only open chair was the one next to Nicholas's. Nicholas was drinking a beer for the first time since Johnny had met him, and when Nicholas got back to the table he rambled about his client's allowance for loan and lease losses and tried to get everyone's opinion on how best to test them. Johnny felt his exasperation boil to the top.

"Nicholas, why are you talking about work at nine thirty on a Friday night? Actually, why are you even here? Shouldn't you be sleeping by now so you can wake up early and start charging some hours?" Immediately after it came out of Johnny's mouth, he regretted it.

The table was silent for a few seconds. Will was about to speak when Nicholas broke the silence. "You're right," he said and promptly got up, threw two twenty-dollar bills on the table, and walked out the front door.

"That was a dick thing to say," Will said, giving Johnny a look of disapproval that Johnny hadn't seen before.

Johnny got up and hustled out of the restaurant, looking right and then left for Nicholas. Public Square was bustling with people, and Johnny searched while dodging around families. He quickly realized Nicholas could have gone one of a dozen different ways, so he gave up the search. He sat down on a bench and stared off into the distance. Nicholas frustrated him, but his comment had been out of line. Nicholas was harmless. Johnny was tired and irritable from the travel. He was highly distracted by his conversation with Juan Carlos and the street fight in Juárez. He was confused about a couple of his conversations with Maureen, and he was constantly stressed by Bob Grayson. It was suddenly all too much.

"Didn't find him?"

Johnny startled a bit when he heard Will's voice. He shook his head from side to side and Will said, "Text him now, and text him again tomorrow. Then drop it. He'll come around, but it has to be on his terms. Let's go back inside."

When they got back inside, Katie had taken Nicholas's seat. "You doing all right?" she asked. "I know he's irritating, but that wasn't like you."

Johnny sighed and looked away. "I don't know," he muttered.

"What's going on?"

"Let's talk about you first, then maybe about me."

Katie nodded and told him that she would be flying to Pittsburgh the coming week to continue discussions about helping to open a new JPG office there. "Do you think I should relocate?" she asked.

Johnny turned his head and thought for a moment. She studied him, looking for signs of what he truly thought. He looked back and asked, "Do you want my professional opinion or my personal opinion?"

She smiled. Johnny loved her smile. "Let's start with professional."

"It's a no-brainer. You should do it. It's rare to be part of something from the ground up. This is JPG, so you know it will be successful. And when someday the office has five hundred people and you are managing partner, you can talk about how you were one of the first twelve people in the office."

Katie blushed a bit and said, "I don't know about that." She leaned in a bit closer. "Now, how about your personal opinion?"

Johnny was about to answer when the server came over to ask for drink refills and bent down near their table. He came up holding a rectangular piece of plastic. "Is there a Nicholas Montgomery here?"

"He left a little bit ago," Johnny said.

"Looks like his driver's license," said the server.

Nicholas must have dropped it in his hurry to throw money on the table. Johnny took it and said he would get it to Nicholas. Reflexively, he looked at the ID for a moment. Five foot nine, 150 pounds, brown hair, brown eyes. Nicholas was wearing his trademark studious brown glasses in the picture. His birthday was listed as November 15, 1998. Johnny thought for a moment and then realized that today was Nicholas's 21st birthday. Most of his friends were turning 24 this year, but Nicholas had started schooling early and graduated high school at 16 years old. He'd spent only three years in college and graduated when he was 19. Tonight was the first legal beer Nicholas had ever consumed, and Johnny realized it was quite possibly his first beer, period. Nicholas had played by the rules and finally relaxed. Johnny had ridiculed him and sent him home in tears. He felt even more awful than he had before.

Around that time, he got a call from the airline. His bag had been found and had made it to the Cleveland airport. They could have someone drop it off at his apartment in 30 minutes. Johnny figured it was about time to call it a night; he had done enough damage.

"Can we continue this later?" he asked Katie. She nodded, and Johnny called a Lyft.

As instructed by Will, Johnny texted Nicholas to apologize that night when he got home and then again the next afternoon. He didn't receive a reply to either text. He decided to follow Will's advice and let it rest. He would have to make amends to Nicholas through future actions.

The next morning, Will and Johnny met at Starbucks. Will told Johnny about his unusual conversations with Bob Grayson, both in the office and at the hospital, and Johnny told Will his suspicions that Bob had had Will whacked and that Maureen was somehow in on it. Will wasn't yet ready to implicate Maureen— she had been such a positive influence throughout his career, and he trusted her to handle the bribery that Johnny had uncovered down in Mexico—so they focused their attention on Bob.

They decided to keep the information to themselves for

now. Bob Grayson was a very highly respected senior partner. Blowing the whistle could be career suicide. In a case of "he said, she said," Bob's word would trump Johnny's in an instant. Plus, Bob wasn't stupid. He certainly hadn't traded the shares in his own account; he had most likely traded them through the account of a friend or two. Further, Johnny was involved to an extent—he had provided Bob with the information. Bob could likely afford good lawyers, and Johnny could end up being a fall guy. They decided to play a waiting game. They figured they had a couple of months until Bob would come knocking again, so they had time to develop a plan.

Finally, Johnny told Will about the discussion he'd had with Juan Carlos.

"We have to go to the FBI," Will said.

"Can we hold off a bit?" asked Johnny. "Juan Carlos is convinced that Jorge is in bed with the local cops, so if we trigger any alarms, Jorge may have Juan Carlos killed."

Will thought and said, "I don't like that one bit, but I understand. We'll give it a little time, but if we hear that Jorge's plans are progressing, we have to notify someone. Yes, we have to think about Juan Carlos, but there are a thousand people there who would be impacted by this."

Johnny agreed and called Juan Carlos, encouraging him to keep digging without getting caught.

The next week, Johnny was so distracted that his charge hours fell off a cliff. Nicholas Montgomery had taken a commanding lead in their competition. Maureen asked if everything was okay, and when Johnny responded that it was, she suggested that he show it in his charge hours, so Johnny poured himself into his work.

CHAPTER 23

Charlotte, North Carolina
December 1–4, 2019

A couple weeks later, Johnny was waiting at the airport gate to catch a flight to Charlotte to meet with another JPG client that was looking to acquire a company in North Carolina. He was checking messages on his phone, periodically looking up to see if Rodney, the JPG partner who would be joining him, was there yet, when a familiar voice startled him.

"Good evening, Johnny," said Bob Grayson.

"Hi, Bob," Johnny said, trying to hide his surprise.

"I'm glad you could join us on this trip," Bob said. "Is Rodney here yet?"

"No," Johnny said as calmly as possible, "I haven't seen him yet." What he was thinking was, *Why the hell are you here?* Rodney must have invited Bob along because he was considered an expert at merger and acquisition issues.

A few minutes later, Rodney walked up. "Hey, guys. Good to see you both here. Not sure I could make it through the next couple of days without you."

"You bet," Bob replied. "It will feel good to get my hands dirty for a couple of days. It seems that most of my time is spent on personnel issues and trying to win clients. I look forward to doing some good old-fashioned work. Someday you'll know what I mean, Johnny. Everyone raves about the work you have been doing. You'll have a long and successful career with the firm."

Johnny managed a grin while thinking, *I'd quit tomorrow if I could.*

The airline attendant called for first-class passengers, and Rodney asked Bob if he was coming. "No," replied Bob, "first class was full by the time I booked."

"I'll send back some drinks." Rodney chuckled.

"You do that." After Rodney was gone, Bob handed Johnny an envelope and said, "You are doing fantastic work for the firm, especially on the PurePower account. I really appreciate your efforts."

Before Johnny could open the envelope, the flight crew called for all rows to board, and Johnny followed Bob onto the plane. Rodney handed them each a beer as they walked past. "I recognized the flight attendant," he explained.

Johnny stowed his carry-on and took his seat on the aisle. He slowly opened the envelope from Bob and nearly shuddered at what he saw: Crisp, new one-hundred-dollar bills. Twenty of them. Two thousand dollars in cash.

Johnny quickly stuffed the envelope into his laptop bag and sat staring at a magazine for a minute. He looked at the beer in the seat pocket in front of him, thought, *What the hell*, and opened it. The flight attendants were starting to come through the aisle, so he didn't have much time. He pounded the beer in under 60 seconds. A few minutes later, as the plane was gaining speed on the runway, Johnny found himself drifting off to sleep. He had a fleeting moment of pleasure imagining all of this was only a dream. But it wasn't. This was real and getting more real by the day.

Johnny's time in Charlotte was miserable. The work was interesting, but Bob's presence was unbearable. For three long days, they were in a conference room with a few members of JPG's Charlotte office. When Bob wasn't in meetings, he sat by Johnny. He insisted they go to lunch together, to dinner together, for drinks together. Bob showed genuine interest in Johnny, and had the PurePower mess never happened, Johnny might have been loving the attention. Bob taught him technical matters, how to analyze client situations, and how to interpret stock market behaviors. When it was only the two of them, Bob would bring up PurePower often—nothing unusual, just discussion about the company and the audit team in general.

Wednesday at 4:00 p.m. could not come quickly enough, and when Johnny boarded that flight home, he was exhausted. Every second he spent with Bob Grayson was strained, but he couldn't show it, which of course strained him even more. He felt dirty after spending so much time with Bob and had been showering both before going to bed at night and upon waking up in the morning.

When the plane touched down in Cleveland a couple hours later, Bob and Rodney, who had both been flying first class, waited for Johnny in the gate area. The three of them walked together toward the airport's exit and prepared to hop into three cabs going in three different directions.

"Johnny, you did a real bang-up job these past few days," Rodney said. "I really appreciate your time and admire your work ethic."

"Yes, Johnny," Bob interjected. "Outstanding job. We will need to work together more often."

"Thanks" was all that Johnny could mutter.

With that, Johnny hopped into a cab and headed straight to Will's house. Will handed him a beer as he walked through the front door, and Johnny drained it in three big gulps. He told Will about the envelope with $2,000 in cash and Will nodded as if that were par for the course.

"We've got about two months until it happens again," Will

said. "Stocks always trade more when year-end earnings are released, so he will be able to get away with trading even more shares than usual."

Johnny nodded solemnly. He understood this but had no idea what to do with the information. "Should I quit the firm?" Johnny asked.

Will took a sip from a bottle of craft soda and thought about it. "I don't think so. You don't have a reason to quit. If you left, Bob would just find someone else to get information from. No, I think we need to frame him. Get him to explain what he is doing, record it, and turn it over to the authorities."

"Just like that?" Johnny asked.

Will nodded.

"And how do we do that?"

"I have absolutely no idea, but I haven't come up with anything better yet. We'll figure it out."

"How about a whistleblower hotline? The SEC has one. PurePower must have one. JPG must have one. We'll call them all."

"I've been thinking a lot about that. But you know who else has? Bob Grayson. He's a brilliant man. I'm sure he is covering his tracks well. Again, it isn't like he is making these trades. He has friends, probably a couple of them, who are already active in the stock market. They probably make big bets as it is, so when they hit a home run, it doesn't send up much of a red flag. An investigation may come of it, but the government would find nothing, and Bob would know the tip came from us. He'd make our lives hell. We can't underestimate him."

"Damn it!" Johnny yelled, getting to his feet. "Then what the hell am I supposed to do?"

"Not you, us. I'm not leaving you alone on this one. We—

again, *we*—are going to frame him. And we are going to do it next quarter."

Johnny nodded.

"Anything new from Juan Carlos?" Will asked.

Johnny shook his head. "Radio silence from Juárez."

"Good. We deal with Bob first, and then we solve the mess in Juárez."

Will grabbed a beer and Johnny asked, "Is that okay? How's your head?"

Will replied, "I feel great. Had a headache for a week, but I'm more or less back to normal."

"No brain damage?"

"None more than usual."

Johnny laughed.

CHAPTER 24

Cleveland, Ohio
December 6–7, 2019

The first Friday in December was always the firm's holiday party. Much to Johnny's relief, Bob Grayson was not in attendance. One of the region's major clients was upset, and Bob was running damage control.

Dress was formal, and Johnny admitted that after seeing everyone in jeans or business casual attire day after day, it was kind of fun to see everyone spiffed up. Significant others were welcome at the party, although the unwritten rule was that if you weren't dating someone seriously, you didn't bring them. Odds of hooking up were decent, and you didn't want to wreck your chances. The firm paid for rooms at the Hilton for those who wanted them, and many of the younger members took advantage of this.

Johnny reserved a room, not because he hoped to hook up, but because he didn't want to have to worry about driving. Will had not booked a room—he was running a 10k race in the morning near his home—but Johnny suspected that Will would celebrate a bit too hard and end up in his spare bed before the night was over.

The firm spared no expense for the party. There were food stations all around the ballroom serving beef tenderloin, crab, and other gourmet foods. There was a popular local band, kind of a blues/soul group who mixed in appropriate rock covers. And, of course, there was an open bar—three open bars, actually.

Around eight o'clock, Andy Becker walked on stage. With

Bob now the central region managing partner, Andy had taken over leadership of the Cleveland office. The crowd died down long enough to hear Andy thank everybody for a great year of work. He passed along a message from Bob Grayson, who said he was sad he could not be there in person but would be there in spirit with anyone drinking a Jack and Coke. After that, Andy invited the band to take over, and the party was back on.

At about eight thirty, Johnny walked to the bar to grab another drink. As he was waiting, a voice next to him asked, "Johnny Fitch? I'm Marco, Maureen's husband." A handsome and stylish Latino man extended his hand toward him.

"Nice to meet you, Marco," Johnny said, shaking his hand. He felt nervous. He would have felt anxious meeting the spouse of the head of the Cleveland audit practice even if he hadn't still harbored suspicions that Maureen was partnering with Bob.

"Likewise," said Marco. "I believe you were recently down in Juárez with Maureen?" Johnny nodded and Marco continued, "My parents were both born in Juárez and lived there until their early 20s. They crossed the border in the middle of the night, and I was born a couple years later in Texas. I've been to several places in Mexico but never Juárez. What did you think about it?"

Johnny had an enjoyable conversation with Marco and liked being able to give him some insights about what Juárez was like today. Marco also seemed to enjoy learning about foreign outsourcing and how factories in Mexico were structured and operated differently than factories in the US.

After they had been chatting for a few minutes, Maureen walked up and slid her body next to Marco's, pressing into him gently. Johnny noticed how intently Maureen watched Marco when he talked. She had a smile on her face that Johnny didn't often see and laughed freely whenever Marco told a joke. Johnny only knew her as tough and powerful, so it surprised him to see this tender side of her. The conversation went so well that Johnny began to question the validity of his suspicions about Maureen. Maybe he *had* jumped to conclusions too quickly.

After a while, Maureen and Marco shook Johnny's hand and walked away arm in arm. Johnny longed for a love like that.

It was, coincidentally, at that moment when he first noticed Katie.

She was wearing a somewhat tight—and somewhat short—black dress along with three-inch heels. She had on black pearls, and her normally straight hair had a bit of a curl to it. She was standing close to an incredibly handsome man, talking and laughing. When she touched him on the arm, Johnny's heart sank. He turned from her and walked over toward the dessert station, where an assortment of bite-size cheesecakes, tiramisus, and other delectables beckoned him. He was contemplating eating everything when he felt someone walk up beside him.

"Hey, Johnny," Katie said. "I want you to meet someone."

Great, thought Johnny. *She can't simply date someone else. She's got to rub it in.*

"This is Craig," Katie said, pointing to the handsome man. "He's a New Start."

He's also a son of a bitch, thought Johnny bitterly.

The music picked up, forcing Katie to talk more loudly.

"We've known each other our whole lives. Now we're dating," he heard her say.

"You're dating?" Johnny's heart sank even further.

"No, we are debating!" she yelled back. "He wants to propose to his girlfriend on Christmas Day, and I told him that was too cliché. What do you think?"

With that, the tension was broken. Johnny offered his hand

to Craig, and the three of them chatted for a few minutes, ultimately deciding that Craig's girlfriend may be expecting a ring on Christmas, so he should surprise her with a proposal two days before. Eventually, Craig excused himself, and Johnny and Katie were alone eating shots of chocolate mousse.

"You here with anyone?" she asked.

"No. How about you? I mean, anyone besides your date Craig?"

Katie threw her head back in laughter. "You always could make me laugh." She smiled. "And no, I'm not here with anyone."

Johnny couldn't think of anything else to say, so he simply said, "Good," and she smiled again, although much more bashfully this time.

"Johnny, can I ask you something?"

"Of course."

Katie paused, took a quick breath, and blurted, "Why'd you do it? Atlanta. Why'd you do it?"

Johnny had expected, perhaps even hoped, that this question would come someday and had rehearsed his answer many times. But now that they were in the moment, he froze. Instead of saying the words he had prepared, he spoke from the heart. "Katie, I can't tell you why it happened. Maybe because I was drunk. Maybe because I'm a guy, and she's a woman. Maybe because Ben left me with no place else to go. I don't know. All I know is there is not a day that goes by that I don't regret it. And that's because of what it did to you, to us."

Katie started to tear up. At that moment, however, Ben walked over to them. By his side was Emily. She had flown up for the party and to be with Ben for the weekend. After a couple minutes of somewhat tense idle chitchat, Emily looked at Ben and said, "I'm sorry. I can't do this." She then looked at Johnny, raised her voice a bit, and said, "What you did to Kim really sucked." She grabbed Ben by the arm and hastily pulled him away.

"What was that all about?" Katie asked. "What did you do to Kim?"

Johnny asked if they could step outside the ballroom to chat. They grabbed a couple glasses of Sangiovese from the bar, found chairs by a wood-burning fireplace, and sat down. They were alone in the room.

"Remember the boys' weekend I went on over Labor Day weekend?" Johnny said.

Katie nodded.

"Well, I *thought* it was a boys' weekend. But Ben had flown up Emily and Kim instead. It was going to be the four of us at the cabin. Shortly after I arrived, we went for a boat ride and stopped at a lakeside café for lunch. Kim was coming on to me."

Katie's eyes dropped.

"Wait. I told her the boat ride was making me a little queasy, but that was a ruse. We got back to the cabin, and I laid down. The three of them chilled out in the sun for a bit. Instead of taking a nap, I got in my car and left. Didn't know what else to do. So Ben calls me up and says Kim is freaking out, and I tell him I don't care. It was his stupid idea to bring her up there. He says he thought I'd like it. I told him"—Johnny swallowed—"I told him meeting Kim was one of the worst things that ever happened to me. Then I hung up. Kim tried calling me a couple times, but I didn't answer. But she did send me a text. Want to see it?"

Wide-eyed, Katie nodded. Johnny fiddled with his phone for a minute and then handed it to her.

The text said, "Johnny, what the hell? Was I that bad? Or are you just gay?"

Katie burst out laughing. She set her wine glass down, stood up from her chair and sat back down on Johnny's knee. She put her arms around his neck, leaned in, and pressed her lips to his. Johnny closed his eyes and kissed her back. It was better than the first time they'd kissed. Much better.

"Why are you here?" he asked softly.

"Because it's the firm holiday party. I love these kinds of events."

"No, I mean why are you here, sitting on my knee? I thought I'd blown my chance with you. It didn't look like you would ever forgive me."

Katie exhaled and said, "From the moment it happened, I could tell you regretted it. You've been nothing but kind to me ever since. But I wasn't going to rush back into things with you. I was going to wait, to see if you would move on or if your feelings were sincere."

"It was a long wait. But it was worth it."

"I've been keeping tabs on you. I love your mind, and I love the way you treat others. Most of the time," she added with a smile. "And you look damn fine in a suit, especially with that burnt-orange tie."

"It's your favorite color," he said. She scrunched her eyes at him, and he continued, "You told me on our first date."

"You remember that?"

"I remember a lot."

She leaned into him and again pressed her lips against his. Their kiss was cut short when a nasally voice asked, "Why am I not surprised to see the two of you in here?" Katie pulled back and Johnny stared at Nicholas Montgomery, who was standing in the doorway holding a can of Coke.

"Nick—" he started, but then the tenderness of the moment softened him. "Nicholas. Are those new shoes? They look sharp."

Nicholas recoiled in surprise and said, "Well, actually, they are. I bought them for tonight. Thank you for noticing." Johnny nodded, and Nicholas said, "Well, you two have a great night now," and he walked out of the room.

Katie watched him leave and then returned her gaze to Johnny. She didn't lean in again, just stared, and her smile got larger the longer she looked. Finally, she whispered, "Let's get out of here."

Johnny felt his whole body warm up in a sort of tingle. He stayed quiet for a few seconds, savoring the moment. Finally, he whispered back, "I have a room upstairs."

The smile on her face gave him his answer. She removed her hands from around his neck, grabbed his hand, and pulled him out of his chair.

As they waited for the elevator, Will passed by. "Looking lovely tonight, Ms. Doyle," he said.

Katie blushed and laughed at the same time.

"Bring it in bro," Will said to Johnny. "Love you, man," he said as he gave Johnny a powerful embrace.

The elevator arrived, and Will stepped aside. He bowed playfully and gestured for them to enter the elevator. Katie and Johnny laughed and got in. The door began to shut, in slow motion it seemed, and Johnny saw Will looking in at him. Will gave him a wink right before the door fully closed, and Johnny smiled, so pleased to have Will's friendship. Will was like the big brother he never had.

When the elevator doors fully closed, Katie turned into Johnny, and they kissed passionately the whole elevator ride up to the 11th floor.

Johnny wanted to sprint down the hallway but settled for a quick walk arm in arm down to room 1124. Katie excused herself to the bathroom, and he sat down on the bed and felt his body warm and his breath shorten.

When Katie emerged a few minutes later, she was wearing one of the white bathrobes provided by the hotel. She walked in front of him, he undid the robe's knot, and a year of anticipation was released.

A bit after midnight, Will offered to give Amanda a ride home. Amanda had been in Will's start group, and they had always been close, but it was unclear if they were dating or what exactly their relationship was. Maybe they would fool around that night, maybe they wouldn't.

Amanda flipped through the Sirius XM radio dial, looking for a good song, and landed on Train's "Hey, Soul Sister."

"Hey, it's your band," she said.

Will smiled, remembering his encore performance at the Spring Bash several months earlier, and started to sing along. Amanda joined in, and soon they were both belting out the lyrics at the top of their lungs.

They were less than a mile from Amanda's house when the final chorus came on. Will shot a glance toward Amanda and sang with a big smile on his face. She smiled back and matched him word for word.

Will saw her eyes shift slightly to her right. Her mouth opened wide. By the time the scream came, Will had already turned his head sharply to the left and was being blinded by headlights.

Will swerved hard to avoid a major collision, but the driver still clipped the back end of his Jeep Wrangler, and it rolled three times. On the third roll, Will's head smashed against the driver's side window. Another motorist saw what happened and called

911, then began CPR on Will. The driver of the pickup truck had serious but non-life-threatening injuries, and Amanda had been knocked unconscious for a few minutes. All three were taken to the county hospital.

At 8:00 a.m., Katie's cell phone rang. It was Angela. Katie didn't answer it at first and cuddled into Johnny, who was struggling to wake up. When Angela called a second time, Katie pulled her body away and pressed the talk button.

"Hello," said Katie.

"Katie. It's Angela." She had been crying.

"Angela, what's wrong?" Katie asked as she sat up. Johnny leaned into Katie and looked into her eyes with concern.

"Have you seen Johnny?"

"Um, actually, he's here with me right now."

"Tell him I'm so sorry."

"Sorry for what?"

Angela paused. "Haven't you heard? Will is dead."

CHAPTER 25

Cleveland, Ohio
December 7–12, 2019

Will was pronounced dead of blunt force trauma to the head shortly after arriving at the hospital. Tests later indicated that Will's blood alcohol content had been 0.15 percent, nearly double Ohio's legal limit. The driver of the other vehicle, a Ford F150, had had very little alcohol in his system. Amanda was shocked. She'd never felt any danger while Will was driving and had thought he'd only had a couple of beers at the party, as he was still recovering from the attack in the PurePower parking lot. Perhaps he'd thrown down some shots at the bar when she wasn't with him.

Johnny didn't want to go home, so he followed Katie to her apartment. She had a roommate who was thankfully out of town for the weekend. Katie had known that Johnny and Will were close but didn't realize how close until Johnny alternated between crying and laughing while telling Katie story after story about Will.

They barely left her couch, but there was no fooling around. When they weren't talking about Will, they were largely silent. Katie ordered a pizza for dinner—Chicago style, Will's favorite. Katie had a couple bottles of wine in the cupboard, but she didn't offer any to Johnny. It wouldn't have mattered, as Johnny wouldn't have had any. Alcohol had claimed the life of one of his closest friends, his mentor, and his role model. He had no plans to drink again anytime soon.

At times, Johnny's thoughts shifted to Bob Grayson and

whether he was involved in the accident. It all seemed too random. Then he began to wonder what he would do now that Will was out of the picture, but he made his mind think of something else very quickly. The loss of Will went far beyond the loss of his only ally in the mess with Bob. A couple of times, he thought about telling Katie about the situation with Bob, but he decided there was no way he could bring her into the scandal. He was now going to have to face Bob Grayson alone.

They didn't leave the couch until after midnight, and they went to bed wearing underwear. Sometime in the middle of the night, Johnny awoke from a dream. He and Will had been having drinks at Sonrisa, laughing and joking. Bob Grayson wasn't there and wasn't mentioned. When the end of the night came, they got into separate Lyft rides and were safely transported home. When Johnny awoke, he was so happy and for a moment wondered if the car crash had all been a dream. But then he noticed he was in Katie's apartment and realized that this was his new reality. He began to tear up and breathe heavily. The noise woke Katie, and she pulled herself into him. Johnny let it out, stronger this time, and cried harder than he ever remembered.

An office-wide memo came out from Andy Becker on Sunday morning:

On Friday night, JPG lost one of the members of its family. In May of 2014, Will Stevens graduated from John Carroll University in University Heights, Ohio, and joined the firm that October. He was a tireless worker, and his enthusiasm was infectious. He was a popular mentor and loved by all.

We are in contact with his family and will provide details about Will's funeral as soon as we have them. The days ahead will be especially difficult for us all. We will be grieving, yet we still have a business to operate and clients who depend on us. Please stay in contact with your engagement manager and partner to let them know if you need some time off. You may take time off without charging your time to PTO—use the charge code for Other Approved Absences. Since many in our family will be grieving, we ask those of you who can to do a little more. Volunteer to pick up some hours for coworkers who need time away.

Will was killed in a two-vehicle accident, and alcohol may have been a factor. If you feel that you cannot drive at any time, work-related or not, please take a cab and submit the expense for reimbursement. No questions will be asked.

Please keep Will's family in your thoughts and prayers.

Johnny woke up on Monday morning without much of a plan as far as work was concerned. He couldn't sleep past six, so he got up and went for a run. The cool air felt wonderful as it filled his lungs. He didn't notice his surroundings. He just ran. He finished his first loop in Edgewater Park and did another, and then another. All sorts of thoughts raced through his mind, and by the time he finished his nine miles of running, he was spent physically and emotionally. The long, hot shower felt so good.

He knew he would go crazy if he spent all day at home, so he decided to try to work for a few hours. In fact, the entire PurePower engagement team showed up, including Maureen and Rodney, the concurring partner on the account. They wanted to grieve together. They did a little bit of work and told a lot of stories. At 4:00 p.m., they all headed to Sonrisa for a drink. A couple people had a second drink, but no one had a third except Johnny, who drank four Cherry Cokes and left at about seven.

Johnny eventually turned on the second half of the Monday

night football game. The Eagles were hosting the hapless Giants. Johnny and Will had been in the same fantasy football league, and Will had had Eagles tight end Zach Ertz on his team. Will needed 11 points from Zach to win his weekly matchup. Ertz had nine catches for 91 yards and scored two touchdowns, including the game winner in overtime. "Thanks, Zach," Johnny said aloud before drifting off to sleep.

Will's funeral was on Thursday at St. James Church in the small town of Cambridge, two hours south of Cleveland. The office of JPG was closed that day, and a temporary receptionist was brought in to answer the phones so Val could attend. Nearly every member of the firm attended, as did many of the inhabitants of Cambridge. Cambridge was a small town, and everyone knew the Stevens family. Many of Will's college friends also made the trek, as did many of his clients, including several employees of PurePower. In all, around 1,500 people attended the funeral, which was also livestreamed to the local high school's gymnasium.

Will's family were devout Catholics, and a full Catholic Mass was included in the funeral. Near the end of Mass, a family member was permitted to give a brief eulogy, and Aaron walked to the front of the church and began to speak.

"William James Stevens was born on December 28, 1991. He died on December 7, 2019. But those dates are not significant. What is significant is how Will spent the nearly 28 years in between. My parents enjoy telling people how Will demanded to be present in the delivery room the day I was born. He was only two at the time, but he felt a sense of responsibility for me.

"That is how Will lived his life, looking out for and including others. In grade school, he ate lunch with the boy no one else wanted to sit with. In junior high, he got a black eye defending the new kid at school. And in high school, he took a girl who didn't have a date to prom. In college, Will volunteered regularly with campus ministry. He never went to Mexico, Texas, or Florida for spring break, but he did go to Haiti two times. Even in his work at JPG, Will included all members of his engagement teams and organized the United Way events.

"I have many fond memories of my brother, but one in particular stands out. When he was fifteen years old and I was thirteen, our parents were at the theater. Will had his driving permit and decided that he should get some extra practice in. My dad had an old Corvette—he still does—that he rarely took out. Will decided to learn how to drive a stick shift that very evening. After about an hour of starting, stopping, jerking, and stalling, he had it down. We had been practicing in the parking lot at our high school, and I begged him to let me drive. Before long, I kinda sorta had the hang of it, and I asked if we could take it on a spin through town. Always up for an adventure, Will agreed.

"On the way into town, we passed a police car going the opposite way, and Will noticed that I was going too fast. When the squad car turned around and put on its lights, Will figured we were in for it.

"I remember beginning to cry and screaming at him, 'What are we going to do?'

"Will asked me if I had my Swiss Army knife on me.

"'You can't stab the police officer!' I remember yelling.

"'Just give it to me,' he replied. He opened it up, took a breath, and slashed it across his forearm. When the cop pulled us over and walked up to the car, Will said, 'Officer, I am sorry we are going too fast. My brother is trying to get me to the hospital.' When the officer saw his arm, he yelled, 'Follow me,' and escorted us.

"Mom and Dad came to pick us up, and Will made up a story about us playing with my knife, him getting cut, and then him deciding to drive us to the hospital, with the first keys we could find being those of the Corvette. The officer never did write a report, and it was never suggested that I was driving. To this day, no one had heard the true version of the story. So, sorry Mom and Dad, but that's what happened. The scar that Will carried around for the rest of his life was our secret, and whenever I saw it, I would remember the way that he had protected me.

"Will did crazy things like that all the time. He was full of adventure but always took the fall or the blame when things went wrong. Honestly, I'm scared about living the rest of my life without my older brother looking out for me. But for 24 years, I got the best friend and brother that anyone could ask for. Thank you, Will. I will miss you so much."

After the Mass and burial, a reception was held at the high school where Will had been a three-sport star. No alcohol was served, out of respect for the way that Will's life was ended. There was an open microphone, and many of Will's family members and friends took time to remember his life. The atmosphere went from somber to jovial depending on who was speaking.

Johnny had decided in advance that he was not going to speak. He wanted this to be more about Will's family and closer friends. But then Bob Grayson took the microphone. Bob spoke for a few minutes about how Will embodied the spirit of JPG: determination, client service, and the highest ethical standards. After hearing the words "the highest ethical standards" come out of Bob's mouth, Johnny couldn't contain himself. He walked to the front of the room and picked up the microphone.

"Hi, I'm Johnny. I worked with Will until last Friday. I related to what Aaron said because I felt like Will was an older brother to me too. I'm devasted at losing him, but I'm also happy for Will. The world we live in is flawed and corrupt"—his eyes lingered on Bob—"but he is now in a better place, looking down on us and wondering what all the fuss is for."

Bob scowled at Johnny as Johnny walked past to return to his seat. When Johnny got back to his table, he leaned down and whispered to Katie, "I need to go now."

Katie grabbed her coat and purse and caught up to him. "Johnny, what's wrong?"

"Nothing."

"You didn't seem like yourself when you spoke about Will."

"One of my best friends died. Give me a break," he gruffly replied as they walked out into the crisp evening air.

Ben was preparing to leave the reception when, out of no-where, Bob Grayson appeared at his side.

"Tough day," said Bob. "Did you get to know Will at all?"

"I think everyone got to know him," Ben replied. "I didn't work on any of his accounts, but that didn't stop him from show-ing interest in me. Whether it was in the break room, at a happy hour, or passing by in the hallway, he always checked in with me to see how I was doing. Amazing guy."

"Yeah," replied Bob. "He will be tough to replace."

Ben tried to hide his shock. "No one can replace Will."

"One thing I have learned," replied Bob, "is that no one is irreplaceable."

Ben was stunned and wanted out of the conversation. "I should get going."

"Say, Ben," Bob said as Ben walked toward the door. "I heard there was kind of a confrontation at the holiday party involving Johnny and that woman from Austin. I don't like confrontations at my parties. What can you tell me about it?"

Ben hesitated. He really didn't feel like sharing his personal life with Bob Grayson. "It was really nothing."

"That's not what I heard," Bob replied. "Who was that woman anyway?"

"That's Emily. She's my girlfriend. She works for our Austin office."

"And why was she so upset?"

"Her best friend Kim also works for the Austin office. She and Johnny had a thing going for a while. But Johnny has always liked Katie better." Upon saying this, Ben almost kicked himself. Bob Grayson didn't ask for nor need that much personal information.

"Katie Doyle?" asked Bob curiously.

Ben nodded and quickly excused himself.

Later that evening, Bob was home in his office sipping on an expensive Meritage wine from Napa Valley and looking through the firm's online directory. He pulled up a list of experienced associates in the Austin office and found her: Kim Santos. He typed Kim's name into LinkedIn's search box, and her profile picture popped up. It was professional, but Bob could tell she was beautiful.

Bob spent the next hour searching through all forms of social media for more information on Kim. On Facebook, Kim's friends had tagged her in a few pictures from a beach party during her college years, and Bob perhaps looked at those bikini pictures a bit longer than necessary. Bob was scrolling through her timeline and was about to call it a night when he saw a post from 2017 that caught his eye. Kim had shared a news story without comment. The story was about a David Santos who had been murdered in a gunfight with police in Mexico City.

Many of the comments on Kim's posting said something to the effect of prayers for her family. One poster said, "I'm so sorry you lost your father. I can't even imagine."

Kim had replied, "It's okay, I hadn't seen him in five years."

Bob took another sip of the Meritage and considered what it meant. He then finished his glass and smiled.

CHAPTER 26

Cleveland, Ohio
December 16–24, 2019

Johnny returned to PurePower nine days after Will's death. Maureen, Rodney, and Bob Grayson had called a meeting for 8:00 a.m., and they were accompanied by someone Johnny didn't recognize.

"Good morning, everyone," Bob began. "I know this has been a tough week on everyone. Will was your leader and your friend. But now we must move on. We're not sure how we can, but we will. We won't forgot about Will. Instead, we will honor him through our actions. We are pretty short-staffed in the office, and we don't have another manager ready to lead the team through this busy season, so we have brought in Jarod Nelson, who is a new manager out of the Kansas City office.

"Jarod will take over day-to-day management of PurePower, although Maureen and Rodney will of course still have ultimate responsibility. I have promised that they will have whatever resources are necessary to get the job done. PurePower has quickly become one of the office's most important clients, and we need to have a great busy season. Maureen, would you like to add anything?"

Bob sat down, and Maureen spoke for a couple of minutes, giving a mix between a remembrance and a pep talk. Johnny wasn't really listening. He was trying to figure out how he would deal with Bob without Will. He wasn't sure exactly how he would pull it off, but one thing was sure: he was going to do it the way that Will had recommended. He was going to frame Bob Grayson.

Johnny and Will had figured that Bob would strike again while the iron was hot. Earnings were due to be released on February 3, 2020, and about two weeks beforehand, the earnings release would be drafted and in Johnny's possession for first review. Johnny knew this, and he knew that Bob Grayson knew this. Sometime in late January, Johnny could expect another call or meeting request or whatever the hell it would be from Bob this time. And he had to be ready.

Johnny dropped into the JPG office on Christmas Eve Day. Jarod was hardly the savior the PurePower account needed, and Johnny was doing what he did best: picking up the slack whenever and wherever possible. Katie had invited him to come with her for Christmas, which she was planning to spend in the small town about two hours south of Cleveland where her family lived, but Johnny had declined. "It seems too early to meet your family" was his official reply, but the truth was that he needed time to come up with a plan to deal with Bob.

The office was like a ghost town; Johnny was one of the only ones still working. Val shut the front doors at one in the afternoon, and by five, the 17th floor of the Stone Tower was completely deserted. Johnny packed up to leave and drive to his family's home a bit after six. He shut off the remaining lights and popped into the bathroom in the hallway by the elevator banks. As the door closed behind him, he heard the elevator door open. A loud, angry voice came from within the elevator and out into the hallway.

"I told you April 30, and that is what the hell I meant!" All was silent for a moment, and then Johnny heard Bob yell again. "Fine. February 5 at the Mirage. But not a day sooner. I can't do it. I'll give you the final six forty plus interest."

Johnny heard the main doors of the JPG office shut. Wher

it was silent again, he realized he was breathing heavier, and his pulse was racing. He peered out into the hallway, didn't see any sign of Bob, and ran over to push the elevator button. He waited for what felt like forever. Suddenly, he heard Bob's voice again.

"This ends in February. I've got to up the stakes. One final time, a big one, and then we are done. How much?" Bob paused and then exclaimed, "Ten more? I've already given you twelve! I thought the deal was seventeen. Now you want twenty-two?"

Bob was coming back through JPG's main door, and the elevator had not yet arrived.

Johnny dashed into the stairwell just in time. As he started sprinting down the stairs, he heard the stairwell door open and Bob yell down, "Who's there? Come back here. This is Bob Grayson, and I own this place. Get your ass back here!"

Johnny, already a good four floors down, kept running and prayed that Bob couldn't see him. When he got to the ground floor, he burst through the lobby and out into the cold, fresh air and looked around in the dark. No one was there except for a couple of homeless men looking for money. Johnny looked back and out of the corner of his eye caught a glimpse of Bob Grayson hustling out of the elevator and into the building's lobby. Johnny took off at a dead sprint and didn't look back. He didn't stop until he was completely out of breath and out of sight of the Stone Tower. When he did stop, he felt a wave of nausea coming. He lunged for a trash receptacle and vomited until there was nothing left.

When he was empty, he texted his mom, "Not feeling well. Will for sure be there tomorrow."

He drove straight home and was still shaking when he walked into his apartment 20 minutes later. He set his laptop down on the kitchen counter and threw his jacket against the wall. "Damn you, Bob Grayson!" he screamed. He fell to the floor and cried, clutching his coat and wishing that Will were there to help him. As he lay on the floor, he looked up at the framed sketch that Dani had done of him sitting alone in the Public Square. He yearned to be the man back in the drawing, back when life was simpler.

Eventually, he got up and flipped on the TV. A college bowl game was in progress, two mediocre programs playing in a meaningless game in front of a small crowd. Johnny hated the college football bowl system and wished they would simply expand the playoffs to 16 teams. He opened the cupboard and found a package of beef sticks. Next, he went to the fridge and instinctively grabbed a bottle of beer. He stared at the bottle for a minute. It was an IPA from a local brewery, one he had gone to with Will. He opened it and poured it into a pint glass. A rich foamy head beckoned him, so he picked up the glass. The smell of citrus was present as he brought the rim to his lips.

Ping. A text on his cell phone interrupted him. *Ping.* Another message. "Hey handsome," the first message said. "Sure you don't want to come down this way?" said the second.

Johnny looked at the glass in his left hand and the phone in his right. He looked back at the glass and again raised it to his lips.

"I miss you."

CHAPTER 27

Bexley, Ohio
December 24–25, 2019

A bit more than two hours later, Johnny pulled into Katie's parents' driveway. Katie ran out to greet him, threw her arms around him, and kissed him.

"Merry Christmas," she said.

"Now it is," he replied as he pulled her tighter and pressed his face into hers.

Katie came from a big family where chaos reigned supreme. Most of her family members were a little buzzed up, but the taste on Katie's lips told Johnny that she was sober just like he was. On his table back in Cleveland, an IPA was sitting lonely in a glass, getting warm and going flat. Katie's "I miss you" text had come through just in time.

Katie was the youngest of five, the only girl in the family. Her brothers were married, and so far there were a total of six grandkids. Everyone was present, including Katie's grandmother, Grandma T. She was a feisty sort of gal who was either buzzed up or just naturally a bit goofy. When Grandma T. went to the piano, the whole group followed her. She couldn't hear very well anymore and thus pounded the hell out of the keys as the group belted out "Deck the Halls." Johnny was bashful at first but quickly joined in. Katie saw him hamming it up with her oldest brother, Marcus, and she beamed at him. An evening that had started so dreadfully was turning out perfectly.

Christmas Day was full of games, great food, and even louder piano playing by Grandma T. At one point, Marcus asked Johnny to help gather more wood for the fireplace. They were out at the woodpile when Marcus asked, "So how long have you known Katie?"

"A couple years," said Johnny. He talked a bit about how he'd had his eye on her during their internship but she'd had a boyfriend at the time.

"Yeah, their breakup was tough on our family. They had been dating so long, he was almost like another brother to us." Marcus paused and then asked, "Did she tell you what happened?"

Johnny shook his head.

"She'd probably get pissed at me for telling you, but I think it is best you know."

Johnny stood frozen for a moment, unsure of what to expect.

"Her ex was the jealous type. Didn't like Katie talking to other guys. A couple times they had been out to the bars, and he'd almost gotten into fights because guys looked at her. Well, anyway, they took a trip to Europe after college, and after rock climbing in Spain, they went to Italy. They were in Rome and went out to a nightclub. Her boyfriend went to the bathroom, and right as he was getting back, some Italian guy walked up to Katie, leaned over to whisper in her ear, and put his hand on her lower back. Her boyfriend saw this and went berserk. Started a fight in the nightclub that spilled outside. Ended up beating the guy into a coma. Last I heard, the guy still hasn't woken up, and Katie's ex is in an Italian jail. His family has money, so they hired a good Italian lawyer. He'll get out this summer and probably come back looking for Katie. She said she's done with him, but I'm not sure he's done with her."

Johnny sat there slack-jawed, unsure of what to say, or even what to think, for that matter. Marcus gave Johnny an open-handed slap to the arm and said, "Just shittin' ya, man!"

Johnny exhaled and chuckled nervously, shallowly at first and then more heartily.

Marcus continued, "She dumped him the summer after college before the European rock-climbing trip. Just bored with him, I guess. He wasn't very interesting or mature. At first, she liked him because he showed interest in her, but after that wore off, there was nothing left."

Johnny smiled and said, "Marcus, you are evil."

"Yeah, I like screwing with people sometimes. So, what would you have done if it had been true? Run like hell?"

"No way. I'm sticking with her," Johnny said, as much to himself as to Marcus.

Marcus nodded his approval and said, "Good choice. You won't find a better woman than my sister."

They finally carried some wood back into the house. Katie came up to them and said, "I wondered where you went. Marcus didn't say anything to scare you away, did he?"

Johnny looked at Marcus, smiled, and said, "Just the opposite."

Luckily, Katie had ridden with one of her brothers to their mom's house, so she was able to ride with Johnny to his parents' home late in the afternoon on Christmas. The celebration at Johnny's parents' was more subdued. They were a quieter bunch.

After a nice dinner and a few presents, Billy flipped on an NBA game. Dani sighed, an artist in a house full of jocks, and plopped down in a small chair on the side of the room to sketch. She kept glancing at Katie periodically.

Katie learned most about Johnny when his dad, Rich, asked if she wanted to tag along on a trip to the gas station to pick up some vanilla ice cream for dessert.

"What was Johnny like as a kid?" she asked.

"He had a quiet confidence, even at a young age," Rich said. "Very determined. He never quit on his homework until he figured it out. He played sports with older kids to challenge himself more. He loved puzzles. When something was missing in the house, we'd ask him to find it."

Katie reflected a bit on Johnny's weekly charge hour battles with Nicholas Montgomery, and they started to make more sense.

"Growing up," Rich said, "he was too short for basketball, so he started wrestling. He went into every match thinking he would win, and he always did."

"Always?" Katie asked.

"Well, his junior and senior years of high school, yes. He was a two-time state champion."

"Wow. I didn't know that. What made him so good?" Katie asked.

"Again, it goes back to his determination. He simply out-worked everyone else. Also, he definitely liked the individual challenge. He figured he could beat anybody one on one."

"Where did he get that from?"

"Probably from his best friend growing up, Pete. Have you heard about him?"

"A bit."

"Because of his bad asthma, Pete couldn't really do a lot athletically. Johnny was fond of saying that he had to win twice as many trophies, one for him and one for Pete. Pete was his biggest fan and would go with to the matches and games, take video, stats, whatever."

"Can I ask you kind of a personal question about Johnny?" Katie asked.

Rich chuckled and nodded.

"What kind of girls has he dated before?"

Rich chuckled again. "Not many."

"Really? But he's so handsome and charming!"

"He's always been so focused he hasn't had a lot of time for girls. He had plenty of them as friends, and plenty that wanted to date him, but he largely ignored them. In fact, I don't think he ever dated any of them for more than two to three months, so honestly, I never really got to know any of them very well."

Rich paid the gas station clerk, and then he and Katie got back in the car. "So you don't think I will be around for very long?" She laughed.

"I wouldn't say that."

"And why not?"

"He's never brought a girl home before. I've seen the way he acts around you."

"And?"

"And I am pretty sure he likes you. A lot. He's going through a lot right now. Please don't hurt him."

"I won't," Katie promised. She was smiling when they walked back into the house.

"Dad," Johnny said, dragging out the "a" sound. "What did you tell her?"

"None of your business, mister," Katie replied.

After the NBA game ended, Dani begged for something different, so they watched *It's a Wonderful Life.* Dani continued to glance over at Katie much of the time, as if she were sizing Katie up. Finally, Dani asked, "So are you Johnny's friend or his girl-friend?"

Katie looked embarrassed and replied, "I don't know. You'd have to ask him."

"She's my girlfriend," Johnny said, hoping that wasn't too presumptuous. The sparkle in Katie's eyes meant that it was quite all right with her, and Dani's immediate grin meant that she liked his answer too.

As they were getting into Johnny's car to leave, Dani ran out and handed a sheet of paper to Katie. Dani had sketched a profile of her, and it was striking.

"I love it," Katie said with great feeling. "It's so beautiful."

"It's beautiful because you are beautiful," Dani replied. "I always wanted a big sister." Katie leaned down a bit, and Dani squeezed her around the neck. "Bring her here more often," Dani ordered Johnny.

"Yes, ma'am." He smiled, picked up his little sister in a big bear hug, and swung her back and forth, much to her delight.

CHAPTER 28

Ciudad Juárez, Mexico
December 28, 2019

Jorge was shaking when he picked up the phone and called Bruno. "The plan is in place, as you requested."

"Tell me," Bruno commanded.

Jorge couldn't believe the words that came out of his mouth. "I will close the facility and drive the product in during the day in a large canopy truck. I will also have a large cube van loaded with hundreds of gallons of diesel fuel. I will douse the product with diesel fuel. On top of the product will be a remote detonation device, which we will trigger by calling a special phone. Once the device is triggered, the diesel fuel will begin to burn. Within a few minutes, a deflagration-to-detonation transition will take place, and the explosion will occur."

"Perfect," Bruno replied. "Did you test it?"

"Yes." Jorge sighed. "On a much smaller scale and in an open field."

"Good. This is very good."

"I still don't understand," Jorge said in a pleading tone. "Isn't there some other way?"

"No," Bruno replied coldly, "there is not."

"Is it all about the money?" Jorge asked.

"It's always all about the money. You are about to become a rich man, Jorge, and you are going to make me very, very rich."

The call ended, and Jorge set down his phone. He walked out of his office and left the facility without saying goodbye to his team, something he normally would have done on a Saturday.

He drove to his ex-wife's home, picked up Ana, and took her to a local park. They kicked a ball back and forth for a while, and Jorge enjoyed the rhythm of it all. Eventually, other children arrived and asked Ana to join them in a friendly match of fútbol. They were running short of players, so they asked Jorge if he would be one of the goalies. He agreed and spent the next hour playing with the children, letting a few shots slip past him at appropriate times. He smiled brighter than he had in some time.

After he tucked Ana into bed that night, though, his smile vanished, and he went back to thinking of any way possible to get out of the hell coming toward him. So far, he had come up with nothing.

CHAPTER 29

Cleveland, Ohio
December 30, 2019

It was six o'clock on a Monday morning when Johnny grabbed his laptop and ventured to the same Starbucks off Clifton where he had first told Will about the Bob Grayson mess. The same table in the back was still open, and he ordered the same tall Sumatra and the same fried egg bagel. It felt good to be in a familiar place where he felt some connection to Will.

After his pleasant Christmas with Katie and their families, Johnny felt refueled and ready to get back to business. He needed to figure out a plan to frame Bob Grayson before Bob started making moves in the new year, and to do that, he probably needed to figure out what Bob had been yelling about on Christmas Eve. From the sounds of it, Bob owed someone money. How, Johnny had no idea. Bob probably pulled in a million bucks per year and could afford most anything.

Johnny was puzzled by the numbers Bob had been throwing around. He repeated them in his head. Based on the calculations he and Will had gone through, Bob may have netted profits of about $7 million from trading PurePower stock, so how had he already come up with $12 million? Given that Bob sounded like he was under enormous financial strain, Johnny doubted that Bob had simply saved up that extra $5 million. Maybe Bob hadn't netted $7 million at all, and maybe Johnny was misinterpreting things. Where was Will when Johnny needed him?

An hour later, Johnny still hadn't made any progress. He went home and laced up his running shoes, hoping he would think better on the trails. Before he left, he got the automated email from the firm showing charge hours by person over the last week. Even on holiday weeks, there was a constant reminder and push for competition. Johnny was midpack at 30 hours. Some associates were listed at 0 hours—presumably, they had taken a week of vacation, but the firm seemed to enjoy reminding them of the deficit they were creating for themselves. As expected, Nicholas Montgomery was first with 52 hours. The office had only been open for three and a half days, so that was quite a feat.

Johnny left his apartment and broke into a jog. He was annoyed at Nicholas Montgomery for working hard on a holiday week, which of course didn't make sense, but it was how he felt. He did one loop through Edgewater Park and was still wound up pretty tight, so he decided to go another round. He was still thinking about the damn charge hours and Nicholas Montgomery. *Freaking Nicholas Montgomery*, he thought. *Why couldn't Bob Grayson have picked him instead?*

Then it clicked, and Johnny stopped dead in his tracks. He turned around and raced home.

Nicholas was sitting in the conference room at American Bank when he got an IM from Johnny.

"Hey, Nicholas. Hoping to chat with you about something. Meet at Merton's after work?"

What in the world? thought Nicholas. Although they'd had a pleasant interaction at the firm's holiday party, he and Johnny rarely socialized, and the last time they did had ended poorly. The best he could tell, Johnny didn't like him, and he didn't know why. Because of that, he didn't really like Johnny either.

"Sorry, man. Gonna be a late night," he wrote back, hoping that would be the end of it.

"I won't take much of your time. You gotta eat. Just let me buy you a Philly at Merton's and you can go back to dominating the charge hour competition."

Nicholas smirked. The auditors' expense accounts were so lavish that Johnny wouldn't be buying anything out of his own pocket. JPG or one of their rich clients would end up paying for it once Johnny's receipt found its way onto an expense report.

"I don't know. Can't you call me? Got a big presentation in the morning in front of Andy," he wrote.

"Andy will still be there after dinner. C'mon. I'll even let you upgrade to the onion rings."

Nicholas thought for a moment. "Six o'clock. Don't be late. Thirty minutes is all I've got." He'd picked six o'clock because it would still be rush hour. He would simply have to walk across Public Square in downtown Cleveland, but Johnny would be driving. A little payback for the way Johnny had treated him, however petty, felt nice.

"Great," Johnny replied. "See you then."

Nicholas didn't reply. It was an unwritten rule that the person with more power didn't finish the conversation. He sat back and smiled, proud of the way he had handled his biggest rival. Twelve years from now, they would both be up for partner. Maybe there would be room for two partners that year, but maybe only one. And if it would only be one, it was damn sure going to be Nicholas Montgomery.

Johnny knew he couldn't be late, and a slight snowfall had the roads tied up something fierce, so he started packing up his stuff at PurePower at a quarter to five.

"Where are you going?" Jarod asked, a hint of annoyance in his voice.

"Got something I need to take care of," Johnny replied. Will never would have questioned Johnny's decision to head out a little early; he'd known he could trust Johnny to get his work done. Despite the slack Johnny had already picked up on the PurePower account, Jarod didn't seem any more inclined to show Johnny that same respect.

"We are already behind schedule," Jarod said as Johnny started to walk out the door. "I need your report by first thing tomorrow morning. Will put us in a tough spot."

Johnny froze, and the entire conference room went silent. Johnny set his laptop bag down and shut the door. He walked over and leaned right into Jarod's face, pointing his finger, and said, "Don't you ever disparage Will Stevens again. Ever. Do you understand me?"

The rest of the conference room stayed silent. Johnny was popular, everyone missed Will, and Jarod was the unwanted team member. They weren't about to stick up for Jarod. They knew Johnny had some serious martial arts training and were wondering if they were about to witness Jarod go flying through the conference room window.

"Chill, bro," Jarod said with all the conviction he could muster.

As Johnny slowly backed away, he said, "You will get your damn report, bro."

Fortunately, traffic wasn't as bad as Johnny had expected. At a quarter to six, Johnny was at Merton's ordering the Philly and onion rings so that they would be ready when His Majesty arrived.

Nicholas walked in at ten past six. He had been sitting at the client's office two blocks away and had been at a good stopping point for a while, but he'd wanted to show up late to show Johnny who was in charge.

"Hi, Johnny," he said as he slid into the booth without apologizing for being late.

"Thanks for coming, Nicholas."

"Well, what's up?" Nicholas said as he picked up his Philly and took his first bite.

"I need to ask you a couple questions, and depending on how you answer, I may need to let you in on some unpleasant information."

Nicholas started chewing more slowly and said, "What the hell?" with a mouth half full of beef, provolone cheese, onions, and banana peppers.

"Who is the signing partner on American Bank?"

"Andy Becker. You know that."

"And who is the concurring partner?"

"Liz Franklin. Where is this going, Johnny?" Nicholas had finished his first bite of Philly and wasn't taking another.

"Does Bob Grayson ever come out to American Bank?"

"Not that I know of."

"Has Bob ever asked you about how American Bank is doing?"

Nicholas lowered his eyes, thought for a moment. "I guess. I mean, whenever I see him, we talk about how things are going in general, how my clients are doing, stuff like that. He's the regional managing partner. That's part of his job."

"Nicholas, has Bob ever asked you if American Bank is going to raise or lower their earnings guidance?"

Nicholas thought for several seconds and took a drink of his ice water. He closed his eyes and leaned his head back against the booth. When he lowered his head and opened his eyes, he softly said, "Yeah. The last two quarters, I think. Why?"

Nicholas's spirit was deflating. The confidence had left his eyes, his mouth was hanging slightly open, and a strand of provolone cheese dangled halfway down his chin.

Johnny's pulse began to race, and he felt his breath getting shorter. He wanted to scream but needed to stay composed in front of Nicholas. "Nicholas," he said, "you can leave now and pretend we never had this conversation. You can take the Philly with you." He paused and then continued, "Or you can stay, and I can let you know what I know, and we can help each other out."

Nicholas had a general idea of where this was headed—though he didn't know how bad it would get. He sat back in the booth and looked out the window. The snow was falling a bit heavier now, and he watched a family walk past on the sidewalk, the kids delighting in the feel of cold snowflakes on their faces.

He knew that if he stayed, Johnny would tell him things that were bad for Bob Grayson, bad for the firm, bad for Nicholas, or maybe all of the above. But if he left, he could plead ignorance and go on his merry way. He had been approached by a couple of headhunters about some cushy jobs in the suburbs and even one with a venture capital firm on the east coast that came with a hefty salary increase, fewer hours, free parking, and maybe some stock options.

Nicholas looked out the window for another minute. Johnny was prepared to give him all the time he needed. When Nicholas was ready, Johnny was going to tell him that his best estimates were that Bob had profited $5 million trading on American Bank, using information provided by Nicholas.

When Nicholas finally looked back, Johnny saw a cold resolve in his eyes. "Sorry, Johnny. You're on your own. I'm outta here. Like you said on my birthday, I've gotta go charge some hours."

With that, Nicholas Montgomery got up and started to walk out of Merton's, leaving his Philly behind. He walked back over and said, "One quick thing. Bob Grayson was at my client this afternoon. He asked why I was running out without packing up, and I told him you'd asked to meet with me. Seemed innocent enough. I figured you'd want to know."

Johnny sat in his booth for a while after Nicholas was gone, staring out the window, feeling lost. He felt that he couldn't do this alone. He couldn't do this without Will.

The following morning, Nicholas shocked the Cleveland office of JPG by announcing that he had accepted a job in Boston. Leaving right at the start of busy season was considered taboo, as it left the firm in a tough spot. Even more shocking, Nicholas did not give the customary two weeks' notice. He packed up his things and left that very day. That night, on New Year's Eve, Nicholas loaded down his Ford Mustang with his clothes and certain personal items. He headed east on Interstate 90, vowing never to return to Cleveland.

There was a part of Johnny that was furious at Nicholas for leaving, but there was another part that had expected it. Nicholas had always been a me-first kind of guy and did not have a reputation as a team player. The partners were generally mixed when discussing him, some focusing on the lack of rapport he had with the rest of the team, others focusing on his astronomical charge hours—after all, charge hours were what generated revenue. Through it all, though, Johnny had hoped that Nicholas had some courage in him. In the end, it seemed he did not.

— Boz Bostrom

CHAPTER 30

Cleveland, Ohio
December 31, 2019

Johnny would have loved to have New Year's Eve completely off to prepare for the impending onslaught of busy season, but PurePower's inventory count was slated to begin at 9:00 a.m. that day. He pulled into the parking lot 15 minutes early. The inventory count was expected to be worse than Johnny remembered from the time he'd spent at a client last year. Batteries were best preserved when stored around 40 degrees Fahrenheit, so Johnny would be spending much of the day in a chilly warehouse.

The client wasn't ready yet, so Johnny, not motivated to do much else, traded messages with Katie. They hadn't seen each other since the day after Christmas and had simply exchanged a few texts and IMs.

"Did you hear about Nicholas Montgomery?" she asked.

"Yeah," he replied. "Pretty surprising."

"It's so odd and so sudden. Do you think something triggered it?"

"Good question." Johnny hated to lie to Katie, but he couldn't yet be honest with her on this one. "What do you want to do tonight? I'm happy to take you out for a fun night on the town if you wish."

"Ben's party?" she replied.

"You'd go?"

"Why not?" she said. "I don't think Kim is coming."

"Very funny," he replied. "Pick you up at seven?"

"Sure. What are you wearing?"

"You?"

"That's not till after the party, mister!"

"Oops."

"I want to dress up a bit."

"Sounds good. I'll wear something that doesn't embarrass you too much."

The client still wasn't ready, so Johnny decided to make a coffee run to the Starbucks a couple of minutes away. As he left the facility, he stopped and chatted briefly with Joan and Jim, the security guards at the gate. They were the only PurePower personnel on duty except for one finance team member helping with the inventory count and one of the warehouse supervisors. Johnny returned from Starbucks 15 minutes later with three tall, hot cups of Sumatra. He figured that warehouse security work was a recipe for boredom and that hot caffeine would be in high demand, especially on a cool December morning. "Black okay?" he asked as he carried the coffees to Jim and Joan.

Johnny visited with them for about 20 minutes. He learned about their families and their interests. Eventually, Jarod pinged Johnny to let him know that the client was just about ready.

"Well, thanks for the coffee," Joan said, "but more than that, thanks for chatting. Most of the corporate types won't even acknowledge us."

"It was my pleasure," Johnny replied sincerely. "I'll look forward to seeing you a year from now. Same time, same place. I'll bring some bagels as well."

"I love it," said Jim. They shook hands, and then Johnny went back inside the warehouse.

It was close to eleven before the client was fully ready for them. The client gave them a tour of the warehouse and explained the types of batteries on hand, repeating much of the information Johnny had learned during his trip to Mexico. PurePower had about $200 million of inventory on its balance sheet, with 90 percent of it located in Parma, so if management reports were accurate, about $180 million of inventory was sitting in front of them. The inventory was neatly organized on pallets in the warehouse, separated in rows with labels at the front of each row and, of course, on each box. Each box contained 100 batteries. Generally, Apple, Samsung, and other big phone manufacturers bought somewhere between 50 and 500 boxes of batteries at a time, which amounted to thousands, if not tens of thousands, of batteries in a single order.

PurePower's inventory system indicated that there were about 75,000 boxes of batteries in the warehouse, so with 100 batteries per box, there were about 7.5 million batteries on hand. Verifying the existence of that many batteries was a daunting task, so JPG trained its auditors on how to effectively use sampling techniques.

Johnny and Jarod started with a simple and low-risk step. They each picked 10 boxes at random in the warehouse and verified that those boxes were listed on management's report. As Johnny walked around the warehouse looking for a box to select, he felt a bit like he was at a grocery store trying to figure out which Honeycrisp apple to put in his shopping cart—except every apple looked a bit different, whereas each box looked exactly the same. The 10 boxes that Johnny selected existed on management's report, as did those that Jarod selected.

The next step was more important. Jarod randomly picked 80 boxes of batteries from the management report, and he and Johnny each hunted down 40 of those boxes in the warehouse to verify their existence. Jarod picked more boxes of the higher-value X+ batteries, given that any discrepancy with those would pose greater risk. The process of finding the boxes, while mundane, went smoothly because the rows, pallets, and boxes were well labeled. Had even one box not been accounted for, it would have meant that management's report was not fully reliable, and they would have had to select and investigate the existence of many more boxes. Thankfully, they found all the boxes that Jarod selected.

The more arduous task was that each time they found a box, they opened it to ensure it contained the type of batteries that the box's label said it contained. Johnny had to take off his gloves for this part, and his hands got cold quickly, although at least that numbed the feeling of all the paper cuts. As he was digging through the fifth box, Johnny thought back to his first accounting course in college, where the professors and recruiters had regularly shown glitzy pictures of students working in cushy high-rise offices, not digging around on all fours in cold, dusty warehouses.

Johnny opened another box, and to no surprise, the batteries inside were the same as what was listed on the box. He dug through the box a bit to make sure that all batteries were the same, and sure enough, they were.

"What a waste of time," he mumbled.

By this point, it was 2:30 p.m. The client asked Jarod if they could reduce their sample size and count fewer batteries. While Johnny was eager to wrap things up so he could get in a workout and then enjoy his evening, he agreed with Jarod's call to hold firm.

Johnny had to use the restroom, partially so that he could warm up, so he walked past the row of pallets filled with X batteries on his way. For whatever reason, on his way back to his side of the warehouse, he stopped and opened an additional box of X batteries. "Going the extra mile," he chuckled to himself. Sure enough, the packaging on the individual battery container was the same as the packaging on the box.

"Just curious, how do you inspect the batteries when they come from Mexico?" he asked one of the warehouse workers.

"Well, we do what you are doing—open a box and make sure the packaging of the individual batteries matches the box's label. We can also open the packaging on an individual battery and check the model number inscribed on the back, but we don't do that too often. It's too tough to repackage a battery once we have opened it, so any that we double-check can't really be sold. They get used for testing or samples or giveaways, although it's not like there's a big market for that, so oftentimes they just get scrapped. If our supplier was a third party, we'd maybe do it more, but our supplier is a wholly owned subsidiary, so they have no incentive to try to short us."

Johnny nodded and said, "I will need to open a couple."

"Well, like I said, that pretty much ruins them. Do you really have to?"

Johnny hesitated for a moment. JPG policy certainly required him to complete this test, but now he felt pressured not to. "I really should do it," Johnny said finally.

"Go ahead, then," said the worker. "That's what you guys get paid to do, I guess."

Johnny opened a box of X batteries and then opened an individual package. Sure enough, he found an X inscription when he flipped the battery over.

The worker shrugged and said with a bit of an edge, "I know we are a huge company, but you basically just took thirty-two dollars and threw it down the drain. Kind of a waste, don't you think?"

Johnny set the battery off to the side and nodded.

His next box was within the X+ batteries, and Johnny decided to check one of those individual batteries as well. If there was a risk, it would be that the more expensive X+ batteries were actually X batteries. He opened a battery package. When he flipped the battery over, he saw the inscription: X+.

"Surprise, surprise," he muttered with more than a touch of sarcasm.

Shortly after, he and Jarod finished up, and Johnny sped off to ring in the new year with Katie.

CHAPTER 31

Austin, Texas
January 7, 2020

Kim arrived at five before noon at Mixon's, a restaurant near her client in West Austin, and told the host she was checking in for her lunch of three. A bit over a week ago, a JPG partner from the Austin office had given Kim a heads-up that Bob Grayson, the partner in charge of the entire central region, would be getting in touch. Bob apparently had a nephew who was considering attending Saint Edward's University, Kim's alma mater, and Bob had wanted to arrange a meeting so his nephew could ask Kim some questions about the school and their accounting program. Kim had been delighted to have the chance to help and was impressed with the way Bob wanted to support his nephew. She wished, not for the first time, that she'd had a father figure like that.

When the host led Kim to a table for two in the back corner of the restaurant, Kim was a bit surprised, but she recognized Bob Grayson's face from his profile picture.

Bob stood up and said, "Hi, Kim. Nice to meet you."

"Hi, Bob. Where is . . ." Kim realized she didn't know the name of Bob's nephew.

"Martin. He is back at the hotel. We flew in yesterday afternoon, and I dropped him off at the dorms. He's a football recruit, and I guess some of the upperclassmen took him out on the town last night and got him intoxicated. He apologizes but sent me with a list of questions for you."

"Stupid guys." Kim smiled.

"This is my first time to Austin. Seems like a great town. Have you lived here your whole life?" Bob asked.

"I was born in Mexico but moved to the States when I was eight," she replied.

"I hope the move was a good one for your family. Did your parents find work here?"

"My dad did odd jobs for cash."

"Are they still in the area?"

"My mom is," she replied after a brief hesitation. She did not want to mention her dad's murder.

The waiter came with their drinks and asked if they were ready to order. "Yes," Kim quickly replied. "House salad with a grilled chicken breast. Raspberry vinaigrette on the side."

No wonder she's in such good shape, Bob thought.

"And you, sir?"

Normally Bob would have ordered the greasiest hamburger or a huge plate of ribs, but he wanted to impress Kim. "I'll take the cup of tomato basil soup with a half turkey sandwich."

"Certainly. Any bread and butter to start with?"

Bob was famished and normally would have devoured half a loaf if he had been at lunch with another man, but since he was with Kim, he said, "I'm fine. How about you Kim?"

Unsurprisingly, she said, "No thanks."

Bob took a sip of his martini. "How do you like working for JPG?" he asked after a brief pause.

"So far, it's pretty good. The hours are long, but I like the people and clients."

The reply Bob normally received to that question was generally more enthusiastic than "pretty good." He sensed that Kim was not completely sold on a career with JPG, and this pleased him.

"What does your nephew want to know about Saint Edward's?" Kim asked.

"Oh, yes." Bob pulled a sheet of paper out of his sportscoat pocket, unfolded it, and asked, "What did you like and not like about the school?"

For the next 15 minutes, Bob feigned interest in Kim's answers to his questions. He made notes that would be thrown away as soon as he left the restaurant. There was no nephew, and Bob was about to get to the real reason for the lunch.

The waiter brought their food, and that gave Bob an opportunity to shift gears. "Curious: have you ever met any of the team in the Cleveland office?"

He watched closely as Kim began chewing her salad a bit more slowly. "I met a couple at training," she replied without looking up.

"I'm always interested in how people are representing themselves. Who did you meet, and how did you like them?"

Kim kept looking down and poked at her salad. "My best friend Emily just got engaged to Ben Murphy. Ben seems like a great guy."

"Engaged! I didn't know that!" Bob exclaimed as if he somehow should have known.

"It happened on New Year's," she replied.

"Ben does a great job for us. Anyone else?"

Kim didn't want to answer, but she also didn't want to lie to a senior partner. "I met Johnny Fitch at training as well. And his girlfriend, Katie Doyle." She exhaled.

Bob paused and let her answer hang in the air. "Everything okay, Kim?" he asked before taking another bite of his sandwich.

"It's fine. I have some history with Johnny. It didn't end well." Bob nodded and took a spoonful of soup, waiting for her to fill the silence. "I really liked him, but I guess he liked Katie better."

Bob watched her eyes flutter quickly a few times. He had predicted that, because her father had abandoned her, she would have a strong longing for approval from men and would feel a fierce sense of betrayal when a relationship didn't work out. It seemed as though his prediction was at least partly correct.

"I'm sorry to hear that," Bob said. "I try not to pry, but people tell me things. I think you are better off without him."

"What do you mean?" Kim asked with surprise.

"Apparently Johnny has been getting around the office. His thing with Katie will likely be over soon, and he will be on to the next woman. It's creating tension, and I'm getting frustrated. I don't want him hurting my people."

Kim was stunned. "Son of a—" she muttered. Bob took another spoonful of soup to let the information fully sink in. "That son of a bitch."

Bob paused dramatically and then asked, "Kim, can I trust you?"

Kim was surprised at the question but, already feeling vulnerable, replied, "Sure, with what?"

"Johnny's actions are starting to divide people in the office. Some side with him, some with the women he has been using. I need to get rid of him. I need him to find a new job before he does any further damage. I could wait until he leaves naturally, but that probably wouldn't be until at least after busy season. I need him gone sooner, before he hurts more women."

Kim gulped. Johnny had indeed hurt her. She started to see her relationship with Johnny in a new light. He had used her for sex and then gone on to the next woman, just like Bob had said. It made her angry, and suddenly she wanted Johnny to hurt.

"What were you thinking?"

"I am thinking that if he were to provide someone, maybe you, with confidential information, we could terminate him. We'd show him the evidence and keep it quiet, but he'd be done. He is charming, as you know, so he'll land on his feet and get a new job quickly. No harm done in the long run."

"What do you want me to do?"

"I hadn't expected this," Bob lied. "Give me a couple minutes to think about it."

Bob excused himself to use the restroom. As he washed his hands, he looked at his reflection in the mirror and grinned proudly. But when he got back to the table, he noticed that Kim's demeanor had changed a bit. "Is something wrong, Kim?"

"I can't do it," she said. "I don't like Johnny—actually, I think I probably hate him—but I can't do it. It doesn't seem right."

Bob was thrown—he hadn't expected this quick turnabout. "I understand," he lied. "But I need you to keep this quiet for me. Can you do that?"

Kim nodded, and they exited the restaurant together.

"Tell your nephew to contact me if he has any further questions," said Kim.

Bob paused, having forgotten that fabricated part of the story long ago. "Thanks, Kim. Will do."

"What position does he play anyway?"

"Offensive guard," said Bob. "More cerebral than athletic."

"Sounds like the making of a good accountant," Kim said as she turned to walk to her car.

"Say, Kim," Bob said, and she turned around. "If you change your mind, you know how to get a hold of me."

Bob watched her leave and then made a call before driving his rental car back to the airport. "Didn't work," he said. "I think you need to send another message. Just to make sure he stays in line."

"I'm in Cleveland right now. I'll take care of it," said the cold voice on the other end of the line.

CHAPTER 32

Cleveland, Ohio
January 7, 2020

Johnny walked into the dojo at eight thirty on Tuesday night. Busy season had started in earnest the day before, and he knew he'd best survive it if he kept active. As he stretched out, he watched the final class of the night winding down. It was a sparring class for all belt levels. His friend Brent was leading the class through some drills, and when Brent broke the class into two groups, he asked Johnny to run the ring with the more experienced sparrers. Johnny put on his gloves and helmet with no face shield and popped in his mouthpiece. There were six people in his group. Two would face off. The first person to score a point would win, and the next would rotate in. There was some good talent, but all were much less experienced than Johnny. He didn't crush his opponents, but he didn't roll over either. He would leave himself exposed for a second, and if his opponent could take advantage of it, he'd let them get the point, but if not, he'd score with a light strike.

One by one, he noticed other instructors showing up and getting limber, waiting for the final regular class to end. At about a quarter to nine, a man Johnny didn't recognize showed up, which happened on occasion. He was a bit older, mid-30s, maybe, and had olive skin. He was tall and seemed fairly big, but Johnny couldn't fully tell due to his loose-fitting clothing. Johnny watched as one of the other instructors walked over and greeted the man. The return greeting was warm, and there were a couple of laughs. Five minutes later, class wrapped up, and the students bowed out and left the mat. Most left, but a couple of 17-year-olds stuck around to watch. They were good, but rules at the after-hours sparring were that you had to be 18 to participate. They were counting down the days until they got to mix it up with the instructors.

At nine o'clock sharp, Brent called the instructors to attention in a semicircle of sorts. They bowed at each other and then found a partner. It was Brent's dojo, so as usual, he sparred with the new guy first, who introduced himself as Alex. Brent pressed a button on an electronic timing device, and there was a ding, sort of like a bell in a boxing match. There would be three minutes of sparring followed by a one-minute break, and that pattern would repeat itself until Brent decided to do some tournament-style matchups.

Johnny watched Brent and Alex out of the corner of his eye. Alex had an unusual style. He shadowed Brent's moves but wasn't light on his feet and didn't bounce. He didn't move, duck, or dodge when Brent threw punches and kicks. Instead, he blocked them effortlessly, stealthily, and instantly threw single blazing-fast counterstrikes. He pulled back each time before striking, showing excellent restraint.

The bell sounded and partners switched. Johnny again noticed how Alex moved slowly until he didn't, in which case he was very fast. The best Johnny could tell, Alex's opponent never landed a single blow. The eerie thing was that, had Alex not been showing restraint, his strikes would have been doing some serious damage. They were all directed at weak spots in the opponent's body—the nose, the chin, the side ribs, and the solar plexus.

The bell sounded again, and Johnny moved into Alex's ring. "I'm Johnny," he said.

"Alex."

"New in town?"

"Just here for a few days on business. I bring the gear with wherever I go and hope to find some action."

"Glad to have you with us." Johnny smiled.

"Are you Johnny Fitch?" asked Alex.

"Yes," Johnny said, somewhat surprised. "Have we met?"

"No, I was at the tournament in DC last summer. I saw your match."

"I got destroyed," Johnny replied.

"You were fighting the best." Alex shrugged.

With that, the buzzer sounded. Johnny and Alex touched gloves and began to size each other up. Johnny bounced side to side, in and out, but didn't throw any strikes. Alex wore a bandana instead of a helmet, so instead of aiming his opening roundhouse kick at Alex's temple, Johnny decided to play it safe and aim it at his midsection. To his surprise, Alex stepped straight at him, knocked down the kick, and countered with a short right-hand strike to Johnny's midsection. But unlike with the other instructors, this time Alex didn't hold back. He caught Johnny flush and, using his body as momentum, struck him with a great deal of force. Johnny dropped instantly, the wind completely knocked out of him. This had happened before, but not in years. He sat up and did some breathing exercises to get his wind back.

Everyone else stopped and gathered around. Brent looked warily at Alex and asked, "Everything okay here?"

Johnny's breath was coming back, and he replied, "All good. He caught me fair and square." A minute later, Johnny pushed himself back to his feet, and Alex extended a hand to assist him. Johnny said, "Thanks." Normally an opponent would check in or give some effort at an apology for striking so hard, but Alex said nothing in return.

The buzzer sounded again, and Brent said, "Everyone take two, and then we will start points." They gathered back together in two minutes and threw a single large, foamy die. There were eight of them, and the first four to roll an odd number would go into one ring, with the other four joining the second ring. Johnny ended up in the second ring with Brent and two of the regulars. They fought round-robin style, and Brent narrowly beat Johnny, who wasn't quite recovered. In the other ring, Alex won his three matches, never giving up a point but never throttling anyone either.

Brent and Alex met for the final match of the night, the evening's championship match—one three-minute round, most points wins, reset after each point.

After bouncing around for a few seconds, Brent blitzed, looking to score a quick point. His left hand went high to block any strike Alex would throw, and his right hand went to Alex's body. But Alex saw it coming. He stepped into the attack and launched a straight right hand directly into Brent's face. Alex connected with an eerie thud, blood went splattering, and Brent went down hard.

Johnny quickly rushed to Brent's side, taking his mouthpiece out to make sure he was breathing. He looked up at Alex and asked, "What the hell was that for?"

"I got the point." Alex smiled.

"Actually, you didn't," said Johnny. "Drawing blood is an automatic DQ." This was something that kept karate sportier and more inclusive than something like mixed martial arts. Fighters thus relied more on hooks and backfists when throwing blows to the head, which kept most contact on the helmet and not square in the face.

"It's too bad. I heard you guys were good. I heard wrong." Alex began to walk off the mat, and Johnny was suddenly quite certain that Alex was not a regular martial artist. Stepping off the mat before bowing out was something they never did.

With Brent out, Johnny was the unquestioned alpha dog among the instructors, so he spoke up. "One more match."

Alex stopped, looked at him, and smiled.

"No, that's enough," Brent gasped between gulps of blood. "Get out of here, and don't come back." He pointed at Alex and then the door.

The other instructors stayed silent. Johnny said, "No, I want this."

Brent slowly got to his feet and surveyed the situation. "Okay, but my dojo, my rules. Tournament style. You guys can fight hard, but this isn't a free-for-all."

Johnny stepped to his line and Alex stepped to his. Brent stepped to the side as the other instructors took their spots around the ring as judges. One stepped to the middle and said, "Fighters, bow."

Johnny bowed, but Alex did not.

"Ready, fight!"

Johnny had seen enough of Alex to know his style was to bait people. Johnny didn't take the bait. For two and a half minutes, he bounced side to side, in and out, threw some fakes, but didn't throw any strikes. Alex mirrored him but likewise did not throw any strikes.

"Thirty seconds," called out one of the instructors. With that, Johnny slid toward Alex like he had in their earlier match. But this time, he faked the roundhouse kick to the midsection, causing Alex's hand to drop. Johnny pulled back ever so slightly and then popped the kick into the side of Alex's head. The move was a weakness of those who blocked with their hands. Johnny's kick was strong enough to wobble Alex a bit.

"Two points, Fitch," said the center judge. "On your lines. Ready, fight."

Up in scoring, Johnny didn't press it. He wanted to win, not hurt Alex back. Play the game right and show Alex who was the best. Down in points, Alex advanced quickly. He threw two hooks, which Johnny evaded, and a judge yelled out, "Time!" Johnny kept his guard up for a second, to make sure Alex wasn't in the middle of a move, and then lowered his hands. Both men took off their gloves and tossed them to the side.

Alex said, "You won, fair and square. I got out of hand. My bad."

Johnny cautiously bowed, and Alex bowed back. Out of habit, Johnny extended his hand, and Alex took it and shook it, firmly but not excessively. As Johnny went to release his grip, he felt Alex pull hard, twist Johnny's arm behind his back, and leg-sweep him to the ground. Johnny landed hard on his chest.

One of the instructors began to move forward. Alex said, "Stay back, or I snap it." Alex had a knee in the middle of Johnny's back with Johnny's arm heavily contorted. Johnny tapped out with his free hand, but Alex only sunk into the hold more deeply. Johnny tapped again, but Alex did not relent.

"Release him," yelled more than one instructor.

Alex leaned down and whispered into Johnny's ear, "Watch yourself." With that, he pushed hard once and released his grip.

A couple of instructors moved quickly toward Alex, but Johnny yelled out, "Let him go!"

Johnny sat up and rubbed his shoulder as Alex walked out the front door, taking off his bandana. He had jet black hair. Mid-30s, olive skin, jet-black hair. The same guy who had whacked Will in the PurePower parking lot. It had to be.

And just as the realization dawned on Johnny, Alex was gone.

An hour later, Johnny was home and showered. He popped open LinkedIn and noticed the five recent messages he had from recruiters promoting jobs. Jobs with higher pay. Jobs with fewer hours. Jobs with less travel. Jobs, most importantly, without Bob Grayson. Johnny stared at the messages for a couple of minutes and picked the one that seemed the least salesy.

"That sounds like an interesting position," typed Johnny.

To no surprise, the recruiter responded immediately. "Thanks for the note, Johnny. It's a really interesting company, and the pay is great. I think it is a great position for someone with your experience. Could we get together to chat about whether it would be a good fit?"

Johnny hesitated and thought about all that had happened in the past few months. Bob's scheme. Will's death. The fight in Mexico. Alex's attack.

It was too much.

"Yes, I'd like that," he replied. "Busy week and then out of town Friday and Saturday nights. Any chance you'd be willing to meet Sunday afternoon?"

"Just tell me when and where, and I'll be there," replied the recruiter.

"Let's do 4 p.m. at the Starbucks off Clifton," Johnny replied. He closed his internet browser and felt a bit guilty. Guilty that he was considering leaving at the beginning of busy season just like Nicholas had. But he also felt some relief, some hope. It was just one meeting, he told himself.

CHAPTER 33

Westerville, Ohio
January 10–11, 2020

Westerville was hosting games on back-to-back nights, so Johnny made the two-hour drive down Interstate 71 to join his family for the weekend. On Friday night, the Sand Gazelles moved their record to 11–0 with an easy 24-point win. Billy was the team's leading scorer, as he usually was, finishing right at his season average of 18 points.

After the game, Johnny and Billy went to enjoy some time on their own while their parents took Dani to an open mic night on campus. It was a warm evening for January, so Billy and Johnny made the five-minute walk into downtown Westerville and went to Mario's, the local Italian restaurant, for some pizza.

"Looking forward to tomorrow night?" Johnny asked. "Or more nervous?" Westerville would be hosting their archrival, Loveland College, the two-time defending national champions who had four of their five starters back. Their record sat at 11 wins with only 1 loss. Their wins were coming by an average of 32 points per game, and their only loss had been a non-conference buzzer-beater upset against one of the top Division One programs in the state.

"I suppose some of both," said Billy. "No one expects us to beat them except our coach." He laughed. "I'm sure I'll get anxious during warm-ups tomorrow."

"How do you prepare for a team like them?"

"Just like any other team. We will watch a couple hours of

film tomorrow morning, figure out where we need to stop them, figure out where we can attack them."

"How's your matchup?"

"I know I can take him. I played against him in tourneys growing up. He's a bit taller but a step slower. I feel like I am the one guy on our team they can't handle. If I can get hot, I think we can beat them. I'm going for it."

Johnny admired Billy's confidence but wondered if he was putting too much pressure on himself. He let it pass and instead asked, "Got your resume dusted off?"

Billy nodded and said, "Yeah, interviews start next month for the sophomore experience programs. Crazy. I've only got three semesters of college under my belt."

"You a 4.0?" Johnny asked.

"Not quite. Got an A- in a theo course last spring. I guess the prof hasn't given out an A in ten years."

"Tick you off?"

"Nah. You always told me 3.9s were better than 4.0s anyway. Means I'm human."

"I only said that because I wasn't smart enough to get a 4.0." Johnny laughed.

"I'm applying to all of the Big Four and a couple regional firms. I was planning to apply to JPG as well. You liking it there?"

Just then, the pizza arrived, which gave Johnny a minute to think of how to answer. A lot was going to change in the next month, and he didn't want to raise any alarms. "I do, quite a bit," he said finally. "They grind you hard but really reward you. It's been tough with Will gone, though."

"Mom told me a little about that," Billy said. "Damn drunk drivers."

Johnny winced. "C'mon, man."

Billy cocked his eyebrow. "What?"

"I know Will was drunk, but I'm still torn up that he's gone."

Billy's eyebrow was still cocked as he asked, "Will was the drunk one? Mom said it was a drunk driving accident, so when she told me the name of the other guy, I assumed he'd been the one who was drunk."

Johnny was about to take another bite of pizza but set it down. "Why's that?"

"He was an assistant basketball coach of mine back in high school. Got canned after showing up plowed to a game. I think he's still hitting it pretty hard. Shit, two weeks before Will's death, one of my buddies ran into him in a restaurant parking lot—he was hammered and trying to get in his car. Said his cousin was a sheriff and could get him out of anything. Messed up, if you ask me."

Johnny nodded.

"Speaking of alcohol," Billy continued, "did you know that Westerville was once the Anti-Saloon headquarters of the United States and was called the Dry Capital of the World. That's where Sand Gazelles comes from. It's an animal that needs very little to drink to survive."

Johnny nodded, but he really wasn't listening. He was contemplating the very real possibility that Will had in fact not been drunk at the time of his death and that a crooked sheriff had somehow falsified the report to protect his drunk cousin.

Johnny spent his Saturday holed up in his hotel room working on the PurePower audit. The rest of the team was on site in Parma, but Johnny had told Jarod that he'd need to work remotely so that he could attend Billy's games. After their previous incident, Jarod had been coming around.

Fifteen minutes before tipoff on Saturday, the gymnasium was rocking, at capacity (2,100 people) for the matchup of two of the best teams in the country. Johnny was walking back to his seat after grabbing some popcorn when a man approached him from the side.

"Johnny Fitch?" the man asked. He was about 60 and wore a very stylish suit.

"Yes," said Johnny, not at all recognizing the man. "Have we met?"

"We have a mutual friend," the man replied. "Enjoy the game." He walked quickly away before Johnny could ask who their mutual friend was.

The sharp-dressed man sat two sections away from Johnny with other fans from Loveland. He seemed somewhat out of place, not in the way he dressed as much as the way he watched the game without emotion. On a few occasions, Johnny looked his way and caught the man staring at him.

Once the ball tipped off, Billy was confident, as Johnny had expected him to be. Billy hit long bombs, drove hard to the hoop, and played tenacious defense. Even a casual observer would quickly discern that he was the most intense player on the court. While he was competitive, he maintained a strong sense of fair play, an attitude instilled in him by his family. When he drove hard to basket and was fouled hard by Loveland's center and they both went down in a heap, Billy popped up first and extended his hand to help his foe off the ground.

The first half was some of the most beautiful basketball one would ever hope to see. The teams made a combined 58 percent of their shots, and it wasn't because the defense wasn't bad. Players were routinely making shots with hands in their faces. With the clock winding down before halftime, Billy nailed a three-pointer, his *10th* of the half, and the arena erupted. The Sand Gazelles had a 66–60 lead, and the teams' 126 combined points set a conference record. Billy ended the half with an incredible 40 points.

When using the restroom over halftime, Johnny crossed paths with the referees. As usual, they were serious and unengaging. He was wondering if they were enjoying what they saw when he heard one of them whisper, "Best shooter I have ever seen." Johnny smiled, proud to be the older brother of the star on the court.

As they walked away, one referee fell behind a bit to tie his shoe. When he stood up, the sharp-dressed man from Loveland leaned into him and whispered. The referee seemingly ignored him, except that he nodded almost imperceptibly. Johnny had an uneasy feeling about the man and was nervous at what he just saw.

A minute into the second half, the referee whistled Billy for a ticky-tack foul while boxing out for a rebound. Billy said something that looked an awful lot like "I barely even touched him" as he walked past the referee. With that, the referee brought his hands together and made them into a T. When Billy gestured and said, "What?" the referee again made his hands into a T, pointed at Billy, and then pointed toward the area of the locker rooms. Billy had just received two technical fouls and been thrown out of the biggest game of the year. When the Westerville coach asked for an explanation, the referee said, "Obscene language." When the coach asked what was said, the referee said he refused to repeat such vulgarity.

While there hadn't seemed to be any vulgarity coming from Billy, the same couldn't be said for the Westerville student section, which rained down chants of "Bullshit" on and off for the next 10 minutes. As Johnny looked around the stadium, he noticed the sharp-dressed man from Loveland standing near the exit door, staring right at Johnny. When they locked eyes, the man smiled at Johnny and gave him a short wave. The man then turned and walked out the exit.

Johnny rushed from his seat down the stairs and toward the exit. He flung open the door and quickly looked around. The sharp-dressed man was gone.

This was no longer between only Johnny and Bob Grayson. Alex was involved, as was the sharp-dressed man from Loveland. And now they were messing with Johnny's family. This was too much, way too much. He needed to get out of JPG now. Tomorrow at 4:00 p.m., he would meet with the recruiter, and if the opportunity looked even half-decent, he would pursue it. And if the opportunity didn't look good, he would find another. He was done at JPG. Bob Grayson could have his millions, and Juan Carlos was on his own in Juárez. These weren't Johnny's fights.

He texted his dad, "I don't think I'm coming back in. Going for a walk."

His dad replied, "Don't blame you. Loveland just scored fifteen straight and is up by nine. This game is over."

Johnny put his phone in his pocket and exhaled deeply. He wanted to drive back to Cleveland, to Katie, but he felt an obligation to stick around and check in with Billy after the game. He stood outside the stadium, watching a somewhat steady stream of students filing out, their spirits low.

"Want to take a walk?" The voice was soft and familiar, but it still startled him. He looked to his right and saw Elena, his former Spanish professor.

"Were you at the game?" he asked.

Elena smiled. "Does it surprise you that I'm a big Westerville basketball fan?"

"It shouldn't, but for some reason it does."

They began to stroll. They walked past the football field, the campus center, some dorms, and the library. Within a few minutes, they were in the center of campus, near a building where Johnny had spent hundreds of hours as a student. Elena stayed quiet, waiting for Johnny to speak. She had seen a similar defeated look on Johnny's face before, when he had been homesick in Chile, and she knew that she could help him best by letting him have the conversation on his own terms.

"Have you ever felt like it is just too much?" he asked. "Felt like you just wanted to get away?"

"Every semester right before finals." She smiled.

Johnny forced a chuckle. "No, I mean deeper than that. Like the whole weight of the world was on your shoulders. Like you were being called into a fight—except it was a fight you felt you couldn't win."

Elena hesitated and then replied, "Two times."

"Will you tell me more?"

Elena took a few more steps before she said, "The first time was at a college in Pennsylvania, where I taught before Westerville. There was an incident involving some students, and administration was proposing to expel them. I discovered the truth through the rumor mill, which showed a different side to the story, but I didn't do anything. I didn't want to get involved, and I didn't want to take the risk."

"What happened?" Johnny asked.

"The students were expelled."

"Do you regret it?"

Elena paused and replied, "It was thirty years ago. How many days is that?"

"About eleven thousand," Johnny said, easily doing the math in his head.

"I have regretted that decision for all eleven thousand of those days," she said. "Every single one. I'm not sure if fighting for those students would have changed the outcome, but I should have done it anyway."

They walked in silence for a minute. "You said there were two times," Johnny said. "What happened the second time?"

"In Pennsylvania, I was on the board of a nonprofit. There was some funny business going on between the executive director and the biggest donor. I brought it up at a board meeting and was told to ignore it. But I couldn't. It just wasn't right. I spoke up and eventually had to work with an investigative journalist to get the story out in the open. I upset a lot of people. I started to get harassed even at home. It got so bad, my family and I eventually moved. I gave up a tenure position at that college to take an adjunct position here at Westerville."

"What happened to the nonprofit?" Johnny asked.

"The journalist's story was released, and the corruption was found. The executive director was ousted, and the biggest donor became persona non grata. The nonprofit survived and to this day does great work for the community."

"But it had a significant impact on you and your family," Johnny pointed out. "Do you regret it?"

"This was a little over eight years ago. How many days is that?"

"About three thousand," Johnny replied.

"Yes, it was stressful to speak out. Yes, it was stressful to move my family out of the community we loved. Yes, it *is* stressful knowing that I gave up the security of a tenure contract. But for the last three thousand days, when I look at myself in the mirror, I like the person I see looking back at me. I know I did the right thing. I feel some redemption from the mistake I made thirty years ago when I didn't stand up for those students."

Elena stopped walking and turned toward Johnny. "Doing the right thing can be tough, but what's tougher is trying to live a life knowing you didn't stand up when it mattered most. You may win, you may lose, or more likely, you will land somewhere in between. Do the right thing, Johnny. You'll never regret it."

At 4:00 p.m. the next day, Johnny wasn't at the Starbucks off Clifton meeting with the recruiter. He was at Katie's apartment, curled up with her on the couch and watching the Chiefs trample the Texans in the Divisional Round of the NFL Playoffs. Johnny wasn't going to leave JPG. He was going to stay and fight.

Boz Bostrom

CHAPTER 34

Cleveland, Ohio
January 21, 2020

Johnny got home from work at 9:00 p.m. The first draft of PurePower's earnings release would be available the next day. He knew that fourth-quarter earnings surpassed management's guidance, but he did not yet know what the outlook was for 2020. One thing he did know was that he would be hearing from Bob Grayson very soon, perhaps as early as tomorrow night.

He realized he hadn't checked in with Juan Carlos in a couple of weeks, so he gave him a call. They had agreed to never text. Call logs could be traced, but at least the content of their conversation could not.

Juan Carlos answered on the first ring. "What's up, my American brother?"

Johnny smiled and replied, "Just knee deep in the PurePower audit. Wrapping up soon though. Any developments down there?"

"Nothing really," said Juan Carlos. "I checked the computer logs, but Jorge is clean there. Of course, he could be using a personal laptop or phone, and I'd never know. But I haven't seen any shipments of ammonium nitrate arriving either."

"I suppose that's good. Hopefully Jorge changes his mind and doesn't go through with it. Keep me in the loop. Any news on Felipe?"

"Oh, I can't believe I didn't tell you. Yeah, Felipe is back, but he's a completely different guy. Barely will talk to me. It's as if he has been ordered not to."

"Probably the case," said Johnny.

"I don't think we are out of the woods. Jorge's attitude continues to deteriorate. Many people wouldn't notice it, but I can tell he is not all there."

"Why don't you think others would notice?"

"We all got at least fifty percent raises, effective on our February 15 payroll, along with a twenty-percent retention bonus. My raise was actually seventy percent. People down here are walking on air."

Johnny furrowed his brow. "A retention bonus? Was it a performance bonus related to 2019?" As part of the audit, he'd specifically noticed that the year-end bonus in Mexico was no longer accrued for. He'd asked about it and been told that the Mexican subsidiary had done away with performance-based bonuses. He was concerned that a year-end bonus was somehow being hidden as a retention bonus in order to shift the expense from 2019 to 2020, which would cause income to be higher in 2019.

"Jorge said retention," Juan Carlos replied. "People don't care what it is called. Last year's holiday bonuses were ten percent, and this year people are getting twenty percent, but it is called something different. They don't care as long as they get the money."

Johnny was about to dig further when Juan Carlos said something that made him altogether forget about bonuses: "The one thing I can't figure out is, Why are we getting these huge bonuses at a time when business is slowing down?"

"What do you mean, slowing down?" Johnny asked.

"You know, the demand for X+ batteries has dropped way off. The group working on that production has been shifted around. Some are working the third shift producing X batteries, some are working Sundays producing X batteries, and some are working more on the contract manufacturing business."

"When did this start?" Johnny asked.

"Probably mid-August. Occasionally some X+ batteries get produced, but not often. Oddly enough, they usually get produced when someone from Cleveland comes to visit. I think the last time was when you were down here."

Johnny quietly processed that information.

"Mid-August," Johnny said aloud in his empty apartment when the call ended. He had been in the Parma warehouse less than a month ago and seen six months of inventory for the X+ batteries. He had not seen revenues by product line for the fourth quarter, but total revenues exceeded expectations, implying that demand for the X+ batteries was not down. He pulled up last year's audit files and saw that inventory of X+ batteries was at right about six months. Somehow, they hadn't produced many X+ batteries at all in the past six months, had sold the inventory they'd had, and still had six months of inventory on hand.

It didn't add up.

Johnny thought about the inventory count he had completed with Jarod. Auditors were taught to do random samplings. When he'd checked the inscription on the individual X+ battery, it just so happened that he'd looked in a box on a pallet very close to the shipping door. Those batteries would have been shipped out within the next week. He wondered if he should have done a couple more tests—in a pallet in the middle of the warehouse and one in the back. Would he have found anything different?

He took out a sheet of paper and did some quick math. He reached a number at the bottom of the page with a lot of zeroes at the end. He scrunched his eyes. He needed to investigate this and inform management.

He also realized he now had the perfect opportunity to take down Bob Grayson.

CHAPTER 35

Cleveland, Ohio
January 22–23, 2020

On January 22, management provided a draft of its earnings release to JPG. Earnings for 2019 came in nearly 10 percent higher than expected, and full-year 2020 guidance was raised nearly 20 percent. Manufacturing efficiencies were driving tremendous profit growth. As Johnny the read the management letter, he kept checking his phone, expecting Bob Grayson to call at any moment.

Sure enough, at 9:00 p.m. he got a text from Bob: "I've got some great news for you, Johnny. Let me buy you dinner tomorrow to chat about some ideas I have for your future with the firm."

At eight o'clock the following evening, Johnny parked his car in Sonrisa's parking lot. He cautiously walked to the front door, his eyes darting in every direction. He half expected to be whacked in the parking lot by that Alex guy or one of Bob's other goons. He'd debated not meeting with Bob but didn't want to raise further suspicions. He had to keep this going for another week, and then it would all be over.

Johnny found Bob already seated at a booth. Bob stood to shake his hand, and shortly thereafter a server showed up. "Get you something to drink?" she asked in Johnny's direction.

"I'm having their black IPA and it's delicious," said Bob.

"Just a Cherry Coke," Johnny said, and the server nodded and walked away.

"I thought you liked your beer."

"I did. I really did," Johnny replied. "But after Will died, I quit drinking for a while."

Bob said, "Yeah, I think about Will a lot. Miss having that guy around."

"Yeah," said Johnny.

Bob let the word hang in the air before shifting topics. "The partners and I were talking, and we love your mind. You have a good sense of whether or not things are right, and there seems to be nothing you can't solve when you put your mind to it."

"Thanks."

"As you know, normal promotions are effective September 1. Three years to senior associate, another three years to manager, and four years after that to senior manager. That's the way it has always been, and frankly, I don't like it. We end up rewarding the superstars and the marginal performers at the same time, and that's not the JPG way. Really, promotions are standard all the way through the senior manager level, and it's just that people will make partner or director at different times. It's very rare someone gets promoted early like we did with Will, but even he didn't get promoted to senior associate for three years. It was only that he got promoted to manager a year early."

Johnny simply nodded as Bob continued, "We are thinking that needs to change, and it is going to start with you. Effective March 1, you will be a senior associate."

Johnny couldn't contain his smile. His uneasiness vanished for a moment. As much as he hated Bob, the thought that the partners wanted to give him an early promotion was incredibly flattering.

"That will come with a ten percent pay raise, and our seniors got their year-end bonuses of ten thousand dollars each, so it only feels right that you should get the same. You've really kept the PurePower team together since we lost Will."

Bob handed Johnny an envelope containing 100 crisp one-hundred-dollar bills. Johnny's eyes widened as he looked at the money. It seemed extremely odd that he was getting paid in cash as opposed to through a check from the firm, but holding $10,000 cash in his hands was an incredible feeling.

"Wow. Thanks, Bob. Thanks so much."

"It's my pleasure, Johnny. We'll make an official announcement once things slow down a bit next month, but we wanted to tell you as soon as possible. Please keep it on the down low for now."

Johnny nodded and thought about what he would do with the money. Katie's birthday was coming up in mid-March, and he wasn't sure she was ready to commit to the Dubai megavacation Johnny had won, so he had been thinking of taking her somewhere for a long weekend. Maybe now they would go for a whole week. Hopefully they would go to a beach, but he feared she would prefer somewhere where they could do some rock climbing. Of course, that all assumed he would keep the money. He was going to stuff it under a mattress until the mess with Bob was over.

The server returned with Johnny's Cherry Coke and asked, "Will you be dining with us tonight?"

"I'm starved," said Bob. "I'll go with the steak fajitas and another beer."

"Certainly," she said and then shifted her gaze toward Johnny. "And for you?"

"Those sound good to me too."

"Two orders of steak fajitas. Thanks, guys."

After she left, Bob predictably shifted the conversation back to PurePower. "How is it, working for Jarod?"

"He's fine, and he's getting better," said Johnny. "But he's no Will."

"I suppose not. No one is. Not sure if you heard, but PurePower was one of the NYSE's top stocks for 2019."

"Hadn't heard that," Johnny said. "But it doesn't surprise me, as I know the stock price has doubled. It seems like every time I look their stock is up a couple points. I know the controller got a bunch of shares in the IPO, and he has been walking around on cloud nine."

"Yeah, and they didn't blink when we raised their audit fees by fifteen percent for this year. They win, we all win."

Johnny nodded. He'd heard that line from Bob many times.

"Is 2020 looking good for them?" Bob asked.

Johnny hesitated and then decided to meet Bob head on, to confirm his suspicions. "You know, Bob, we've talked about PurePower's earnings a couple times before, and I'm not trying to question you, but is it okay if I tell you? I mean you're the regional managing partner, but not a partner on the account. So would I be giving you information I shouldn't?"

"That's a great question," Bob replied after a brief hesitation. "And I apologize for not being clearer. Yes, as the regional managing partner, and the office managing partner before that, I have responsibility for all accounts in our office, so it's generally considered okay for me to be in the loop."

"Is there a specific rule that permits it?" Johnny inquired. "I'm curious."

"Another great question. No, not really. The rule focuses on only discussing sensitive information with members of the engagement team. But at JPG, managing partners are generally considered an extension of all engagement teams of their respective offices and regions." Johnny nodded along. "If shit hits the fan, you better believe I will be at the board meeting with Maureen and Rodney explaining things, so I like to stay in the loop in advance—kind of know where potential surprises may be coming."

"Do you ever talk directly with the engagement partners?" Johnny inquired, a bit afraid of the reaction his question might elicit.

But Bob stayed calm. "Of course I do. All the time. But sometimes they tell me what I want to hear. They are fiercely independent and sometimes think I'm meddling if I check in too much. Plus, they got to the positions they are in, in part, by knowing how to bullshit, and they sometimes try to feed it to me. Younger folks tend to give it to me straight. I try to keep the lines of communication open with everyone."

Johnny nodded. He didn't believe a word that Bob said but played along. "Well, okay. I got PurePower's management letter yesterday," he said, saying something he was sure that Bob already knew. Bob leaned in ever so slightly as Johnny continued, "They crushed their fourth-quarter estimates. They are raising 2020 guidance by a ton. They are killing it."

Bob couldn't fully control his grin and giggle. "That's great. Great news for them is great news for us."

And great news for you, you son of a bitch, Johnny wanted to say. The way that Bob reacted was the final confirmation Johnny needed.

When Johnny went to bed later that night, PurePower's share price was $95. Average share volume had been steady around 525,000 shares per day. The next day, 725,000 shares were traded. That figure increased to 750,000 shares on Monday and 775,000 on Tuesday. An extra 675,000 shares had been traded over a three-day period. Johnny expected PurePower's share price to go from $95 per share to over $110 per share once earnings were released. That put the total earnings from extra shares at just over $10 million.

"Ten more?" Johnny remembered Bob Grayson yelling into the phone on Christmas Eve. Thanks to Johnny's help, Bob was in line to get his 10. Or so Bob thought.

CHAPTER 36

Cleveland, Ohio
January 24–25, 2020

The following night, Johnny left PurePower at six and went straight to the gym. Since the altercation with Alex at karate and the presence of the sharp-dressed man from Loveland, Johnny had picked up the intensity of his workouts. He felt slow and soft. Between sets with the weights, he would do plyometrics: box jumps, jumping lunges, squat jumps, burpees, really whatever he could think of. In 45 minutes, he was a pool of sweat. He was determined to be stronger and faster whenever the next altercation took place.

He showered quickly and put on his best pair of jeans, a tight black T-shirt, and a black sportscoat. It was a look he knew Katie was fond of. He picked Katie up at eight, and they arrived in the city of Pepper Pike at eight thirty. Ben and Emily had gotten engaged over New Year's, and Ben's parents were throwing an engagement party for them.

After parking the car, Johnny grabbed his phone and noticed a text. "Just a heads up," the text from Ben read, "Kim's here." Johnny exhaled.

"What is it?" Katie asked. Johnny handed her his phone and she shrugged. "You've convinced me she is ancient history."

"That couldn't be more true," Johnny said as he pulled Katie in for a strong kiss.

It took Johnny a couple of minutes in the house before he saw Kim. She was dressed to the nines, as always, and was drinking a glass of red wine. Johnny saw her head jerk when she recognized him. She confidently started walking toward him and Katie. Johnny felt suddenly glad that Katie was wearing dark clothing—it looked like she might shortly be wearing Kim's wine. His heart raced as Kim grew closer and her wine glass came up, but she simply transferred the wine glass into her left hand, extended her right hand toward Katie, and said, "You must be Katie. I'm Kim."

Katie politely shook her hand and said, "Nice to meet you."

"Johnny," Kim said without shaking his hand. "I think your lovely date needs something to drink. Why don't you go find her something?"

Johnny glanced at Katie, who nodded once, and walked toward a small bar area that had been set up in the corner of the living room. When he returned a few minutes later, he found Katie and Kim laughing like old friends.

The party was excellent. Ben's parents spared no expense when it came to having a good time. At nine thirty, a three-piece band began playing, and there was drinking and dancing and celebrating the happy couple.

It was about eleven when Kim first saw the woman. Kim noticed her because she was gorgeous. Kim took a lot of pride in her appearance and aimed to be the most attractive woman in any room she walked into. Up until now, it had worked. Katie was beautiful, but she didn't stop traffic in the same way that Kim did. This new woman, though, had legs a little bit longer, hair a little bit wavier, lips a little bit fuller, and chest a little bit larger. Kim hated her for it and decided to keep one eye on her.

Johnny knew the woman. Her named was Alessandra, and she was from Brazil. She had been college classmates with Johnny and Ben as well as a star on the women's basketball team. When

Ben had first met her, he had flirted endlessly, trying every trick in the book to win her over. Eventually, Alessandra had quietly let him know that he had no chance.

"Why is that?" Ben had asked.

"Because you have the wrong parts," Alessandra replied.

With the prospect of a relationship ruined, sexual tensions had eased and a strong friendship had blossomed. Alessandra had gone over to Johnny and Ben's college apartment often, and she always joked that they would all have to fight her over any beautiful women that came by.

Kim didn't know this though. She assumed Alessandra was straight.

Johnny had stepped into Ben's parents' kitchen to wash his hands when Alessandra came up behind him and covered his eyes.

"Guess who?" she said in a moderately thick Brazilian accent.

"Ah-lay!" Johnny exclaimed. He spun around, and she draped her arms over his shoulders. He pulled her in for a tight squeeze. They separated a bit, and Johnny recalled the Brazilian custom of cheek kissing. He couldn't remember if he was supposed to lean his face to the right or lean left and aim for Alessandra's right cheek. He guessed incorrectly, aiming right when he should have aimed left, and ended up kissing Alessandra on the mouth. It wasn't the first time it had happened.

Alessandra laughed and said, "Just like old times, Johnny."

Johnny smiled and said, "I've missed you, Ah-lay."

When Kim saw Johnny kissing Alessandra, she was shocked. Bob Grayson had told her a couple of weeks earlier that Johnny was playing the field, but a part of her hadn't wanted to believe it. Now she had very public proof that what Bob had been saying was true. Bob's words rang in her head: "His thing with Katie will likely be over soon, and he will be on to the next one."

Angry with Johnny and Alessandra and maybe even herself for having fallen for a player like Johnny in the first place, Kim went to the bathroom, thought for a moment, and pulled out her phone. She typed, "I've changed my mind. What do you need me to do?"

She waited a minute, and Bob responded, "How soon can you be in Cleveland?"

A short while later, Kim was in Bob's home, which was conveniently located in the same neighborhood as Ben's parents' home. She sat on his couch with a glass of wine and listened to his plan. It sounded wrong, too extreme. But so much in her life had gone wrong. This would just be one more thing.

"I'll do it," she whispered.

Bob smiled and said, "You are doing the right thing. Should I take you back to the party?"

Kim thought for a moment. She was buzzed and more emotional than normal. She shook her head and all of a sudden began to cry.

Bob moved his hand to her knee and said, "Don't worry, Kim. It will all be over soon."

She looked at his hand and the lack of a wedding ring, then up at his face. He must have been a very handsome man when he was younger. Added weight and years of hard living had caught up to him. Still, she was angry and upset and knew only one surefire way to feel good.

A while later, when it was over, she lay in Bob's bed and listened to him snore. She felt disgusting. She dressed, walked to her car, grabbed her overnight bag, and called an Uber. She texted Emily and let her know she had gone to a hotel and would be back in the morning to get her rental car. "Thank Ben's parents for a great party," she said.

She then showered, probably the longest and hottest shower of her life. She scrubbed her body with soap in an effort to remove every last drop of Bob's sweat.

Johnny got back from a morning run through Edgewater Park and checked his phone. He had one text message: from Kim.

"I need to discuss something with you."

Johnny felt uneasy but replied, "What's up?" He remembered that Kim had suddenly disappeared from the party and was curious if she was okay.

"My client is in the middle of a big acquisition, and they have some very tricky accounting issues. I need your brain for a little bit. Everyone is crazy busy with year-end stuff right now. I'm sure you are too, but I thought maybe you'd be willing to help me out."

Johnny thought about his own packed schedule. "Not really a good time. PurePower releases earnings in ten days."

Kim replied, "Look, my best friend is marrying one of your good friends. We need to get along. Let's say that if you help me out on this one, we'll call it even. And you'll get some charge hours out of the deal, and we all know you love those."

Johnny grunted. He didn't love charge hours—they just happened. Now that Nicholas Montgomery was gone, he had the most in the office at the associate level, and that came with a reputation of sorts.

"What would it entail?" he asked.

"I've got a pretty big charge code," Kim said. "My flight

doesn't leave until one. Could you spare a couple hours for coffee?"

"Fine. Only this one-time shot though."

"That's it. Not like I really want to spend any more time in your crappy city anyway."

Johnny let the dig at Cleveland slide and replied, "Where should we meet?"

"Your place?"

"You have got to be kidding me."

"Yes, I am kidding you. God, you're arrogant. Just pick a coffee shop or something and text me the address."

Johnny felt embarrassed and did not at all like the way that Kim was messing with him, but once again he decided to be the bigger person and let it slide. "There is a Starbucks in my neck of the woods. I'll look up the address and send it to you."

Johnny told Katie of the plan, not wanting to keep any secrets, and she gave him a little crap. "How would you like it if I started hanging out with an old boyfriend?" she asked.

"The one in the Italian jail?" Johnny asked, thinking about his conversation with her brother Marcus on Christmas.

"What?" she asked.

"Never mind," he said. "Honestly, I wouldn't like it. We'll be at the Starbucks for a couple hours, then she's leaving, hopefully forever. I seriously wouldn't mind if you wanted to come hang out there as well."

"Like, sit and do my work with you?"

"Well, I think her deal is still confidential, so maybe a couple tables away."

"You think I'm that much of a loser that I have nothing better to do than to sit in a Starbucks and monitor you?"

"Of course not," Johnny said. "I don't like this either."

"Just this once?" Katie asked.

"That's what she said," Johnny replied.

Two minutes before nine o'clock, Kim's Uber pulled up in front of Starbucks. She got out and straightened out her waist-length winter coat and smoothed her well-fitted pair of jeans before entering the coffee shop. Johnny stood up and waved when he saw her. She walked over. He, clearly at a loss for how to greet her, extended his hand at the same time she leaned in for a hug. The result was his hand resting against her slender waist. It brought back memories. Disgusted with herself, Kim brushed Johnny's hand aside, gave him a quick squeeze, and said, "Let me get some coffee and we can get on with this."

For what she was about to do, Kim really, really wanted to order a tall black coffee, piping hot. Scalding hot. A whole pot maybe. Instead, she ordered an iced mocha with two extra shots of caramel, the stickiest substance she could think of.

She picked up her drink and began walking toward Johnny. He was facing her but had his nose buried in his laptop. When she was one table away, a somewhat disheveled patron abruptly got out of his chair and rammed into her. She stumbled toward Johnny and used her left hand to catch herself on the table where he was seated. The momentum of her fall caused the contents of her drink to go flying—right into Johnny.

"Aaaaahhhh," Johnny yelled when the 20 ounces of cold coffee, milk, chocolate, and caramel hit his face and chest. He looked at the man who rammed into Kim and said, "What the hell?"

"So sorry, man," the stranger said. "I'll get some towels." The stranger walked toward the front of the coffee shop but bypassed the towels and went straight out the door.

Kim grabbed some towels from the staff and brought them to Johnny. "I'm so sorry. I mean, that guy just rammed me."

"I know," said Johnny, exasperated. "I need to get cleaned up. Can you watch my stuff?"

"Of course," Kim replied.

Once Johnny was in the bathroom, Kim quickly slid into his chair. Thankfully, his screen was still unlocked, and his email was open. Had it been locked, she would have had to resort to a different plan.

She clicked on the icon to compose a new email and entered her own name. She then typed, "Hey, Kim. Sorry things didn't end well for us. I want to make it up to you. My client, PurePower, is going to have a great earnings release in a few days. If you want to make a nice profit, have a friend buy some shares or purchase some call options. Can't miss, but be careful! Johnny."

After hitting send, she went to his sent folder and deleted the message, then went to his deleted folder and permanently deleted it. Though it would be permanently gone from Johnny's sight, IT could still find it for quite some time if needed.

She then picked up Johnny's phone, which was locked. She quickly unlocked it using the security code he had mentioned to her in his drunken stupor on that fateful night in Atlanta; she had a great memory for numbers. She found the text conversation between the two of them and deleted it. She wasn't sure she needed to do that, but she wanted to cover her bases. Now there would be no easy trace that she had ever asked Johnny to meet with her while she was in Cleveland.

A few minutes later, Johnny emerged from the bathroom with a stained shirt. Kim sat with her coat on and laptop still in her bag. Johnny, confused, asked her, "Do you want to get to work?"

"This is crazy. I got a text saying that my client's deal is off.

There is nothing to analyze. I wasted your time, and you ended up wearing my mocha."

Johnny laughed. "That would have been a nice text to have gotten an hour ago!"

Kim nodded and said, "I'm going to explore a bit. I called an Uber while you were cleaning up. Thanks for being willing to meet though. It means a lot."

"So are we even?" Johnny grinned.

"Yes, we are even." Kim smiled. "I'd give you a goodbye hug, but you are wet and filthy. I'll see you at Ben and Emily's wedding."

Johnny shook her hand gently and said, "Sounds good."

Kim began to walk out the door but turned around. "Johnny?" He lifted his head a bit, beckoning her to continue. "I really enjoyed meeting Katie last night. She's awesome. You be good to her."

Johnny smiled.

Kim left the Starbucks and got into the Lincoln Town Car with tinted windows. In the driver's seat was the man who had rammed into her in the coffee shop. In the back seat sat Bob Grayson.

"Everything go according to plan?" Bob inquired.

"Exactly," said Kim. She pulled out her iPhone and forwarded to Bob the email regarding PurePower's earnings, sent from Johnny's email account to her own.

"Have some time to kill before your flight?" Bob raised his eyebrow in what he probably thought was a seductive gesture.

Kim nearly threw up, actually tasting a bit of vomit in her mouth. "I don't think so," she managed to reply. "Could I get dropped off downtown?"

Bob easily acquiesced. Kim had already given him much

more than he'd expected.

CHAPTER 37

Cleveland, Ohio
January 30, 2020

It was the eve of the last trading day before PurePower's earnings would be released. Johnny left PurePower's office at seven. Instead of driving home, he went to PurePower's nearby warehouse. He pulled up to the gate, where a familiar face was working.

"Hey, Johnny," said Jim. "Great to see you again, man! Bring my coffee and bagels?"

Johnny reached into the passenger seat and handed Jim a hot cup of Sumatra. "The bagels didn't look very good. Probably been sitting out since this morning. Chocolate chip cookie okay?"

Jim said, "You the man, Johnny. We weren't expecting any visitors tonight."

"Yeah, I got asked to run out here at the last minute. Audit's wrapping up, and there is one more thing we need to look at. Do you want me to have someone give you a call to approve my visit? I'd be happy to do so."

Johnny felt awful lying. He felt awful using the coffee and cookies as a bribe of sorts. But the truth was, if he didn't dig into this, PurePower was going to have a major problem that would affect everyone from the C-suite all the way down to the warehouse security guards.

"Nah, you're good, man. Joan's inside. I'll let her know you're coming."

Johnny thanked Jim as the gate raised. He drove to the front door, and Joan was waiting for him. He carried coffee and a big cookie to her, and they walked inside, out from the cold.

"Good to see you, Johnny. Need to check a couple more things out?" When Johnny nodded, she said, "It's not that I don't trust you, but I have to walk around with you. Company policy. Hope you understand."

"Of course. I prefer it this way. I need to get a couple updated samples."

"What do you guys do, anyway?" asked Joan.

"PurePower states that it has about two hundred million dollars of inventory. We need to verify it."

"Why?" she asked.

"Sometimes, companies will overstate their inventory to make their financials look better. And this may help them get loans with more favorable terms or make them look more valuable and increase their share price. Auditors are safeguards for the public. We let the public know that the company's financial information, as they present it, is correct."

Joan smiled and said, "Thanks for explaining that. No one ever has before."

The warehouse looked about the same as the last time he'd been out there. If he had to guess, there were a similar number of total batteries here as there had been at the time of the inventory count on New Year's Eve, with probably even fewer of the X+ model and more of the X model. He walked to the first pallet of X+ batteries at the front of the closest warehouse. He opened a box, grabbed a package that said X+, opened it, and saw the X+ inscription.

He showed it to Joan, and she gave him a kind of puzzled look. "That's a good thing, right?" she asked.

"Yep," Johnny replied. "Let's take a walk."

Four minutes later, they were at the back of the warehouse, where the most recent shipments of the X+ batteries were stored.

He opened a box, grabbed a package that said X+, opened it, and showed it to Joan.

"X," she said. "They put the wrong battery in the package."

Johnny nodded glumly and said, "We need to figure out how long that has been happening."

He walked up to pallet 600 and opened an X+ box. X battery. The same thing happened at pallet numbers 500, 400, 300, 200, and 100. He walked to pallet 90. X. Pallet 80. X. Pallet 70. X. Pallet 60. Finally, an X+. He backtracked and found that the final X+ batteries were in pallet 67, with the X batteries starting in pallet 68. Instead of the 6 million X+ batteries they were supposed to have in the warehouse, they had a bit more than 400,000. That was enough to last about two weeks.

Joan looked at him with great concern and asked, "What are you going to do now?"

"I'm going to talk to management first thing in the morning. We caught this just in time. It's going to get really busy here over the next couple of days."

"I don't understand," Joan said.

"When this is fixed, we'll grab lunch and I'll explain it to you," he replied.

"What should I do if people ask me questions?"

"Just be honest. You didn't do anything wrong. I don't think I'd bring it up to Jim or anyone else in the meantime. People will probably start asking questions tomorrow."

Johnny got home around nine thirty and put the final touches on his presentation. It was a short presentation, four slides long, but it explained the problem. PurePower's inventory was overstated by $50 million, so after taxes, net income would get clobbered by $40 million. In all probability, PurePower would have to disclose the control weakness, and it would look very bad.

But on the bright side, a crisis had been averted. Had Johnny not intervened, PurePower would have started shipping the wrong batteries to its customers. Transit time to the customers and wait time in the customers' warehouses would probably have meant that the problem wouldn't have been discovered for another month after shipping. Once the problem had been discovered, it would have taken another week for PurePower to get X+ batteries produced and to the customers. There was a limit on how many X+ batteries could be produced, even at full capacity in Juárez, and it would have taken about a month to get caught up. Production of certain models of iPhones and Androids would have stopped for at least a couple of weeks. That was about $500 million of revenues that Apple and Samsung would have lost, which truthfully wasn't that material to them, but the fallout to PurePower would have been enormous. In a best-case scenario, PurePower would have offered a huge price concession to Apple and Samsung to make amends. In a more likely scenario, Apple and Samsung would have pressured the hell out of PurePower and then dumped them for another supplier as soon as one could be found. You didn't mess with a trillion-dollar company like Apple without paying the price. The end of PurePower certainly would have been a possibility, perhaps even a likelihood.

Johnny pulled up Maureen's contact information on his phone. She hadn't exhibited any odd behavior in a couple of months, and Johnny was still questioning his original assumption that she was involved with Bob. Because of that, and because he didn't know where else to start, he'd decided to present the information to her and let her bring it to the attention of PurePower management. They would be forced to report much lower earnings in 2019 and disclose what had happened.

PurePower's stock price would probably drop at least 25 percent. Though it would rebound, perhaps even somewhat quickly, Bob Grayson, who had already made his large trades on PurePower (or so the trading volumes seemed to indicate), would pay dearly when the margin account he had likely invested through got called and liquidated. Johnny was sure Bob would be able to trace his losses back to him, but Johnny would say that he'd only recently figured out there was a problem with PurePower's numbers. Bob may or may not believe him, but it wouldn't matter. The damage would be done.

Maureen agreed to meet with Johnny first thing in the morning. With the plan officially in motion, Johnny headed to bed. He was sure he wouldn't sleep well, but he'd need whatever rest he could get.

He had almost managed to fall asleep when he received a phone call from someone he hadn't expected to hear from ever again.

Bob saw the incoming call from Maureen and answered. "Kind of late to be calling, isn't it?"

"Tell me you didn't make the trades yet," Maureen said.

"Of course I made them," Bob replied. "Tomorrow's the last day of trading before the release. You never wait until the last day. Why?"

"Johnny texted me. There is a fifty-million-dollar inventory error and a major control weakness at PurePower."

"Who knows about this?" Bob asked softly.

"I don't know. I'm guessing Johnny told me first, so probably just us."

"What time does the board meet?"

"They met all day today and will be meeting most of the day

tomorrow—probably until about two thirty."

"And earnings are still scheduled for a seven o'clock release Monday morning?"

"Yes."

"The markets will open at eight thirty. I don't care what we have to do, but Johnny's information cannot get leaked until after nine on Monday."

"What would you like me to do?" she asked.

"Hang tight. I'll come up with a plan and call you back. But no texts, just calls."

"Of course not," she replied. "I want to get you through this and then be done with it."

Bob hung up the phone and briefly reflected on Maureen's reaction. Condoning his insider trading was one thing, but for her to now let a false earnings announcement go through was way too much. She was definitely working with the authorities. She had to be. But it didn't matter. Once the markets opened on Monday, Bob would close his position and be long gone.

He punched a new number into his phone and prepared to make some calls. After his final call was done, he walked to his safe, loaded the Glock 19 he'd purchased after Sage had attacked him in Vegas, and sketched out a plan.

Across town, Maureen also made a call. "Are we good to go?" she asked.

"Just say the word," the man replied.

"Sometime overnight Tuesday into Wednesday morning," she said. "Book our flights."

CHAPTER 38

Ciudad Juárez, Mexico
January 30, 2020

Jorge was facing the bathroom mirror, wearing a T-shirt and underwear and holding a toothbrush in his mouth, when he heard his cell phone ring in the kitchen. Ana was at his house for the night, fast asleep in her room. When Ana was with her mom, Jorge kept his phone in the bedroom in case any emergencies happened. But Ana was with him now, and nothing else really mattered, so he'd left his phone in the kitchen, not wanting any distractions while he slept. He wasn't sure who would be calling him at bedtime, but whoever it was, they could wait until the morning for a reply.

When his phone rang a second time, he rinsed his mouth and spat into the sink. When the phone rang a third time, he cursed under his breath and walked to the kitchen. He looked at his caller ID and saw that all three calls had been from Bruno. Jorge's heart sank. There could only be one reason Bruno was calling with such urgency.

When the phone rang for a fourth time, Jorge answered with a simple "It's late."

"Shut up and listen," Bruno replied. "The time has come. Everything ends next week. I will be arriving at your home tomorrow night and staying until it is done. Make sure your daughter is not around."

"But it is my weekend to have her," Jorge said. "Her mother will be out of town."

"You listen to me: make sure your daughter is not around."

"No, you listen to me." Jorge mustered up all his courage and said, "We can't do this. I can't do this. I don't know what your motive is, but this is crazy. I will pay you back the advance."

"Are you saying you won't do it?"

"That's correct."

Bruno laughed, an evil chuckle. "I warned you what would happen if you tried to back out." The phone went dead.

Jorge scrambled and began packing a bag. He was going to take Ana and flee that instant. He would get them to a safe place, call Ana's mother, and figure something out. He put on a pair of jeans and some sandals. He packed one change of clothes, some medications, and the contents of his safe, which weren't much. He walked quickly down the hallway to Ana's room and paused at her door to catch his breath. He needed to express urgency, but he also did not want to scare her.

He quietly opened her door and felt a breeze come in through the windows. That was odd, as Ana always slept with her windows shut. Jorge turned on the light and noticed three things. First, the windows were indeed open. Second, Ana was nowhere to be seen. Third, Bruno was sitting on the edge of her bed, revolver in hand and a slick grin on his face.

"I knew we couldn't trust you, Jorge. Ana is safe with my men, and she will be returned to you when the job is done."

Jorge's mouth fell open. All he could do was stare.

Bruno made a shooing motion with his hand. "I'm tired now, Jorge. I need to rest. Ana's bed is so comfortable. We will talk in the morning. Oh, and one final thing. If you don't complete the job, or if you harm me in any way, Ana will be sold to a cartel to do with as they please."

Jorge clenched his jaw and his fists. Tears poured down his face, and he felt all the rage in the world boil inside of him.

Bruno lay back on Ana's bed and said, "See you in the morning, Jorge. Please shut off the light on your way out."

CHAPTER 39

Cleveland, Ohio
January 31, 2020

When he arrived at PurePower at a quarter to seven, Johnny recognized Maureen's car in the parking lot. She had asked Jarod to join them, and they were both waiting in the conference room when Johnny walked in. Without preamble, Johnny told them what he had found: that PurePower had 14 days of X+ inventory instead of 6 months, that inventory was overstated by $50 million, and that PurePower management needed to be notified as soon as possible. He said he had been acting on a hunch when he'd stopped by PurePower the night before and left out the discussion with Juan Carlos that had originally tipped him off. Jarod told him that he should have asked before going to the PurePower warehouse a second time. Maureen told Jarod to shut the hell up.

"PurePower was planning to report net income of $240 million, but my calculations show it will be $200 million," Johnny concluded. "Earnings for the year aren't going to be $2.00 per share. They will be $1.67, much lower than expected."

Silence hung in the air as Maureen stared at the short presentation Johnny had placed in front of her. Johnny sat down, his pulse racing. He had sweat through his light-blue dress shirt. Jarod looked like he was about to vomit.

Timing was critical. This information needed to get to the board of directors before earnings were finalized, and production of X+ batteries needed to ramp up in a hurry.

"Wait here," Maureen said as she grabbed the presentation. "And start typing that up into a memo."

Eventually, other team members filled the conference room. They noticed an odd tension between Johnny and Jarod but stayed quiet. Johnny figured Maureen was sharing the news with the C-suite and that they were trying to figure out how to handle it.

After three long hours, Maureen came into the conference room and said, "Bob Grayson wants to meet with us in his office in half an hour."

Johnny had expected this. Bob would be furious—not because of Johnny's findings but because his insider trades would soon be underwater. Johnny packed up his files, saved the work on his computer, and started to head to his car. Jarod did likewise and was waiting for an elevator when Maureen walked into the elevator lobby.

"What are you doing?" she asked.

"Coming with?" Jarod looked at Maureen quizzically.

"You should have inspected more boxes when you did the inventory count. Pack your bags, you worthless son of a bitch. Take your ass back to Kansas City, and never come back."

Jarod stood stunned for a minute before deciding to go for a walk instead of heading back into the conference room. He could think of nothing worse than having to pack up his things under the questioning stares of his coworkers right now. He felt ashamed. The truth was that he had known he was in over his head on the PurePower account. His father was the CFO for a Fortune 100 company, and everyone was always saying that Jarod was following in his dad's footsteps. Jarod had said yes to every opportunity thrown his way, including relocating to Cleveland to lead the PurePower team, because that was what his dad always did. Jarod enjoyed accounting and the work he did, but the shoes were too big to fill. This time, he should have said no, because he had screwed everything up.

Back at the Stone Tower, Johnny and Maureen walked into Bob Grayson's office and shut the door.

Bob, as expected, was fuming. Pop was splattered everywhere, and Johnny could see a small dent in the wall courtesy of a fastball by Bob.

"Maureen tells me there is a problem," Bob said.

"Yes, you see—" Johnny started.

"I wasn't finished," Bob said. "Don't *ever* interrupt me again. What I want to know, Mr. Fitch, is why this wasn't brought to our attention earlier."

"I found out about it last night," said Johnny. It wasn't entirely true, but it wasn't entirely untrue either. Johnny had waited to validate his suspicions until he'd been sure Bob had made his large trades. Though he definitely felt guilty about not speaking up sooner, it had been the only plan he'd had to bring Bob down.

"Bullshit!" Bob replied. "You don't find out about stuff like this at the last minute. You were on to something long ago, and for some reason you waited until now to bring it up."

Bob nodded at Maureen, who went to the door and opened it. A muscular man with olive skin and jet-black hair—the man Johnny knew as Alex but whom Bob knew as Sage—walked in and shut the door. This time, he wasn't wearing loose-fitting clothing. He was an incredible specimen in his tight black T-shirt. His body tone resembled that of an NFL defensive end.

Johnny sat frozen until Sage said, "Stand up."

"What?" Johnny said with a great deal of surprise and a healthy amount of fear.

"You heard me."

Johnny stood up, and Sage roughly but efficiently patted him down, emptying his pockets of his keys, cell phone, and access cards to both PurePower and JPG. Sage set those items on Bob's desk and said, "Now, sit back down."

"That's all," said Bob.

"I'll be outside if there are any problems," said Sage. He walked out, and Bob's office was silent.

"That was the guy who whacked Will with a baseball bat, the psycho who almost broke my arm at a karate class. You ordered hits on two of your own team members?"

"I have no idea what you are talking about."

They again sat in silence. They were waiting for something, and Johnny wasn't sure what for.

The silence was broken when the door opened, and in walked a familiar face.

"Kim?" Johnny asked, bewildered.

Bob, not even trying to hide his lust, looked her up and down with a smirk on his face. The thought that something had happened between them was repulsive to Johnny.

Kim looked at Bob, who nodded, and then back at Johnny as she said, "I was stunned at first when I received your email, but it is all starting to make sense now."

"What email?" said Johnny. He was pretty sure he'd never sent her any emails, only texts, but either way, he wasn't sure what that had to do with anything.

Kim pulled out her phone and said, "It was sent on Saturday, January 25. 'Hey, Kim. Sorry things didn't end well for us. I want to make it up to you. My client, PurePower, is going to have a great earnings release in a few days. If you want to make a nice profit, have a friend buy some shares or purchase some call options. Can't miss, but be careful! Johnny.'"

Johnny sat completely still. His mind raced back to last Saturday, when Kim had been in town. The smokescreen of needing help with a client, the spilled coffee: it was all making sense. It was a setup. But why? They had been getting along so well at the party.

Johnny looked at Bob and then back at Kim. "Why? Why would you do this to me?"

"I wondered the same thing when you sent me the email," she replied coldly. "I guess I didn't know you as well as I thought."

"She's lying!" Johnny yelled to Maureen, who simply shook her head disapprovingly.

"Goodbye, Johnny," Kim said. She leaned in to give him a kiss on the cheek and slid her face up to his ear. "Payback's a bitch, isn't it? Maybe 'Ah-lay' can bail you out of jail."

Johnny couldn't figure out why Kim was bringing Alessandra into this.

Kim stepped away and out the door. In walked a face Johnny had not seen in a month: that of Nicholas Montgomery.

"Nicholas gave me some troubling news regarding you, Johnny," Bob said, "so we have been following you. It seems like you have been inquiring about confidential information and then passing it along."

"What!" Johnny shouted.

"It's true," Nicholas said. "Johnny bought me dinner at Merton's and asked what I knew about American Bank's earnings. It wasn't the first time. I even saved a screenshot of the IMs where he said he wanted to meet with me."

"You liar," Johnny whispered.

"But it didn't stop there, did it, Johnny?" Bob said. "You

have always been pretty keen on PurePower's earnings as well."

Johnny shook his head in disbelief as things spun out of control.

"We wondered what your motives were, so we did some checking around. And wouldn't you know it, but one Joe Doyle happened to profit two quarters in a row on trades involving PurePower and American Bank. Joe Doyle has a daughter who works here, doesn't he, Johnny? I believe Katie is her name. And wouldn't you know it, but this morning Joe sold short some PurePower stock. Kind of convenient, isn't it, Johnny? The share price is at an all-time high. Joe short-sells the stock. You embellish some story about inventory in hopes that the share price crashes."

Bob leaned back in his chair and said, "Johnny, securities fraud is punishable by imprisonment. You are looking at up to twenty years."

Johnny shook his head. This whole twist involving Katie's dad was perplexing, and now Bob was talking about prison. Nicholas had called Johnny the night before, warning him that something was up and to play along and do what came naturally. Had that been part of the scheme as well?

"Nicholas, that's enough. Please wait outside. The FBI will probably want a statement from you."

"Sorry, pal," Nicholas Montgomery said as he stood to leave. "I always win. It was nice knowing you."

Nicholas extended his hand to Johnny, his back to Bob and Maureen.

Bob, uncomfortable, said, "Nicholas, you can go now."

Out of instinct, Johnny weakly grasped Nicholas's hand. Nicholas winked at Johnny, leaned down, and whispered in his ear, "I'll take care of Katie for you. Really good care."

Johnny stood and lunged at Nicholas. Nicholas, knowing he

was no match for his much stronger and irate colleague, wrapped his arms around Johnny and held on for dear life. Within seconds, Sage was back in the room, separating the two of them and putting Johnny back into his chair.

"Goodbye, Johnny," said Nicholas, straightening his shirt and walking out the door.

"I can't believe you guys," Johnny said to Bob and Maureen. Maureen was staring off into space, clearly uncomfortable yet trying to act oblivious to what was happening.

"You sure have gotten yourself into a shit sandwich here, Johnny," Bob said. "One call to the FBI and you're history. Maybe you can share a cell with your girlfriend's dad. You could still be screwing one of the Doyle family, think of it that way."

"You disgusting pig."

"Well, Johnny, this disgusting pig may be able to help you out. You see, we don't really want to have to bring your findings to PurePower's attention, or we'd have to admit we screwed up the audit. It was a good catch by you, to be sure, but we will figure out a way to tip PurePower off after earnings come out. They will deal with it however they want, on their own time. They may go through some tough times, but they'll be back. When it comes out that they need to revise earnings downward, we won't take any of the blame. They'll have plenty of time to figure out how to spin it. Maybe they'll even find a way not to have to go public with it. Chalk it up as restructuring or something like that. All I know is that if we give them this information today, they'll probably have to postpone their earnings release for a couple days, which will only delay the inevitable bad news. They will fire us immediately, say we didn't do our jobs, maybe even sue us for good measure. We can't have that.

"So here's the deal: If you keep your mouth shut, we'll help you find another job within a couple of weeks. You can say you got burned out. Your girlfriend will be none the wiser."

"And if I don't?"

"Then I call the FBI. Nicholas Montgomery testifies against you. Your email to Kim is used as evidence. You and your girlfriend's dad go to prison for insider trading."

"How do you know I won't agree to this and then change my mind?"

"The statute for insider trading is five years. You talk within five years, and we call the FBI. You talk after five years, and everyone will have forgotten about this and look at you as some sort of bitter lunatic. Frankly, five years from now, I don't give a damn what you do."

"So I really only have one option, don't I?"

"That's how I see it."

Johnny thought for a minute and then exhaled. "Maureen, you know this isn't right."

Maureen was void of emotion as she replied, "I don't know why you did what you did. When you discovered the inventory error, you should have let us know. But instead, you waited and used the information as part of an insider trading scheme. I've never been more disappointed in anyone in my life."

Johnny couldn't believe what he'd just heard. Defeated, he looked at Bob and said, "Okay, I'll cooperate. But first, Maureen, I need to talk with Bob alone."

Maureen looked at Bob, who said, "It's okay. Go ahead. I will stop by your office once Johnny and I are done."

Once Maureen had left and closed the door, Bob smiled and said, "So, Johnny, what's on your mind?"

"You got me. You win. I want to know how you did it. Off the record."

Bob stared at Johnny for several seconds, and then several more, before saying, "Of course we're off the record. Why do you think we had you searched?"

With that, Bob set Johnny's cell phone on the ground, placed a leg of his chair on top of it, and sat his large body down. Pieces went flying everywhere.

"Can't take any chances, can we?"

"What are you going to do with the money?" Johnny asked.

Bob looked a bit taken aback. "Excuse me?"

"The money. The ten more. The seventeen that turned into twenty-two?"

"You're a nosy little prick, aren't you?"

"What are you going to do with the money?"

"Well, Johnny, it's none of your business. But let's say I have a friend who found a great international business opportunity that required, shall we say, a sizeable investment."

"Can I guess that this friend is a financial advisor?"

"Something like that."

"Perhaps the same advisor that convinced Katie's father to place some well-timed trades on PurePower?"

Bob smiled. "Perhaps."

"Fair enough. Why'd you choose me, and why'd you choose Nicholas Montgomery?"

"It was nothing personal, Johnny. You happened to be staffed on the two companies that showed the most potential for extreme earnings swings. Just dumb luck."

"How did you frame Nicholas and get him to cooperate?"

"His favorite uncle may have made a bit of money recently on American Bank."

Johnny shook his head. "The best I can tell, you make twenty-two million dollars profiting from insider trading and set up a couple young and innocent kids. How do you live with yourself?"

"It's what they call a victimless crime, Johnny. I'm richer and no one's poorer. It's perfect."

"Victimless," Johnny muttered under his breath.

"Just one question before you go, Johnny." Johnny looked at Bob. "How did you figure out we'd involved Nicholas Montgomery?"

"What the hell. I may as well tell you. I was in the bathroom on Christmas Eve when you came storming in. That's when I heard you throwing around those numbers. I'd already suspected you of insider trading based on our two previous conversations and estimated that you'd made almost seven million on those transactions. You'd said you already had twelve, which meant you had to have made another five million somewhere else. I figured Nicholas would be the most likely target, as he was young but had a lot of responsibility and probably had access to things like management reports. I pulled up the master schedule of which clients he was on and checked their earnings history. Sure enough, over the last two quarters, there was unusually higher trading volume on the American Bank account right before they released earnings. When I multiplied the increased volume by the increase in share price once earnings were released, I got over five million."

"Hot damn. You're good, kid."

"But then I messed it up for you when I talked to Nicholas, because he quit. Then you got pressure to come up with the money sooner, probably from that goon standing outside your door, or more likely his boss. You were hoping to spread out another ten million of profits over two quarters and two clients, and now you had to come up with twice as much money, and all in one shot. You're sitting on six hundred seventy-five thousand shares right now, probably in a highly leveraged margin account, with some call options thrown in for good measure, but not too many, as those raise suspicions."

Bob leaned back in his chair and shook his head. "That's brilliant. You are going to need work, Johnny. Maybe we should stay in touch."

"Yeah, right," Johnny said. "One final question."

"Sure, what the hell."

"Why did you do it?"

"I told you. It was a once-in-a-lifetime investment opportunity perhaps spurred on by the need to clean up some gambling debt. Once I stepped over the line, I figured I may as well go all in."

"You've traded a lot of shares. FINRA and the SEC will know something is up. You'll get caught. It's twenty-two million dollars."

"They'll investigate, but they won't find anything, at least not until I'm long gone. It's an elaborate scheme. A week from now, I'll be ten thousand miles from here. Maybe I'll send you a postcard, kid."

Johnny got up to leave.

"So we've got a deal?" Bob asked.

"Screw you."

"That wasn't my question."

"Yes, we have a deal. And screw you."

"Please send me your email of resignation this afternoon."

Bob smiled as Johnny walked out the door. Maureen stopped into Bob's office, shut the door, and glared at him.

"Are you going to stop this?" Bob asked nervously.

She simply said, "No. This is the last time, and then we move forward clean."

Bob knew Maureen's response should have made him feel uneasy. The only reason she was cooperating was because Johnny's discovery would hurt the insider trading case she and the authorities were building against him. If the share price went down, Bob would lose money, which meant it would be harder for them to nail him. The government wanted to make a big example out of him, to make him a poster child for SEC enforcement actions. This was one of the most shocking and high-profile insider trading cases in history. It was bigger than a single earnings release and the careers of a few young associates.

But for the first time in a while, Bob wasn't concerned. He would have the money he needed after this. He would be long gone before Maureen and the authorities could touch him.

Because the auditors used a hoteling concept, Johnny didn't have any personal items in the office. He walked down the hallway knowing he would never set foot in the building again. He reached the reception area and elevator bank and saw Val, who had been on lunch break when he'd arrived.

"Have a great weekend, Johnny! Need some Sumatra for the road? Someone told me you were here, so I brewed a batch."

What the hell, he thought and nodded at Val.

She poured him a cup, covered it with a travel lid, and handed it to him.

"I'm going to miss you, Val," he said.

She looked oddly at him and replied, "I'll be right here Monday morning, unless you know something I don't!"

Johnny chuckled bitterly and said, "Have a great one, Val You're the best."

When the elevator reached the bottom, Johnny walked ou of the Stone Tower for the final time. It was one o'clock in th afternoon, and the sun was shining brightly, so his eyes squinted a bit. It was a tick under 50 degrees. He realized he had nowhere to go, and he had nothing to do other than resign from JPG. He started to put his hand in his pocket to look for his phone, then remembered that Bob had crushed it. He'd have to go home to log in with his laptop and send his final email as a JPG employee. He took a sip of his Sumatra and arched his head back, staring up at the sun. He thrust his free hand into his pocket, where he brushed a small object. He took it out and saw a timer ticking up: 25:15, 25:16, 25:17.

"What the hell?" he mumbled.

He looked around and saw Nicholas Montgomery leaning against the wall of the Stone Tower, grinning.

"She still running, I hope?" Nicholas called out as he walked toward Johnny.

"Think so," said a confused Johnny.

"Did you get him to fess up?"

"Yes," said Johnny, starting to realize what had happened.

"I shoved it in your pocket when we were wrestling."

"Honestly, when you called me last night, I didn't know what to believe."

"I told you to stay the course, no matter what."

"I know, but I haven't always been good to you."

"True, but you're no Bob Grayson."

Johnny thought for a moment and said, "The PurePower board meeting should last for about another hour—let's go!"

Johnny tossed the cup of Sumatra into a nearby garbage can—it was a shame to waste it—and he and Nicholas took off running toward the parking garage.

"You're driving," said Nicholas. "I'm going to figure out how to download that puppy. By the way, sorry about what I said about Katie. I had to piss you off enough to make you attack me."

Johnny laughed and said, "You bastard!"

Weekend traffic combined with a tractor-trailer rollover had the freeway out to PurePower messed up something fierce. "Damn it!" said Johnny. "If we can't get to the board in time, they'll never agree to adjust their earnings. Bob Grayson will be laughing his ass off halfway around the world when the market opens on Monday."

But traffic eventually loosened, and they pulled into PurePower's headquarters at 2:15 p.m. The final day of the board meetings regularly ran until 2:30 p.m., at which time the board members would speed to the airport to fly off to wherever they came from.

Johnny and Nicholas jogged toward the front door, and standing guard were two huge goons, like Sage but on steroids.

"We were told that you guys may be coming. Why don't you turn around now?"

"I'll run interference," whispered Nicholas. He sprinted between them as if he were a football nose guard occupying two offensive linemen so that the linebacker could make the tackle.

The goons tackled Nicholas, and Johnny began to run around them. One of the goons reached toward Johnny, who brushed off his weak attempt at a single leg takedown.

Johnny ran to the elevator bank and pressed the up button. The receptionist looked at him curiously. None of the elevators came quickly enough, and he heard one of the goons come running through the lobby at him. He saw the doorway to the stairwell and dashed up it as quickly as he could. When he got to the fifth floor, he realized that his access card was sitting on Bob Grayson's desk. He began banging on the door. Seconds later, Jarod opened it.

"Johnny?"

Johnny pushed him back and yelled, "Don't open the door for anyone else. No one else. Do you hear me?"

A moment later, a goon was pounding on the door, demanding entrance. Jarod backed slowly away, went back into the conference room, and closed the door. His staff stared at him. "What are you looking at?" he snapped. "Let's get to work."

Johnny ran past the executive secretary and toward the board room. "You can't go in there," she commanded just as he burst through the door.

The CEO, a burly man in his late 50s, was making a point and gesturing to the others when the door flew open. The 11 board members looked at Johnny, who was red, sweaty, panting, and out of breath.

"I'm terribly sorry for interrupting," he said, "but I have some information that you need to hear."

"Young man," the CEO replied. "I'm going to ask you once to leave before I call security."

"No, I'm an auditor with JPG. I discovered an error in your financials. You can't release them on Monday."

The CEO nodded toward the secretary, who had followed Johnny into the board room, and she quickly left the room to call security. "Young man, we value the role of auditors and that is why we met with Maureen and Rodney yesterday afternoon. They assured us they saw nothing in our release that was materially wrong. If you had a problem with something, you should have brought it to their attention before yesterday. Again, you need to leave right now."

"But I just found out last night!" Johnny pleaded. "Our managing partner has been trading on your shares."

A beefy security guard entered the room and grabbed

Johnny. "Please, your financials are wrong. You don't have the inventory!" Johnny yelled as he was dragged out of the room.

The CEO maintained his composure and said, "Thank you. We will take it under advisement."

As the door was closing, Johnny heard a voice ask, "Disgruntled employee?" and another laugh in reply, "Most likely."

Fifteen minutes later, the earnings release was approved, the board meeting ended, and no further mention of Johnny was made.

The security guard pushed Johnny out the front door of PurePower headquarters and said, "Get lost."

Nicholas was waiting for Johnny by the front door.

"They didn't listen," Johnny gasped. Nicholas's eyes fell.

They walked dejectedly toward the parking lot, where the two goons were joined by Sage. The three of them stood near Johnny's car in the parking lot, the same lot where Will had been assaulted.

Nicholas lowered his head and muttered, "We're totally screwed."

"It's okay," Johnny said. "We have the recording. We may not be able to stop Bob Grayson from getting rich, but we can clear our names."

They walked toward Johnny's car, trying to ignore Sage and the goons. As they drew near, the goons stepped aside, and Sage slid near the front of a black Town Car that was parked right next to Johnny's Corolla. The front passenger side window lowered, and it was Bob Grayson.

"Well boys, I thought we had a deal. Guess what? Deal's off. Talk all you want because by this time Monday, I will be half a world away. I don't think anyone is going to believe you anyway."

Johnny saw Bob's and Sage's eyes both dart to something in the distance behind him. Before he could look, Sage charged at him and tackled him to the ground. To his surprise, Sage rolled onto his back and pulled Johnny on top of him, a move popular in jujitsu. Johnny broke free of Sage and sat up into a full mount. The adrenaline of the moment and the strain of the past two months overwhelmed him, and he rained down punch after punch toward Sage's face, though Sage blocked almost all of them.

Just then, two squad cars flew into the parking lot, lights flashing and sirens blaring. The view they had was of Johnny throwing punches at a seemingly helpless Sage.

"Get your hands up!" one officer yelled as he rushed out of his parked car.

Nicholas and Johnny looked at each other and raised their hands above their heads. Within moments, they were shoved to the ground, handcuffed, and put in separate squad cars.

"Where are we headed, officer?" Johnny asked.

"County jail."

"What's the charge?"

"Trespassing on private property was what we were called for, but obviously now there is probable cause of assault."

"What happens then?"

"You'll see the judge, who will set bail and then a court date."

"How soon till I can get out?"

"Once bail is set, as soon as you post it, you can leave."

Johnny exhaled in relief. "Do we go straight to the bail hearing, then?"

The officer started laughing. "Court is done for the day, son. You won't see the judge until about ten Monday morning."

Ten on Monday. PurePower's earnings would be released,

and the markets would be open. Bob Grayson would be $10 million richer and long gone. Johnny and Nicholas would eventually come out of this, thanks to the recording, but not without a lot of legal haggling.

The recording. He had given the recorder to Nicholas, who had copied the recording onto Johnny's hard drive and then given it back. Johnny's hands were cuffed, so he asked the officer to please grab the recording from his pocket and listen to it.

The officer reluctantly patted Johnny's pockets. "Nothing in here," he said.

Johnny's heart sank. The recorder was gone. It had probably fallen out of his pocket when he'd been running or fighting with Sage. *At least we got it on my computer,* he thought. But then he remembered Sage and the goons standing by his car and realized that there was no way his computer was still there. It was in Bob Grayson's possession, and Johnny would never see it again.

Bob was home free. He certainly was going to throw the blame on Johnny and Nicholas. They would be convicted of securities fraud and spend time in prison, along with Katie's dad and Nicholas's uncle. Life as they knew it was over.

Will had warned Johnny that they shouldn't underestimate Bob. Will had been right. Johnny had had the perfect plan to frame Bob Grayson, but instead, Bob had framed him.

CHAPTER 40

Cleveland, Ohio
January 31, 2020

Maureen showed back up at PurePower to apologize for Johnny's behavior and to reassure her team that everything would be okay. When she popped her head into the conference room, she noticed Jarod sitting in the corner, head in his hands.

"Jarod, I told you to leave," she said.

She watched as Jarod grabbed his bag and left. No good-byes were said.

The rest of the team sat in stunned silence.

"I'm sorry to say that Johnny kind of lost it today," Maureen told them. "He hasn't been the same since Will died. We are going to sort things out, but I don't think you'll see him anymore at JPG.

"I tell you what—you all have been working very hard. Take the rest of the day off. Take the whole damn weekend off. We'll have a meeting right here at eight o'clock Monday morning to regroup."

Katie was working away at a client in the southern suburbs of Cleveland when her IM started to light up. "Did you hear what happened?" she was asked by several coworkers.

Katie tried to call Johnny, but his cell phone went straight to voicemail. It was somewhere in pieces in the bottom of Bob Grayson's briefcase.

"His car is still in PurePower's parking lot, but there is no sign of him," a message said.

Katie packed her things, promised her manager she would

check in soon and be back online later, and dashed to her car.

"They took him to jail," the next message said.

As Katie was driving toward the jail, fighting back tears, her phone rang. It was her mother.

"Mom," she said as the tears started to flow, "Johnny is in trouble."

"Katie, what is going on? An investigator is at our door. Something about insider trading, securities fraud, and the company PurePower."

"What?" Katie asked.

"Gotta go. The investigator needs to talk to me." The call ended.

Katie was still heading for the jail, but now she wasn't sure that she wanted to go in. Insider trading on PurePower? Maybe she didn't know Johnny that well after all. She pulled over at an exit, drove her car to the back of a fast-food parking lot, and pounded on her steering wheel in anger.

Jarod pushed the elevator button and waited. He wondered again how things had gone so wrong. The elevator had not yet come when the door to the offices opened. He heard the voices of the other auditors coming out. He didn't want to see them—he was too ashamed—so he hustled to the stairwell to begin the five-floor descent.

Two flights down, a flash of light caught his eye. As he got closer, he realized the light was reflecting off of a small device. It was an odd-looking piece of electronic equipment, so he picked it up to examine it. It had only two buttons. He pressed one of them. The display lit up, and he noticed numbers scrolling by. He was recording himself.

"A voice recorder," he said aloud, and then pressed the

button again to stop the recording. "Better turn it in."

He reached the bottom of the stairs and brought the recorder to the receptionist. He handed it to her and said, "Someone lost this, I think." Then he left the building and walked out into the sunshine. He would drive to the airport and drink himself silly while waiting for the next flight to Kansas City.

Two board members in dark suits walked past and said, "That kid was crazy. Insider trading? I heard there was a fight in the parking lot and they took him to jail."

They must have been talking about Johnny. Jarod hung his head. He was so confused. Johnny's story had seemed legitimate, but now he was going to jail. How had that happened? Johnny had sure looked determined the last time that Jarod had seen him, in the stairwell . . .

"Ma'am," Jarod said with conviction back at the reception desk. "I realized that the recorder may belong to a friend. May I look at it a second, please?"

She handed it back to him, and he walked back outside and pressed play.

"A voice recorder," he heard himself say, from when he'd accidentally recorded himself a few minutes ago. He pressed another button, and the recorder skipped to another track.

"I'll take care of Katie for you. Really good care." Jarod didn't recognize the nasally voice. After a bunch of banging around and muffled noises, the same voice said, "Goodbye, Johnny."

"I can't believe you guys," said another voice. It was Johnny.

Jarod continued to listen and heard enough of Johnny's discussion with Bob Grayson to know what was going on.

In the distance, he saw the two board members still talking

in the parking lot. He watched them shake hands and then get in their respective rental cars, prepared to drive to the airport and head home for the weekend.

Jarod took off at a dead sprint and reached the nearest car before it began to back up and pull away. He knocked on the window, and the man lowered the window an inch.

"Please, sir," Jarod pleaded. "I'm a manager with JPG, and I have something you need to hear." The board member lowered his window further and Jarod exhaled, relieved that he had caught the man in time. "Here, I'll play it for you."

The man snatched the recorder out of Jarod's hand and said, "I've got to catch a flight. I'll have to listen to it later. I don't know what it is with JPG, but we will be starting the search for new auditors next week."

He rolled up his window and began to pull away. Jarod ran alongside the car, yelling, pleading with him to stop. The man drove out of sight and tossed the voice recorder onto the passenger seat.

Jarod looked down at his phone and for whatever reason checked the markets. They were closed, and PurePower had ended the week at an even $98 per share, an all-time high.

Johnny briefly saw Nicholas when they were brought into the booking area. They tried to communicate, but the officers said, "Stop talking," and took them into separate rooms. The whole booking process—mug shots, fingerprints, paperwork, change of clothes, and the like—took about two hours.

Johnny was brought into a holding cellblock that only had a few other inmates. He was led past them and into a cell. The jailer shut the door behind him and said, "I guess you have a buddy in here with you. You guys aren't permitted to talk, so you will spend your next three nights in your cell."

"May I please make a phone call?" Johnny asked.

"Maybe in a bit, after your buddy is settled in," the jailer replied and shut the door behind her.

"What was he arrested for?"

"Aiding and abetting is what I heard."

"Aiding and abetting *who*?" Johnny asked.

"My guess is that that would be you."

Johnny looked around his cell. Two steel bunks, crappy bedding, a toilet, mirror, and sink. Nothing to look at, nothing to read, nothing to do except pace and think.

"This is a pretty bad setup," Johnny mumbled as the jailer started to leave.

"I'm not sure what you expected," she said. "Jail isn't supposed to be fun."

About 15 minutes later, he watched them lead Nicholas to his cell. His eye was puffy and his cheek was swollen, something Johnny had failed to notice earlier. One of the goons at PurePower had likely roughed him up a bit.

"Can I make a phone call now?" Johnny pleaded.

"You've got ten minutes," said the jailer. "And don't forget your inmate phone card."

It took Johnny about five minutes to figure out how to use the phone card, and the guard was getting testy. When the phone finally starting ringing, Johnny felt his heart race.

"Hello?" said Katie, not recognizing the number.

"Katie, it's me. Look I'm at the Cuyahoga County Jail. I was framed. Bob Grayson is the real crook. I need you to call around and find a criminal defense attorney for Nicholas Montgomery and me."

"Johnny, my dad shorted PurePower today, and an investigator is saying you advised his financial planner to do so. How could you?"

"Katie, no! I didn't do anything wrong. Please listen."

"Johnny, I don't . . . I can't." And the phone went dead.

"Time's up," said the jailer. She led Johnny back to his cell, where he sat in stunned silence for the better part of an hour. Eventually, he started to pace until he thought he would go crazy.

He buzzed the jailer and asked, "Anything to read?"

"I'll find you something."

When she returned 10 minutes later, she held a single book: *The Firm* by John Grisham.

"Want this one?" she asked, sliding it through a slot in the door.

"Why not?" he said. "I'm living it right now."

At six, the guard slid dinner through the slot: two pieces of wonder bread, two pieces of bologna, a slice of cheese, an orange, a piece of chocolate cake, and a carton of two-percent milk. Looking at his meal, Johnny shook his head.

How did I get here?

At 10:00 p.m., the TV played the local news in the jail's common area. Johnny never watched the news anymore, instead consuming it all online, but he had nothing else to do. He peered through the bars and watched, seeing if there was any mention of his adventures, but there was nothing yet. The weather came on. It was going to be nice this weekend, not that he would notice. He'd be surrounded by cinder. As the station went to commercial break, he heard the announcer say, "Next, in sports, a matchup of titans in Loveland."

Johnny recalled that Westerville's rematch with Loveland

had been that evening. The teams each still had one loss, and the matchup was highly anticipated, with the conference championship likely at stake. Johnny had planned to drive to the game but, in the chaos of the past few days, had completely forgotten.

After what seemed like a hundred commercials, the news segment started and cut to a reporter in front of the basketball arena in Loveland.

"It was all Loveland tonight as the home team led by 30 points at the half en route to an 85–50 victory." The announcer shared statistics from a couple of Loveland's players before ending with "Westerville's sophomore star Billy Fitch was held scoreless, missing all 10 of his shots from the field."

Johnny's heart sank, and he wished desperately he could call Billy. He couldn't help but wonder if Billy knew he was in jail. The knowledge might have been what threw him off.

The lights went out at 10:30 p.m. Johnny hadn't slept at all the night before but was still keyed up. The bedding was awful, and he tossed and turned and figured he would never get to sleep. But within 10 minutes, he was out and didn't wake up until the lights came back on at 7:00 a.m.

CHAPTER 41

Cleveland, Ohio
February 1–2, 2020

Breakfast was Corn Flakes, skim milk, a banana, and orange juice. Lunch came at noon and consisted of a peanut butter and jelly sandwich along with a small salad that wasn't much more than iceberg lettuce and cheap French dressing, a pear, and a small carton of apple juice. At this pace, Johnny was pretty sure he would lose 10 pounds by Monday morning. He mused that he should have followed this diet back when he was trying to cut weight in his high school wrestling days.

It was three o'clock on Saturday afternoon when a guard notified Johnny that he had a visitor. He wasn't sure who it would be, but he was hoping Katie had found a lawyer and had sent one to visit him. When he took the phone off the hook and the video screen illuminated, he was stunned at who was on the other end.

"Jarod?" he asked. "What are you doing here?"

When Jarod said he'd found the voice recorder, Johnny's eyes widened. When he said he'd given it to a board member, Johnny's eyes lit up even more. When Jarod said that the board member had driven off with the recorder and that he hadn't heard anything since, Johnny's eyes dropped.

"Do you think he listened to it?" asked Johnny.

"I don't know," replied Jarod. "But my gut tells me he didn't, or we would have seen a news release from PurePower."

"Jarod," Johnny pleaded. "I don't know how, but you need to find that recorder and get someone to listen to it before seven a.m. on Monday."

Jarod left and went to a nearby coffee shop. He drank coffee and thought hard. He had been there for nearly an hour, and had just received a refill, when he had an idea. He pulled out his laptop and found a listing of PurePower's Board of Directors. He identified the man he had given the recorder to: Lance Kessling, CEO of Fireside Instruments in Seattle. Jarod went to Fireside's website and found a long biography about Lance. Although contact information for Lance was not provided, a few quick Google searches let Jarod know that the standard email format for employees at Fireside was firstname.lastname@fireside.com. He drafted a quick and direct message to lance.kessling@fireside .com. He had no idea if it would go through or what Lance would think if it did.

Jarod waited and after a few minutes still did not see an "Undeliverable" email, which implied that his email to Lance had gone through. But Lance did not respond.

A bit more than 2,000 miles away, Lance Kessling looked at his phone for the first time in an hour. He had missed a phone call from his sister. He had 3 texts, all from friends talking about their excitement for the Super Bowl the following day, and he had 30 new email messages.

A year ago, when he'd been burning out in his role as CEO and had sought professional coaching, his coach had recommended that he only check texts and voicemail on weekends. That way, he could still be reached with urgent matters but wouldn't have to think about the smaller stuff until his executive assistant handled his email first thing Monday morning.

As a result, Lance called his sister back and then set his phone down without checking his email.

By Sunday, Johnny was beginning to go stir-crazy. He'd read *The Firm* and another Grisham novel, *A Time to Kill*, but he could no longer focus on reading so instead spent most of his time lying on his back and staring at the bunk above. He tried not to think about what would happen if the voice recorder was lost, but his thoughts kept drifting that way. Life as he knew it would be over. He tried to focus on the best-case scenario but kept coming back to the worst one: he would face prison time and job loss, his CPA license would be revoked, and his relationship with Katie would be over. His family, especially Dani, would be devastated.

At ten o'clock in the morning, Jarod visited again.

"Johnny, I'm sorry. I still haven't heard from the board member. I sure hope he hasn't thrown the recorder away. I swung into the police station, and they took some information from me, but they said that without evidence, they couldn't simply spring into action. They encouraged you to get a lawyer and to take it from there. I had a short conversation with Maureen, but she accused me of fabricating the story in order to cover up my error on the inventory audit."

"I was hoping you would come back," Johnny said. "I've racked my brain, and there is one other thing you could try. But you are going to have to hustle."

Lance Kessling picked up his phone and saw no missed calls or texts. He set his phone aside and helped his wife prepare their home for guests. It was Super Bowl Sunday, and the slightly favored Kansas City Chiefs would be facing the San Francisco 49ers. They were hosting a small gathering with three other couples. He picked up his phone again, seeing he was now up to 45 new email messages. *What could be the harm in checking a few?*

he asked himself. The first message was from an investor upset at the growth estimates Fireside provided in its latest earnings release. Lance felt his blood begin to boil and heard his professional coach's voice in his head: "If you keep checking emails on the weekends, you are going to eventually say screw it and quit."

He set the phone down and poured chips into a nice serving bowl. He went to the fridge to grab a jar of salsa and poured it into the bowl, a hollow space in the middle to keep it separated from the chips. He looked at his phone and looked away, and then picked it up. Forty-four new emails, it displayed. He set the phone back down and decided he would let his assistant take care of the emails on Monday.

When Mitch Wishnowsky kicked off for the 49ers in the Super Bowl game, Lance Kessling was in his theater room with his wife and three other couples. During the first commercial break, he heard his doorbell ring upstairs.

His wife started to get up, but Lance said, "I'll grab it." He walked up the stairs, confused as to who would be at his door during the sacred time that was the Super Bowl.

He looked through the window and saw a face that was familiar but that he couldn't quite place. The face conjured memories of confusion, not unease, so he opened the door partway.

"Mr. Kessling," Jarod said. "I really need you to listen to that voice recorder."

By the time Patrick Mahomes kept the ball on an option play from the one-yard line to put the Chiefs up 7–3, all 11 members of PurePower's Board of Directors were on a conference call. PurePower's CEO spent the rest of the night on the phone with PurePower's general counsel, head of investor relations, and his contact at the New York Stock Exchange.

At 10:00 p.m., the company issued a very brief press release. Due to "previously undetected accounting issues," the earnings release was being postponed.

CHAPTER 42

Cleveland, Ohio
February 3, 2020

A bit after ten o'clock in the morning, when visiting hours started, the intercom in Johnny's cell buzzed, and a voice said, "Visitor. Go to the phone and pick it up."

Johnny's cell buzzed open, and he hurriedly walked over to the phone. After a couple minutes of staring at a blank screen, it illuminated, and he saw Katie's face. She started beaming when she saw him.

"Hi, Katie," he said in a hopeful but cautious voice.

"Hey, darling!" she said, much more warmly than the last time they had spoken. He didn't know why she was suddenly so enthused, but he sure was happy about the change.

"PurePower is all over the local news. Lots of speculation going on right now. The company canceled its earnings release and is going to issue another press release tomorrow. Some crazy guy broke into their building and tipped off the board on Friday that some funny business was going on. Know him at all?"

For the first time in several days, Johnny felt like he could breathe.

"I'm so sorry for doubting you," Katie said. She got choked up and repeated, "I'm so sorry."

Johnny felt a lump in his throat and his eyes started to water.

"I got in touch with a lawyer and gave him the lowdown," Katie continued. "He's going to meet you when you get brought to the courthouse. I have bail money ready to go for you, but the lawyer said he watched your story on the news and doesn't think bail will be necessary."

"Thank you," he said with feeling. "By the way, you look great. Even through a crappy TV screen."

She laughed, and they spent the next 15 minutes talking about what had happened.

"Why'd you hide all this from me?" she finally asked.

"I didn't want to get you involved," he replied. "Plus, I thought it would be fun to have you visit me in jail. Say, is everything going to be okay with Nicholas? He saved the day with the idea of the voice recorder."

"Yeah, as soon as we are done talking, his mom is right here, and she is going to use this phone to talk with him."

"Can't wait to see you."

"I'll be back this afternoon to take you home," she replied. "I'll probably check out the court proceedings."

He smiled, and without thinking about it said, "Okay, see you then. Love you."

Her face got red. "Jail makes you talk funny. See you, hon."

Johnny met with the lawyer late in the morning, and at one o'clock that afternoon, Johnny and Nicholas walked in shackles in front of the judge. The prosecutor had also seen the news story and declined to press trespassing charges. Sage had disappeared, so the assault and aiding and abetting charges were forgotten as well. It took a couple of hours to complete some paperwork and the rest of the exit process, so it was after three when they were both released into the waiting room. Katie sprinted to Johnny and hugged him fiercely while Nicholas's mom wept and generally embarrassed the heck out of her only child.

Johnny walked over to Nicholas and extended his hand.

"Nicholas, I know we've had our differences, but I want to thank you for what you did. You saved me. That took real courage."

Nicholas nodded and bit his lower lip. He had been told a million times that he was smart, hardworking, and ambitious, but no one had ever called him courageous. He pulled Johnny toward him and squeezed him hard for a long time.

"Thank you," he whispered.

"What would you like to do?" Katie asked Johnny as they walked out of the courthouse into the brilliant sunshine.

"I'm starving," he said, "and I need a new phone." They stopped at a Chipotle five minutes away and then made their way to a Verizon store.

"Make sure to call your family first," Katie said. "Your parents are worried sick about you, and Dani is pretty ticked off. She said she'd warned you to be careful."

Johnny smiled and made the call. He promised to come home soon, and yes, he promised Dani, he would bring Katie along.

Next, they went back to his apartment so that he could change into a fresh set of clothes and get cleaned up. The water pressure in the jail showers had certainly left something to be desired. He stood in the shower for 20 minutes, cranking the heat as high as possible without burning himself. When he was done, he reached for the towel and found the rack empty. The clean clothes he had set on the bathroom sink were also nowhere to be found. Grinning, he opened the bathroom door and walked into his bedroom, where Katie was lying on her side on his bed, her clothes also nowhere to be found.

He lay down next to her and whispered, "I meant what I said earlier. I love you, Katie."

She smiled and pulled him close. "And I love you, inmate number 274198422."

"You memorized by inmate ID number?" Johnny asked incredulously.

"I think it's kind of sexy," she said.

They both laughed and held each other close.

CHAPTER 43

Cleveland, Ohio
February 4, 2020

At exactly 7:30 a.m. the next morning, a press release hit the newswire. While a full earnings release was expected to be published in a week, due to a significant internal control weakness related to inventory and their Mexican manufacturing facility, PurePower's earnings were expected to be about $1.63 per share, 20 cents lower than the guidance given when third-quarter earnings had been released. Guidance for 2020 was suspended until further notice. A review of PurePower's external auditor was also underway due to possible independence concerns.

Bob Grayson checked premarket trading and saw that PurePower's stock, which had closed trading on Friday at $98 per share, was at $70. His margin account would call his order, and all $12 million would be gone.

At 8:15 a.m., there was a knock on his front door. Bob was upstairs in his home office. He looked out the window and saw a news van at the end of his driveway and another pulling up. The knocking on his door continued.

He reflected on his life. He had made great money but wasted some on drinking and the rest on gambling. He had chased away the two women who had loved him and was estranged from his three daughters. He lived in his large home by himself. Maureen had turned against him. He was an overweight practicing alcoholic facing a prison sentence. When he got out, he would still have his gambling debt, which would be in the millions with interest. His CPA license would be gone, and he would have no way to make real money with a felony on his record. He would be dodging shadows for the rest of his life with no friends and nothing to offer society.

Bob walked to his closet. He punched the combination on his safe and took out his Glock 19. He heard the reporters still at his front door, knocking louder. Bob pointed the gun at his office door, then rotated it a full 180 degrees.

In the comfort of his home office, Bob Grayson put the Glock 19 in his mouth and pulled the trigger.

Sage was hiding in a home two doors down from Bob. He had cased the house months ago and knew that the empty nesters who lived there left for work by seven thirty each morning. Sage was preparing to kill Bob himself. The remaining gambling debt would be lost, but he couldn't risk Bob talking to the authorities. Sage watched the news vans show up at Bob's door, heard a single gunshot, and saw an ambulance pull up 20 minutes later.

Good riddance, he thought.

Sage received an enraged call from his boss. Sage offered to find Johnny and Nicholas and kill them, but his boss directed him to wait. Months from now, when this had all blown over, they would use Johnny and Nicholas to recoup the gains that should have been theirs. Sage relented and quietly left Cleveland.

Johnny called Jarod and then Nicholas to again thank them profusely for what they'd done. Jarod was planning to look for another job, the stress of the last two months having worn him out. He was going to find work that suited him and no longer live in the shadow of his father. Nicholas indicated that he would likely return to JPG in Cleveland—he had a gap to make up in his charge hour competition against Johnny.

Johnny walked down to check his mail from the past few days. There was a somewhat large envelope addressed in calligraphy to a Mr. Jonathan Fitch. He opened it up to find a wedding invitation from Ben and Emily. They were in love and couldn't wait to be married. The wedding would be on March 20, a Friday night, in Austin.

"Let's think about it," Katie said, and Johnny agreed. March 20 was also Katie's 24th birthday. Johnny had promised to take her away for the weekend, and they weren't sure Austin was where they wanted to go.

At 9:00 a.m., CNBC ran a story about PurePower. Rumors were rampant. Bob Grayson's picture was shown, and it was speculated that he was dead. Johnny's and Nicholas's mug shots were shown, Nicholas looking like a complete thug with his bruised face. The story was told about how Johnny and Nicholas had helped derail a large insider trading scandal.

Across town, a former JPG auditor watched the news segment with great satisfaction. He sent a quick text to Johnny: "Thanks for taking down that bastard."

Johnny didn't know the context or the reason for the angst, so he replied with a simple "You're welcome. Hope you are well, Josh."

Down in Austin, Kim read a news report and was confused. Bob was the bad guy? She thought for a moment and pulled up the Facebook app on her phone. She clicked on Johnny's profile and searched for "Alessandra" in his friends. There was one hit, an Alessandra Batista from Brazil. She clicked on Alessandra's profile picture and recognized the beautiful woman, who was pictured along with another woman. She clicked on the About section and quickly found that Alessandra was engaged—to a woman. Kim's heart sank as she realized she had misinterpreted Johnny's actions and had been used by Bob Grayson. She began typing an apology to Johnny, realized it was insufficient, and threw down her phone. She felt sick to her stomach, and her head began to spin. She had a gnawing feeling that she should cooperate with the authorities to clear Johnny's name regardless of how it would impact her.

Katie turned off the TV and asked Alexa to play some music. Johnny preferred alternative rock, but she was slowly introducing him to old-school country. For a moment, Johnny relaxed and hadn't a care in the world. He pulled Katie in close and thought about the madness of the past few months.

He allowed himself to be fully present in the moment. He saw nothing except the blue clear sky out his window. He closed his eyes and heard nothing but the steel guitar in a George Strait song. He smelled nothing except a second fresh pot of Sumatra brewing in the background. He felt nothing but the warmth of Katie's skin. And he tasted nothing except her lips as she leaned in to give him a kiss. He was at peace and wanted to stay there.

He sat like that for a minute and probably would have for another hour had his cell phone not started buzzing. He figured it was a friend who was going to ask him about the news segment, so he let it go to voicemail. He would listen to it later, maybe not even today. When his phone buzzed a second time, he considered answering it, but Katie nestled in deeper, and again he let it go. When his phone buzzed a third time, he unwound a bit from Katie and reached toward the coffee table. He pushed the talk button without looking at the caller ID.

"Johnny." He recognized the voice, although he had never heard it speak with such panic and urgency. "It's Juan Carlos. Jorge's going through with it. It's going down tonight."

CHAPTER 44

Ciudad Juárez, Mexico
February 4, 2020

At six o'clock that evening, Johnny crossed the border that separated Arizona and New Mexico. His rented Toyota Tundra was cruising smoothly at 80 miles per hour, 5 over the posted speed limit. Juan Carlos had told him to "rent the biggest thing he could find" and that he would explain later.

Johnny was a bit more than two hours from El Paso, and if the border crossing went well, he would be in Juárez by nine. He looked to his right and saw Katie staring out the window, perhaps wondering how she had gotten herself into this mess.

Johnny had gone into his bedroom to talk to Juan Carlos and had closed the door behind him. When he'd emerged, Katie had demanded answers. He'd initially balked, but when he'd said he was leaving and wouldn't be back for a few days, she'd grabbed him and wouldn't let go until he talked.

He'd given her the short version, and when he'd finished, she'd proclaimed that she was coming with. He'd told her it was too dangerous, but she'd again told him she was coming with. His firm "Hell no" had been met with an even firmer "Hell yes," and he'd relented.

They'd both grabbed their laptops and quickly scoured the travel sites to find how they could still get to Juárez that day. Their best option was an 11:00 a.m. flight that would touch down in Phoenix at about 2:00 p.m. It would take six hours to drive to El Paso, and then it was hopefully a quick border crossing into Juárez. They booked a one-way flight. They had no idea when or from where they would be returning.

As they drove to the Cleveland airport, they called the police, who then patched them through to the FBI. The agent they talked to was skeptical when she heard their story and said the best she could do was contact the CNI in Juárez. Since the bomb was not on US soil, the FBI had no jurisdiction and couldn't show up in Juárez and start raising hell.

When Johnny and Katie landed in Phoenix, they had a message from the FBI agent. The CNI had done a brief investigation and found nothing, although they would continue to monitor the situation. Johnny expected that the CNI had contacted the police, who had "investigated" and said they found nothing because they had been paid off by Jorge. The FBI agent said her hands were tied but encouraged Johnny to contact her if he gained more information.

A bit after seven in the evening, the lights of Las Cruces, New Mexico, came into view, and shortly thereafter Interstate 10 veered sharply to the south toward the Mexican border. When Las Cruces was in the rearview mirror, the car became quiet, and only the sounds of classic country music coming from the radio were audible. For some reason, the turn south reminded Johnny of a turn toward hell, or at least the hell that potentially awaited them at their destination.

Forty-five minutes later, they were pulling into El Paso, looking for signs for Bridge of the Americas. They crossed the bridge without incident, and at almost exactly 9:00 p.m., they walked into the lobby of Hotel Lucerna, home again for Johnny.

Juan Carlos was waiting for them. Rather, he was waiting for Johnny.

"Who's she?" Juan Carlos asked, gesturing to Katie.

Before Johnny could speak, Katie stepped forward and said,

"I'm Katie. Johnny told me everything. I think you will find I am quite useful in unpredictable situations."

Johnny shrugged, and Juan Carlos began to speak, repeating much of what they had already discussed: "Around five this morning, Jorge sent out an email to all plant employees. He told us that there had been a power failure at the plant, and the electric company did not expect to have it fixed for several hours. As a result, he told us to take the day off and enjoy the day with our families. He said it would be a paid day off, so naturally everyone was happy. Given all that has gone on, I smelled a rat, so I drove to the facility. I guess I should say I drove close to the facility, but I stayed out of sight. I saw a large, old canopy truck enter the facility, and by the look of its tires and axles, it was carrying a heavy load. From a distance, I saw the plant's two security guards approach, and then Jorge himself emerged and handed them each what looked like an envelope, likely full of cash. They quickly drove away with big smiles on their faces. Jorge then let the truck in through the loading door, and after it was in, he looked around and quickly shut the door. The man who drove the canopy truck into the facility left on foot. Jorge stayed in the facility for several hours, finally leaving around dinnertime. He came back awhile later, not in his pickup truck, but in a large cube van. A man I have never seen before was with him."

"You're sure it's going to happen tonight?" asked Johnny.

"Definitely," said Juan Carlos. "If everyone shows up to work tomorrow and sees a big canopy truck with unexplained chemicals in the back, people will start asking questions. They will dig around and figure it out. It's happening tonight, without question."

"What time?" asked Katie.

"I've been thinking about that quite a bit," Juan Carlos

replied. "Despite what you might be thinking, Jorge is intrinsically a really good guy."

"Good guys don't blow up buildings," Katie interrupted.

"True," Juan Carlos replied, "and that's exactly why I need to stop him: to save him from himself. I haven't figured out his motive yet. It just doesn't make sense."

"Is he maybe hoping to collect on the insurance money?" Katie asked.

"But the policy would be under the company's name," Johnny said. "And the funds would be used to simply rebuild the facility."

"Not necessarily," Katie replied. "I don't think they would rebuild in Juárez after something like this. I wouldn't doubt if Jorge overinsured everything and could get a cut of the insurance money somehow."

Juan Carlos said, "I think someone got to him and threatened him."

"Bob Grayson?" asked Katie, looking at Johnny.

"I was thinking about that, but he was betting on the value to go up, not down," Johnny replied.

For a few minutes they explored other options, but nothing seemed plausible. Was Jorge disgruntled? There was no evidence of that. Was Jorge being paid off by a competitor? Possibly, although blowing up the facility seemed a bit too bold if that were the case. Perhaps it was something to do with his daughter. They again discussed going to the police but quickly determined that the police had been paid off handsomely and may very well hold off until the night was over so that Jorge's plan could go through.

"Well, what's our plan?" Katie asked of Juan Carlos.

"There is a hospital about three hundred yards away. I am assuming they don't want to impact more than needed, so th range of the explosion may be two hundred yards. I am sure there will be some sort of remote detonator. Jorge and the other guy will want to be a ways away, at least a quarter mile, when they push the button. When they leave the plant, we have to grab them and the remote detonator before they blow up the building."

Katie repeated the question she had asked a few minutes earlier: "What time will it happen?"

"Like I said, Jorge's a good guy. He will want to minimize the chance of anyone getting hurt. There are a few restaurants around the facility that will stay open until about one. They should be cleared out by two. The first shift of workers will arrive at six in the morning. So probably sometime between three and four in the morning. There are no homes near the facility, but there are a few other manufacturing plants. In the middle of the night, they should all be closed unless one is open for a third shift."

"So where are we going to wait?"

"This is where it gets tricky. The facility is right off Avenida Bermúdez, a major road that runs north and south. I've been camping out by a FedEx office a block south and watching with binoculars. The problem is, if we are there and they go north on Avenida Bermúdez, we may never catch up to them. I think we need a lookout at the FedEx. We then need one of us waiting a bit up the road, where there is a Carl's Jr., and one of us waiting a bit down the road, where there is a Catholic church. The lookout makes the call, and the person the van is driving toward springs into action. The avenida should be dead at that time of night. I think we ram the van with our trucks. Hopefully that will stun them. I've got some pepper spray and zip ties to control them. Within a few seconds, all three of us should be on them, and I think we can take them down. At that point, we could tip off the cops."

"So I'm waiting down the road, and if they drive my way, I wait until they get close and ram them with my truck?" Johnny asked. "I've never done anything like that before. Have you?"

Juan Carlos reflected back over his time in the gangs in his teenage years and shrugged. "A couple times, yes. Hopefully they will come my way so I can handle that part."

"Guns," said Katie, as much of a statement as it was a question.

Juan Carlos shook his head and said, "I thought about it but decided against it. We are trying to save this plant and the employment and livelihood of one thousand people, but we have to stop short of killing anyone." He looked Johnny's way and said, "If needed, I can fight, and I know you can fight."

"Why don't you ask the girl if she can fight?" Katie interjected. "I grew up with four older brothers, and we fought all the time. I'm not afraid to gouge some eyes or deliver a swift kick to the groin if needed. That's a weakness of you tough guys, you know."

Juan Carlos shook his head no and said, "I don't want you getting involved until we have them on the ground. It's too dangerous."

Katie said, "Okay, good luck then," and extended her hand. Johnny watched with curiosity as Juan Carlos took her hand to shake it. Using a move she had learned from Johnny, Katie quickly twisted his hand and bent his wrist back, bringing him to his knees.

"Well?" she asked.

"Okay, you can help," gasped Juan Carlos, and she released her grip.

Katie stood up and smiled at Johnny. "How'd I do?"

Johnny laughed while shaking his head and said, "Couldn'

have done it better myself, babe."

Juan Carlos got to his feet and glared at Katie. "Okay, but if this goes south, we all haul ass out of here. There is a real chance that the building will blow tonight despite our best efforts. I'm going to do all I can to prevent that from happening, but there is a chance."

"Two accountants and an IT guy trying to stop a building from blowing up," Johnny said. "We are way out of our league."

Juan Carlos nodded. "I know it sounds crazy. But without the help of this company and Jorge, I would be dead or in prison. I've got to give this a shot. If you both need to leave, I understand."

Katie looked at Johnny, who simply said, "I'm in."

"Me too," Katie replied. Katie looked at Johnny and said, "Given what you found with the shortage of X+ batteries, how would an explosion impact PurePower from a business standpoint?"

"It would be a big blow," Johnny said. "The question is whether the facility in Reynosa could keep them afloat for a few months until they got a new supply chain."

Juan Carlos looked uneasy and when pressed said, "Remember, we don't make the X+ model out of Reynosa. That was always the plan, but due to budgets, it never materialized. Reynosa makes only the X. Juárez makes some of the X and all the X+."

Johnny nodded because he knew this. He let the gravity set in, and then said, "If this facility gets taken out, it could end PurePower altogether. If they have nothing to sell, even for a short time, their big customers will get their needs met elsewhere and never come back. PurePower employees—three thousand people, including one thousand in Mexico—would lose their jobs, their health care, and their pensions. This would be devasting to thousands of families. This isn't about trying to save a faceless company. This is about trying to save the people behind it."

"Exactly," affirmed Juan Carlos.

"Then we better not mess up," Katie said with quiet confidence.

They were all quiet for a few moments until Johnny broke the ice. "I'm starving," he said, thinking about the long night ahead. "Let's grab a burger at the Carl's Jr. and get in position."

A few minutes later, all three of them ordered large meals along with tall black coffees. They found a booth near the back, and Juan Carlos sat facing the door. It was 10:30 p.m., and traffic in the restaurant was busy. For a few minutes, they made idle chit-chat. They'd eaten everything but their fries when Juan Carlos's eyes drifted toward the entrance, and his mouth flew open.

"Holy shit!"

Johnny and Katie started to turn their heads, but Juan Carlos said, "Stop. Stay perfectly still."

CHAPTER 45

Ciudad Juárez, Mexico
February 4–5, 2020

Juan Carlos continued to stare at the entrance.

"What is it?" whispered Johnny.

"Jorge and another man just walked in. Through the door over your left shoulders." Johnny and Katie stayed completely still as Jorge continued, "If he sees me here, he may think it is coincidental. But he'd probably come over to talk to me. Once he sees you"—Juan Carlos gestured to Johnny—"he'd know something was up. No doubt the bomb is all ready to go and they have the detonator on them. If they see you, they'll flee right now and blow the facility. The facility would be lost, and possibly some innocent people could get caught by the debris. Right now, they are staring at the menu. They are going to place their order in a minute and then get bored and start looking around."

Johnny said, "There is no way we can walk out. There's no cover."

They were silent for what seemed like an eternity before Katie stood up and said, "He doesn't know me. When I have his attention, exit out the other door. I'll meet you at the car in a few minutes. Rendezvous at the hotel if something goes awry." Johnny reached for her arm, but she pulled it away quickly, turned, and gracefully walked to the front, empty coffee cup in hand.

When she got to the counter, she intentionally stepped into the men's line of vision. She caught the cashier's eye and asked for a refill. After she handed her cup to the server, she casually turned and said, "Hola," to Jorge and his companion. The way

Katie was dressed was highly effective for distracting men. She was wearing blue jeans that fit her well and a tank top that cut off just above her belt line, exposing enough of her midsection to be tantalizing.

Jorge's friend returned the greeting and gave her a once over. "I'm Bruno," he said as he extended his hand.

Katie felt uncomfortable under his lingering gaze but did her best to ignore it. "Katie," she replied. "¿Hay un bar para bailar?" she asked as she gestured out the near-side door. She didn't know much Spanish, but she felt it would distract and intrigue the men if she spoke in their language, if only for a moment. With that, the men turned their heads, and Juan Carlos and Johnny got up and walked quickly across the back of the restaurant and then up the aisle toward the far-side door.

Bruno gestured out the near-side door, and then two things happened at once: the cashier handed Katie her refilled coffee and Jorge began to turn and gesture to the far-side door, presumably to point out a bar in that direction. In a second, he would see Johnny and Jorge, and all hell would break loose.

While Katie was surprised, she didn't lose focus. She screamed, not a loud scream but a startled scream. Accompanying her scream, she dropped her coffee cup right at their feet. Jorge turned his gaze toward Katie and then downward and watched the coffee cup hit his shoe. Hot coffee went flying everywhere. He jumped back as Katie apologized profusely.

"Perdón, perdón, perdón."

With the distraction, Johnny and Juan Carlos managed to slip out the far-side door. Johnny shot a quick glance back toward Katie and the men. He certainly recognized Jorge, but oddly enough the other man looked somewhat familiar as well.

The cashier tossed some towels over the counter toward

Katie and then went to fetch the mop bucket. A couple minutes later, the mess was cleaned up, and Katie, Jorge, and Bruno were left with somewhat damp shoes.

"So where are you from?" Bruno asked.

"Oh—" Katie started before catching herself. She realized if she said Ohio, the men may make the connection to PurePower's corporate headquarters.

"Oh?" asked Bruno.

"Oh-regon," Katie said, somewhat proud that she had come up with a substitute state on the spot.

"Oregon. What part?" asked Bruno. "I have an aunt there."

Katie's mind spun at 100 miles per hour. She had never been to the Pacific Northwest and didn't spend a lot of time thinking about the area. "Seattle," she blurted out and instantly realized her mistake.

"Seattle is in Washington State," Bruno replied, "which is north of Oregon."

Katie couldn't think of anything to say, so she kind of stared anxiously.

"Is everything okay?" Bruno asked.

For a moment, Katie was unsure of how to reply. She didn't want to raise any suspicions, especially not when these men were probably already on high alert. She straightened up and said, "I don't go around telling strange men where I live. Sorry about your shoes—and have a good night."

With that, she slipped out the door. She walked to the back of the parking lot and saw Johnny's rented truck. She checked to make sure she wasn't being watched, slipped in the back door, and then lay down on the back seat to avoid being seen. As Johnny pulled out of the parking lot, Bruno stepped outside and looked both ways for Katie before going back into the Carl's Jr.

They breathed a collective sigh of relief.

"Okay, crisis averted," Johnny said, "but we've got a big problem. They are outside the facility. Who knows if they are even going back in. We've got to tail them somehow."

"Unless," Juan Carlos said, "we jump them right here."

"Too risky," said Katie. "There are people all around who would call the cops. Two Americans and their Mexican friend jump a couple Mexicans in the Carl's Jr. parking lot? We'd get hauled off to jail, and the facility would blow as planned."

They sat at a nearby gas station and watched the doors of the restaurant. The men didn't emerge from the Carl's Jr. for what seemed like forever but was probably a half hour. Presumably they were in no hurry. Johnny watched them get into their cube van and drive back south on Avenida Bermúdez, toward the facility. Johnny began to follow from a safe distance and said repeatedly under his breath, "Please turn in, please turn in." When the right turn signal came on and the van turned in, all three of them breathed a sigh of relief.

They saw the cube van enter the building through a large door. The lights inside were off, so they couldn't see anything, although they weren't sure what 10 tons of ammonium nitrate would look like anyway. They drove on and meandered aimlessly for a few minutes before heading back to their lookout spot at the now closed FedEx.

Johnny said, "Well, not that I doubted you, Juan Carlos, but I think this confirms that you were correct. They grabbed a meal and ate slowly like they had time to kill. Anyone have an idea why they went back in as opposed to waiting outside the facility?"

Katie chimed in, "They probably need a place to hang out. They want to be close enough when the blast happens so they can see that it worked. If they went a few miles away, they wouldn't know if it worked."

"And they probably want to guard the facility," Juan Carlos added. "The police may have told them that the CNI was investigating."

They parked in the FedEx facility at one, and if their estimates were correct, they had about two hours to kill. No one was in the mood for idle chitchat, so they listened to regional Mexican music on low volume, watching the door to the facility. At one thirty, they agreed it was time to split up and get in position in case the party started early. Juan Carlos repeated that they likely would leave Avenida Bermúdez to the north, so he volunteered to sit at the Carl's Jr. location. This was more his fight than Johnny's. Johnny went in the rented Tundra to the Catholic church and waited. He couldn't stop thinking about the man who was with Jorge in the Carl's Jr., so he called Katie.

"Did you talk at all to the guy who was with Jorge?"

"A bit. He said his name was Bruno. Are you jealous?"

Johnny ignored her question and said, "Did he speak English or Spanish?"

"English. Why?"

"How was his English?"

"Now that you ask, it was flawless. Although he certainly appeared to be a native-born Mexican, if we had been speaking via phone, I would have thought I was talking with someone born and raised in the United States with English-speaking parents."

Johnny stayed silent for nearly a minute. Eventually, Katie asked, "Johnny, what is it?"

"I felt like I had seen the guy with Jorge before, though I couldn't place it. But I think I know where I saw him."

"Where?"

"Katie, I think that man is Maureen's husband. I'm

forgetting his name, but it's not Bruno. I saw him at the Christmas party. I chatted with him for a while before I saw you that night. Come to think of it, it's almost like he sought me out. He asked me about my trip to Juárez right away."

"This makes no sense," said Katie. "He is going to blow up the facility where his wife is the partner on the account? Do you know what he does for a living?"

"I don't," Johnny said, "but I will in a moment."

He Googled Maureen's name and found that Maureen Davis and a Marco Chavez were tagged in a donation to a nonprofit in Cleveland. He then typed "Marco Chavez" into a LinkedIn search and instantly found him. He tipped Katie off, and she did the same.

"That's him all right," Katie said, recognizing the menace behind his otherwise beautiful eyes. "He works in investment banking at Morgan Stanley as a managing director."

"Oh gosh," said Johnny. "Last week I was monitoring activity and volumes related to PurePower. The stock price continued to rise, presumably due in part to the trade that Bob was making, but the put options were going the other way. Someone was buying put options instead of call options."

"They were betting that the stock price was going down," Katie said.

"I chalked it up to someone betting that PurePower would miss its earnings, but now it's clear: Marco has a huge bet against PurePower. When the plant explodes, the company's value will drop like a rock, possibly all the way to zero, and Marco will make a killing. Probably tens of millions."

"Do you think Maureen knows?"

"Absolutely. She was somehow in with Bob Grayson on the insider trades. When Bob confronted me in his office, she was way too quiet. And she knew about Will getting hit with the baseball bat. Marco approached me at the Christmas party. Maureen must have sent him."

"We have to tell Juan Carlos," Katie said.

"I'll patch him in so we can—"

"Johnny," Katie interrupted. "The door to the plant, it's opening."

It was 3:00 a.m.

CHAPTER 46

Ciudad Juárez, Mexico
February 5, 2020

Johnny quickly patched in Juan Carlos as Katie spoke.

"The van has left the plant. They seem to be waiting for the door to shut behind them—yes, it's shut now. They are slowly driving toward the gate on Avenida Bermúdez. Okay, the gate is opening. They are through the gate, seem to be waiting for it to shut. Okay, it's shut now. They are rolling again, coming up to the avenida."

Johnny held his breath. Katie's next words would dictate his actions. Either the van would turn left and go north, in which case he'd wait a few seconds before starting pursuit, or the van would turn right and go south, right toward him, in which case a hellacious collision was coming his way. In a few seconds, he would know, and in a few seconds, he would spring into action.

Images flashed through his mind. Images of his father, mother, Billy, and Dani. Images of easier times, only a couple of years ago, when he'd been in college. Images of a few weeks ago when he'd been with Will. Images of Katie, who was sitting about 1,000 feet away, whom he had officially fallen for and was not guaranteed to see ever again.

After what felt like an eternity, Katie finally said, "They are turning right, going south, right toward Johnny."

Johnny closed his eyes for a moment. He tapped his front pocket and felt the small tube of pepper spray Juan Carlos had given him. He put the rented Tundra in neutral so he could more quickly pop it into drive when the time was right. Johnny peered north, up the dimly lit avenida, and saw the shape of the van coming his way. The van was, unsurprisingly, driving with its lights off, letting the streetlights guide its path. As it neared, the rented Tundra suddenly felt small. Johnny wished he had rented a tank, or at least a Hummer.

When the van reached a predetermined point, Katie said, "Okay, Johnny, hit it."

Johnny put the Tundra in drive and pushed the accelerator hard. He didn't floor it until it got going a bit—he didn't want the tires to squeal and give him away. He saw the dark shape of the van coming closer and, in a moment of nerves, instinctively lifted his foot a bit to slow the Tundra. The slip was fortuitous because it got the van more properly lined up. When Johnny floored it again, the Tundra was due to clip the van's front bumper. He turned the wheel hard to the left at the last moment, and the Tundra successfully smashed into the van's front right wheel going about 45 miles per hour, which he hoped was enough to disable the vehicle and stun Jorge and Marco without actually killing anyone.

The airbag deployed, and Johnny smashed into it. He was stunned for a few seconds himself, and then he reached for the door. He leaped from the Tundra, sprinted to the cube van's passenger door, and threw it open to reveal a somewhat-dazed Marco. Johnny took the pepper spray and shot it into Marco's face. He waited for several seconds and then grabbed Marco and flung him down from the cab, glad Marco had not been wearing a seat belt. He grabbed Marco's left wrist and twisted, not enough to break it, but enough to make Marco scream and go limp. Johnny knelt with one knee on Marco's back and maintained firm control of Marco's wrist with his right hand. Soon Katie would be there to help put zip ties on Marco's wrists. Then this would all be over.

Johnny looked to his left as Juan Carlos drove by, brakes

screeching as he disappeared around the other side of the van. He heard the truck door open and listened for the sounds of a struggle. He prayed Jorge was dazed enough that the struggle would be brief.

He heard a few footsteps but no commotion. Juan Carlos must have been struggling to find Jorge in the dim light. He heard Juan Carlos call out, "Johnny?" and was about to reply when he felt the cold steel of a pistol press against the back of his neck.

"Release him," said Jorge.

Johnny went limp. He dropped Marco's arm, and Marco rolled away, drawing his own pistol as he tried to wipe the pepper spray from his face. Juan Carlos came into view on the far side of the Tundra, and Marco, still struggling to keep his eyes open, pointed his gun straight at him.

"Both of you, against the van," Marco ordered. Juan Carlos moved around the Tundra to stand next to Johnny. Behind them, smoke from the collision rose in the air and a hissing sound emanated from the Tundra's engine.

"Jorge," Juan Carlos exclaimed, "what are you doing? This is insane. This is not who you are. I don't know how this man talked you into this, but it's not too late to stop it."

Jorge hesitated, and Marco yelled, "Shut up!" He then turned to Jorge and, gesturing toward the van, said, "See if we can drive it."

Within seconds, Jorge was in the van. He put it into gear, and it pulled forward. The metal made an evil groaning sound as the vehicles separated.

Marco flung the back door of the van open and, to Johnny and Juan Carlos, yelled, "In the back. Now!"

Johnny and Juan Carlos climbed into the van, and Marco slammed the door shut, enclosing them in darkness.

Johnny flipped on the flashlight on his phone. The back of the van was almost completely empty, although it reeked of diesel fuel. He saw damp areas on the floor and realized that they were likely spills from diesel fuel that had been transported into the plant to ignite a fire and cause the explosion.

Juan Carlos began kicking at the door, trying to bust it open, but it was useless. They would be stuck in the back of that cube van while the facility was blown up, and then who knows what would happen to them.

Katie had been sprinting down the sidewalk across the avenida toward the mess of vehicles when Juan Carlos had gone flying by. She'd seen Jorge jump from the van, wobbly from the impact of the collision and clutching at his eyes after having been hit by some errant pepper spray. Jorge had righted himself and quickly moved around the wreck before Juan Carlos could get to him. When Katie had made it to the van's driver's side, she'd heard the commotion on the other side and had stopped to listen.

She could hear Marco yell at Jorge to try to start the engine, so she lay down and wiggled under the van, loose pieces of asphalt digging into her knees. There was enough room for her to lie flat, with maybe six inches to spare. She heard the van start, and then it began to slowly roll forward. She crawled forward, terrified that she would be exposed, but then the van stopped again. She heard Marco yell at Johnny and Juan Carlos to get in the back, and she lay as quietly as possible. The door shut, and the van started to drive away.

As soon as the vehicle cleared her head, she scrambled to her feet and took off at a dead sprint. At first there were about 20 feet between her and the van. She quickly closed the gap to 10 feet, and then more slowly to 5 feet. When she got to within 2 feet of the van, she felt it begin to pull away ever so slightly, so she leaped. Every rock she'd climbed, every pull-up she'd completed, every weight she'd lifted, and every gymnastics routine she'd performed were called into action as she propelled herself into the air and reached for a handle on the side of the back of the cube van. She caught the handle with both hands and clung for dear life, her legs dangling in the air. Her fingers strained, her lats burned, and she wasn't sure how long she could hang on.

"We need to kill them," said Marco.

"No, no death. You promised. This is about money, not death."

"They know too much. We will blow the building, and then we will kill them," Marco said coldly. "Why are you slowing down? What are you doing?"

"Red light." Jorge gestured forward.

"Run the damn thing. Run it!"

"We don't need to attract attention. A cop sees us run a red light and pulls us over, they'll hear those guys banging in the back."

"Pay them off," Marco replied.

"It will take only a few seconds," Jorge said as he slowed to a stop. Suddenly, the lights of a sedan came on, parked on the other side of the intersection.

"Shit!" yelled Jorge. "The cops!"

"It's okay. She's with us," Marco replied. "She's been waiting for us."

The van began to slow, and Katie pulled her legs onto the back of the van and pulled herself upright. As quietly but quickly as possible, she unlatched the rear door and began to raise it.

Johnny's light illuminated Katie's face, and his heart exploded with joy, going from despair to hope in mere seconds. The van rolled to a stop, and he and Juan Carlos jumped into action, sure that Marco would detonate the bomb any second. Johnny ran around the passenger side, and Juan Carlos ran around the driver's side. They flung open the doors, almost simultaneously, just as Jorge was beginning to accelerate again. Juan Carlos climbed up and hammered a fist into the bridge of Jorge's nose. Blood splattered everywhere as Juan Carlos continued to deliver blow after blow. Jorge slammed the van into park before it fully rolled into the intersection.

Johnny caught a backfist to the nose from Marco, and his eyes began to water and his vision blurred. When Marco went to throw another backfist, Johnny caught it with his left hand and held on tightly. He was off balance and threw an awkward right hook toward Marco, who ducked his head so that Johnny's fist smashed against the hard part of his skull. Johnny yelled in pain, then slid his hand down, found Marco's throat, and began to squeeze, the adrenaline numbing the pain in his hand. Marco held a phone in his left hand that Johnny guessed was the detonator for the bomb. Johnny shifted his hand to Marco's wrist and applied hard pressure. Marco didn't drop the phone, but he couldn't use his fingers either.

At the exact moment when Marco was about to give in and release the phone, a voice called out. "Marco!"

It was a female voice, and it was familiar, but it did not belong to Katie. Johnny's focus wavered for a moment, and he felt Marco's forehead smash into his nose, once, twice, three times. Johnny's grip loosened, and Marco freed his left arm enough to toss the phone over Johnny's head and into the waiting arms of the woman in the dark.

Johnny leaped from the van and took one step toward her.

"Wait!" she called. "I push one button and it's done. Get back! All of you, out here, right now!"

Johnny's eyes adjusted to the lighting, and he saw that the familiar voice belonged to Marco's wife—and Johnny's boss on the PurePower account.

"Maureen! What the hell are you doing?" Johnny said.

Juan Carlos exited the van, followed by a bloody but still coherent Jorge. They stood in a circle, all except Katie, who'd remained out of sight when Johnny and Juan Carlos had rushed the van a second time. Maureen held the phone out in front of herself in warning, and Marco drew his gun.

Maureen said, "This facility is blowing one way or the other. The only question is if you will live. We don't want to hurt you, and Johnny, this doesn't concern you. Now, get back in the van, and Jorge, make sure to secure the damn door this time, you fool."

Jorge was a bit taken aback—Marco or Bruno or whatever his name was had been the one to close the door originally—but he remained quiet.

Maureen continued, "We will blow the facility and then drive you to an empty warehouse parking lot. Someone will find you for sure by tomorrow. By then, we will be long gone. We have a private jet waiting for us at the airport right now. You will never see us again."

"You shorted PurePower through put options, didn't you?" asked Johnny.

"You always were a smart one," said Maureen.

"How much?"

Maureen paused and Johnny repeated, "How much?"

"Assuming PurePower goes bankrupt and the stock becomes worthless, north of one hundred."

One hundred million dollars.

Jorge cocked his head a bit, as if just now realizing the full extent of what he was tangled up in. He had been told to make the manufacturing plant as profitable as possible before blowing it up, and now he understood why.

Johnny, unfazed despite the enormous dollar amount involved, asked, "Then why was Bob Grayson involved?"

"That was dumb luck," Maureen said. "We figured we could perhaps earn forty million using put options in a normal market, but then Bob got in on the action, buying as much as he could and passing the info on to others. That kept the put options at a good price for us and prevented the regulators from getting tipped off. When people are on one side of a position, it looks like inside information, but when people are on both sides, it looks like speculation."

"But the stock has already crashed. Why not just take the profit you've made and leave the plant alone?"

Marco snorted. "We don't just want some of the profit. We want it all."

"But you two make great money!" Johnny pleaded. "When is enough, enough?"

"We will make more money tomorrow morning, once the stock crashes, than we could working seventy-hour weeks for the rest of our careers," Marco replied.

"But Maureen, why?" Johnny implored. "You'll be on the run for the rest of your lives. You are going to ruin a company and the livelihood of thousands."

"Ruin a company?" Maureen asked, although it wasn't really a question. "Let me tell you a story. My father worked in manufacturing for a major US corporation. He picked up overtime whenever he could get it to support our family, and he stuck with the company despite higher offers from competitors. A true company man, they liked to say, until one day the company announced it was moving all manufacturing to Mexico. They called a meeting at the end of the day and handed people their final paychecks on their way out the door. They gave employees a hundred-dollar severance for every year of service. After twenty years, all my dad got was two thousand dollars.

"Manufacturing jobs dried up, and he couldn't find work. The bills started piling up. He and Mom argued constantly. Without telling us, he took out a big insurance policy, caught a bus to Niagara Falls, and jumped. The insurance company denied us the money because his suicide happened too soon after purchasing the insurance contract. That insurance company went on to earn two billion dollars in profit that year. So pardon me if I don't give a damn about ruining a big company who would ruin the lives of its employees and their families if it thought it would make a few extra bucks.

"I've been taking orders for the last fifteen years. Taking orders from sexist bastards who thought that as a woman I was not good enough to be a partner. Taking orders from clients who didn't like how I ran my teams or who thought my fees were too high." She shook her head, almost breathless. "No. I'm done. I am never taking orders from anyone ever again."

Johnny was speechless, unsure of how to change Maureen's mind.

"Now, get in the truck," Maureen commanded.

They moved toward the back of the van. Johnny stepped in.

As Juan Carlos prepared to step into the van, Katie, who had climbed to the roof of the van when she'd heard Maureen's voice and had been monitoring the whole conversation, flung herself off the van and at Maureen. The collision knocked the phone out of Maureen's hand. Johnny tensed to hear a mighty explosion, certain Maureen would push the talk button in the chaos, but none came.

Katie raced to pick up the phone as Marco whirled and pointed the gun straight at her. Johnny watched Marco's finger begin to pull back.

"Katie!" Johnny yelled, and she looked right into the barrel. Johnny leaped from the van, and time seemed to slow down. He realized there was no way he would make it to her in time, and at point-blank range, there was no way Marco would miss.

And Marco didn't miss.

CHAPTER 47

Ciudad Juárez, Mexico
February 5, 2020

Juan Carlos was much closer to Katie than was Johnny. Without hesitation, he dove in front of Katie and took two bullets to the chest. He went down hard, clutched at his chest, and took short breaths.

Everyone froze.

"You said there would be no killing," Jorge snarled at Marco.

"It was his fault," replied Marco. "These kids got in the way."

Maureen, back on her feet, lunged for Katie and the phone. Katie stepped to the side and countered with a hard elbow across the side of Maureen's face, sending Maureen tumbling to the ground.

Marco kept one eye on the fracas as he pointed his gun at Johnny, so he didn't see Jorge approach him. Jorge, his face full of blood, balled up his fist and, filled with fury and regret over everything that had happened in the past year and a half, smashed Marco in the solar plexus. The punch was so hard that a couple of Marco's ribs broke. Marco dropped the gun. Jorge grabbed him by the shoulders and pulled forward as he drove his knee into Marco's midsection, once, twice, and a third time for good measure. Marco crumbled to the ground. Jorge kneeled next to Marco and grabbed him by the hair with his left hand. With his right hand, he grabbed Marco's balls and began to squeeze. Marco shrieked, and Jorge squeezed harder. Jorge covered Marco's mouth with his left hand and continued the pressure.

"When I lift my hand," Jorge said, "I am going to ask you for the address of where Ana is. If you don't tell me, or if you give me a false address, I'll continue to squeeze harder and harder. Seeing as how the building is not blowing up tonight, I figure I've got all the time in the world."

Jorge uncovered Marco's mouth and released the pressure on his balls. As it turned out, Marco wasn't such a tough guy after all, and he immediately provided an address that was only 10 minutes away.

Katie scooped up Marco's dropped gun but kept it at her side. Both Marco and Maureen were incapacitated.

Johnny sat and cradled Juan Carlos's head in his arms. Juan Carlos was soaked in his own blood, and his breaths were shallow and labored.

"Thank you, Johnny," Juan Carlos said. "Thank you so much." His voice was a soft whisper.

"Stay with me," Johnny pleaded as tears poured down his face. "Call an ambulance," he said desperately, looking to Jorge.

Jorge began to take his phone out of his pocket, but Juan Carlos ever so slightly shook his head from side to side. "It's okay. Everyone is safe." With that, he closed his eyes and took one final breath.

Jorge kneeled and put his hand on Juan Carlos's neck, feeling for a pulse. Finding none, he lowered his head and then softly asked, "Got any way to tie these two up?"

Using the ties Katie produced, Jorge zip-tied Marco's and Maureen's wrists and ankles. He retrieved some duct tape from the cab of the van and used it to seal their mouths. Johnny helped him hoist Marco and Maureen into the back of the van.

Johnny and Katie leaned down to pick up Juan Carlos. Jorge stepped in and said, "Please. Let me." With great effort, he gathered Juan Carlos into a fireman's carry and gently set him in the back of the van. Johnny had taken Katie in his arms, and both were emotional.

Jorge extended his arms toward them, his palms up. "Please forgive me. This is not who I am. Terrible things were going to happen to my daughter if I did not cooperate. I got desperate."

Johnny looked at him quizzically, and Jorge gave them an abridged version of what had happened over the past 18 months. Then, they returned to the facility together, and Jorge quickly disassembled the bomb.

"I could use your help with one final thing," he said. "Will you wait here? I should be back soon, but if I am not back in an hour, leave the country as quickly as you can."

Johnny and Katie shrugged, largely numb from the night's events. Jorge took Juan Carlos's truck, and 15 minutes later, Ana was in her father's arms, unharmed but terrified. Marco's two thugs each had a bullet hole in their foreheads.

An hour after that, Jorge drove the large, old canopy truck to an empty field about five miles from the facility. Johnny followed about half a mile behind in Juan Carlos's truck with Ana laying on Katie's lap in the back seat.

Jorge parked the truck and climbed into the back, reassembling the detonator. He jogged over to Juan Carlos's truck, picked up the special cell phone, and dialed a number. Within a minute, they saw smoke pouring from the truck. Jorge said, "Let's go."

Johnny and Jorge kept their eyes on the truck's mirrors as they drove away, so they saw the incredible explosion pierce the night sky.

CHAPTER 48

Ciudad Juárez, Mexico
February 5, 2020

By the time they arrived back on Avenida Bermúdez, Johnny's rented Tundra was gone. "Someone likely took it for parts. Tell the rental company it was stolen," Jorge advised.

They agreed that Jorge would call the police to report that Marco and Maureen, still tied up in the back of the van, had murdered Juan Carlos.

"Is Marco simply going to pay off the cops again?" Johnny asked.

"Not with a guy like Juan Carlos dead," Jorge replied. "When the gang members kill each other, the police will turn the other way. When innocent people are murdered, they hold firm. Marco is going to be locked up for a long time, and you aren't going to see Maureen again anytime soon."

Johnny asked, "What will happen to you now?"

"A team from the US is arriving this afternoon to review the inventory shortage. I will admit to what I did with the inventory, but I won't tell them why, and I won't tell them about the bomb. I will help them understand what needs to be fixed, and then I will resign. I have friends at other factories and will eventually find other work. It is what I should have done once this all began. I will find a way, and it will be the right way."

Johnny thought of the $12,000 in cash tucked away safely in his apartment—$2,000 that Bob had given him in Charlotte and $10,000 that Bob had given him as a bonus when Johnny had supposedly been promoted early to senior associate, a promotion that Johnny now realized had never been discussed with any other partner at JPG and thus would not happen. Johnny hadn't been sure what to do with that dirty money, but now it was clear to him.

"As soon as I get back to Cleveland, I am going to send you some cash to help you get back on your feet," Johnny said to Jorge.

With tears in his eyes, Jorge nodded and then pulled them in for a strong embrace, first Katie and then Johnny.

"Thank you so much. I am so sorry," he said.

Johnny replied, "I don't have any children yet, but I imagine I would also do anything for them."

Johnny drove Juan Carlos's car to an all-night pharmacy for antibiotics and bandages. Per Jorge's instructions, they dropped the truck at Juan Carlos's home, locking the keys in his house. His mother would handle his affairs. Johnny and Katie then took a taxi back to Hotel Lucerna. They bathed carefully, applied the medication, and wrapped up Katie's knees and Johnny's nose. At seven o'clock in the morning, they finally lay on the bed, and despite the adrenaline, they fell asleep within minutes due to physical and emotional exhaustion.

They were awakened after noon by a banging at their door. They heard a female voice calling out in Spanish.

"Un minuto," Johnny replied, trying to find a shirt.

"I think she is telling us it is past checkout time and we need to leave," Katie said groggily.

Johnny glanced at his phone, saw that it was a quarter past twelve, and grinned at Katie. "I thought you didn't know much Spanish."

"I don't," she replied. "But I know context."

They quickly packed and went down to the hotel's restaurant for lunch. A television was on in the background, and a news reporter appeared to be discussing a mysterious explosion that had happened overnight.

"Ready to get out of Mexico?" Johnny asked Katie as he looked at his laptop. "There's a three o'clock out of El Paso that connects through Chicago and would have us back to Cleveland before midnight. We could be back in the office tomorrow. They have probably been missing us."

Katie grabbed Johnny's laptop and typed a bit. When she slid the laptop back to him, he saw that she had booked two one-way flights to Cancún.

"We will figure out the rest later," she said.

EPILOGUE

Puerto Morelos, Mexico
February 5–12, 2020

Katie told Andy Becker, the new partner in charge of the office, that Johnny and she would be back "in a few days."

Andy replied, "Take your time. When you get back, we need you to make a big decision. We would like you to move to Pittsburgh and help open the office there. As part of the move, you'd receive an early promotion to senior associate, a corresponding raise, and a nice bonus. You are a star, and we need you there."

Katie decided to keep this information to herself for now. She and Johnny had been through a lot, and she wanted to relax with him for a while before deciding whether to accept an offer that would physically separate them.

Katie called a friend, who called a friend, and when they arrived at the airport there was a driver waiting for them. The driver whisked them 20 minutes south to the sleepy fishing village of Puerto Morelos. They stayed right in the middle of the beach, in the suite of a private rental home named Arenas Blancas: White Sands.

Before turning off his phone and completely detaching, Johnny sent a single text, "I fought, and I won."

"I knew you would," came Elena's reply.

Johnny and Katie spent their days reading and swimming in the ocean and their evenings in the cantinas, tipping the local bands. On their final night before returning to Cleveland, they cabbed into Playa del Carmen, where they dined at El Fogón, a restaurant popular with locals and tourists alike for its reasonable prices and large portions of arrachera. Johnny ordered his first beer since Will's death, and in honor of Juan Carlos, it was a Bohemia with two lime slices. After dinner, they enjoyed a walk along the magnificent La Quinta Avenida. They walked past an internet café, which made Johnny think of his friend Juan Carlos, the IT guy.

"Jonathan Carl Fitch," he said.

"What's that mean?" asked Katie.

"If we ever have a son, I would like to name him Jonathan Carl, after Juan Carlos, the man who died saving your life."

Katie spun in front of him, stopped him in his tracks, and said with a smile on her face, "That would require a proposal."

Johnny leaned in and wrapped his arms around her waist. He pulled her close and kissed her on the lips. The sea breezes gently caressed their faces, and the scent of her perfume mixed in with the salty air.

When they pulled apart, a teenage boy approached them and showed them his phone. He had taken their picture and, for five dollars, would send it to them. Johnny looked at the picture. The boy had caught them midkiss and had perfectly captured the backdrop of the busy avenida. Johnny handed the boy a twenty-dollar bill and told him to keep the change.

Johnny sent the picture to his sister Dani and asked if she would sketch it. She did, and Johnny framed it and hung it in his apartment next to the first picture she had made for him. It was beautiful.

Author's Note and Acknowledgments

This book never would have happened without the people who read it and believed in it. Thanks to Katie Doerer, the world's best campus recruiter, for being the first one to think my short story could become something more. Thanks to my good friend and colleague Ben Trnka for providing multiple reviews of the book and continued insights into the world of auditing. Thanks to my dad, "Big Daddy" Mort Bostrom, for providing several reviews. Thanks to "British" Craig Parsons for your thoughtful comments—I wish you could have gotten the chance to see the final copy, but I am thankful you are no longer in pain and are now in a better place.

Thanks to the various "book clubs" who met and batted around ideas of earlier drafts: former students Jake Thorsten, Hailey Sabin, Maria Van Hove, Chris Condon, Kristin Rezac, and Grant Fuchs; Saint John's guys Brandon Novak, Will Gillach, and Jake Kirsch; Stillwater buddies Mark BURNS, John Holland, Doug Wolff, and Derek Debe; and Heidi Gandsey and the women of the Benson Bring Your Own Book Club. Thanks to Elena Sánchez Mora and Tania Gómez for insights on Latinx issues. Thanks to other readers Sofia Regina, Danny Tripps, Mike Enke, and Dan Vanelli. Thanks to Logan Hershey, Patrick Cotter, and Craig Foltin for letting me bounce things off you.

Thanks to my incredible editor, Jamie Lauer. You challenged me and made me sound like I actually know how to write—no small feat. I hope you know how grateful I am for your work. Jamie may be reached at www.jamielauer.com.

Thanks to Maria Hart, "Mar Har," for the great cover artwork and for joining Sofia and me on our research road trip to Ohio. Thanks to John Ziton and Dianne Swanson at Bayport Printing for your work on design and printing.

The most special thanks to my amazing wife of 23 years, Kacey. You have listened to me talk about this book for 6 years and always encouraged me to keep pushing forward. You make me feel like I can accomplish anything. I love you.

The characters Johnny, Katie, Billy, Dani, Jarod, Elena, Craig, Joan, and Jim are named after friends of mine. The rest of the names just sounded good.

Boz attended Saint John's University in Minnesota, where he majored in accounting, minored in Spanish, and was a Second Team Academic All-American guard for Coach John Gagliardi, college football's all-time wins leader. Boz spent the first nine years of his career in public accounting and was with Arthur Andersen at the time of the firm's demise (although he thankfully never worked on the Enron account). Boz joined academia in 2004 and is a professor of accounting and finance at the College of Saint Benedict and Saint John's University. Boz is active as a CPA and speaks nationally on the topics of ethics and leadership.

Boz and his wife Kacey live in central Minnesota with two of their children, Wyatt and Sofia. In his free time, Boz attends church, college sporting events, and live music performances. He grows potatoes, peddles accounting shirts, and bench presses with the Saint John's football team. Boz is the author of two memoirs: *A Legacy Unrivaled: The Story of John Gagliardi* and *I Believe,* which he wrote with Saint John's legend and philanthropist Bill Sexton.